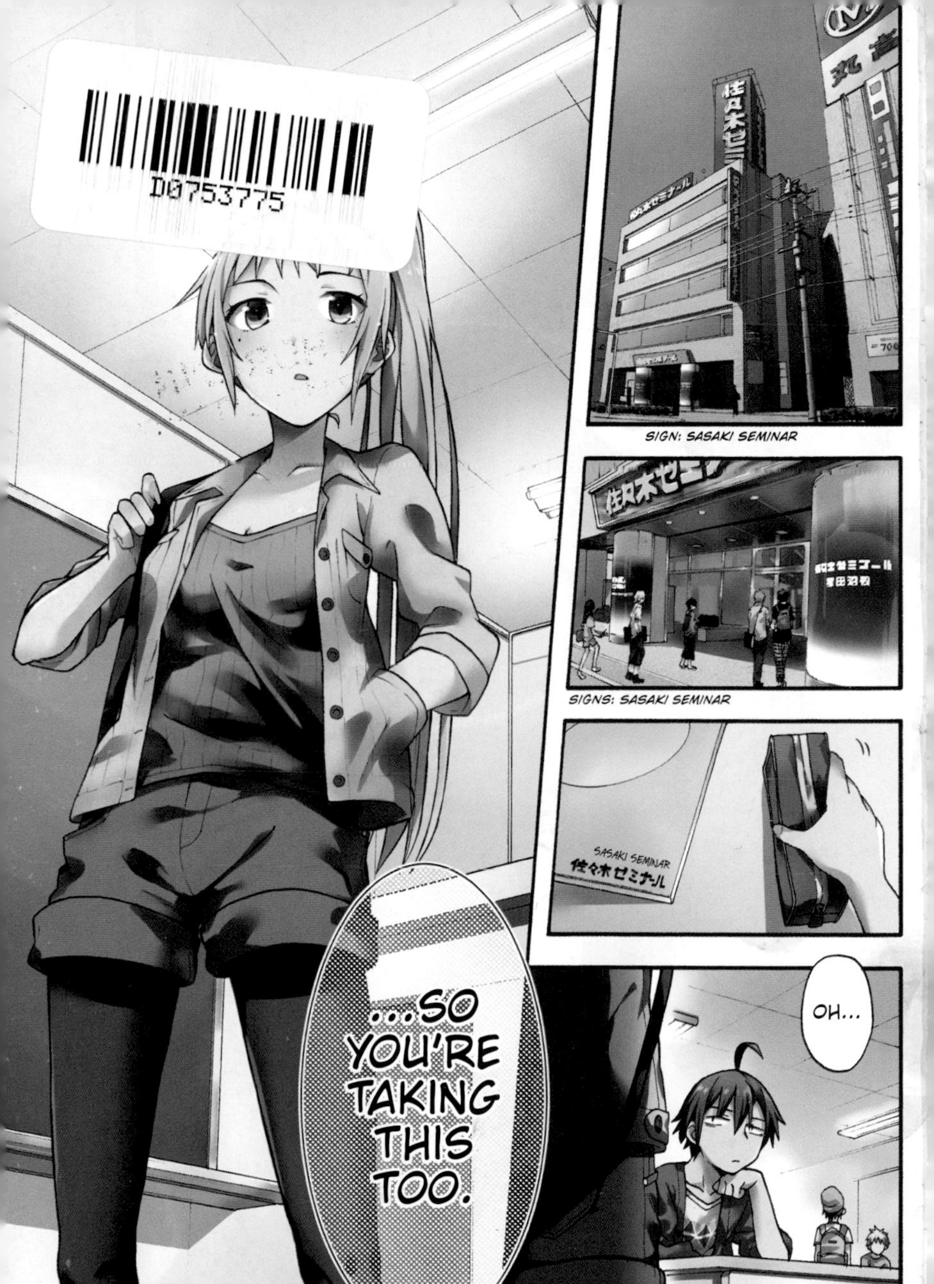
SIGN: SASAKI SEMINAR
SIGNS: SASAKI SEMINAR
SASAKI SEMINAR
OH...
...SO YOU'RE TAKING THIS TOO.

CHAPTER 30 ... SURE ENOUGH, HE'S FORGOTTEN SAKI KAWASAKI.

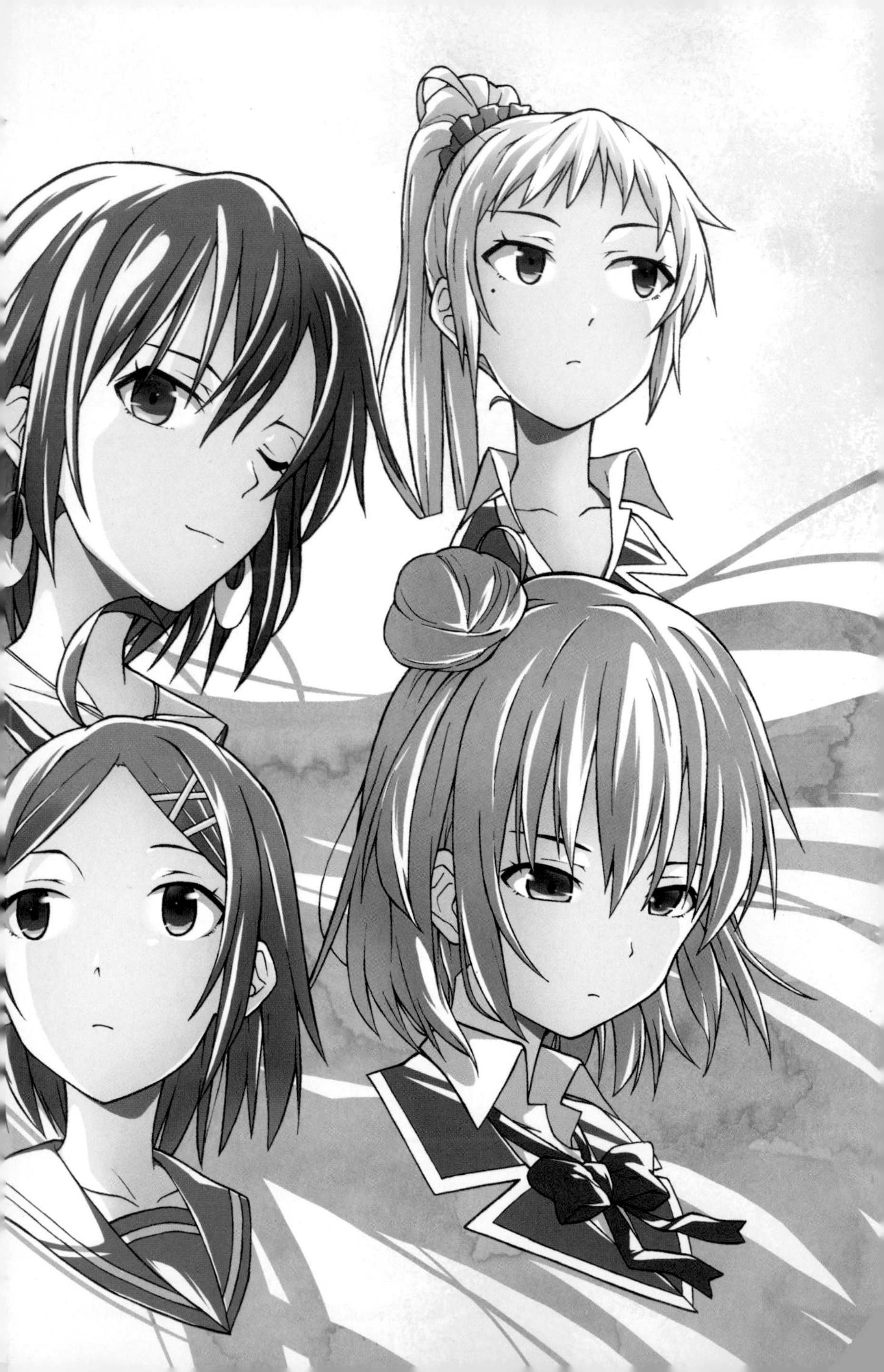

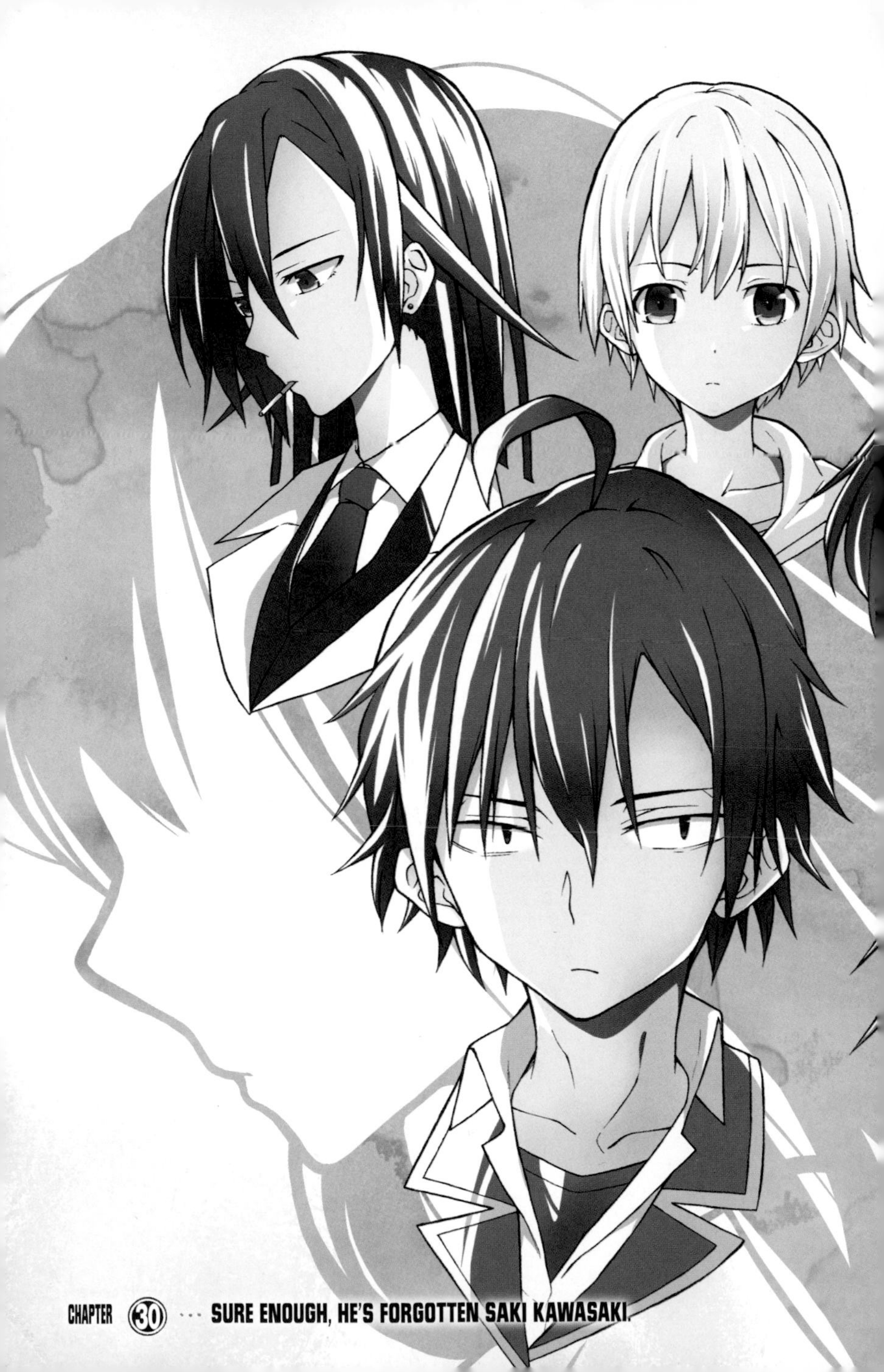

CHAPTER 30 ··· SURE ENOUGH, HE'S FORGOTTEN SAKI KAWASAKI.

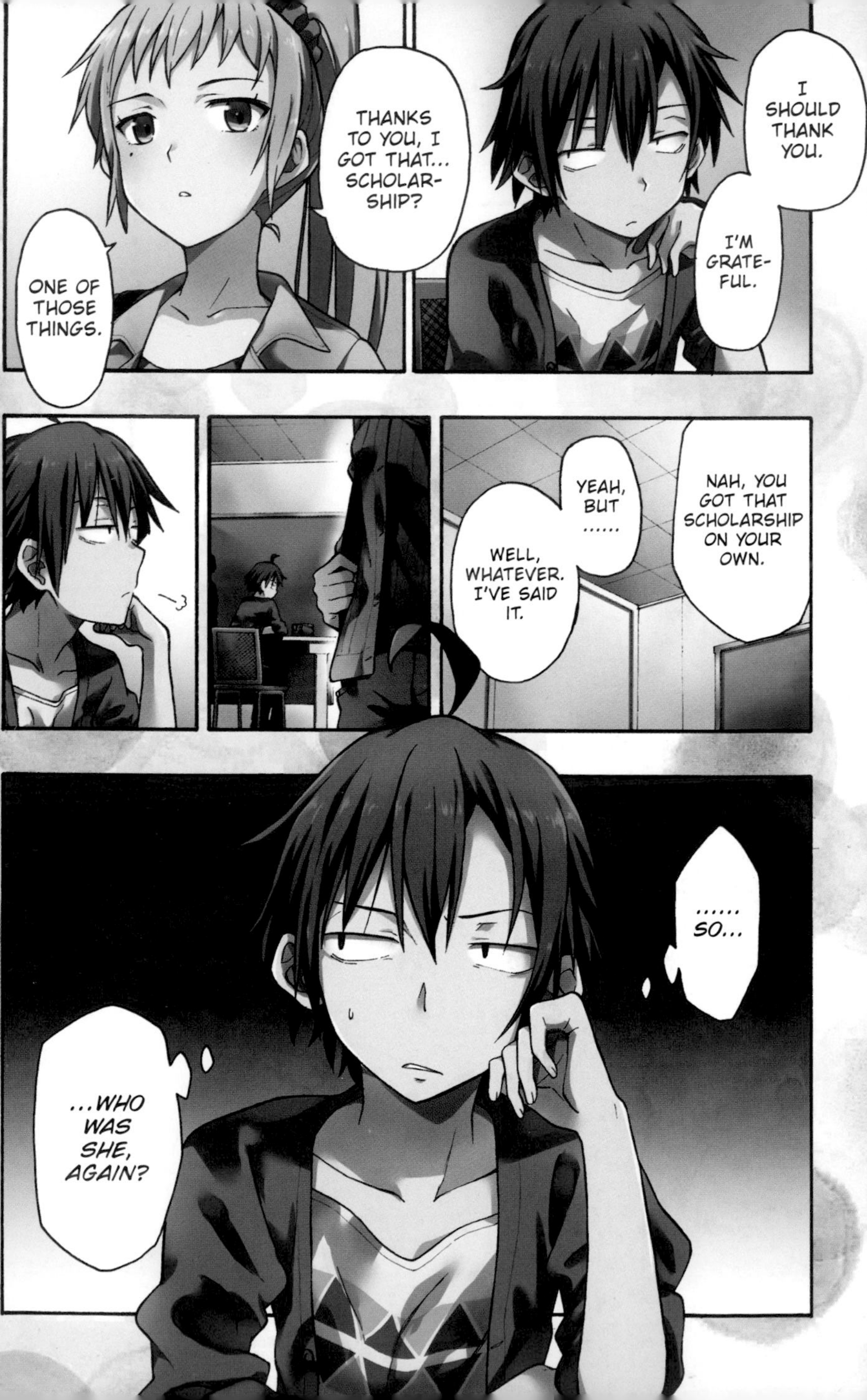
I SHOULD THANK YOU.
I'M GRATE-FUL.
THANKS TO YOU, I GOT THAT... SCHOLAR-SHIP?
ONE OF THOSE THINGS.
NAH, YOU GOT THAT SCHOLARSHIP ON YOUR OWN.
YEAH, BUT ......
WELL, WHATEVER. I'VE SAID IT.
...... SO...
...WHO WAS SHE, AGAIN?

MY YOUTH ROMANTIC COMEDY iS WRØNG, AS I EXPECTED @comic 06

▌Original Story
Wataru Watari
▌Art
Naomichi Io
▌Character Design
Ponkan ⑧

MY YOUTH ROMANTIC COMEDY IS WRONG, AS I EXPECTED @COMIC
CHARACTERS + STORY SO FAR

HACHIMAN HIKIGAYA

➤ LONER AND A TWISTED HUMAN BEING. FORCED TO JOIN THE SERVICE CLUB. ASPIRES TO BE A HOUSEHUSBAND.

YUKINO YUKINOSHITA

➤ PERFECT SUPERWOMAN WITH TOP GRADES AND FLAWLESS LOOKS, BUT HER PERSONALITY AND BOOBS ARE A LETDOWN. PRESIDENT OF THE SERVICE CLUB.

YUI YUIGAHAMA

➤ WITH HER LIGHT-BROWN HAIR, MINISKIRT, AND BIG BOOBS, SHE SEEMS LIKE THE SLUTTY TYPE...BUT SHE'S ACTUALLY A VIRGIN!? MEMBER OF THE SERVICE CLUB.

KOMACHI HIKIGAYA

➤ HACHIMAN'S LITTLE SISTER. IN MIDDLE SCHOOL. EVERYTHING SHE DOES IS CALCULATED!?

SAIKA TOTSUKA

➤ THE SINGLE FLOWER BLOOMING IN THIS STORY. BUT...HAS A "PACKAGE."

SHIZUKA HIRATSUKA

➤ GUIDANCE COUNSELOR. ATTEMPTING TO FIX HACHIMAN BY FORCING HIM INTO THE SERVICE CLUB.

SAKI KAWASAKI

➤ HACHIMAN'S CLASSMATE. TACITURN AND MYSTERIOUS.

YOSHITERU ZAIMOKUZA

➤ AFFLICTED WITH M-2 SYNDROME, HE ASPIRES TO BE A LIGHT NOVEL AUTHOR.

HARUNO YUKINOSHITA

➤ YUKINO'S SISTER. UNIVERSITY UNDERGRADUATE. IS QUITE INTERESTED IN HACHIMAN.

HACHIMAN HIKIGAYA, SECOND YEAR AT SOUBU MUNICIPAL HIGH SCHOOL IN CHIBA CITY, IS A LONER. BUT EVER SINCE HE WAS FORCED INTO JOINING THE SERVICE CLUB, A MYSTERIOUS CLUB CAPTAINED BY THE MOST BEAUTIFUL GIRL IN SCHOOL, YUKINO YUKINOSHITA, HIS LONER LIFE HAS RAPIDLY BEEN VEERING OFF IN AN UNDESIRABLE DIRECTION. WHEN HACHIMAN WITNESSED THE YUKINOSHITA FAMILY LIMOUSINE ROLLING AWAY ON THE FINAL DAY OF THE CAMPING TRIP, HE COULDN'T HELP BUT FEEL SHE WAS CONNECTED TO HIS ACCIDENT. HE KEEPS HIS THOUGHTS TO HIMSELF AS HE SPENDS THE REST OF HIS SUMMER VACATION AT HOME. BUT THEN SUDDENLY, YUI COMES TO VISIT...

MADE IN COOPERATION WITH THE CHIBA CITY LOCATION SERVICE

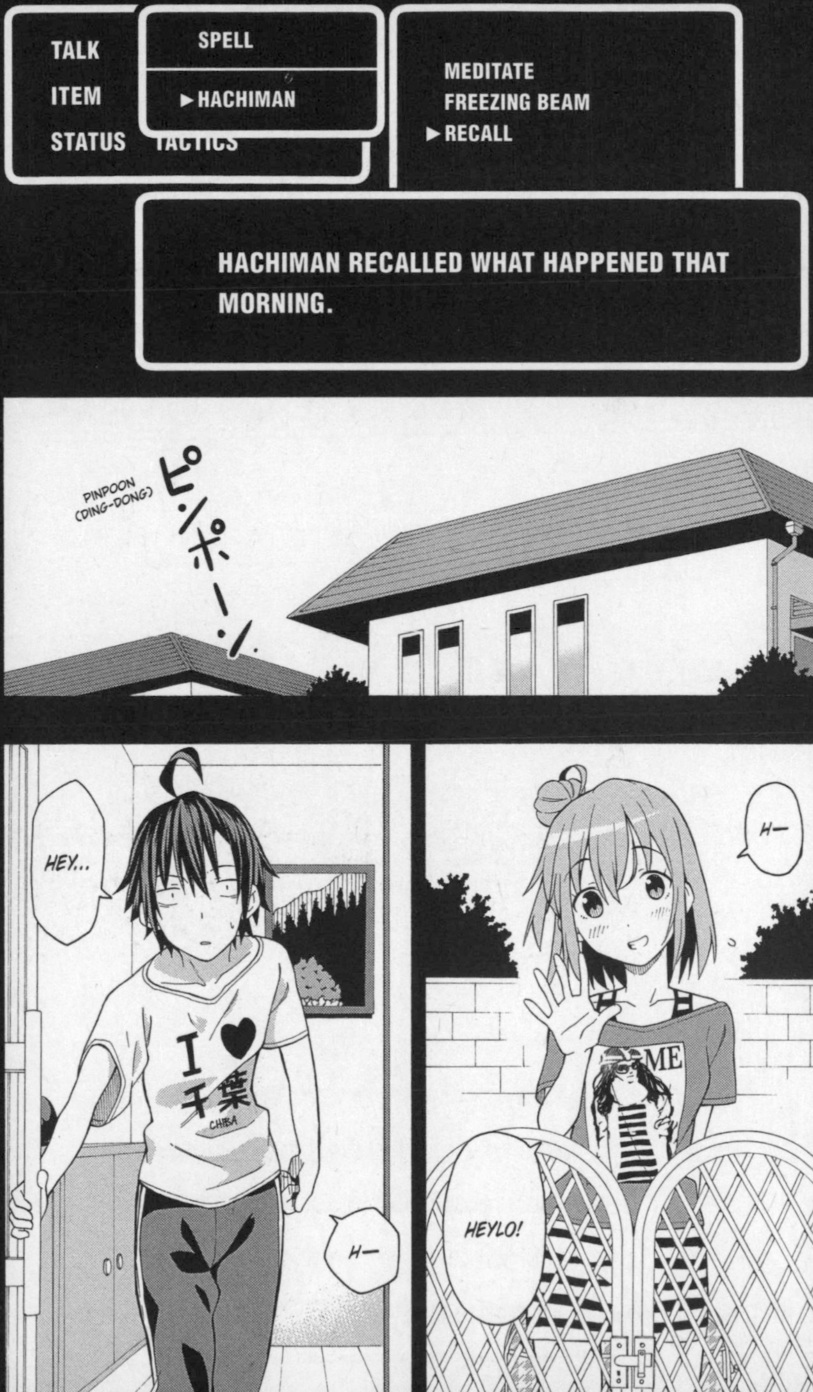
TALK
ITEM
STATUS
TACTICS
SPELL
▶HACHIMAN
MEDITATE
FREEZING BEAM
▶RECALL
HACHIMAN RECALLED WHAT HAPPENED THAT MORNING.
ピンポーン
PINPOON (DING-DONG)
H—
HEYLO!
ME
HEY...
H—
I ♥ 千葉
CHIBA

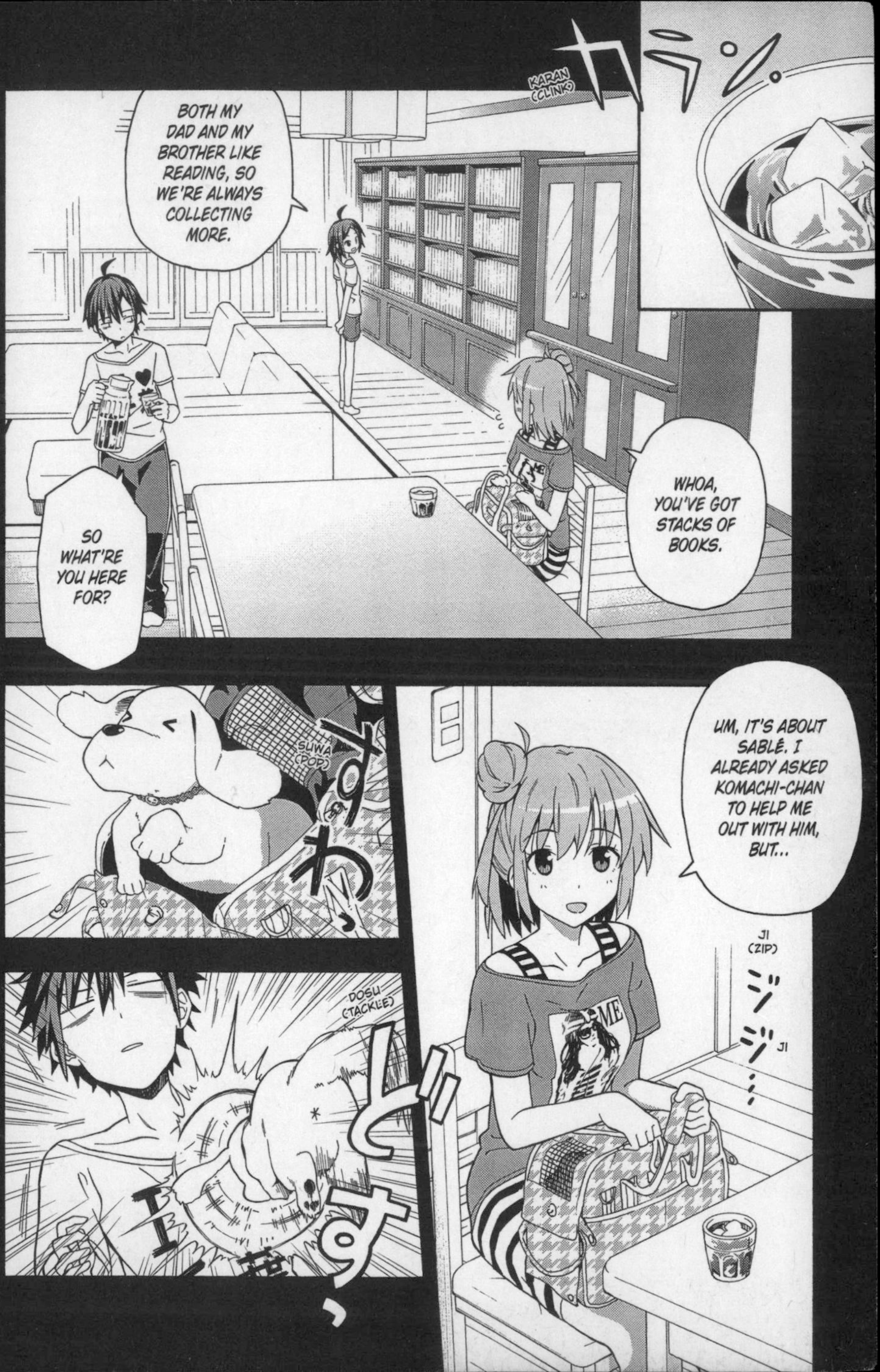
KARAN (CLINK)
WHOA, YOU'VE GOT STACKS OF BOOKS.
BOTH MY DAD AND MY BROTHER LIKE READING, SO WE'RE ALWAYS COLLECTING MORE.
SO WHAT'RE YOU HERE FOR?
UM, IT'S ABOUT SABLÉ. I ALREADY ASKED KOMACHI-CHAN TO HELP ME OUT WITH HIM, BUT...
JI (ZIP)
JI
SUWA (POP)
DOSU (TACKLE)

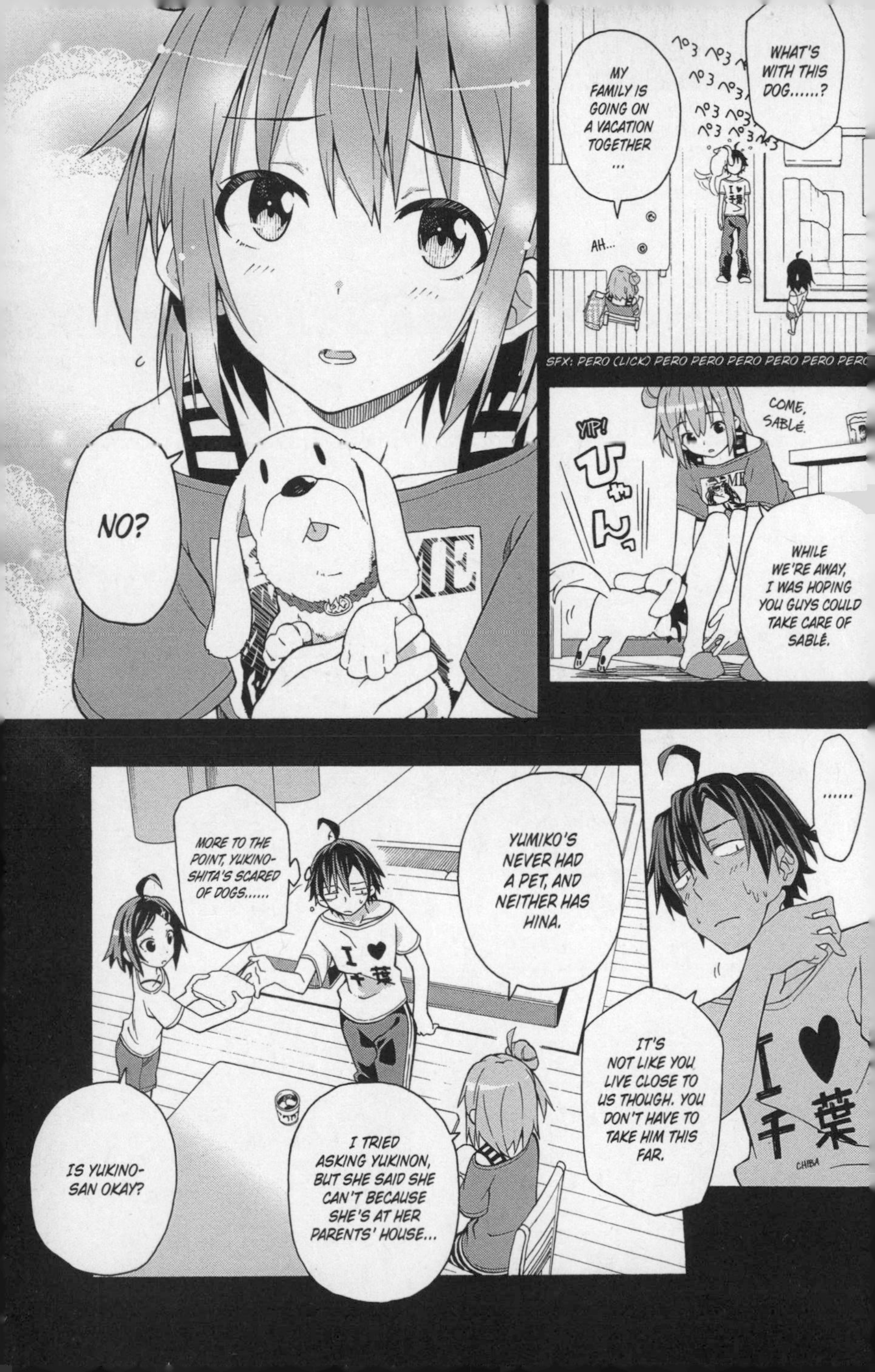

WHAT'S WITH THIS DOG......?
MY FAMILY IS GOING ON A VACATION TOGETHER...
AH...
SFX: PERO (LICK) PERO PERO PERO PERO PERO PERO
COME, SABLÉ.
YIP!
ひゅん
WHILE WE'RE AWAY, I WAS HOPING YOU GUYS COULD TAKE CARE OF SABLÉ.
NO?
......
IT'S NOT LIKE YOU LIVE CLOSE TO US THOUGH. YOU DON'T HAVE TO TAKE HIM THIS FAR.
I ♥ 千葉
CHIBA
YUMIKO'S NEVER HAD A PET, AND NEITHER HAS HINA.
MORE TO THE POINT, YUKINOSHITA'S SCARED OF DOGS......
I TRIED ASKING YUKINON, BUT SHE SAID SHE CAN'T BECAUSE SHE'S AT HER PARENTS' HOUSE...
IS YUKINO-SAN OKAY?

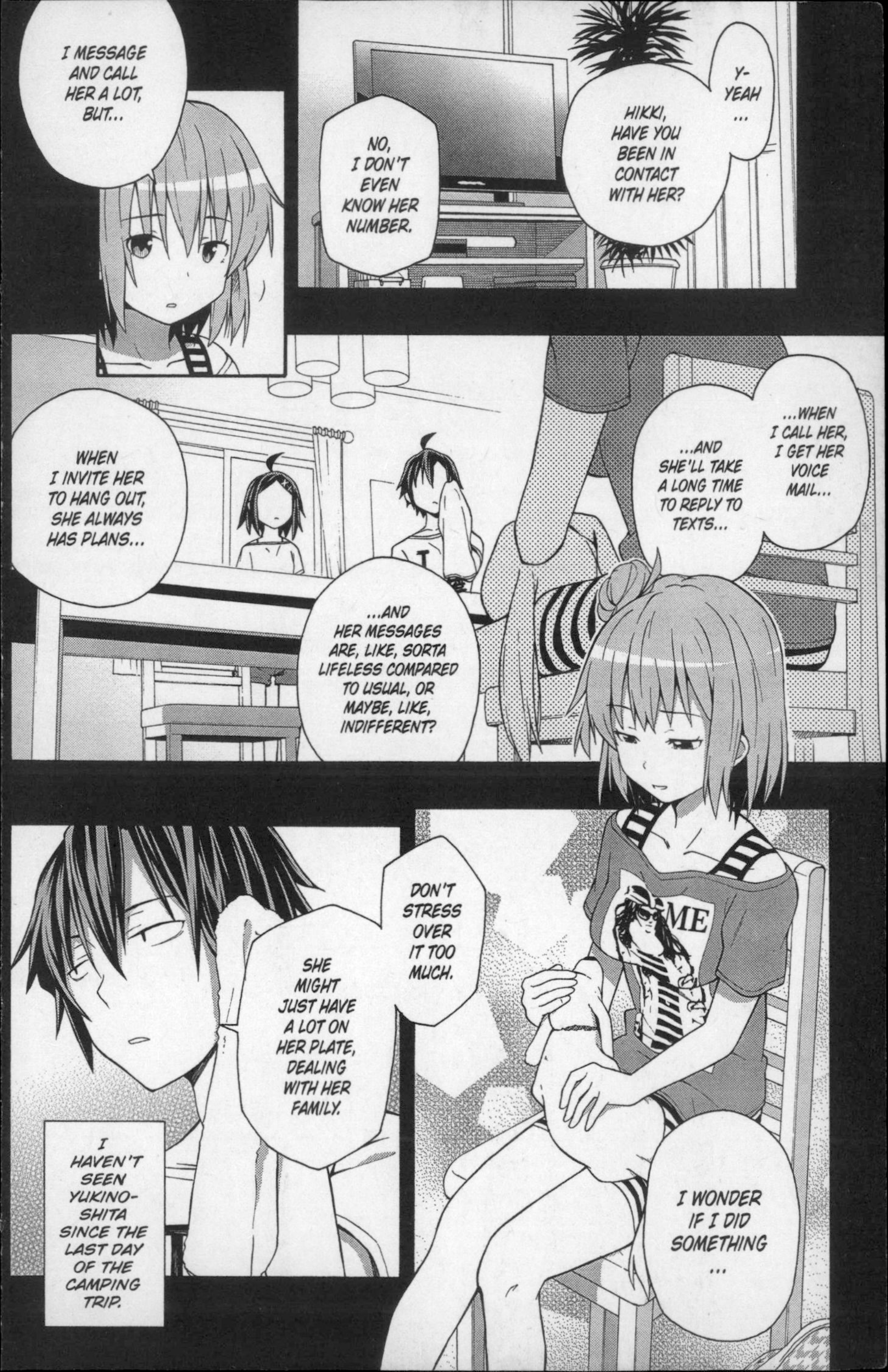
Y-YEAH...
HIKKI, HAVE YOU BEEN IN CONTACT WITH HER?
NO, I DON'T EVEN KNOW HER NUMBER.
I MESSAGE AND CALL HER A LOT, BUT...
...WHEN I CALL HER, I GET HER VOICE MAIL...
...AND SHE'LL TAKE A LONG TIME TO REPLY TO TEXTS...
WHEN I INVITE HER TO HANG OUT, SHE ALWAYS HAS PLANS...
...AND HER MESSAGES ARE, LIKE, SORTA LIFELESS COMPARED TO USUAL, OR MAYBE, LIKE, INDIFFERENT?
I WONDER IF I DID SOMETHING...
DON'T STRESS OVER IT TOO MUCH.
SHE MIGHT JUST HAVE A LOT ON HER PLATE, DEALING WITH HER FAMILY.
I HAVEN'T SEEN YUKINOSHITA SINCE THE LAST DAY OF THE CAMPING TRIP.

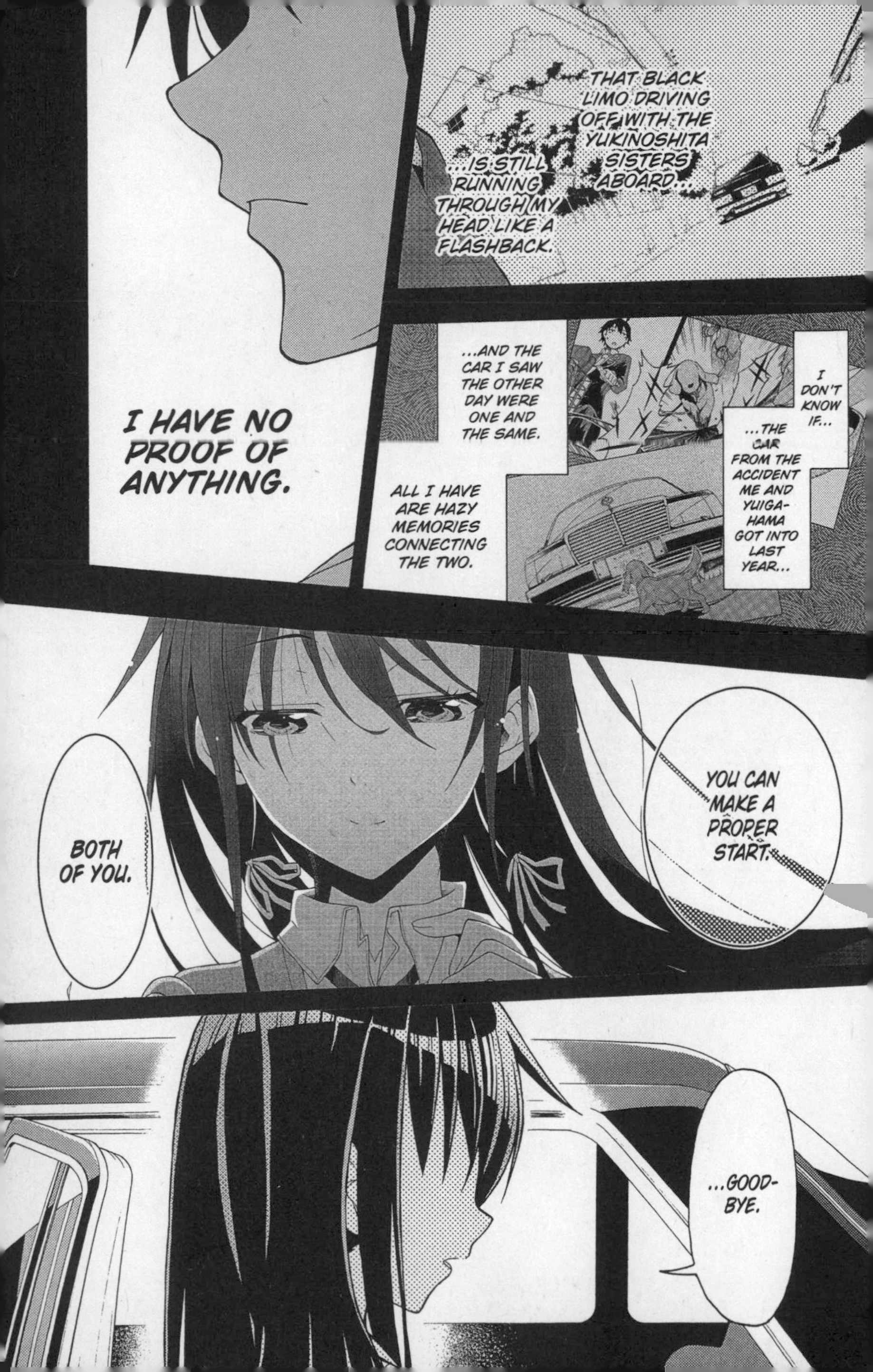
THAT BLACK LIMO DRIVING OFF WITH THE YUKINOSHITA SISTERS ABOARD...
...IS STILL RUNNING THROUGH MY HEAD LIKE A FLASHBACK.
I DON'T KNOW IF...
...THE CAR FROM THE ACCIDENT ME AND YUIGA-HAMA GOT INTO LAST YEAR...
...AND THE CAR I SAW THE OTHER DAY WERE ONE AND THE SAME.
ALL I HAVE ARE HAZY MEMORIES CONNECTING THE TWO.
I HAVE NO PROOF OF ANYTHING.
YOU CAN MAKE A PROPER START.
BOTH OF YOU.
...GOOD-BYE.

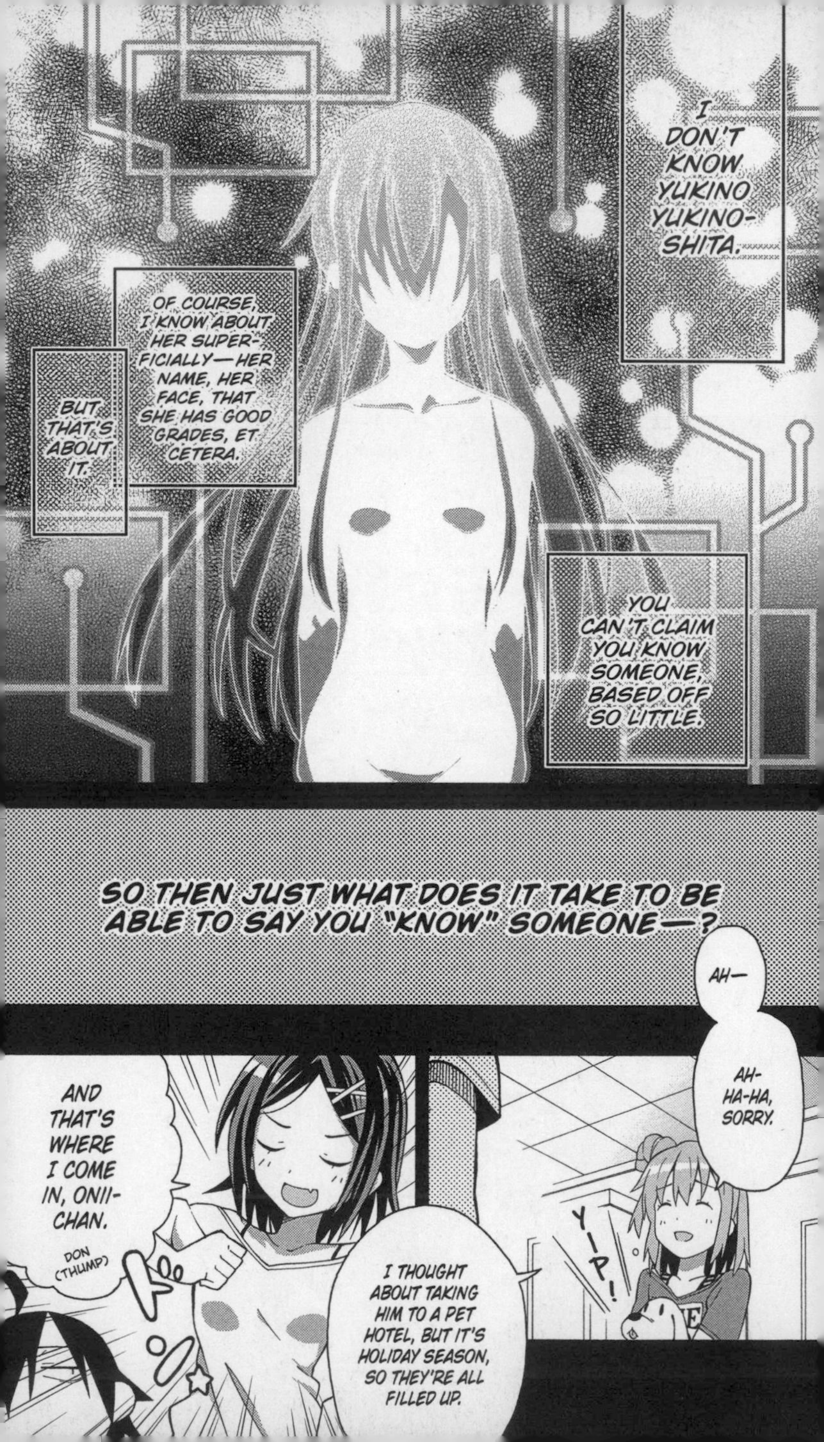
I DON'T KNOW YUKINO YUKINOSHITA.
OF COURSE, I KNOW ABOUT HER SUPERFICIALLY—HER NAME, HER FACE, THAT SHE HAS GOOD GRADES, ET CETERA.
BUT THAT'S ABOUT IT.
YOU CAN'T CLAIM YOU KNOW SOMEONE, BASED OFF SO LITTLE.
SO THEN JUST WHAT DOES IT TAKE TO BE ABLE TO SAY YOU "KNOW" SOMEONE—?
AH—
AH-HA-HA, SORRY.
YIP!
I THOUGHT ABOUT TAKING HIM TO A PET HOTEL, BUT IT'S HOLIDAY SEASON, SO THEY'RE ALL FILLED UP.
AND THAT'S WHERE I COME IN, ONII-CHAN.
DON (THUMP)

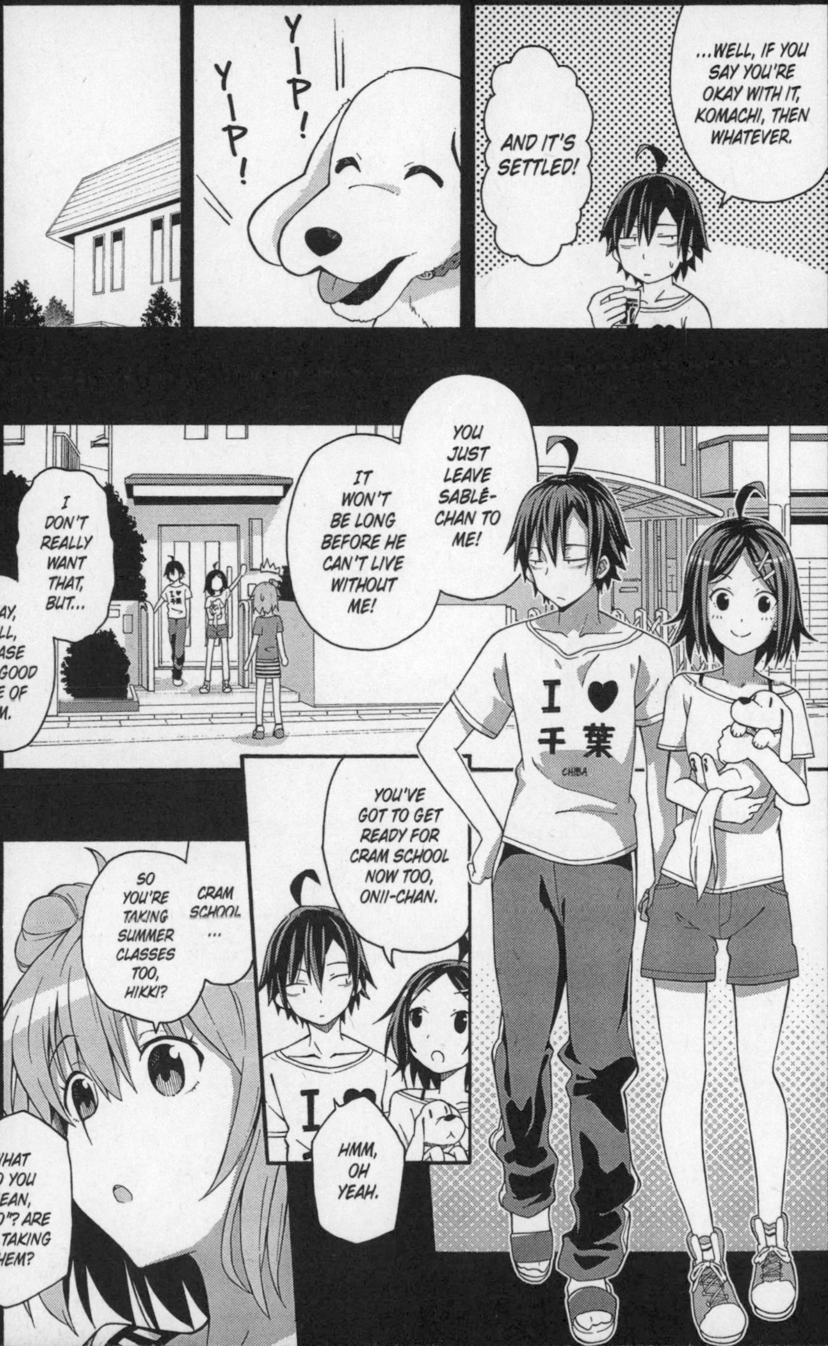
...WELL, IF YOU SAY YOU'RE OKAY WITH IT, KOMACHI, THEN WHATEVER.
AND IT'S SETTLED!
YIP! YIP!
YOU JUST LEAVE SABLÉ-CHAN TO ME!
IT WON'T BE LONG BEFORE HE CAN'T LIVE WITHOUT ME!
I DON'T REALLY WANT THAT, BUT...
OKAY, WELL, PLEASE TAKE GOOD CARE OF HIM.
I ♥ 千葉
CHIBA
YOU'VE GOT TO GET READY FOR CRAM SCHOOL NOW TOO, ONII-CHAN.
CRAM SCHOOL...
SO YOU'RE TAKING SUMMER CLASSES TOO, HIKKI?
HMM, OH YEAH.
WHAT DO YOU MEAN, "TOO"? ARE YOU TAKING THEM?

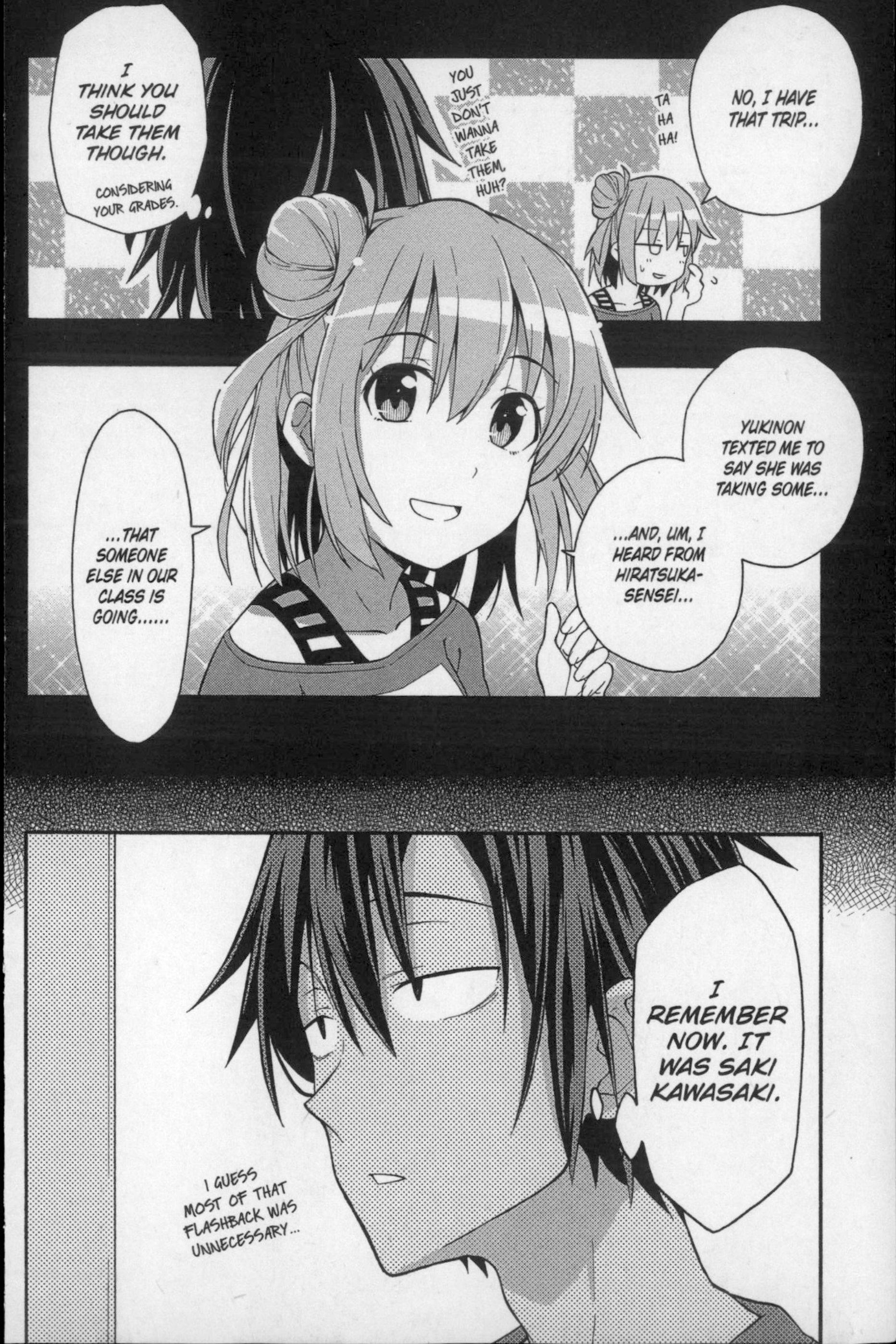
NO, I HAVE THAT TRIP...
TA HA HA!
YOU JUST DON'T WANNA TAKE THEM, HUH?
I THINK YOU SHOULD TAKE THEM THOUGH.
CONSIDERING YOUR GRADES.
YUKINON TEXTED ME TO SAY SHE WAS TAKING SOME...
...AND, UM, I HEARD FROM HIRATSUKA-SENSEI...
...THAT SOMEONE ELSE IN OUR CLASS IS GOING......
I REMEMBER NOW. IT WAS SAKI KAWASAKI.
I GUESS MOST OF THAT FLASHBACK WAS UNNECESSARY...

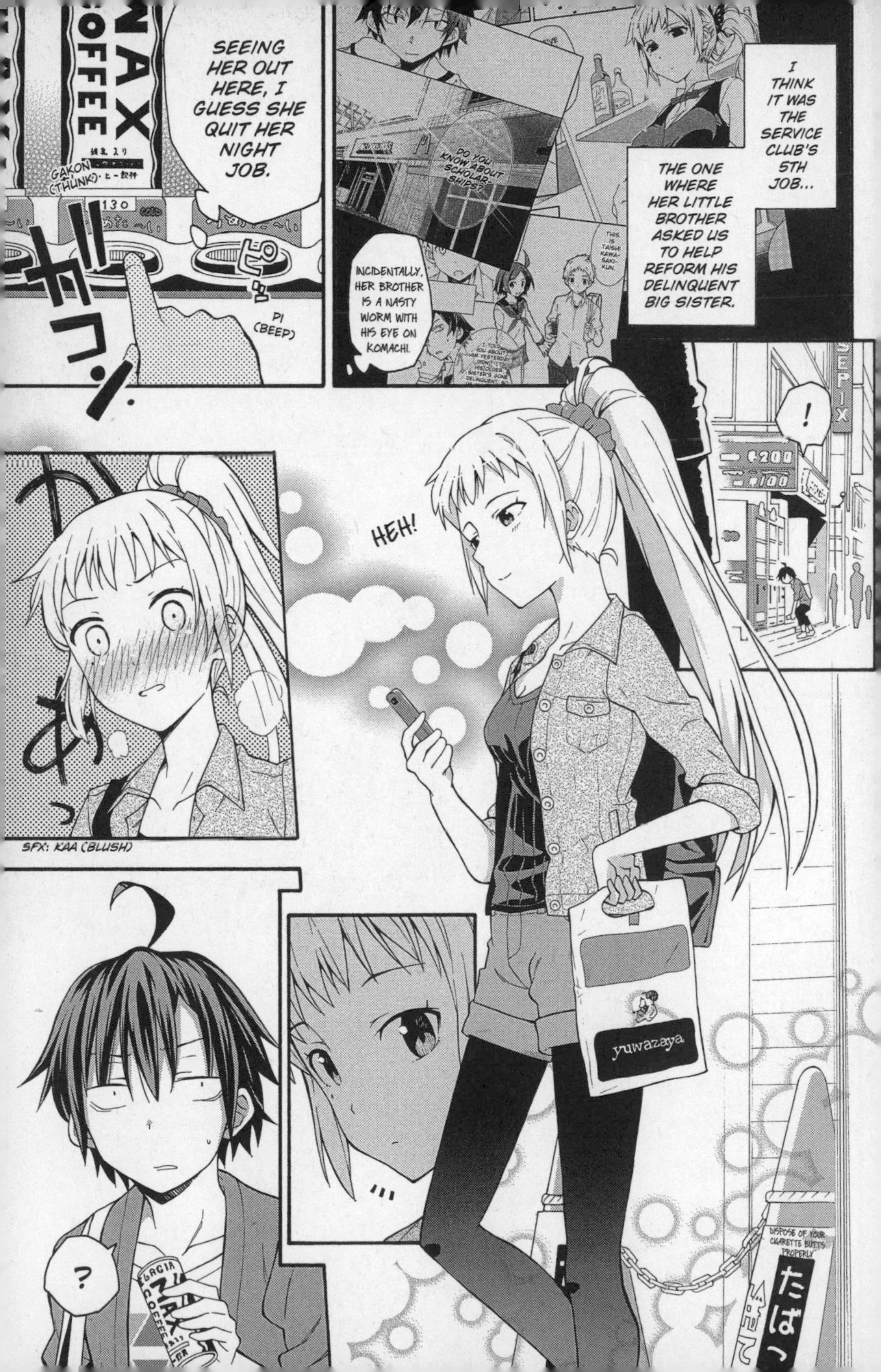
I THINK IT WAS THE SERVICE CLUB'S 5TH JOB...
THE ONE WHERE HER LITTLE BROTHER ASKED US TO HELP REFORM HIS DELINQUENT BIG SISTER.
DO YOU KNOW ABOUT SCHOLARSHIPS?
THIS IS TAISHI KAWASAKI-KUN.
INCIDENTALLY, HER BROTHER IS A NASTY WORM WITH HIS EYE ON KOMACHI.
SEEING HER OUT HERE, I GUESS SHE QUIT HER NIGHT JOB.
MAX COFFEE
GAKON (THUNK)
PI (BEEP)
!
HEH!
SFX: KAA (BLUSH)
yuwazaya
...
?
DISPOSE OF YOUR CIGARETTE BUTTS PROPERLY

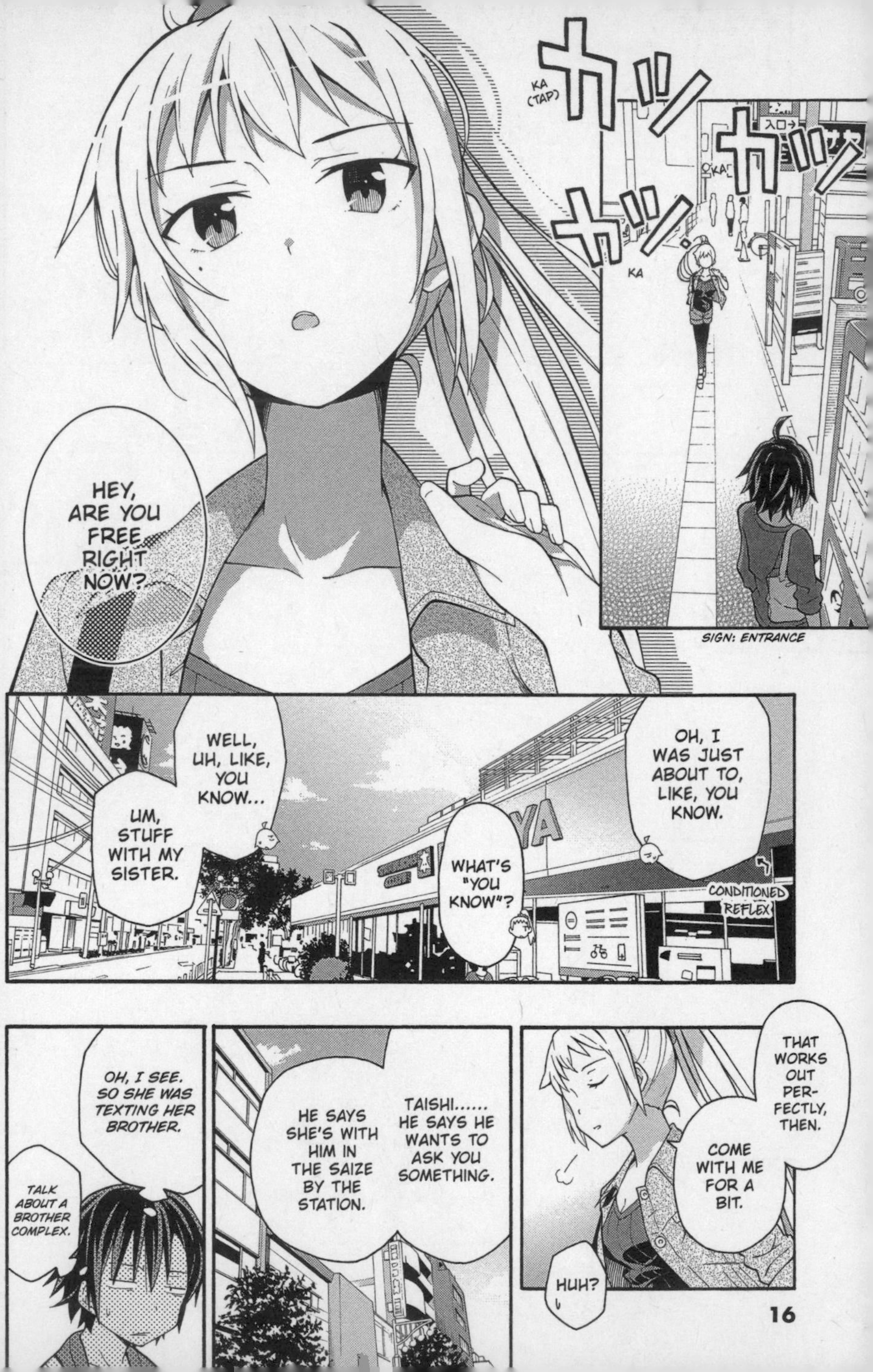
KA (TAP)
KA
KA
SIGN: ENTRANCE
HEY, ARE YOU FREE RIGHT NOW?
OH, I WAS JUST ABOUT TO, LIKE, YOU KNOW.
CONDITIONED REFLEX
WHAT'S "YOU KNOW"?
WELL, UH, LIKE, YOU KNOW...
UM, STUFF WITH MY SISTER.
THAT WORKS OUT PER-FECTLY, THEN.
COME WITH ME FOR A BIT.
HUH?
TAISHI...... HE SAYS HE WANTS TO ASK YOU SOMETHING.
HE SAYS SHE'S WITH HIM IN THE SAIZE BY THE STATION.
OH, I SEE. SO SHE WAS TEXTING HER BROTHER.
TALK ABOUT A BROTHER COMPLEX.

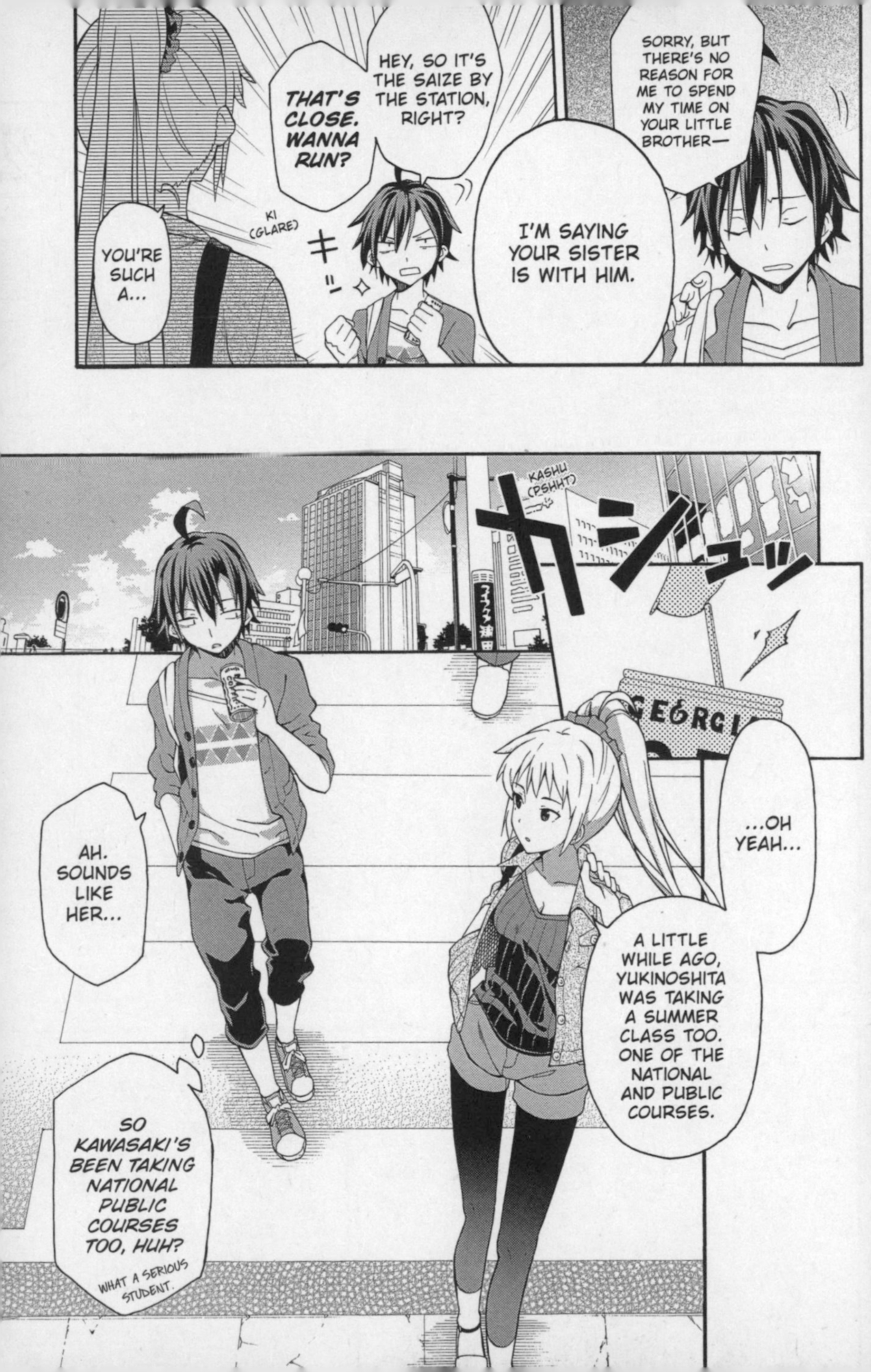
SORRY, BUT THERE'S NO REASON FOR ME TO SPEND MY TIME ON YOUR LITTLE BROTHER—
I'M SAYING YOUR SISTER IS WITH HIM.
HEY, SO IT'S THE SAIZE BY THE STATION, RIGHT?
THAT'S CLOSE. WANNA RUN?
KI (GLARE)
YOU'RE SUCH A...
KASHU (PSHHT)
...OH YEAH...
A LITTLE WHILE AGO, YUKINOSHITA WAS TAKING A SUMMER CLASS TOO. ONE OF THE NATIONAL AND PUBLIC COURSES.
AH. SOUNDS LIKE HER...
SO KAWASAKI'S BEEN TAKING NATIONAL PUBLIC COURSES TOO, HUH?
WHAT A SERIOUS STUDENT.

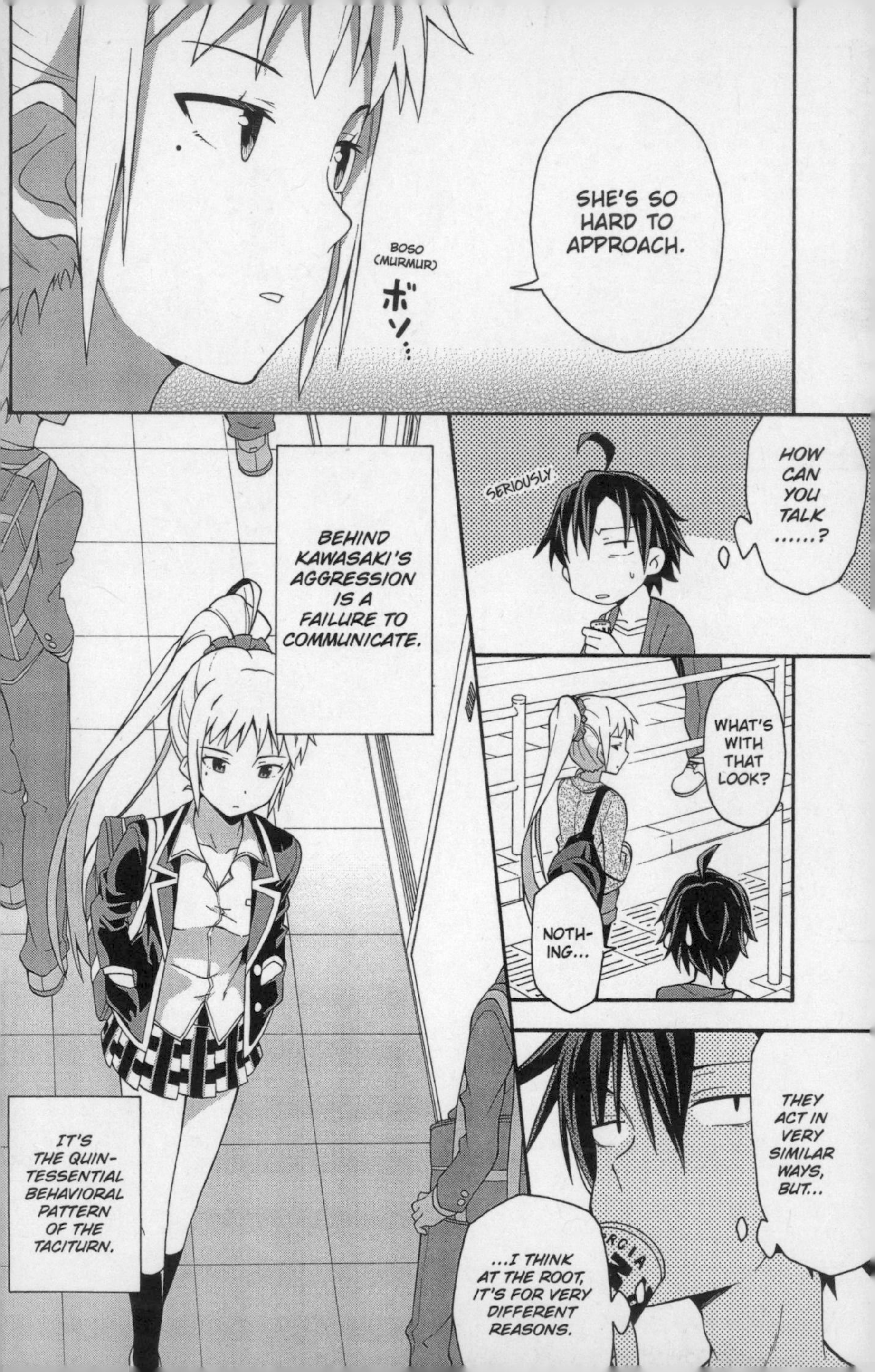
SHE'S SO HARD TO APPROACH.
BOSO (MURMUR)
ボソ…
HOW CAN YOU TALK ......?
SERIOUSLY
WHAT'S WITH THAT LOOK?
NOTH- ING...
THEY ACT IN VERY SIMILAR WAYS, BUT...
...I THINK AT THE ROOT, IT'S FOR VERY DIFFERENT REASONS.
BEHIND KAWASAKI'S AGGRESSION IS A FAILURE TO COMMUNICATE.
IT'S THE QUIN- TESSENTIAL BEHAVIORAL PATTERN OF THE TACITURN.

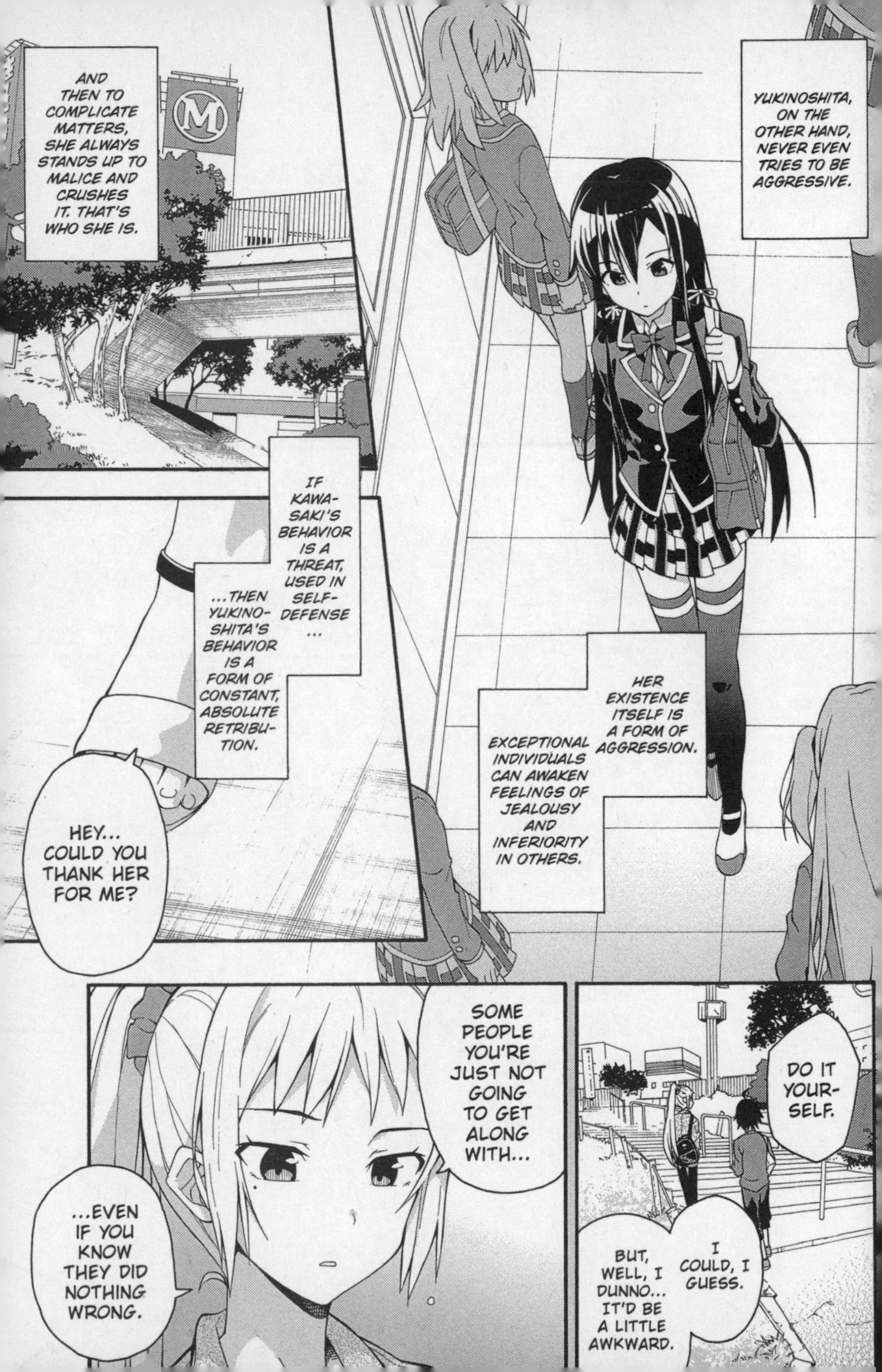
YUKINOSHITA, ON THE OTHER HAND, NEVER EVEN TRIES TO BE AGGRESSIVE.
HER EXISTENCE ITSELF IS A FORM OF AGGRESSION.
EXCEPTIONAL INDIVIDUALS CAN AWAKEN FEELINGS OF JEALOUSY AND INFERIORITY IN OTHERS.
AND THEN TO COMPLICATE MATTERS, SHE ALWAYS STANDS UP TO MALICE AND CRUSHES IT. THAT'S WHO SHE IS.
IF KAWASAKI'S BEHAVIOR IS A THREAT, USED IN SELF-DEFENSE...
...THEN YUKINOSHITA'S BEHAVIOR IS A FORM OF CONSTANT, ABSOLUTE RETRIBUTION.
HEY... COULD YOU THANK HER FOR ME?
DO IT YOURSELF.
I COULD, I GUESS.
BUT, WELL, I DUNNO... IT'D BE A LITTLE AWKWARD.
SOME PEOPLE YOU'RE JUST NOT GOING TO GET ALONG WITH...
...EVEN IF YOU KNOW THEY DID NOTHING WRONG.

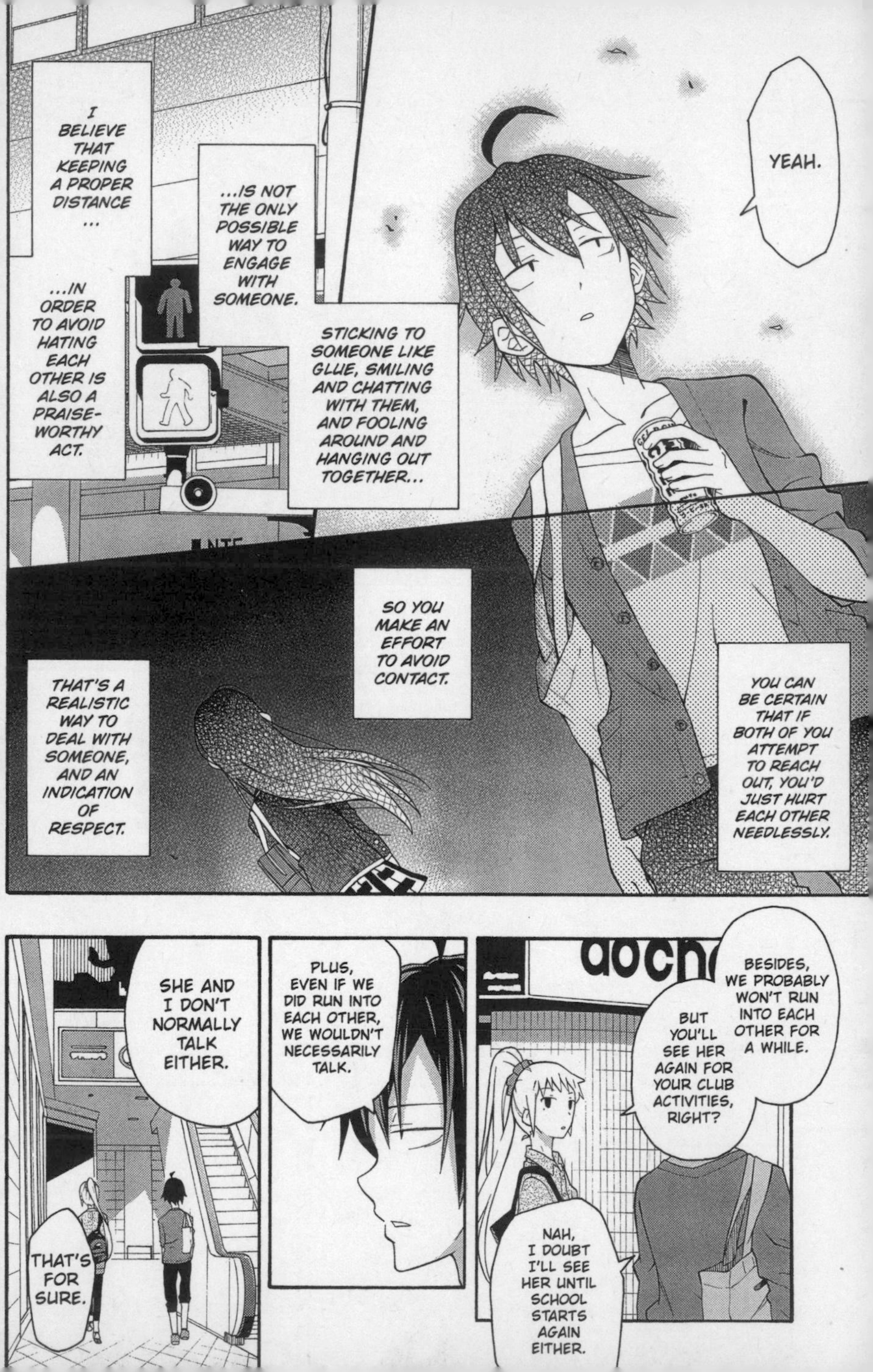
YEAH.
STICKING TO SOMEONE LIKE GLUE, SMILING AND CHATTING WITH THEM, AND FOOLING AROUND AND HANGING OUT TOGETHER...
...IS NOT THE ONLY POSSIBLE WAY TO ENGAGE WITH SOMEONE.
I BELIEVE THAT KEEPING A PROPER DISTANCE...
...IN ORDER TO AVOID HATING EACH OTHER IS ALSO A PRAISE-WORTHY ACT.
YOU CAN BE CERTAIN THAT IF BOTH OF YOU ATTEMPT TO REACH OUT, YOU'D JUST HURT EACH OTHER NEEDLESSLY.
SO YOU MAKE AN EFFORT TO AVOID CONTACT.
THAT'S A REALISTIC WAY TO DEAL WITH SOMEONE, AND AN INDICATION OF RESPECT.
BESIDES, WE PROBABLY WON'T RUN INTO EACH OTHER FOR A WHILE.
BUT YOU'LL SEE HER AGAIN FOR YOUR CLUB ACTIVITIES, RIGHT?
NAH, I DOUBT I'LL SEE HER UNTIL SCHOOL STARTS AGAIN EITHER.
PLUS, EVEN IF WE DID RUN INTO EACH OTHER, WE WOULDN'T NECESSARILY TALK.
SHE AND I DON'T NORMALLY TALK EITHER.
THAT'S FOR SURE.

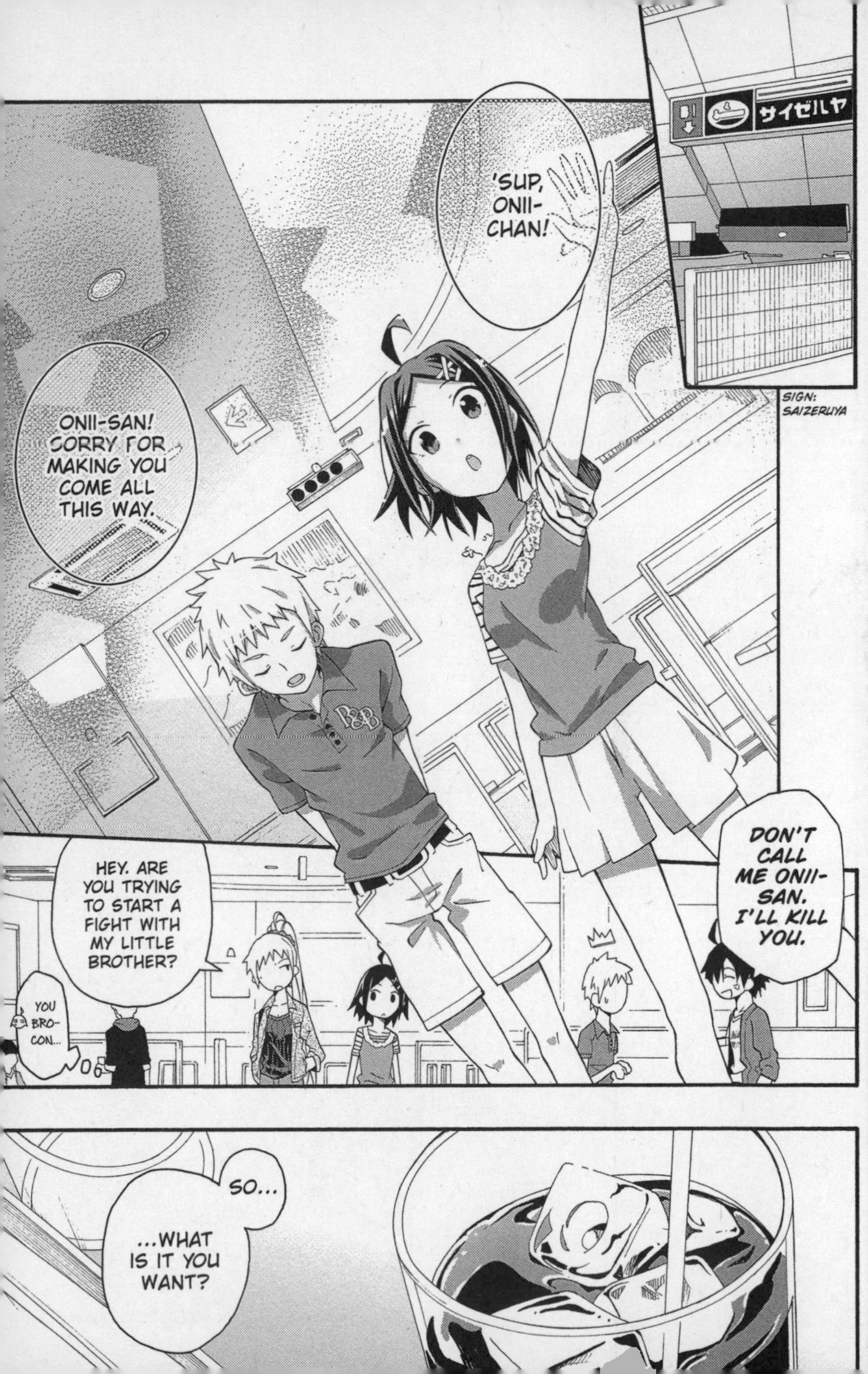
サイゼルヤ
SIGN: SAIZERUYA
'SUP, ONII-CHAN!
ONII-SAN! SORRY FOR MAKING YOU COME ALL THIS WAY.
DON'T CALL ME ONII-SAN. I'LL KILL YOU.
HEY. ARE YOU TRYING TO START A FIGHT WITH MY LITTLE BROTHER?
YOU BRO-CON...
SO...
...WHAT IS IT YOU WANT?

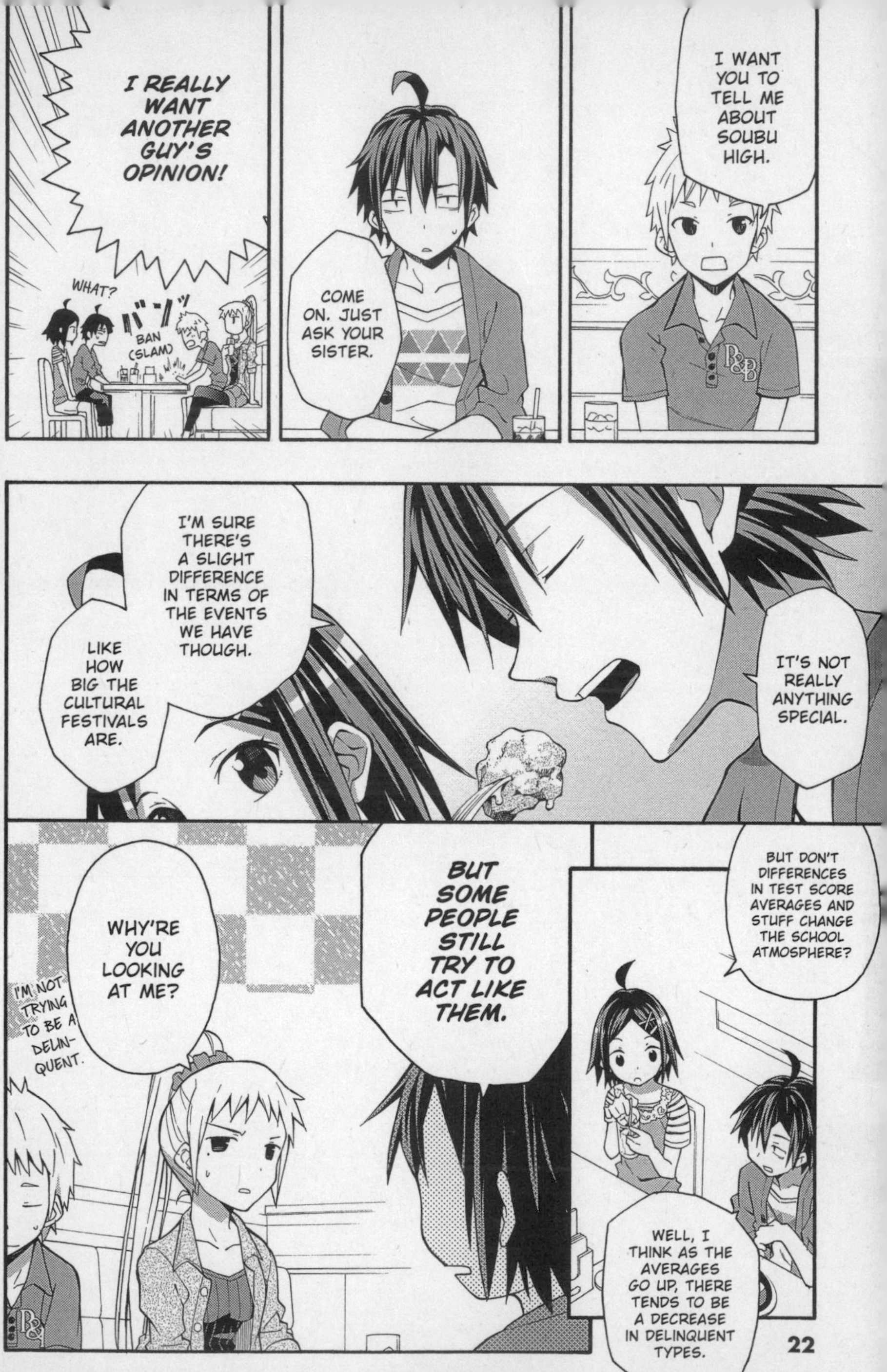
I WANT YOU TO TELL ME ABOUT SOUBU HIGH.
COME ON. JUST ASK YOUR SISTER.
I REALLY WANT ANOTHER GUY'S OPINION!
WHAT?
BAN (SLAM)
IT'S NOT REALLY ANYTHING SPECIAL.
I'M SURE THERE'S A SLIGHT DIFFERENCE IN TERMS OF THE EVENTS WE HAVE THOUGH.
LIKE HOW BIG THE CULTURAL FESTIVALS ARE.
BUT DON'T DIFFERENCES IN TEST SCORE AVERAGES AND STUFF CHANGE THE SCHOOL ATMOSPHERE?
WELL, I THINK AS THE AVERAGES GO UP, THERE TENDS TO BE A DECREASE IN DELINQUENT TYPES.
BUT SOME PEOPLE STILL TRY TO ACT LIKE THEM.
WHY'RE YOU LOOKING AT ME?
I'M NOT TRYING TO BE A DELINQUENT.

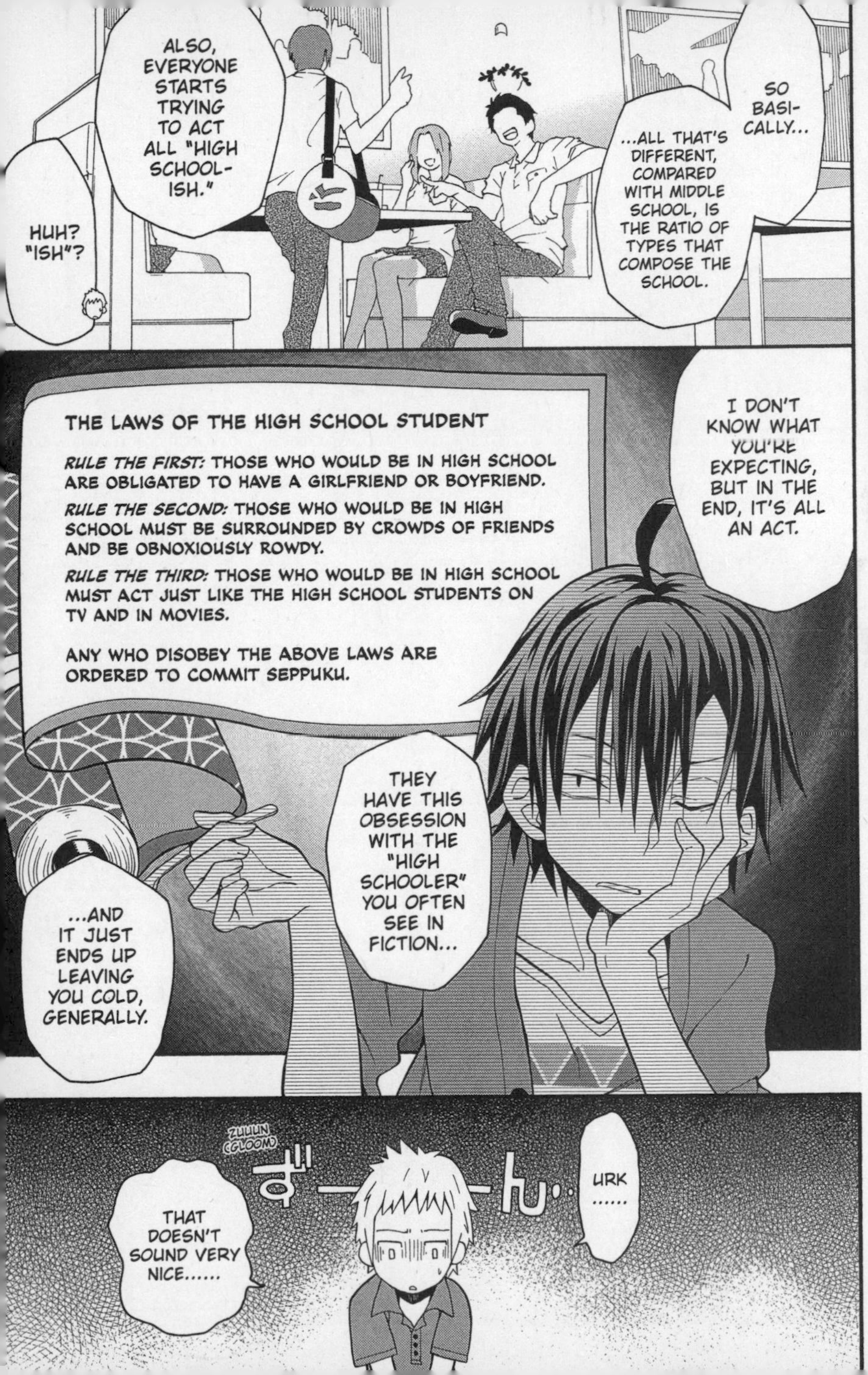
SO BASICALLY...
...ALL THAT'S DIFFERENT, COMPARED WITH MIDDLE SCHOOL, IS THE RATIO OF TYPES THAT COMPOSE THE SCHOOL.
ALSO, EVERYONE STARTS TRYING TO ACT ALL "HIGH SCHOOL-ISH."
HUH? "ISH"?
I DON'T KNOW WHAT YOU'RE EXPECTING, BUT IN THE END, IT'S ALL AN ACT.
THE LAWS OF THE HIGH SCHOOL STUDENT
RULE THE FIRST: THOSE WHO WOULD BE IN HIGH SCHOOL ARE OBLIGATED TO HAVE A GIRLFRIEND OR BOYFRIEND.
RULE THE SECOND: THOSE WHO WOULD BE IN HIGH SCHOOL MUST BE SURROUNDED BY CROWDS OF FRIENDS AND BE OBNOXIOUSLY ROWDY.
RULE THE THIRD: THOSE WHO WOULD BE IN HIGH SCHOOL MUST ACT JUST LIKE THE HIGH SCHOOL STUDENTS ON TV AND IN MOVIES.
ANY WHO DISOBEY THE ABOVE LAWS ARE ORDERED TO COMMIT SEPPUKU.
THEY HAVE THIS OBSESSION WITH THE "HIGH SCHOOLER" YOU OFTEN SEE IN FICTION...
...AND IT JUST ENDS UP LEAVING YOU COLD, GENERALLY.
URK ......
ずーーん・・
ZUUUN (GLOOM)
THAT DOESN'T SOUND VERY NICE......

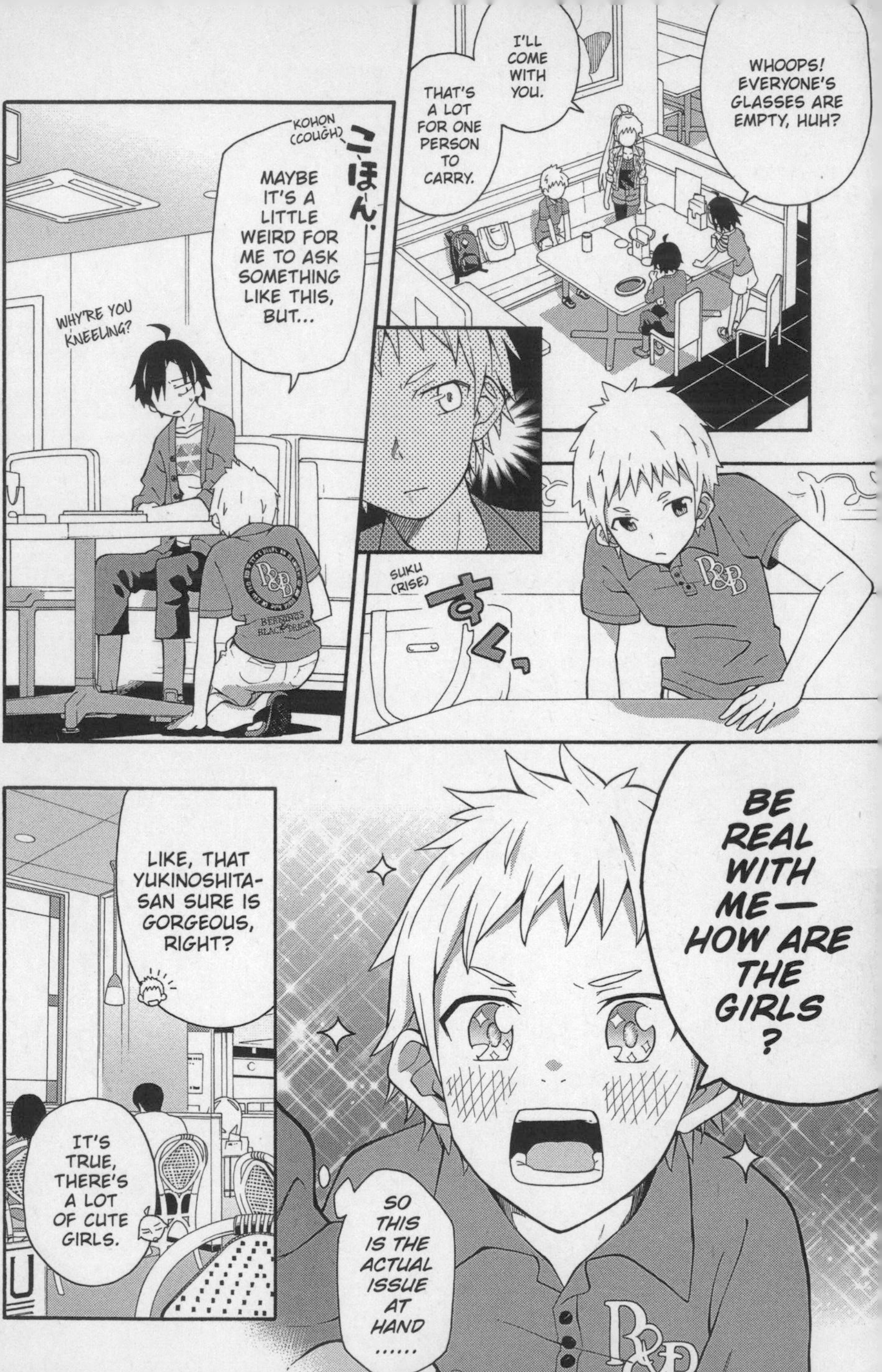
WHOOPS! EVERYONE'S GLASSES ARE EMPTY, HUH?
I'LL COME WITH YOU.
THAT'S A LOT FOR ONE PERSON TO CARRY.
SUKU (RISE)
すく、
KOHON (COUGH)
こほん、
MAYBE IT'S A LITTLE WEIRD FOR ME TO ASK SOMETHING LIKE THIS, BUT...
WHY'RE YOU KNEELING?
BE REAL WITH ME—HOW ARE THE GIRLS?
SO THIS IS THE ACTUAL ISSUE AT HAND......
LIKE, THAT YUKINOSHITA-SAN SURE IS GORGEOUS, RIGHT?
IT'S TRUE, THERE'S A LOT OF CUTE GIRLS.

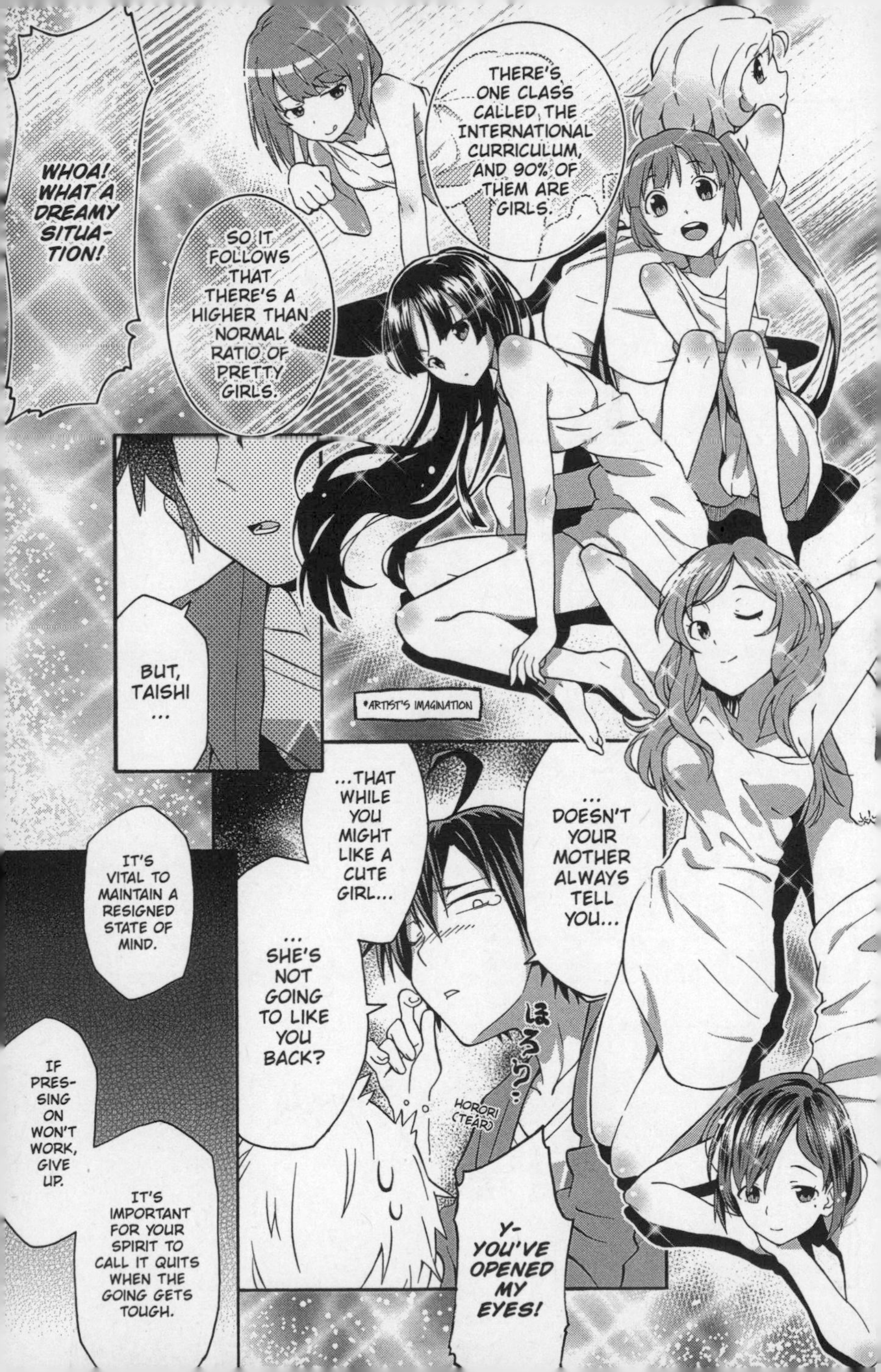
THERE'S ONE CLASS CALLED THE INTERNATIONAL CURRICULUM, AND 90% OF THEM ARE GIRLS.
SO IT FOLLOWS THAT THERE'S A HIGHER THAN NORMAL RATIO OF PRETTY GIRLS.
WHOA! WHAT A DREAMY SITUA-TION!
*ARTIST'S IMAGINATION
BUT, TAISHI ...
... DOESN'T YOUR MOTHER ALWAYS TELL YOU...
...THAT WHILE YOU MIGHT LIKE A CUTE GIRL...
... SHE'S NOT GOING TO LIKE YOU BACK?
ほろり
HORORI (TEAR)
Y-YOU'VE OPENED MY EYES!
IT'S VITAL TO MAINTAIN A RESIGNED STATE OF MIND.
IF PRES-SING ON WON'T WORK, GIVE UP.
IT'S IMPORTANT FOR YOUR SPIRIT TO CALL IT QUITS WHEN THE GOING GETS TOUGH.

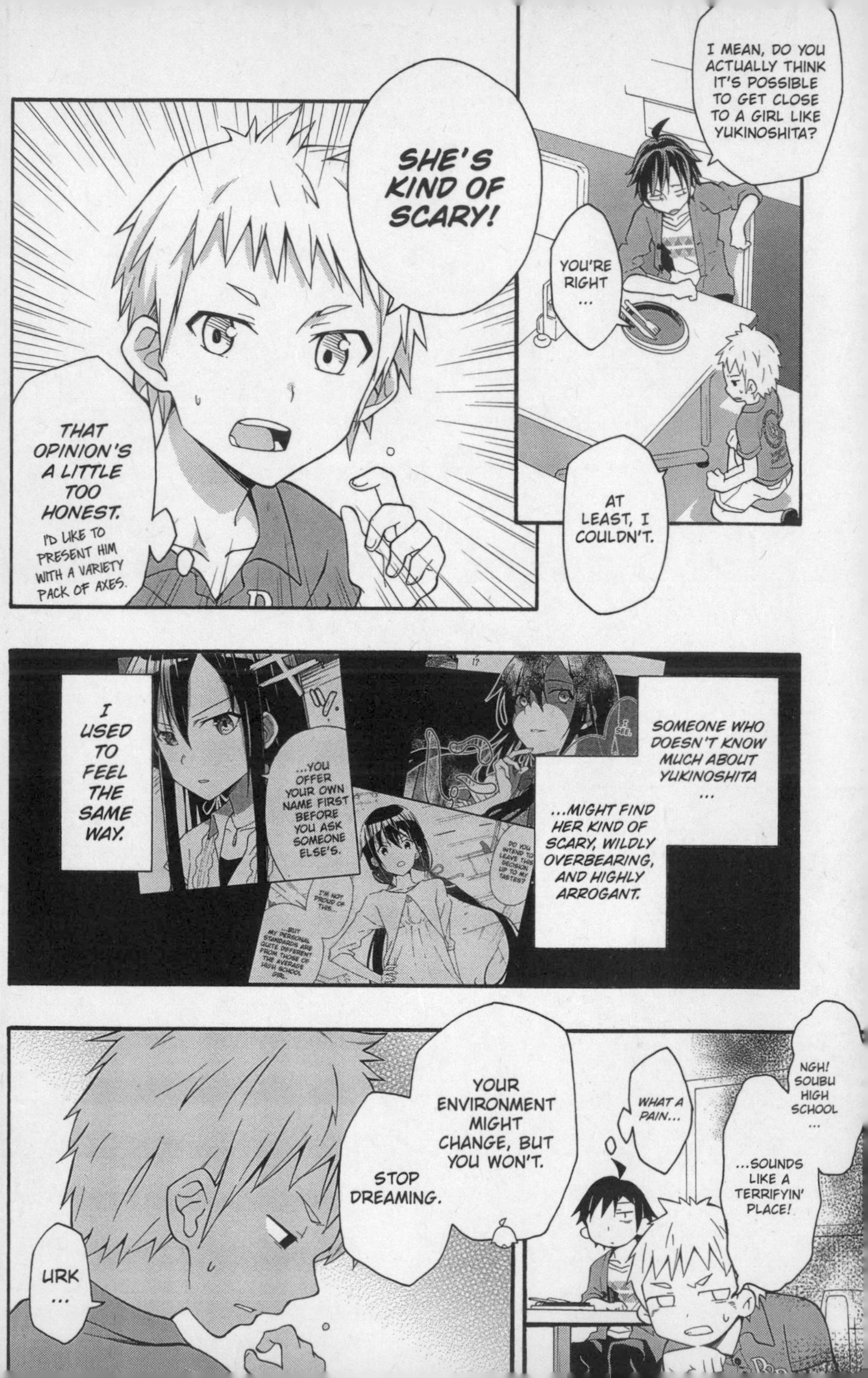
I MEAN, DO YOU ACTUALLY THINK IT'S POSSIBLE TO GET CLOSE TO A GIRL LIKE YUKINOSHITA?
YOU'RE RIGHT...
AT LEAST, I COULDN'T.
SHE'S KIND OF SCARY!
THAT OPINION'S A LITTLE TOO HONEST.
I'D LIKE TO PRESENT HIM WITH A VARIETY PACK OF AXES.
SOMEONE WHO DOESN'T KNOW MUCH ABOUT YUKINOSHITA...
I SEE.
...MIGHT FIND HER KIND OF SCARY, WILDLY OVERBEARING, AND HIGHLY ARROGANT.
DO YOU INTEND TO LEAVE THIS DECISION UP TO MY TASTES?
...YOU OFFER YOUR OWN NAME FIRST BEFORE YOU ASK SOMEONE ELSE'S.
I'M NOT PROUD OF THIS...
...BUT MY PERSONAL STANDARDS ARE QUITE DIFFERENT FROM THOSE OF THE AVERAGE HIGH SCHOOL GIRL.
I USED TO FEEL THE SAME WAY.
NGH! SOUBU HIGH SCHOOL...
...SOUNDS LIKE A TERRIFYIN' PLACE!
WHAT A PAIN...
YOUR ENVIRONMENT MIGHT CHANGE, BUT YOU WON'T.
STOP DREAMING.
URK...

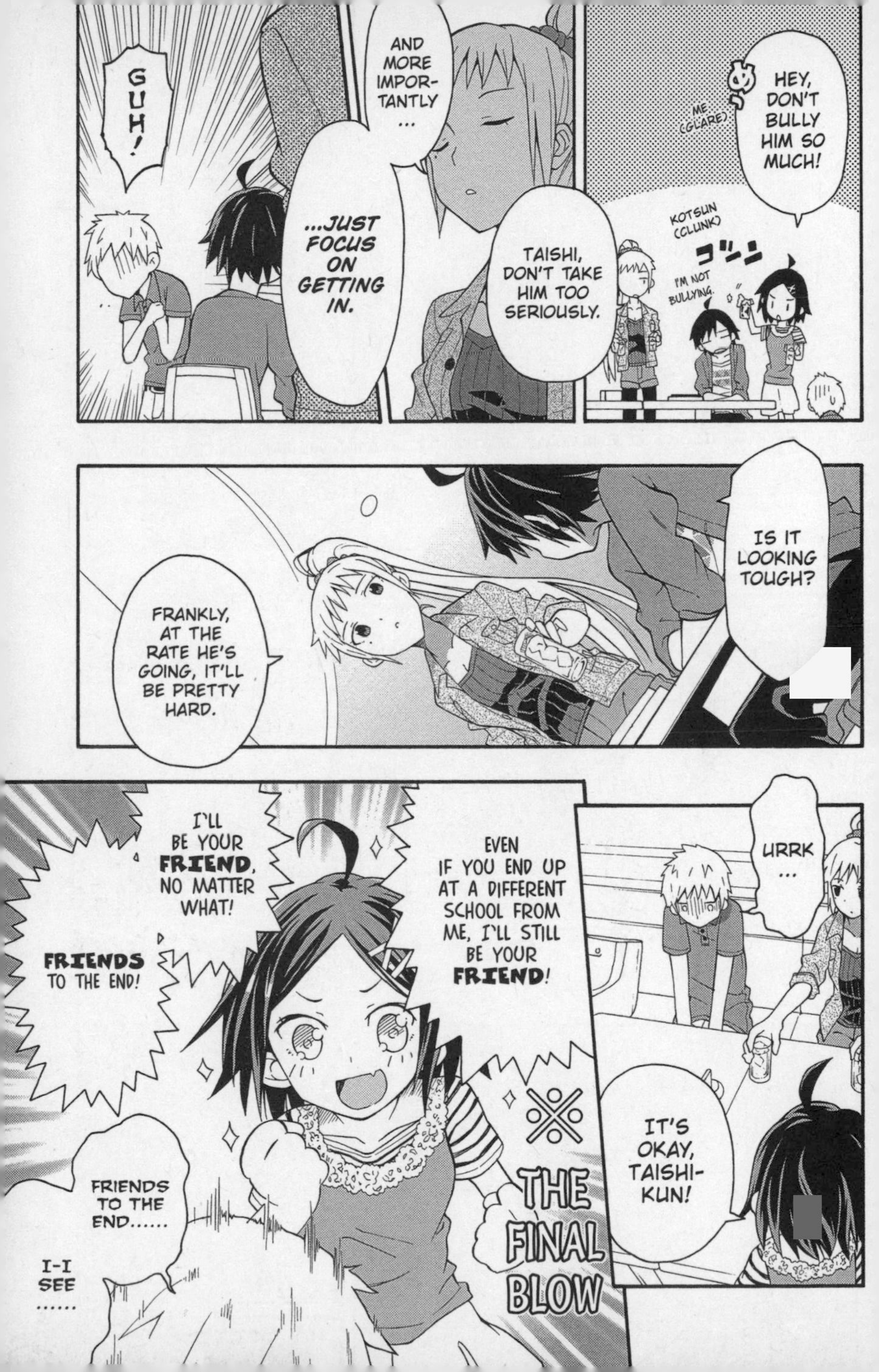
HEY, DON'T BULLY HIM SO MUCH!
ME (GLARE)
KOTSUN (CLUNK)
コツン
I'M NOT BULLYING.
TAISHI, DON'T TAKE HIM TOO SERIOUSLY.
AND MORE IMPORTANTLY...
...JUST FOCUS ON GETTING IN.
GUH!
IS IT LOOKING TOUGH?
FRANKLY, AT THE RATE HE'S GOING, IT'LL BE PRETTY HARD.
URRK...
IT'S OKAY, TAISHI-KUN!
EVEN IF YOU END UP AT A DIFFERENT SCHOOL FROM ME, I'LL STILL BE YOUR FRIEND!
I'LL BE YOUR FRIEND, NO MATTER WHAT!
FRIENDS TO THE END!
THE FINAL BLOW
FRIENDS TO THE END......
I-I SEE......

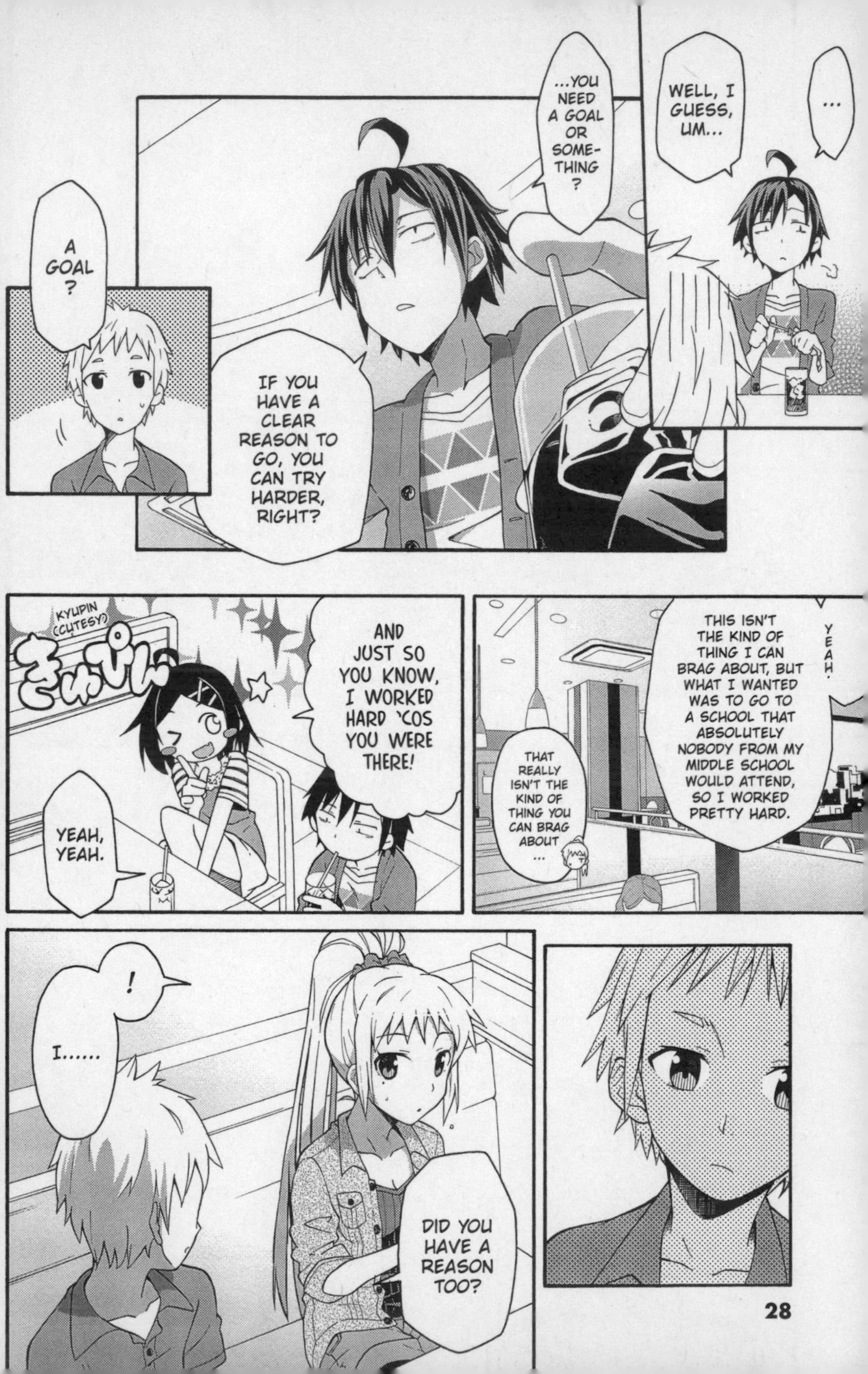
...
WELL, I GUESS, UM...
...YOU NEED A GOAL OR SOME-THING?
IF YOU HAVE A CLEAR REASON TO GO, YOU CAN TRY HARDER, RIGHT?
A GOAL?
THIS ISN'T THE KIND OF THING I CAN BRAG ABOUT, BUT WHAT I WANTED WAS TO GO TO A SCHOOL THAT ABSOLUTELY NOBODY FROM MY MIDDLE SCHOOL WOULD ATTEND, SO I WORKED PRETTY HARD.
YEAH.
THAT REALLY ISN'T THE KIND OF THING YOU CAN BRAG ABOUT...
AND JUST SO YOU KNOW, I WORKED HARD 'COS YOU WERE THERE!
KYUPIN (CUTESY)
きゅぴん
YEAH, YEAH.
DID YOU HAVE A REASON TOO?
!
I......

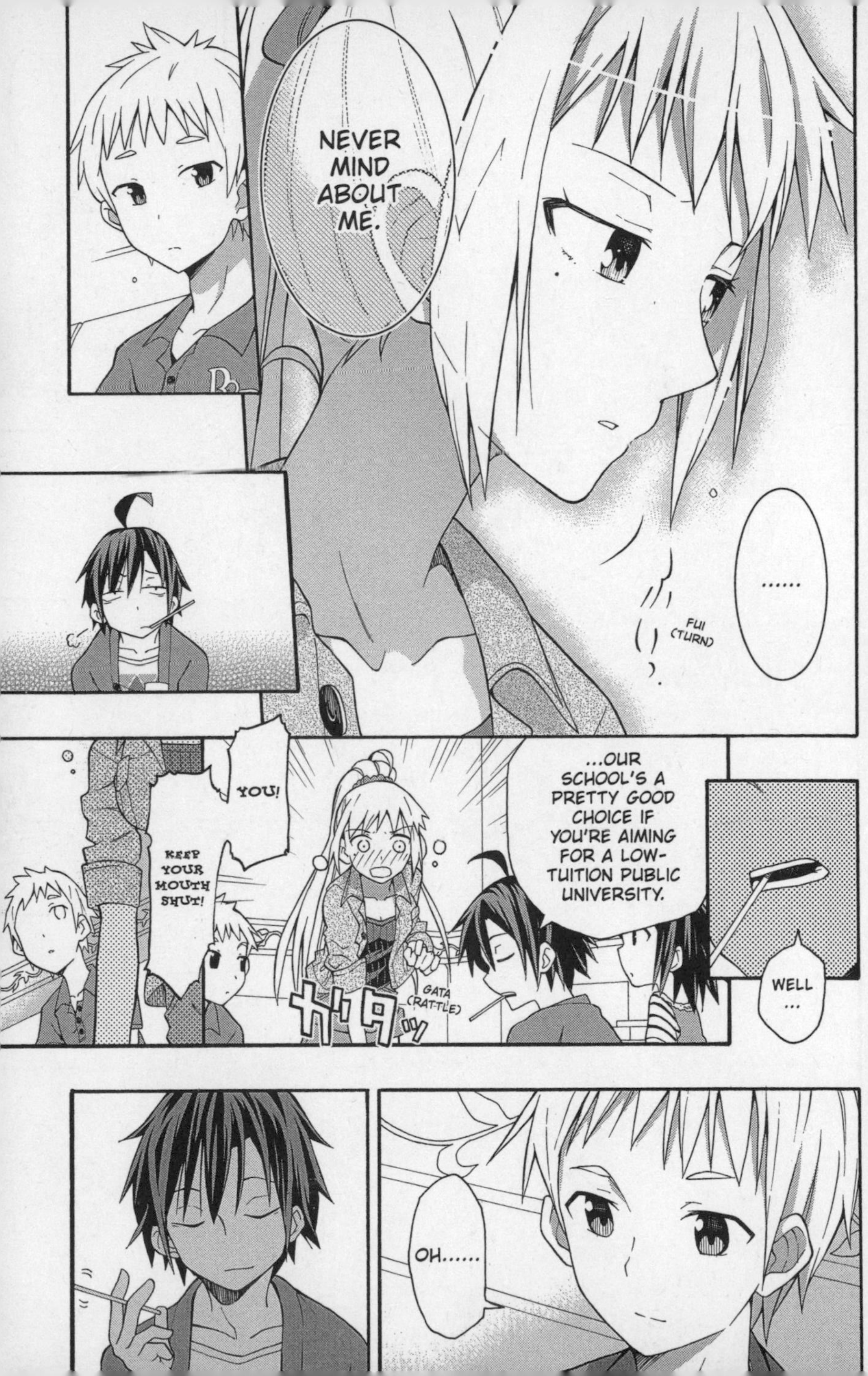
NEVER MIND ABOUT ME.
......
FUI (TURN)
WELL ...
...OUR SCHOOL'S A PRETTY GOOD CHOICE IF YOU'RE AIMING FOR A LOW-TUITION PUBLIC UNIVERSITY.
ガタッ
GATA (RATTLE)
YOU!
KEEP YOUR MOUTH SHUT!
OH......

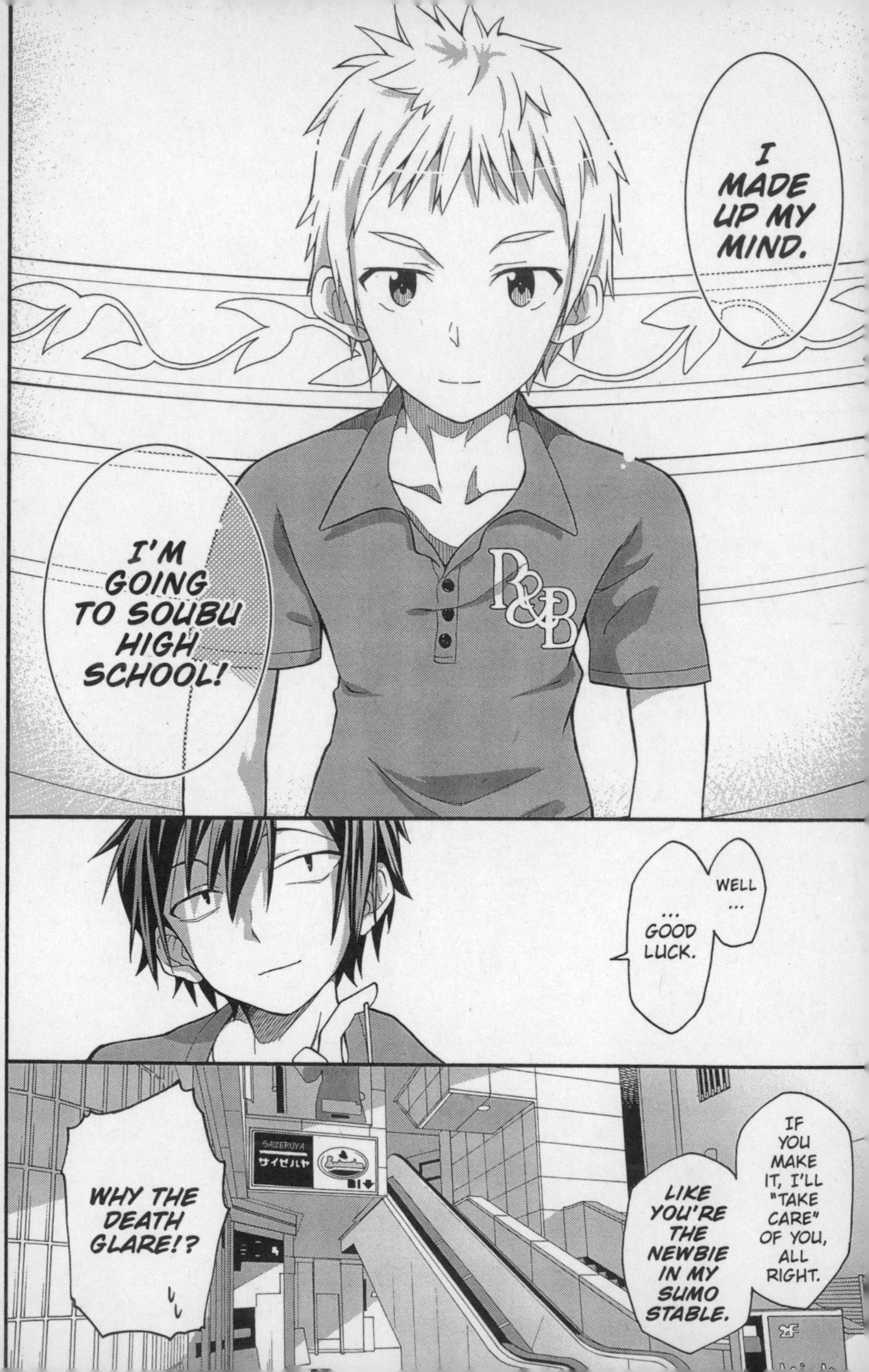
I MADE UP MY MIND.
I'M GOING TO SOUBU HIGH SCHOOL!
WELL...
...GOOD LUCK.
IF YOU MAKE IT, I'LL "TAKE CARE" OF YOU, ALL RIGHT.
LIKE YOU'RE THE NEWBIE IN MY SUMO STABLE.
SAIZERUYA
サイゼリヤ
B1
WHY THE DEATH GLARE!?

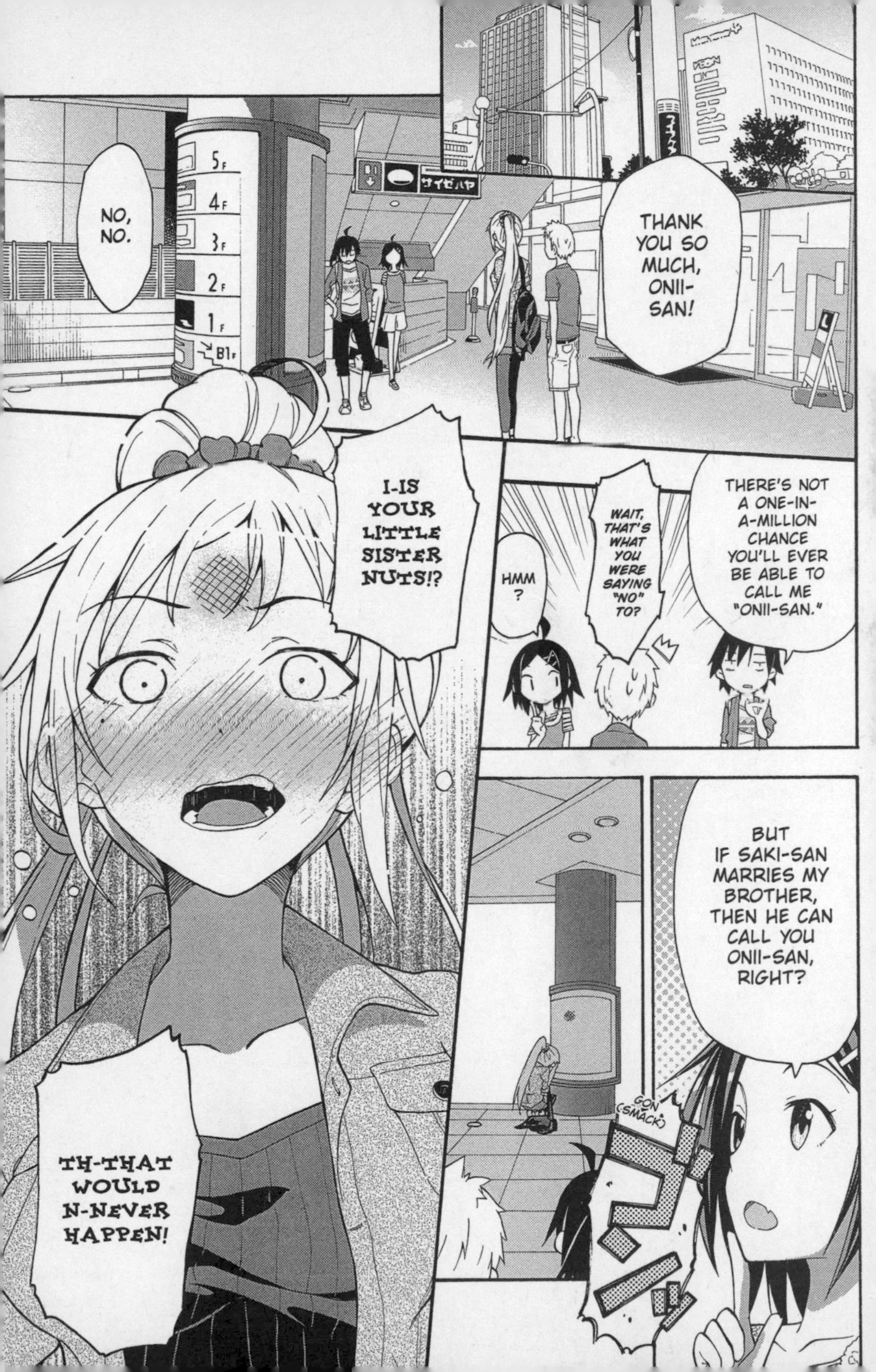
THANK YOU SO MUCH, ONII-SAN!
5F 4F 3F 2F 1F B1F
NO, NO.
THERE'S NOT A ONE-IN-A-MILLION CHANCE YOU'LL EVER BE ABLE TO CALL ME "ONII-SAN."
WAIT, THAT'S WHAT YOU WERE SAYING "NO" TO?
HMM?
BUT IF SAKI-SAN MARRIES MY BROTHER, THEN HE CAN CALL YOU ONII-SAN, RIGHT?
GON (SMACK)
I-IS YOUR LITTLE SISTER NUTS!?
TH-THAT WOULD N-NEVER HAPPEN!

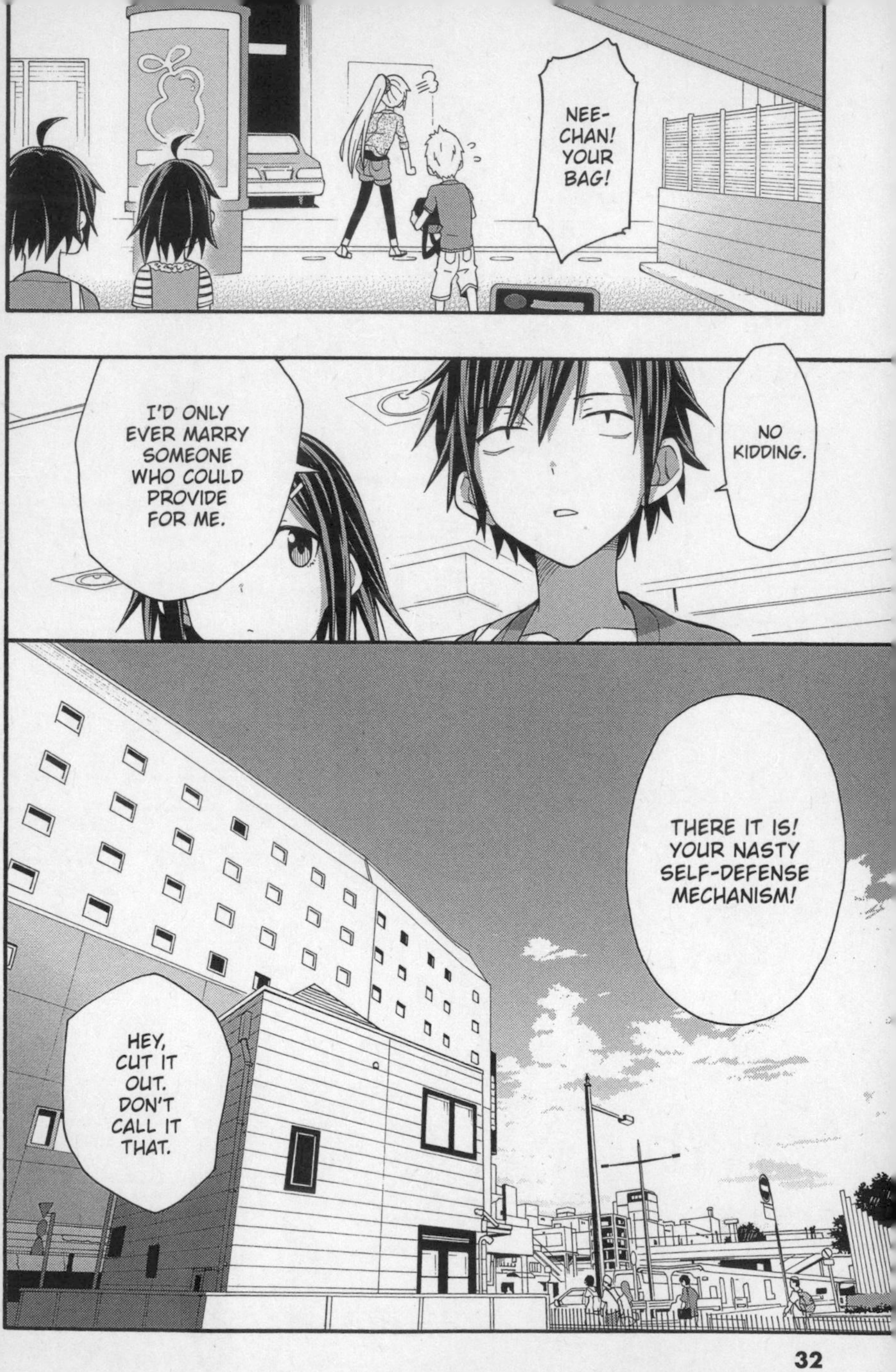
NEE-CHAN! YOUR BAG!
NO KIDDING.
I'D ONLY EVER MARRY SOMEONE WHO COULD PROVIDE FOR ME.
THERE IT IS! YOUR NASTY SELF-DEFENSE MECHANISM!
HEY, CUT IT OUT. DON'T CALL IT THAT.

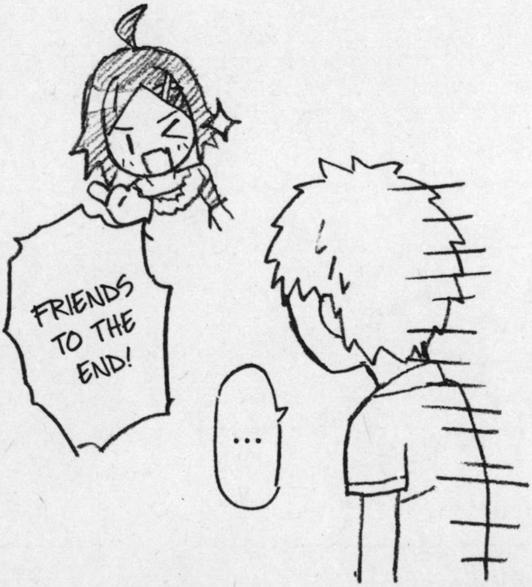
...
FRIENDS TO THE END!

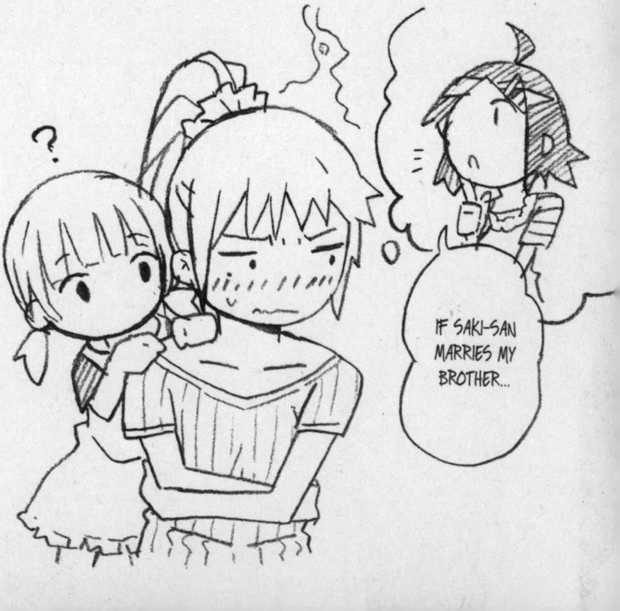
?
IF SAKI-SAN MARRIES MY BROTHER...

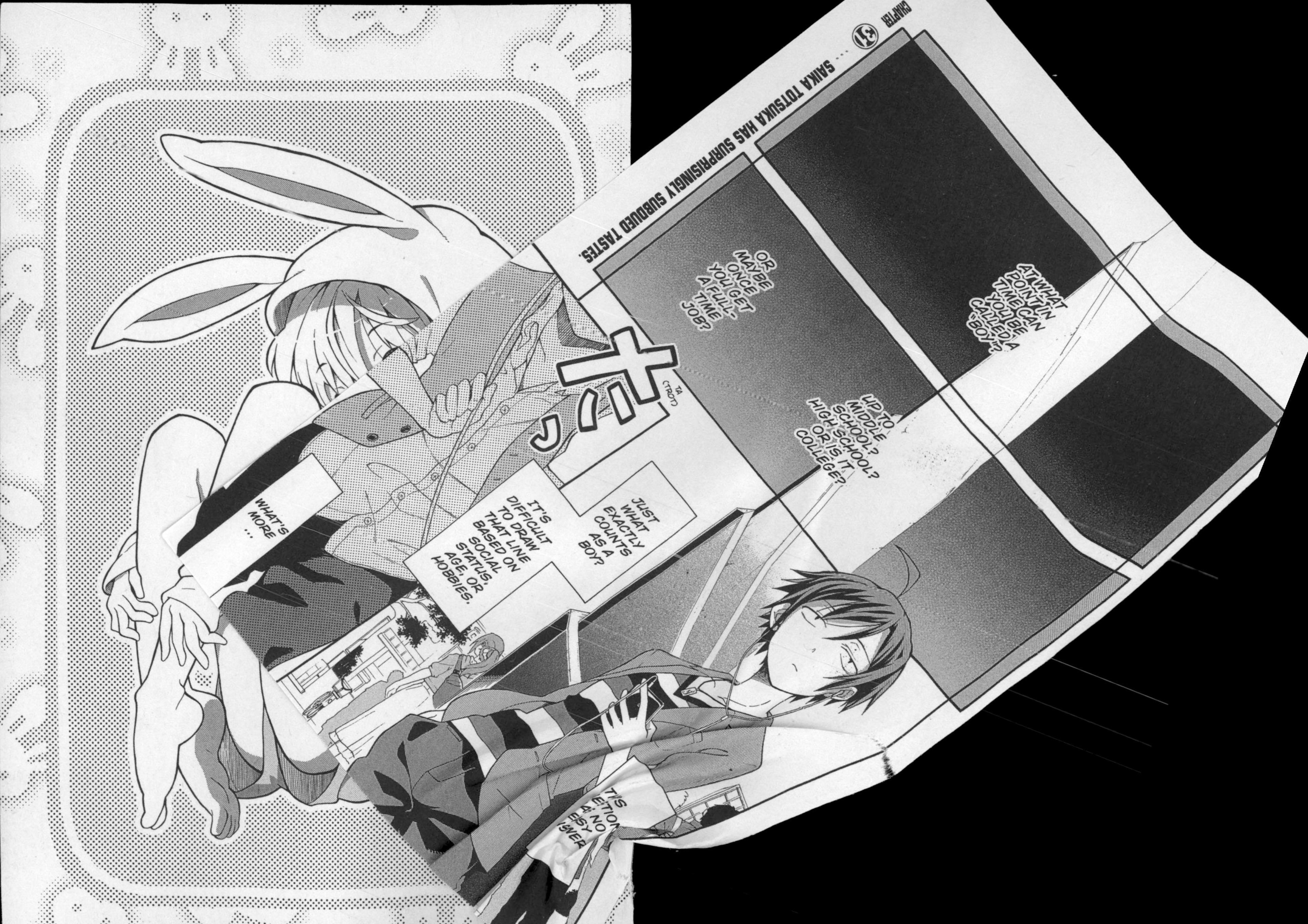
CHAPTER 31 SAIKA TOTSUKA HAS SURPRISINGLY SUBDUED TASTES.
TA (TROT)
JUST WHAT EXACTLY COUNTS AS A BOY?
IT'S DIFFICULT TO DRAW THAT LINE BASED ON SOCIAL STATUS, AGE, OR HOBBIES.
WHAT'S MORE...
UP TO MIDDLE SCHOOL? HIGH SCHOOL? OR IS IT COLLEGE?
OR MAYBE ONCE YOU GET A FULL-TIME JOB?
AT WHAT POINT IN TIME CAN YOU BE CALLED A "BOY"?

CHAPTER 31 ··· SAIKA TOTSUKA HAS SURPRISINGLY SUBDUED TASTES.

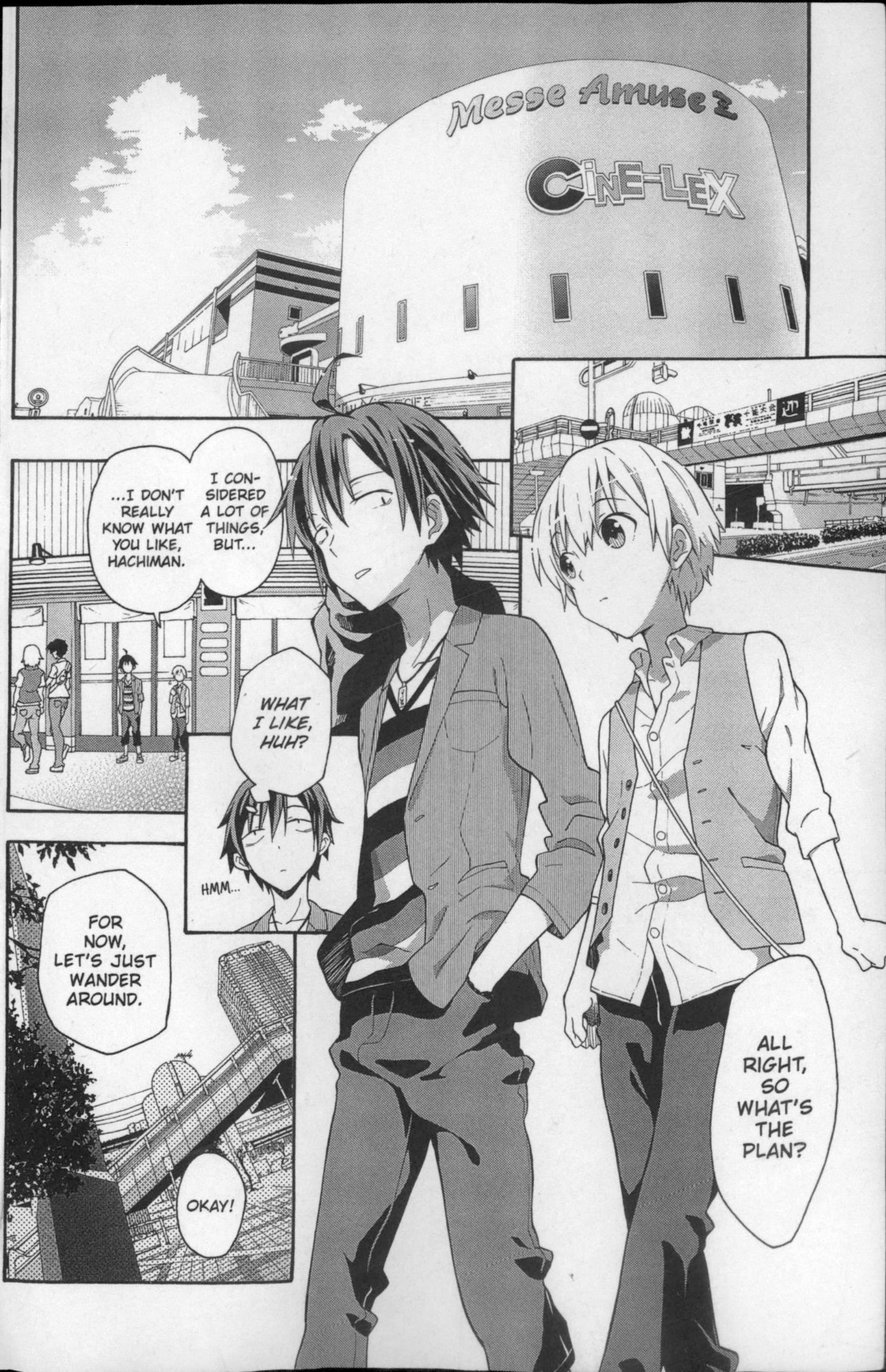

Messe Amuse 2
CINE-LEX
ALL RIGHT, SO WHAT'S THE PLAN?
I CONSIDERED A LOT OF THINGS, BUT...
...I DON'T REALLY KNOW WHAT YOU LIKE, HACHIMAN.
WHAT I LIKE, HUH?
HMM...
FOR NOW, LET'S JUST WANDER AROUND.
OKAY!

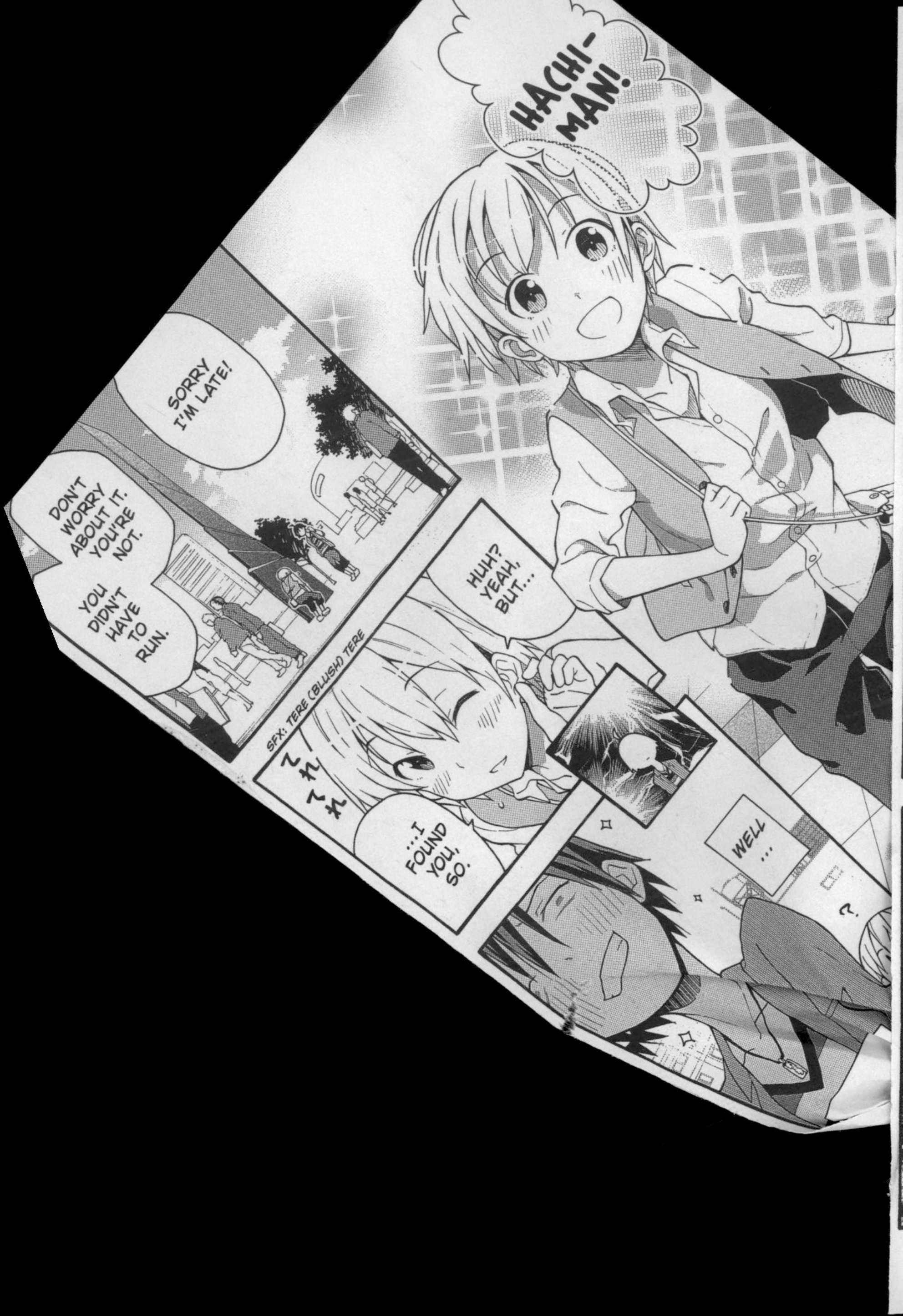

HACHI-MAN!
SORRY I'M LATE!
DON'T WORRY ABOUT IT. YOU'RE NOT.
YOU DIDN'T HAVE TO RUN.
HUH? YEAH, BUT...
...I FOUND YOU, SO.
SFX: TERE (BLUSH) TERE
WELL...

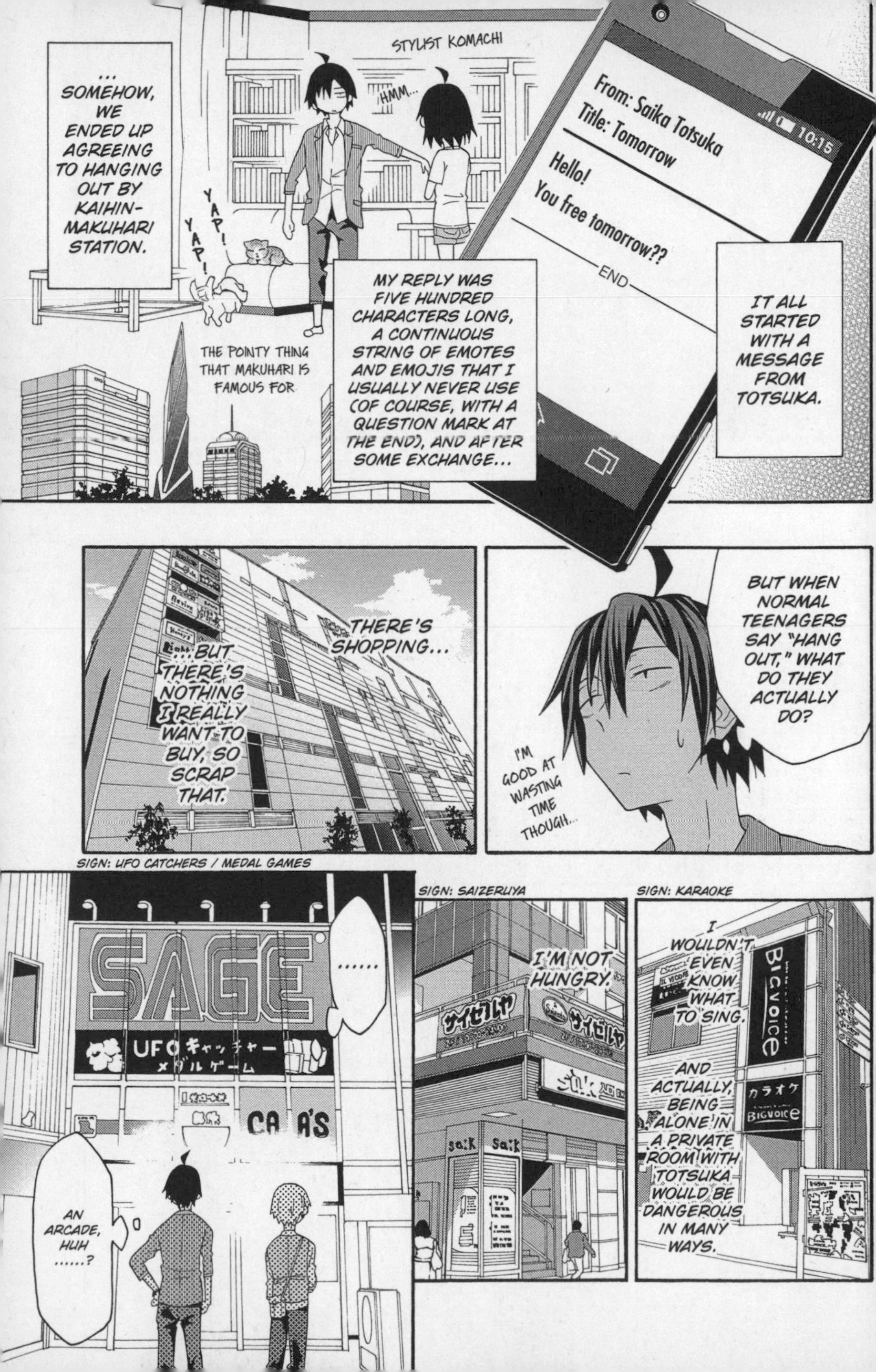
From: Saika Totsuka
Title: Tomorrow
Hello!
You free tomorrow??
END
10:15
IT ALL STARTED WITH A MESSAGE FROM TOTSUKA.
MY REPLY WAS FIVE HUNDRED CHARACTERS LONG, A CONTINUOUS STRING OF EMOTES AND EMOJIS THAT I USUALLY NEVER USE (OF COURSE, WITH A QUESTION MARK AT THE END), AND AFTER SOME EXCHANGE...
STYLIST KOMACHI
HMM...
YAP! YAP!
... SOMEHOW, WE ENDED UP AGREEING TO HANGING OUT BY KAIHIN-MAKUHARI STATION.
THE POINTY THING THAT MAKUHARI IS FAMOUS FOR
BUT WHEN NORMAL TEENAGERS SAY "HANG OUT," WHAT DO THEY ACTUALLY DO?
I'M GOOD AT WASTING TIME THOUGH...
THERE'S SHOPPING...
...BUT THERE'S NOTHING I REALLY WANT TO BUY, SO SCRAP THAT.
SIGN: KARAOKE
I WOULDN'T EVEN KNOW WHAT TO SING.
AND ACTUALLY, BEING ALONE IN A PRIVATE ROOM WITH TOTSUKA WOULD BE DANGEROUS IN MANY WAYS.
BIGVOICE
カラオケ
SIGN: SAIZERIYA
I'M NOT HUNGRY.
サイゼリヤ
SIGN: UFO CATCHERS / MEDAL GAMES
SAGE
UFOキャッチャー
メダルゲーム
......
AN ARCADE, HUH ......?

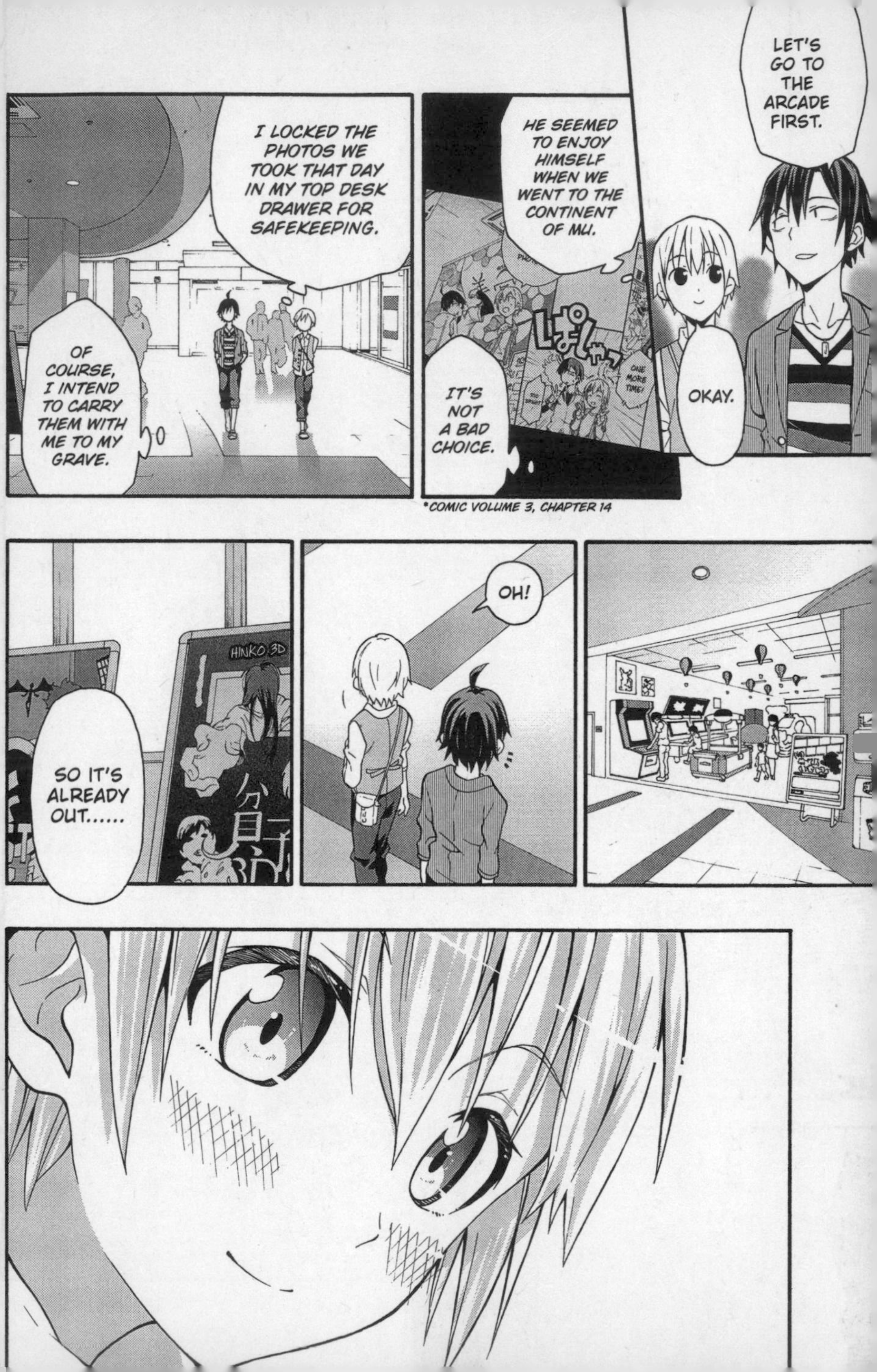
LET'S GO TO THE ARCADE FIRST.
OKAY.
HE SEEMED TO ENJOY HIMSELF WHEN WE WENT TO THE CONTINENT OF MU.
ONE MORE TIME!
IT'S NOT A BAD CHOICE.
I LOCKED THE PHOTOS WE TOOK THAT DAY IN MY TOP DESK DRAWER FOR SAFEKEEPING.
OF COURSE, I INTEND TO CARRY THEM WITH ME TO MY GRAVE.
OH!
HINKO 3D
SO IT'S ALREADY OUT......
*COMIC VOLUME 3, CHAPTER 14

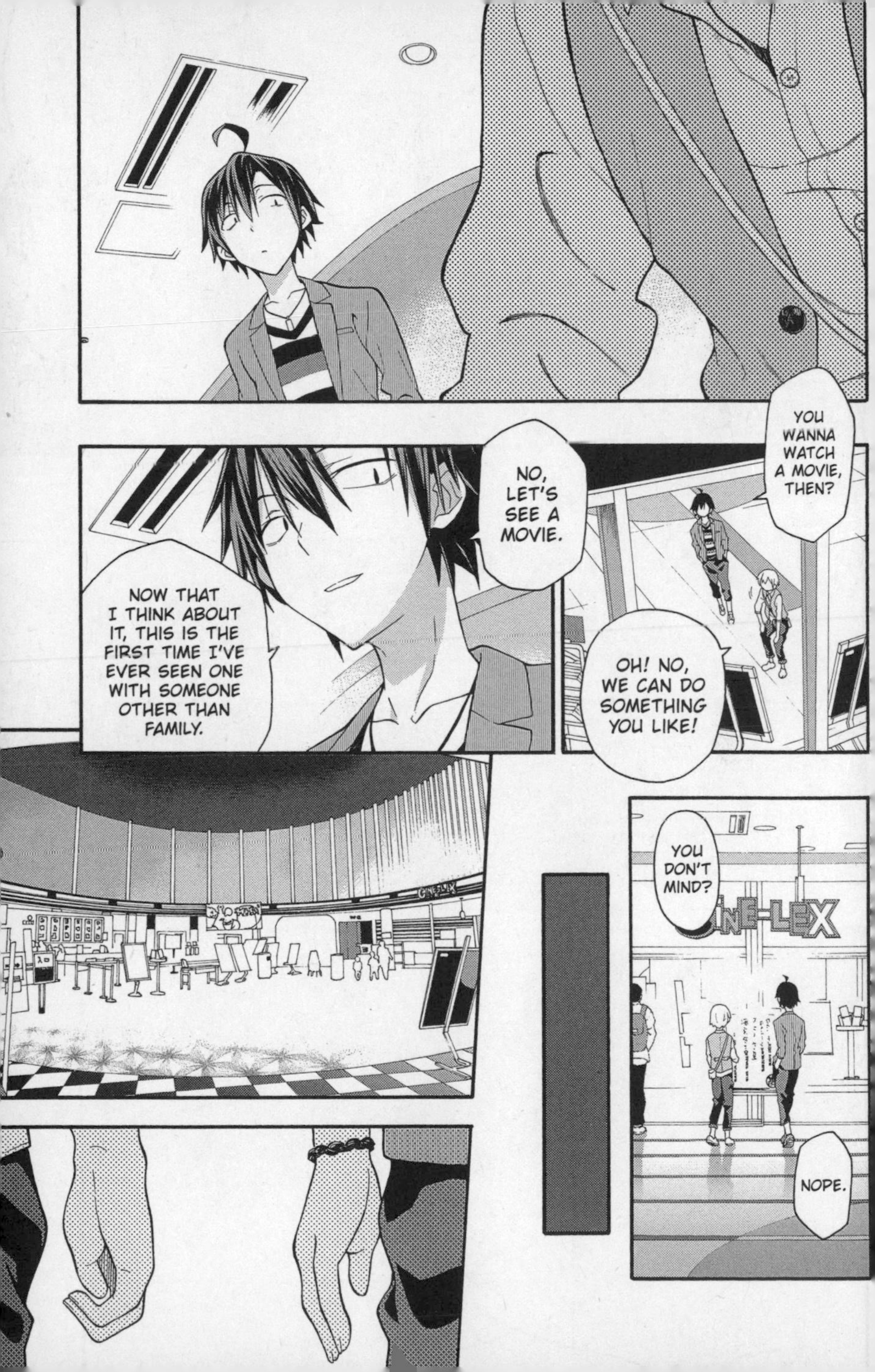
YOU WANNA WATCH A MOVIE, THEN?
OH! NO, WE CAN DO SOMETHING YOU LIKE!
NO, LET'S SEE A MOVIE.
NOW THAT I THINK ABOUT IT, THIS IS THE FIRST TIME I'VE EVER SEEN ONE WITH SOMEONE OTHER THAN FAMILY.
YOU DON'T MIND?
NOPE.

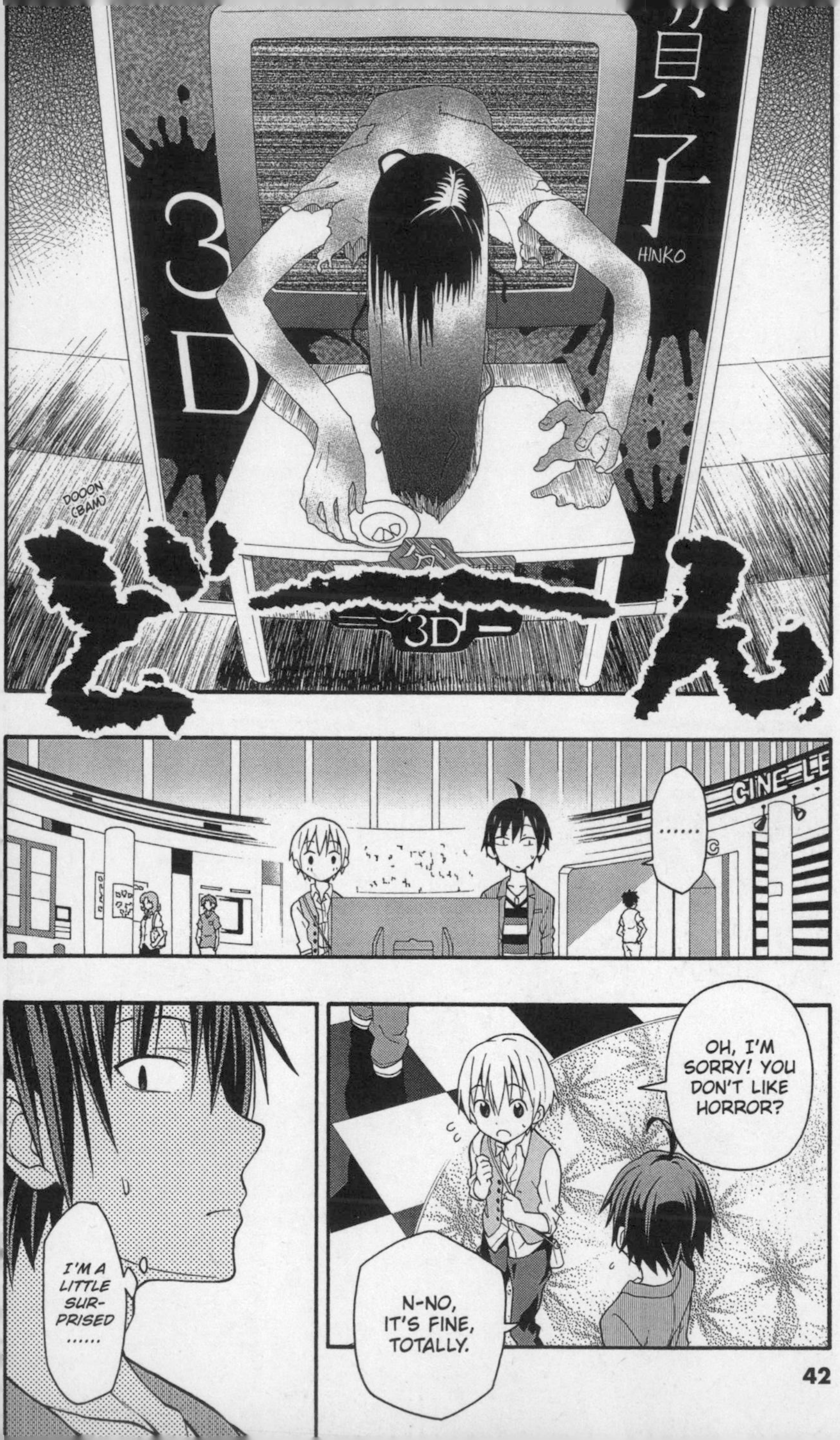

3D
HINKO
DOOON (BAM)
どーん
3D
......
CINE LE
OH, I'M SORRY! YOU DON'T LIKE HORROR?
N-NO, IT'S FINE, TOTALLY.
I'M A LITTLE SURPRISED ......

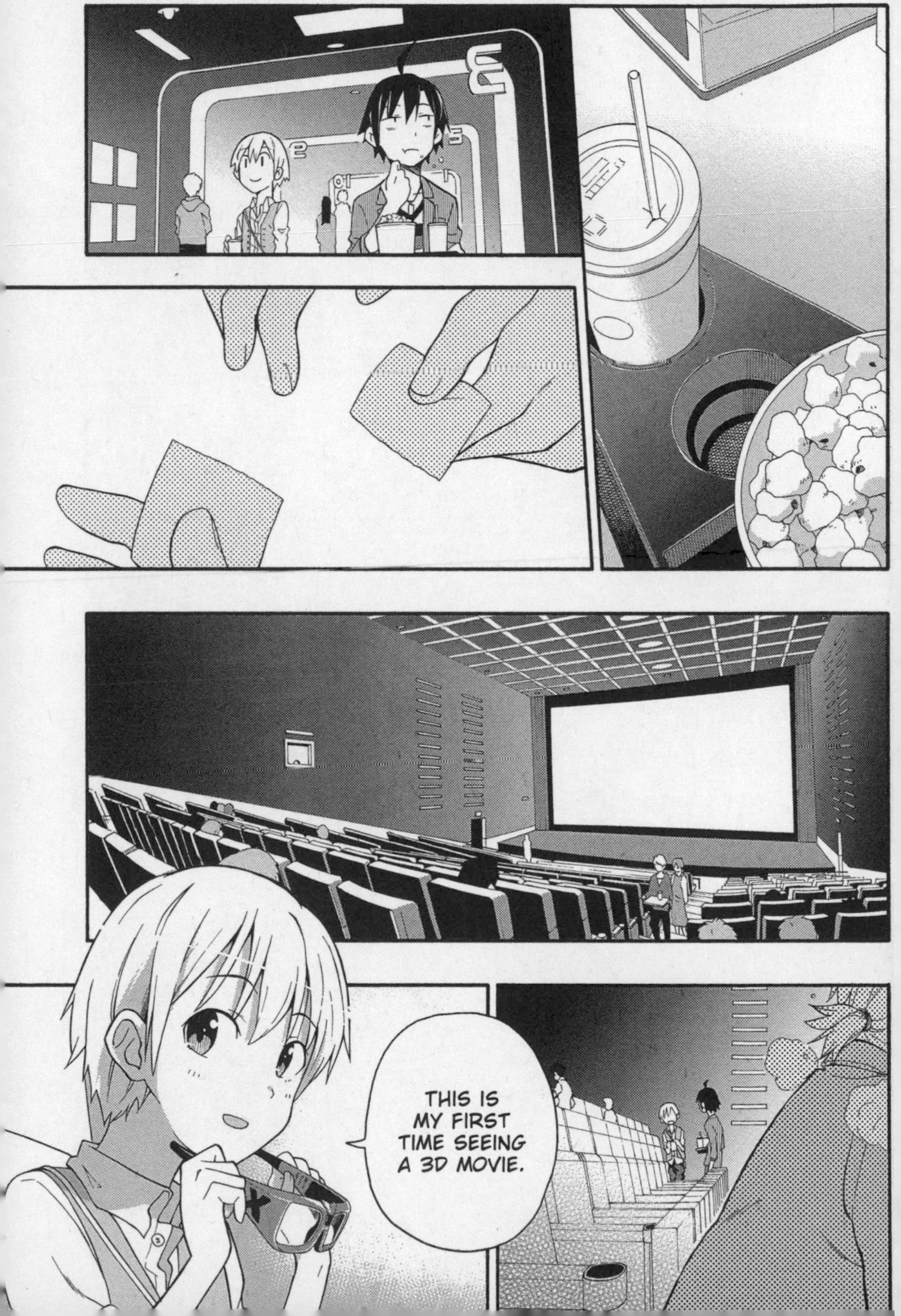
THIS IS MY FIRST TIME SEEING A 3D MOVIE.

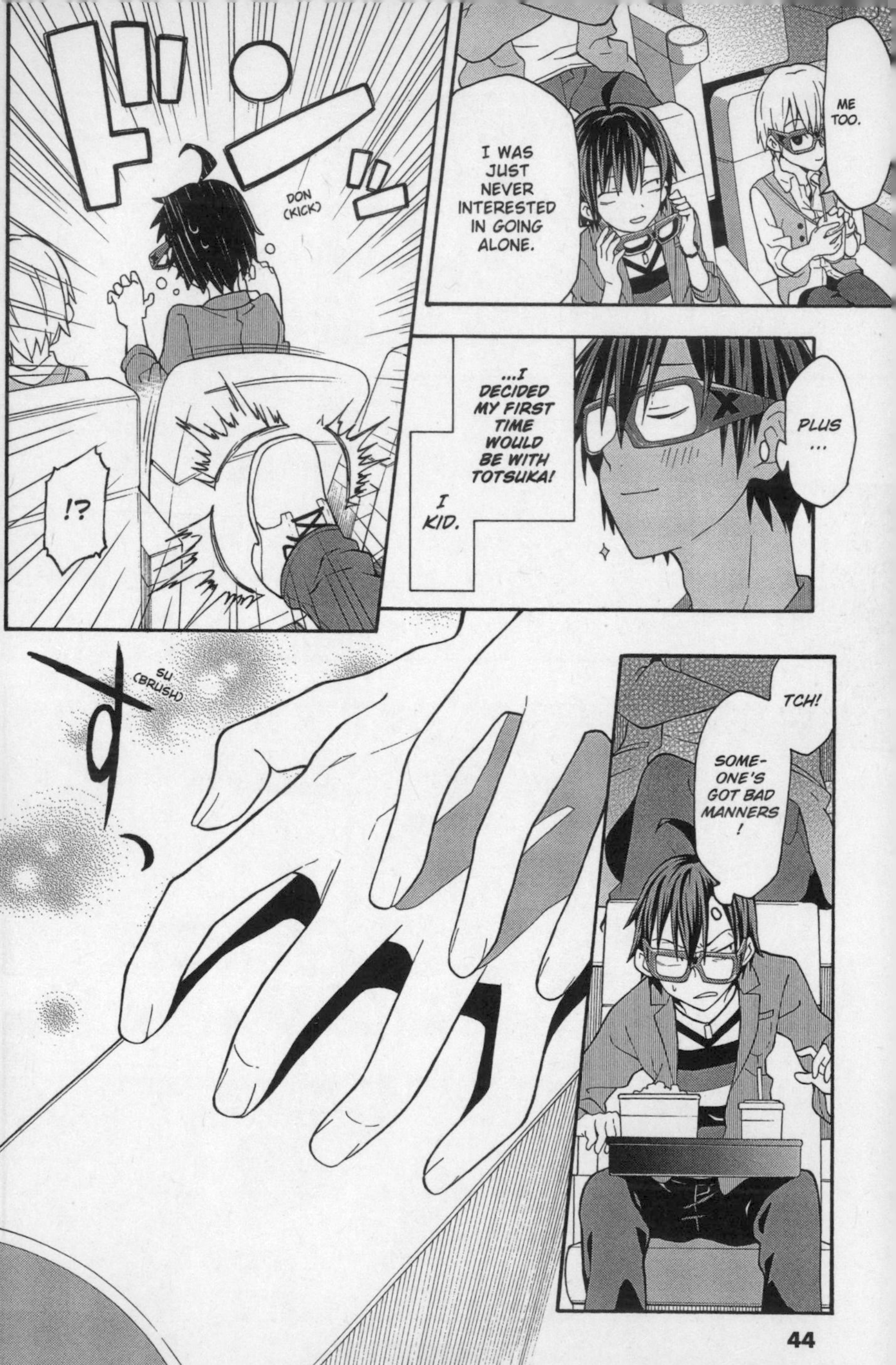
ME TOO.
I WAS JUST NEVER INTERESTED IN GOING ALONE.
PLUS ...
...I DECIDED MY FIRST TIME WOULD BE WITH TOTSUKA!
I KID.
DON (KICK)
!?
TCH!
SOME-ONE'S GOT BAD MANNERS!
SU (BRUSH)

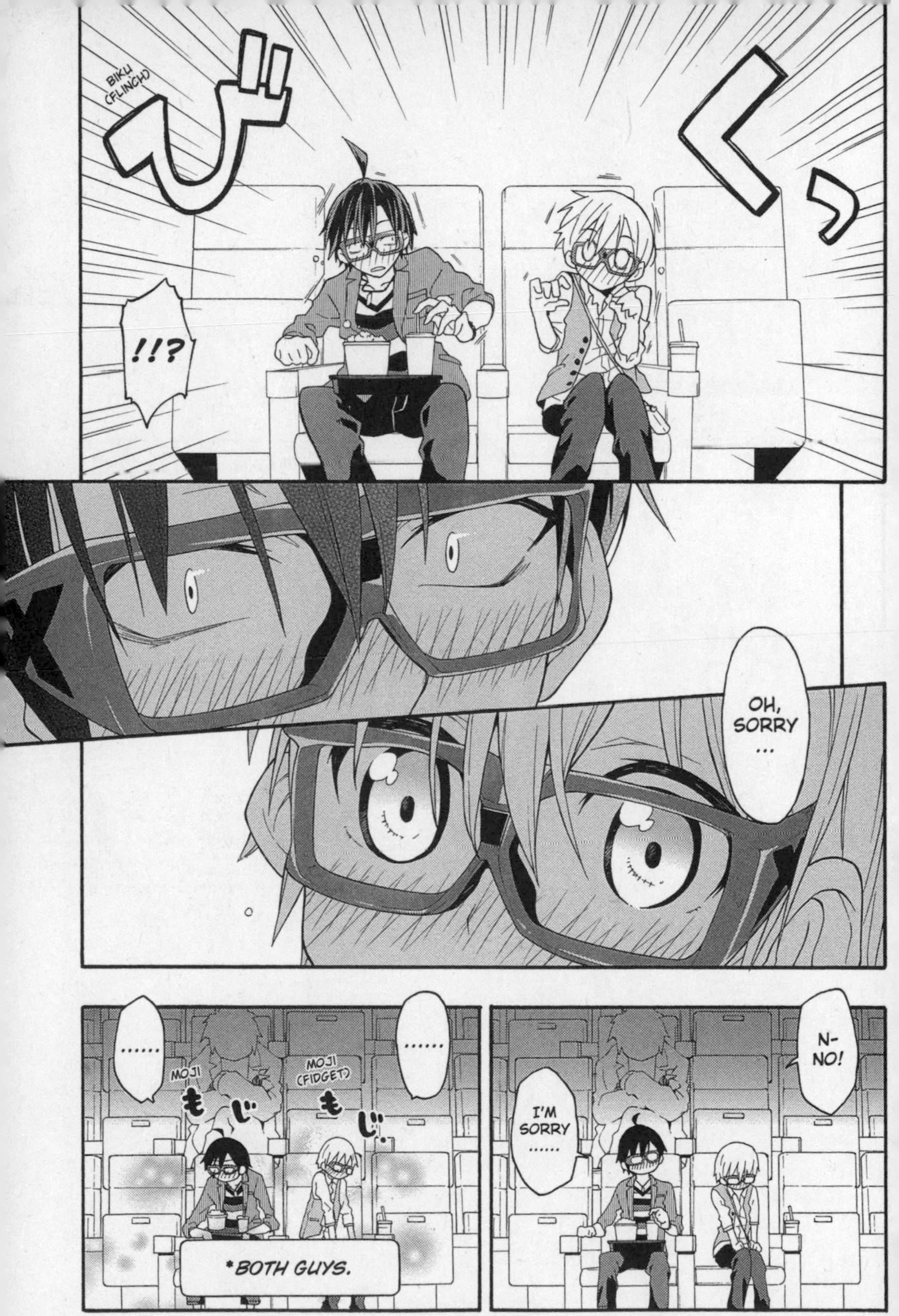
BIKU (FLINCH)
!!?
OH, SORRY ...
N- NO!
I'M SORRY ......
......
MOJI (FIDGET)
......
MOJI
*BOTH GUYS.

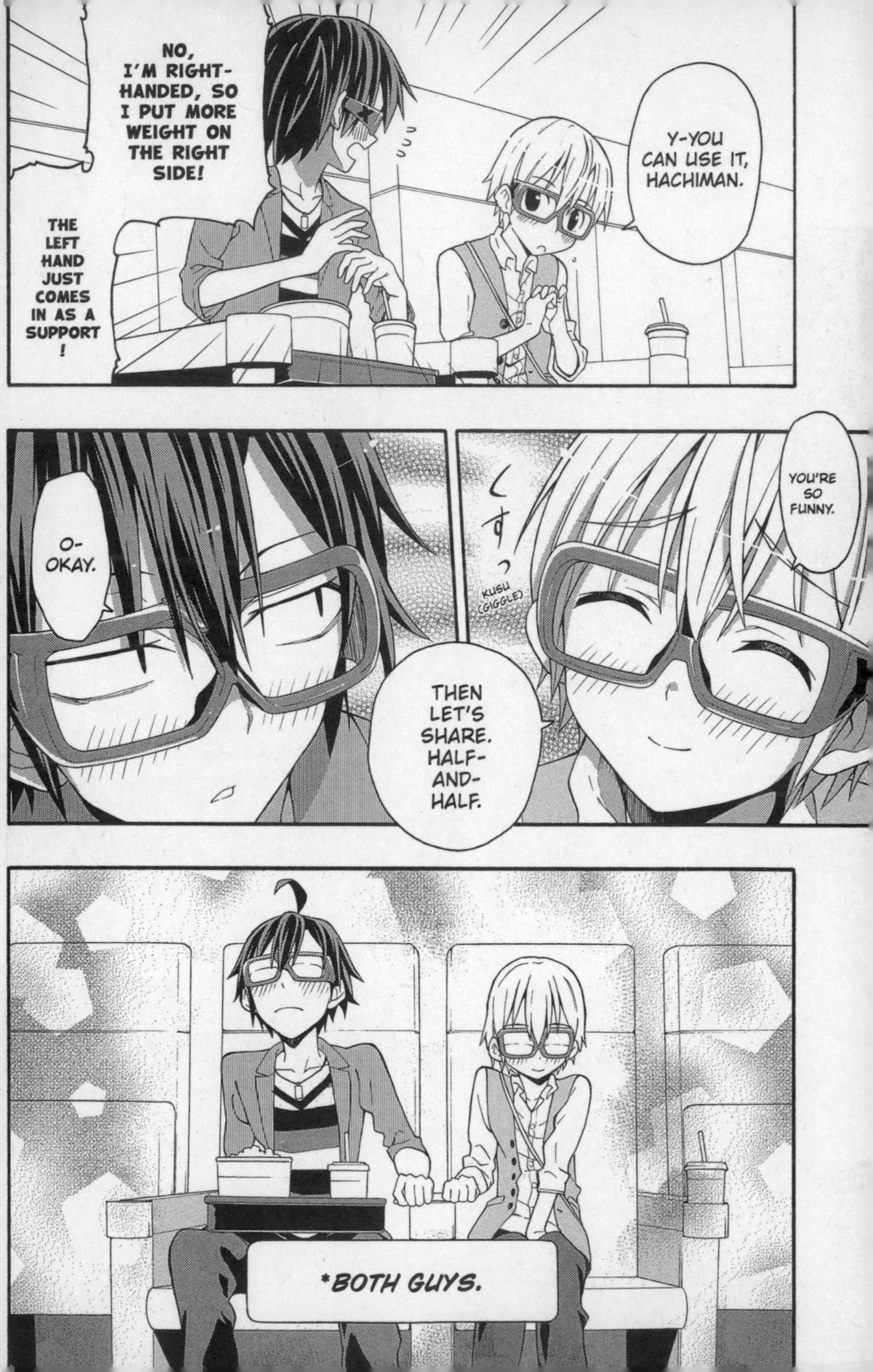
Y-YOU CAN USE IT, HACHIMAN.
NO, I'M RIGHT-HANDED, SO I PUT MORE WEIGHT ON THE RIGHT SIDE!
THE LEFT HAND JUST COMES IN AS A SUPPORT!
YOU'RE SO FUNNY.
くすっ
KUSU (GIGGLE)
THEN LET'S SHARE. HALF-AND-HALF.
O-OKAY.
*BOTH GUYS.

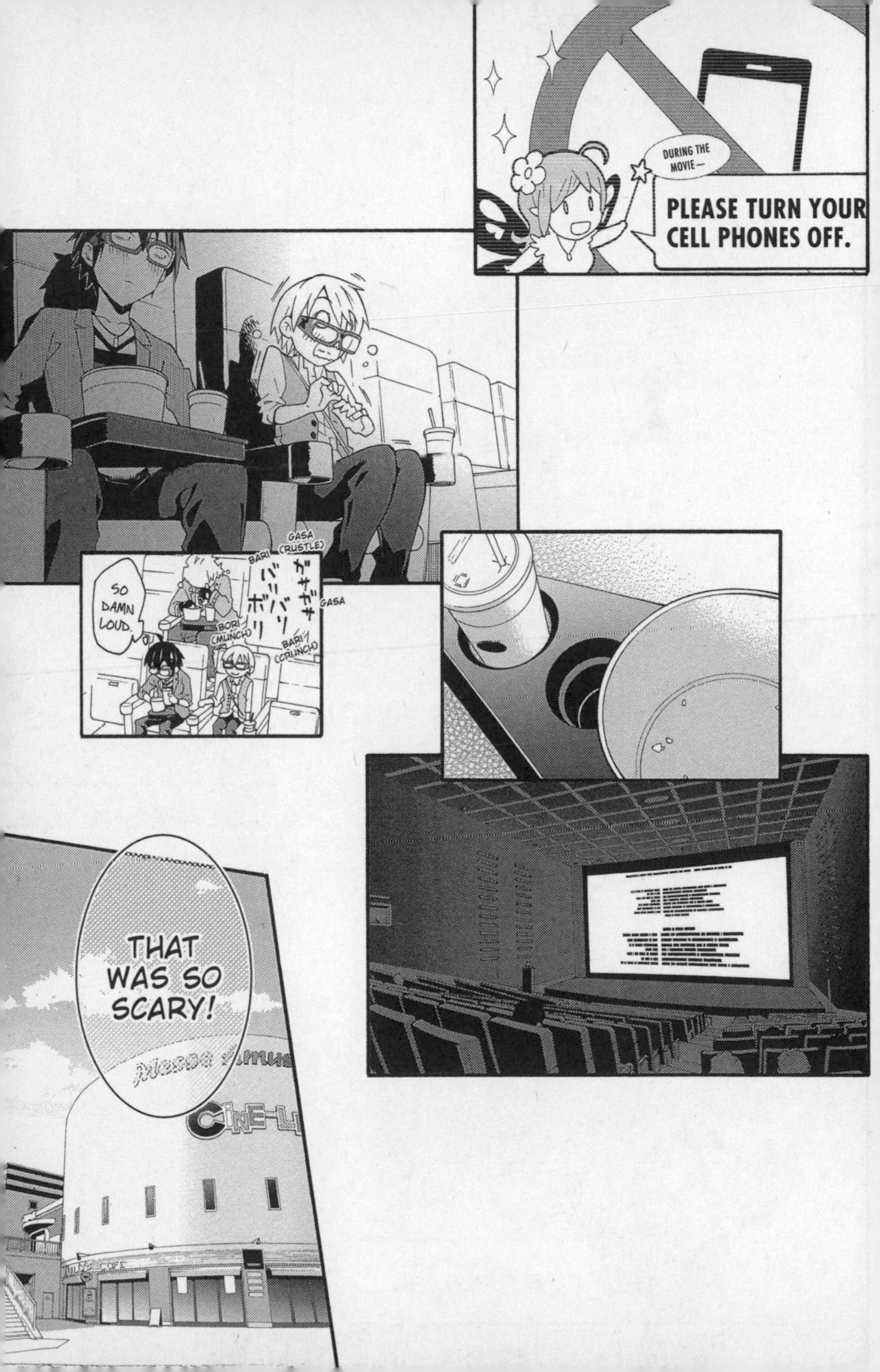
DURING THE MOVIE—
PLEASE TURN YOUR CELL PHONES OFF.
GASA (RUSTLE)
ガサガサ
GASA
BARI
BORI (MUNCH)
BARI (CRUNCH)
SO DAMN LOUD.
THAT WAS SO SCARY!

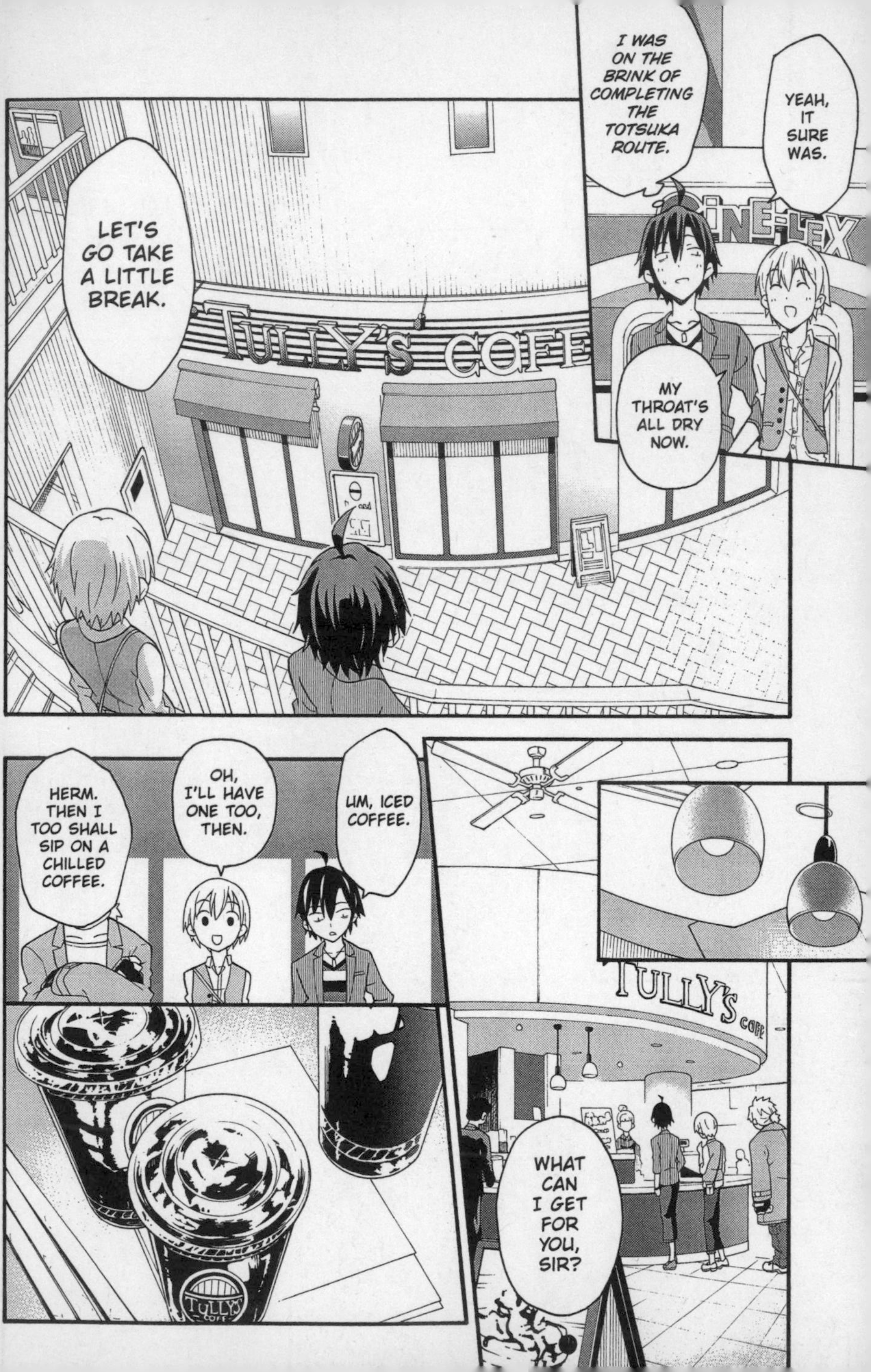
I WAS ON THE BRINK OF COMPLETING THE TOTSUKA ROUTE.
YEAH, IT SURE WAS.
MY THROAT'S ALL DRY NOW.
LET'S GO TAKE A LITTLE BREAK.
WHAT CAN I GET FOR YOU, SIR?
UM, ICED COFFEE.
OH, I'LL HAVE ONE TOO, THEN.
HERM. THEN I TOO SHALL SIP ON A CHILLED COFFEE.

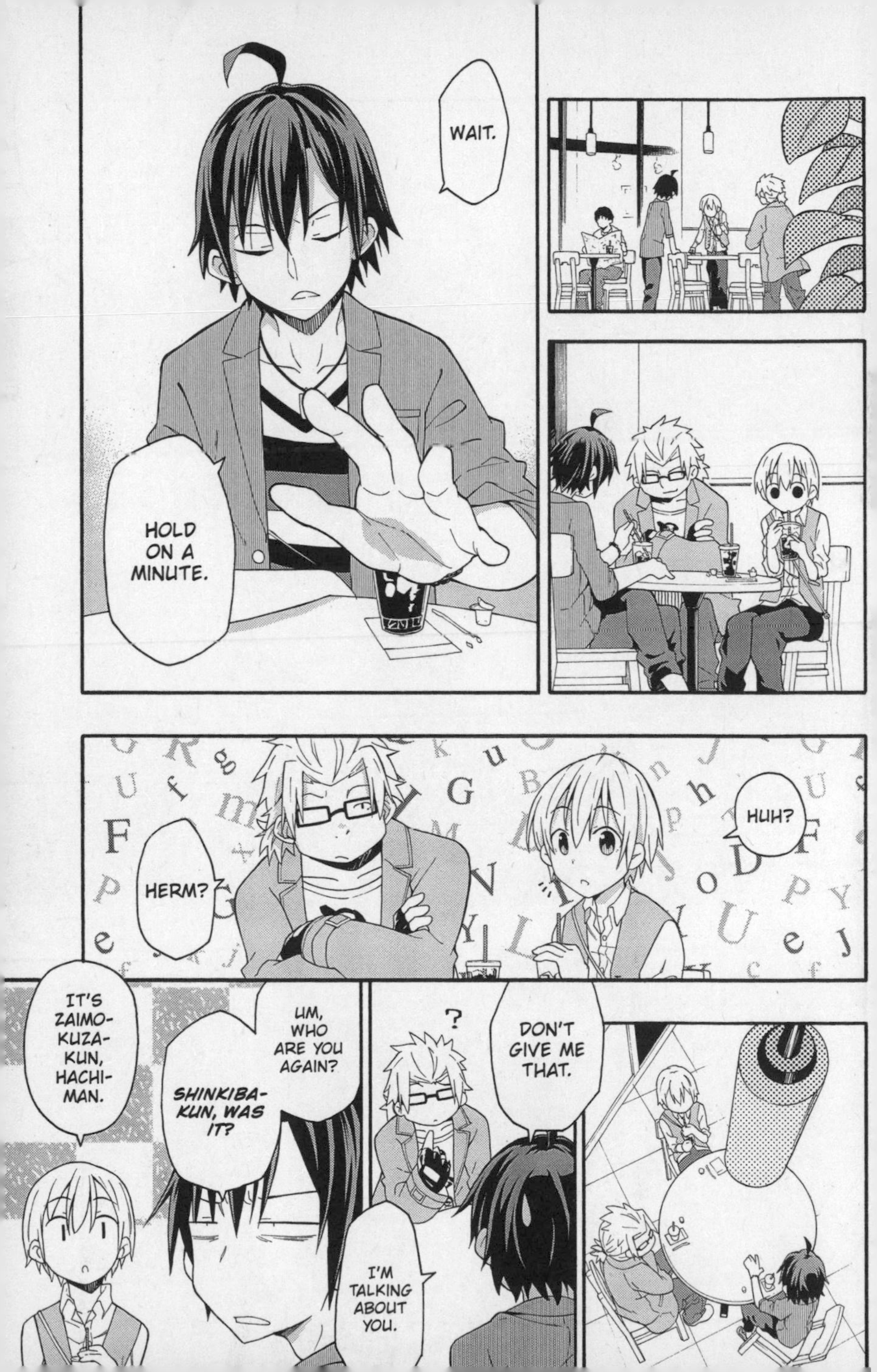
WAIT.
HOLD ON A MINUTE.
HUH?
HERM?
?
DON'T GIVE ME THAT.
I'M TALKING ABOUT YOU.
UM, WHO ARE YOU AGAIN?
SHINKIBA-KUN, WAS IT?
IT'S ZAIMO-KUZA-KUN, HACHI-MAN.

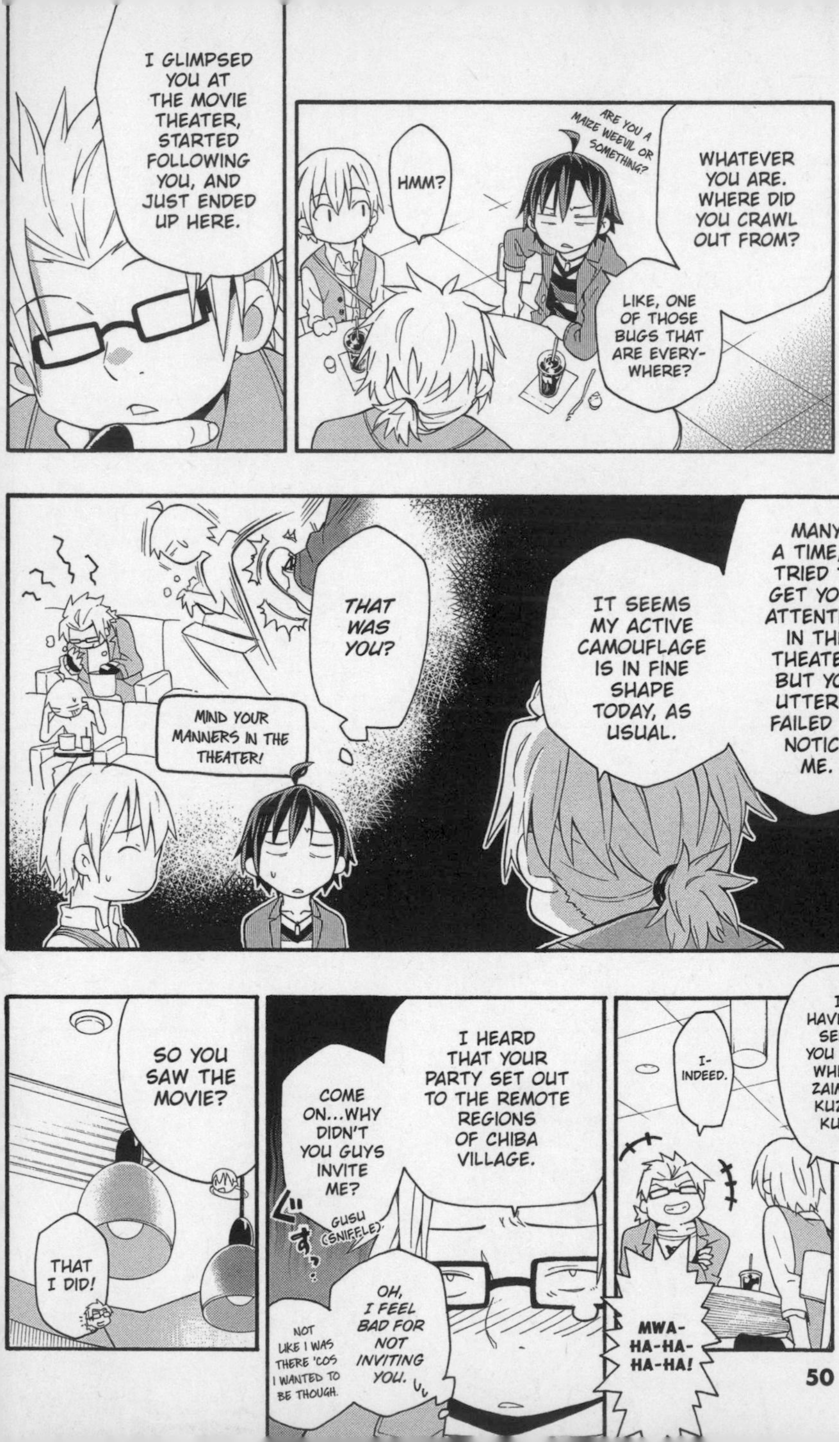
WHATEVER YOU ARE. WHERE DID YOU CRAWL OUT FROM?
ARE YOU A MAIZE WEEVIL OR SOMETHING?
HMM?
LIKE, ONE OF THOSE BUGS THAT ARE EVERY-WHERE?
I GLIMPSED YOU AT THE MOVIE THEATER, STARTED FOLLOWING YOU, AND JUST ENDED UP HERE.
MANY A TIME, I TRIED TO GET YOUR ATTENTION IN THE THEATER, BUT YOU UTTERLY FAILED TO NOTICE ME.
IT SEEMS MY ACTIVE CAMOUFLAGE IS IN FINE SHAPE TODAY, AS USUAL.
THAT WAS YOU?
MIND YOUR MANNERS IN THE THEATER!
I HAVEN'T SEEN YOU IN A WHILE, ZAIMO-KUZA-KUN.
I- INDEED.
MWA-HA-HA-HA-HA!
I HEARD THAT YOUR PARTY SET OUT TO THE REMOTE REGIONS OF CHIBA VILLAGE.
COME ON...WHY DIDN'T YOU GUYS INVITE ME?
GUSU (SNIFFLE)
OH, I FEEL BAD FOR NOT INVITING YOU.
NOT LIKE I WAS THERE 'COS I WANTED TO BE THOUGH.
SO YOU SAW THE MOVIE?
THAT I DID!

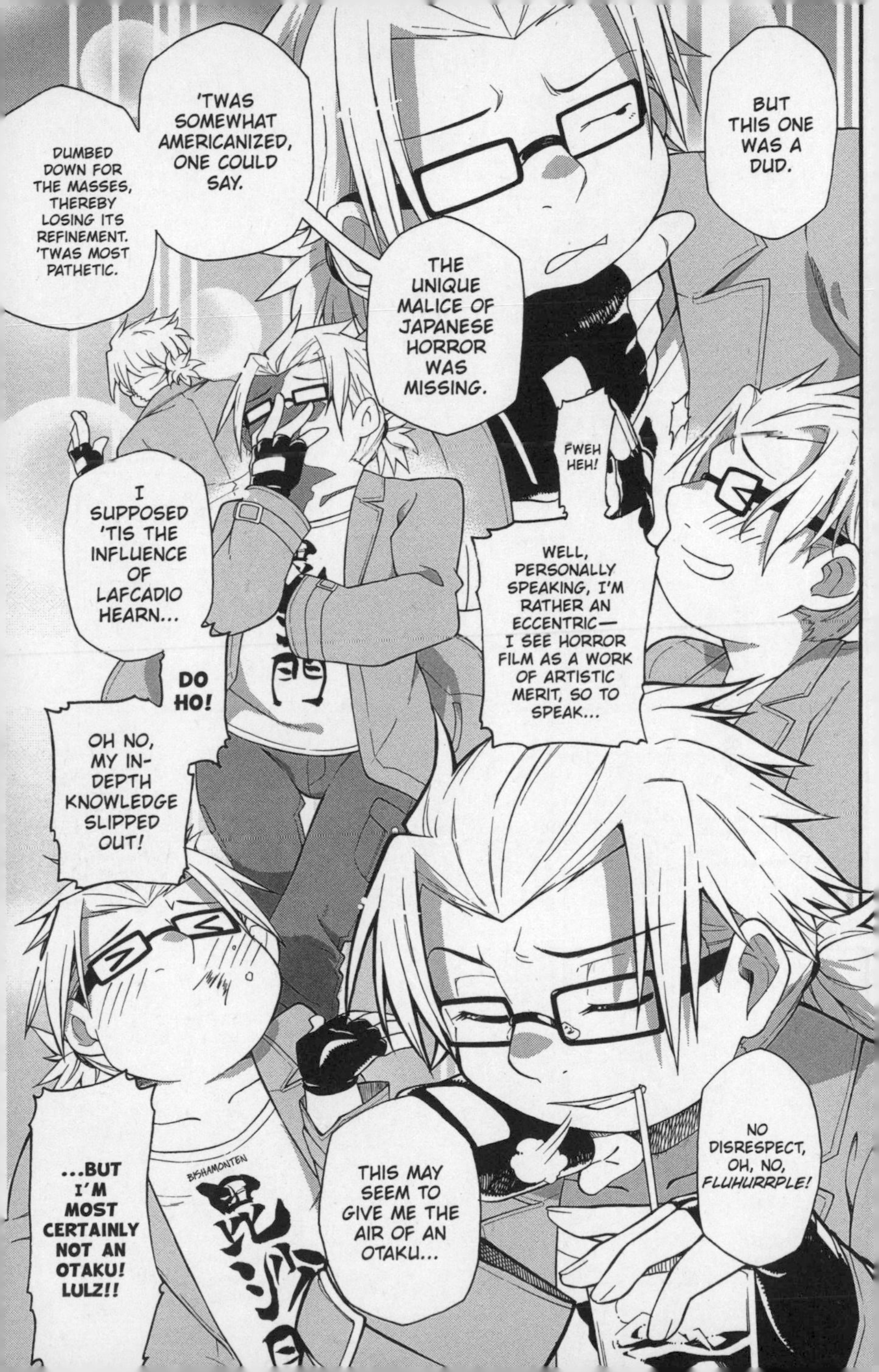
BUT THIS ONE WAS A DUD.
'TWAS SOMEWHAT AMERICANIZED, ONE COULD SAY.
DUMBED DOWN FOR THE MASSES, THEREBY LOSING ITS REFINEMENT. 'TWAS MOST PATHETIC.
THE UNIQUE MALICE OF JAPANESE HORROR WAS MISSING.
FWEH HEH!
WELL, PERSONALLY SPEAKING, I'M RATHER AN ECCENTRIC— I SEE HORROR FILM AS A WORK OF ARTISTIC MERIT, SO TO SPEAK...
I SUPPOSED 'TIS THE INFLUENCE OF LAFCADIO HEARN...
DO HO!
OH NO, MY IN-DEPTH KNOWLEDGE SLIPPED OUT!
NO DISRESPECT, OH, NO, *FLUHURRPLE!*
THIS MAY SEEM TO GIVE ME THE AIR OF AN OTAKU...
BISHAMONTEN
...BUT I'M MOST CERTAINLY NOT AN OTAKU! LULZ!!

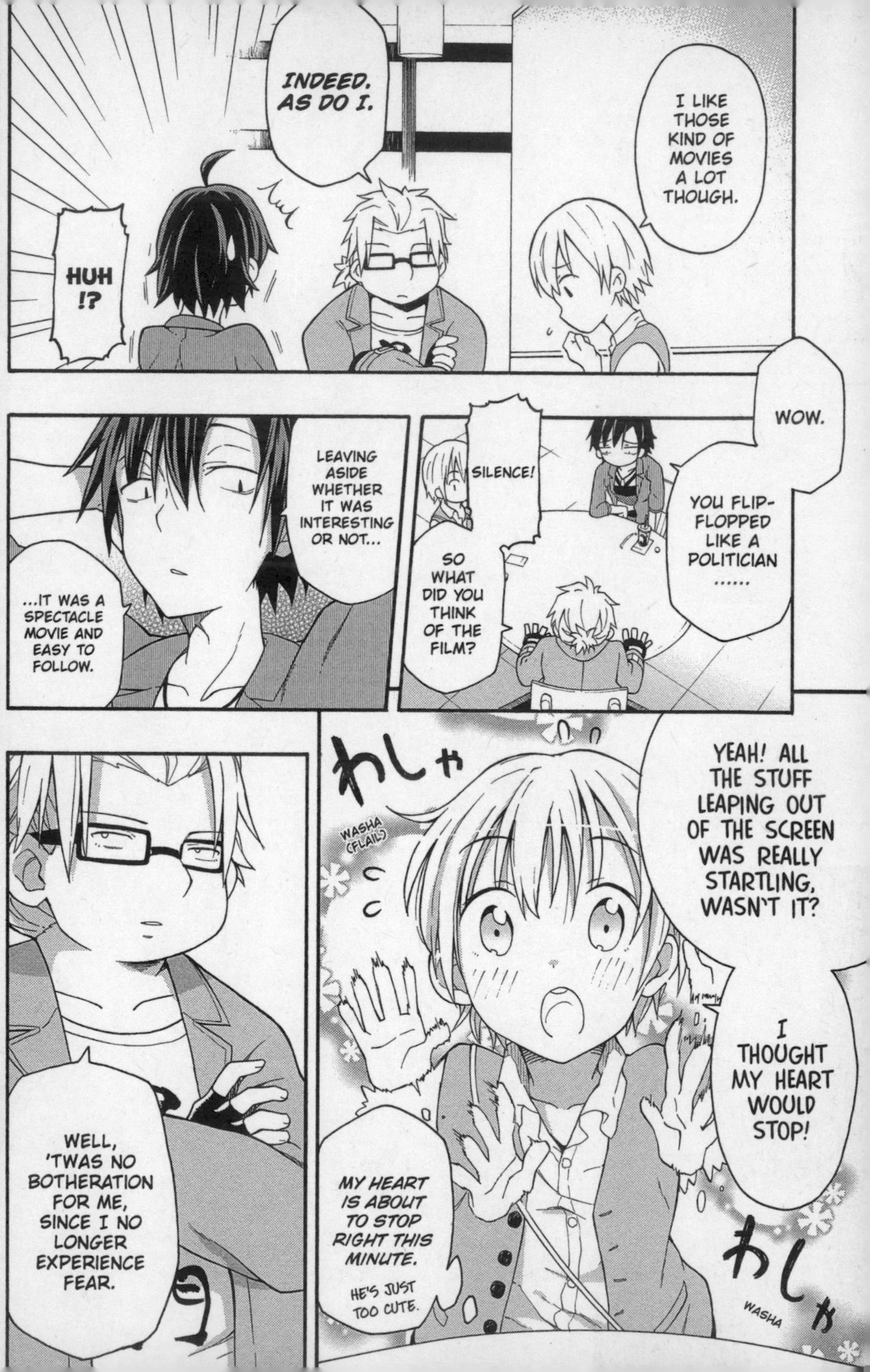

I LIKE THOSE KIND OF MOVIES A LOT THOUGH.
INDEED. AS DO I.
HUH !?
WOW.
YOU FLIP-FLOPPED LIKE A POLITICIAN ......
SILENCE!
SO WHAT DID YOU THINK OF THE FILM?
LEAVING ASIDE WHETHER IT WAS INTERESTING OR NOT...
...IT WAS A SPECTACLE MOVIE AND EASY TO FOLLOW.
YEAH! ALL THE STUFF LEAPING OUT OF THE SCREEN WAS REALLY STARTLING, WASN'T IT?
わしゃ
WASHA (FLAIL)
I THOUGHT MY HEART WOULD STOP!
わしゃ
WASHA
MY HEART IS ABOUT TO STOP RIGHT THIS MINUTE.
HE'S JUST TOO CUTE.
WELL, 'TWAS NO BOTHERATION FOR ME, SINCE I NO LONGER EXPERIENCE FEAR.

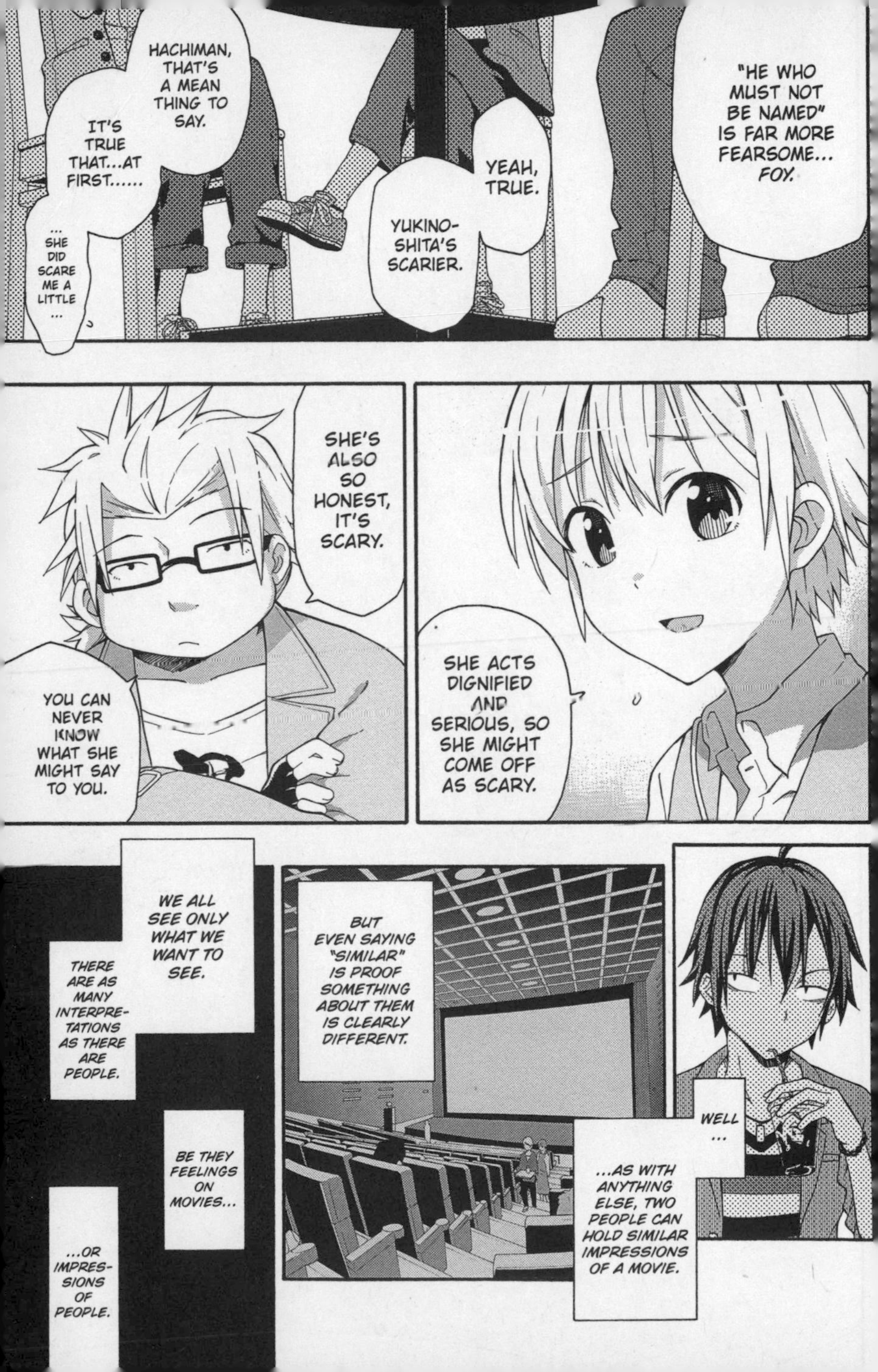

"HE WHO MUST NOT BE NAMED" IS FAR MORE FEARSOME... FOY.
YEAH, TRUE.
YUKINO-SHITA'S SCARIER.
HACHIMAN, THAT'S A MEAN THING TO SAY.
IT'S TRUE THAT...AT FIRST......
...SHE DID SCARE ME A LITTLE...
SHE ACTS DIGNIFIED AND SERIOUS, SO SHE MIGHT COME OFF AS SCARY.
SHE'S ALSO SO HONEST, IT'S SCARY.
YOU CAN NEVER KNOW WHAT SHE MIGHT SAY TO YOU.
WELL...
...AS WITH ANYTHING ELSE, TWO PEOPLE CAN HOLD SIMILAR IMPRESSIONS OF A MOVIE.
BUT EVEN SAYING "SIMILAR" IS PROOF SOMETHING ABOUT THEM IS CLEARLY DIFFERENT.
WE ALL SEE ONLY WHAT WE WANT TO SEE.
THERE ARE AS MANY INTERPRETATIONS AS THERE ARE PEOPLE.
BE THEY FEELINGS ON MOVIES...
...OR IMPRESSIONS OF PEOPLE.

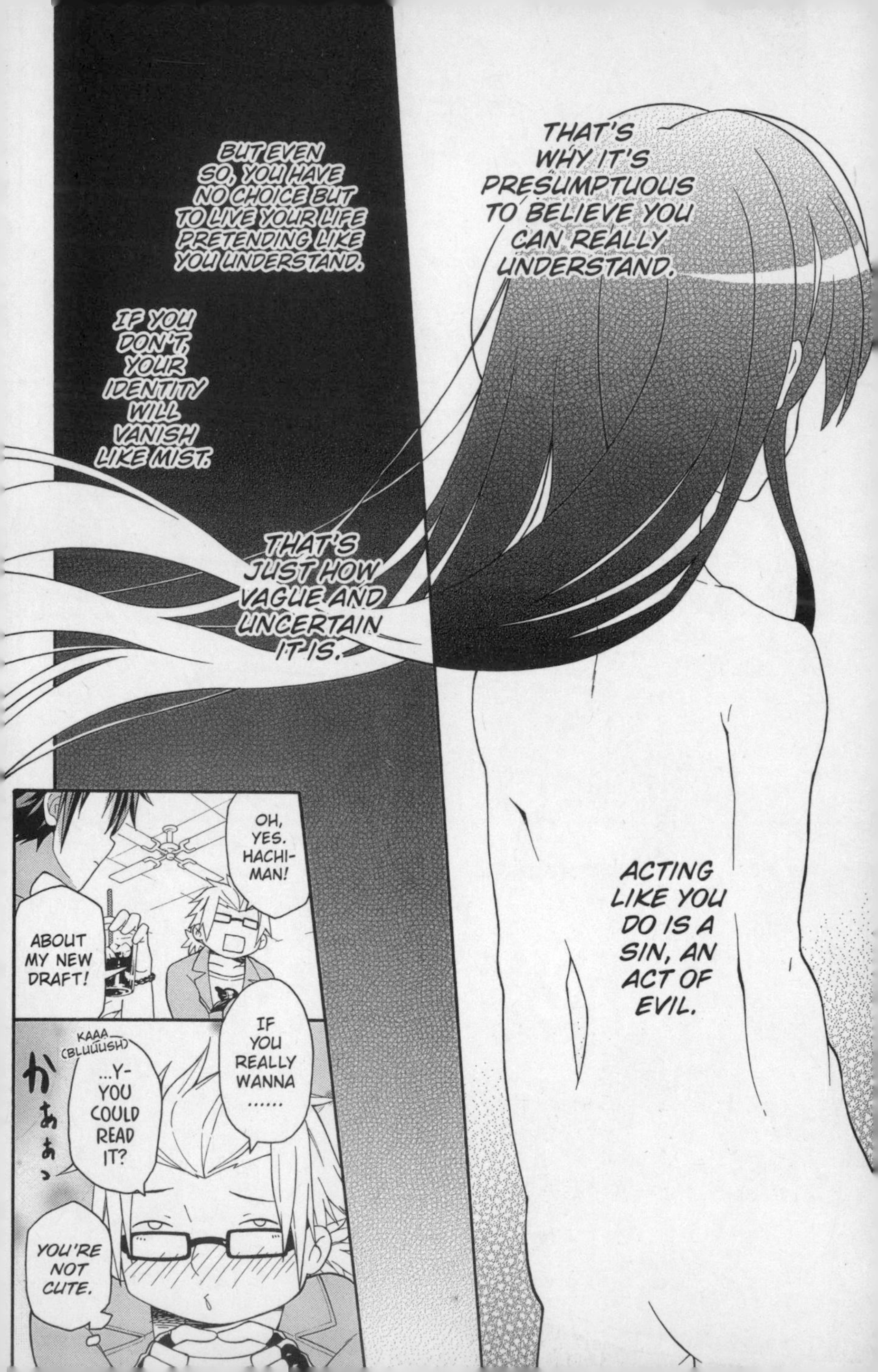
THAT'S WHY IT'S PRESUMPTUOUS TO BELIEVE YOU CAN REALLY UNDERSTAND.
ACTING LIKE YOU DO IS A SIN, AN ACT OF EVIL.
BUT EVEN SO, YOU HAVE NO CHOICE BUT TO LIVE YOUR LIFE PRETENDING LIKE YOU UNDERSTAND.
IF YOU DON'T, YOUR IDENTITY WILL VANISH LIKE MIST.
THAT'S JUST HOW VAGUE AND UNCERTAIN IT IS.
OH, YES. HACHIMAN!
ABOUT MY NEW DRAFT!
IF YOU REALLY WANNA ......
かぁぁっ
KAAA (BLUUUSH)
...Y-YOU COULD READ IT?
YOU'RE NOT CUTE.

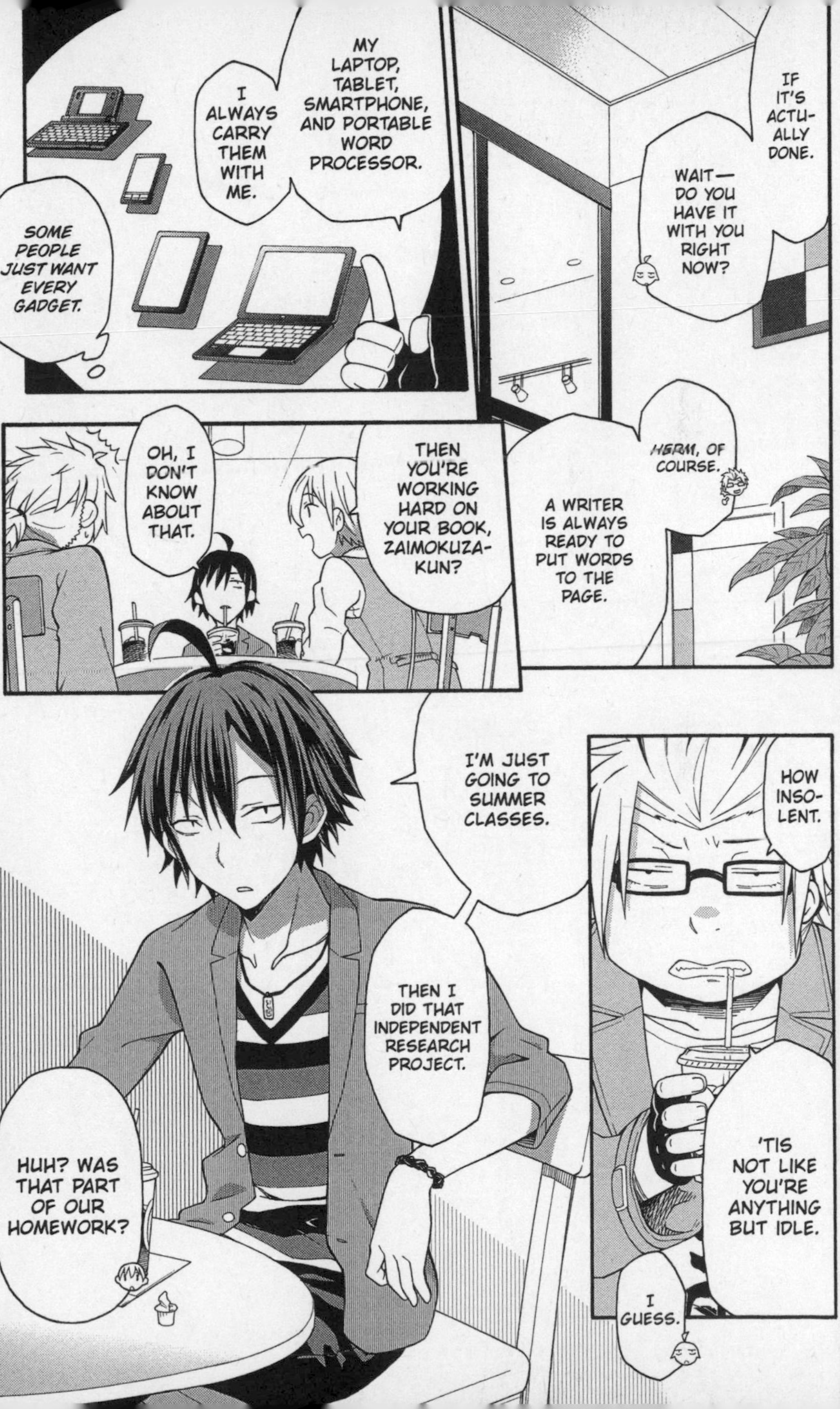
IF IT'S ACTU-ALLY DONE.
WAIT— DO YOU HAVE IT WITH YOU RIGHT NOW?
MY LAPTOP, TABLET, SMARTPHONE, AND PORTABLE WORD PROCESSOR.
I ALWAYS CARRY THEM WITH ME.
SOME PEOPLE JUST WANT EVERY GADGET.
HERM, OF COURSE.
A WRITER IS ALWAYS READY TO PUT WORDS TO THE PAGE.
THEN YOU'RE WORKING HARD ON YOUR BOOK, ZAIMOKUZA-KUN?
OH, I DON'T KNOW ABOUT THAT.
HOW INSO-LENT.
'TIS NOT LIKE YOU'RE ANYTHING BUT IDLE.
I GUESS.
I'M JUST GOING TO SUMMER CLASSES.
THEN I DID THAT INDEPENDENT RESEARCH PROJECT.
HUH? WAS THAT PART OF OUR HOMEWORK?

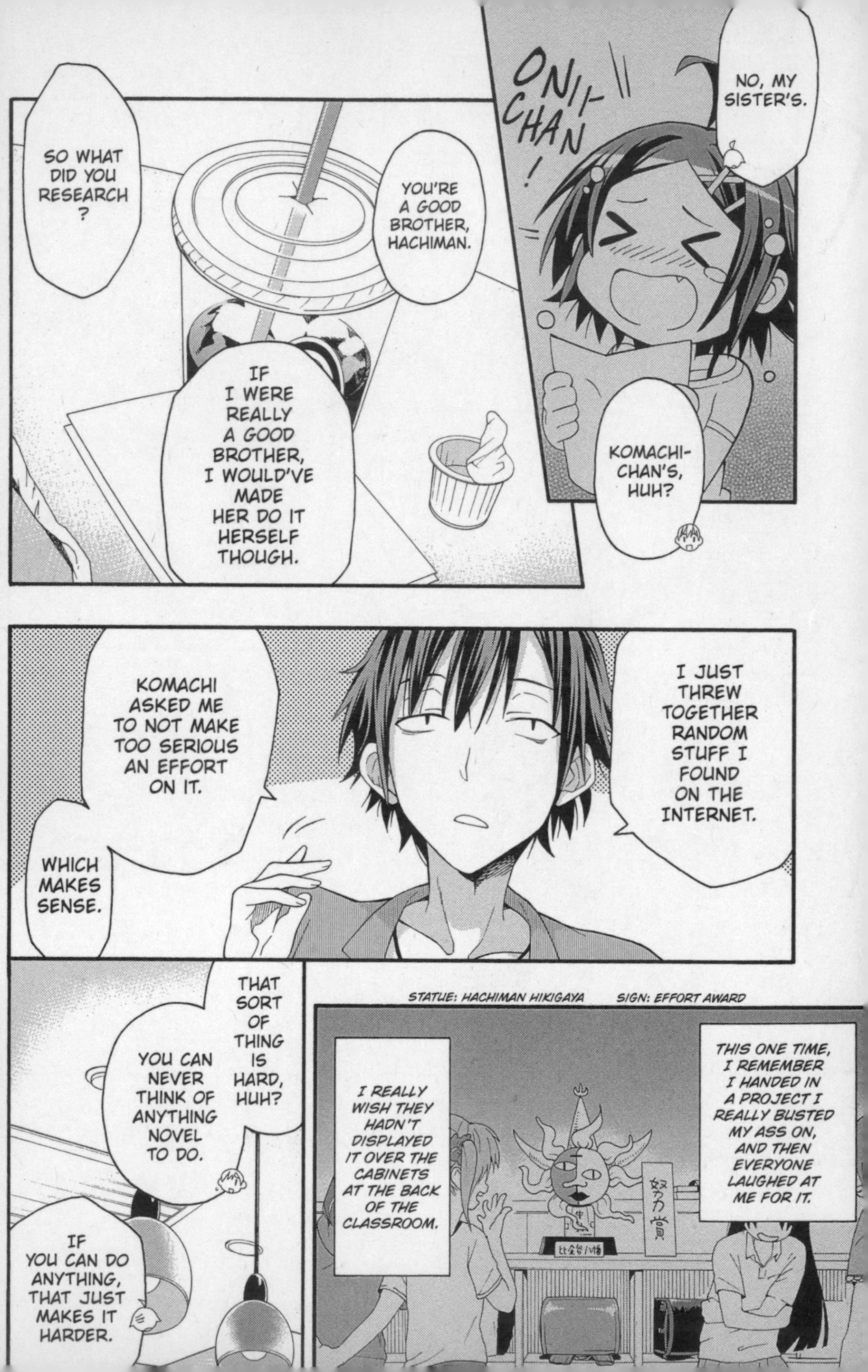
NO, MY SISTER'S.
ONII-CHAN!
KOMACHI-CHAN'S, HUH?
YOU'RE A GOOD BROTHER, HACHIMAN.
IF I WERE REALLY A GOOD BROTHER, I WOULD'VE MADE HER DO IT HERSELF THOUGH.
SO WHAT DID YOU RESEARCH?
I JUST THREW TOGETHER RANDOM STUFF I FOUND ON THE INTERNET.
KOMACHI ASKED ME TO NOT MAKE TOO SERIOUS AN EFFORT ON IT.
WHICH MAKES SENSE.
STATUE: HACHIMAN HIKIGAYA
SIGN: EFFORT AWARD
THIS ONE TIME, I REMEMBER I HANDED IN A PROJECT I REALLY BUSTED MY ASS ON, AND THEN EVERYONE LAUGHED AT ME FOR IT.
I REALLY WISH THEY HADN'T DISPLAYED IT OVER THE CABINETS AT THE BACK OF THE CLASSROOM.
THAT SORT OF THING IS HARD, HUH?
YOU CAN NEVER THINK OF ANYTHING NOVEL TO DO.
IF YOU CAN DO ANYTHING, THAT JUST MAKES IT HARDER.

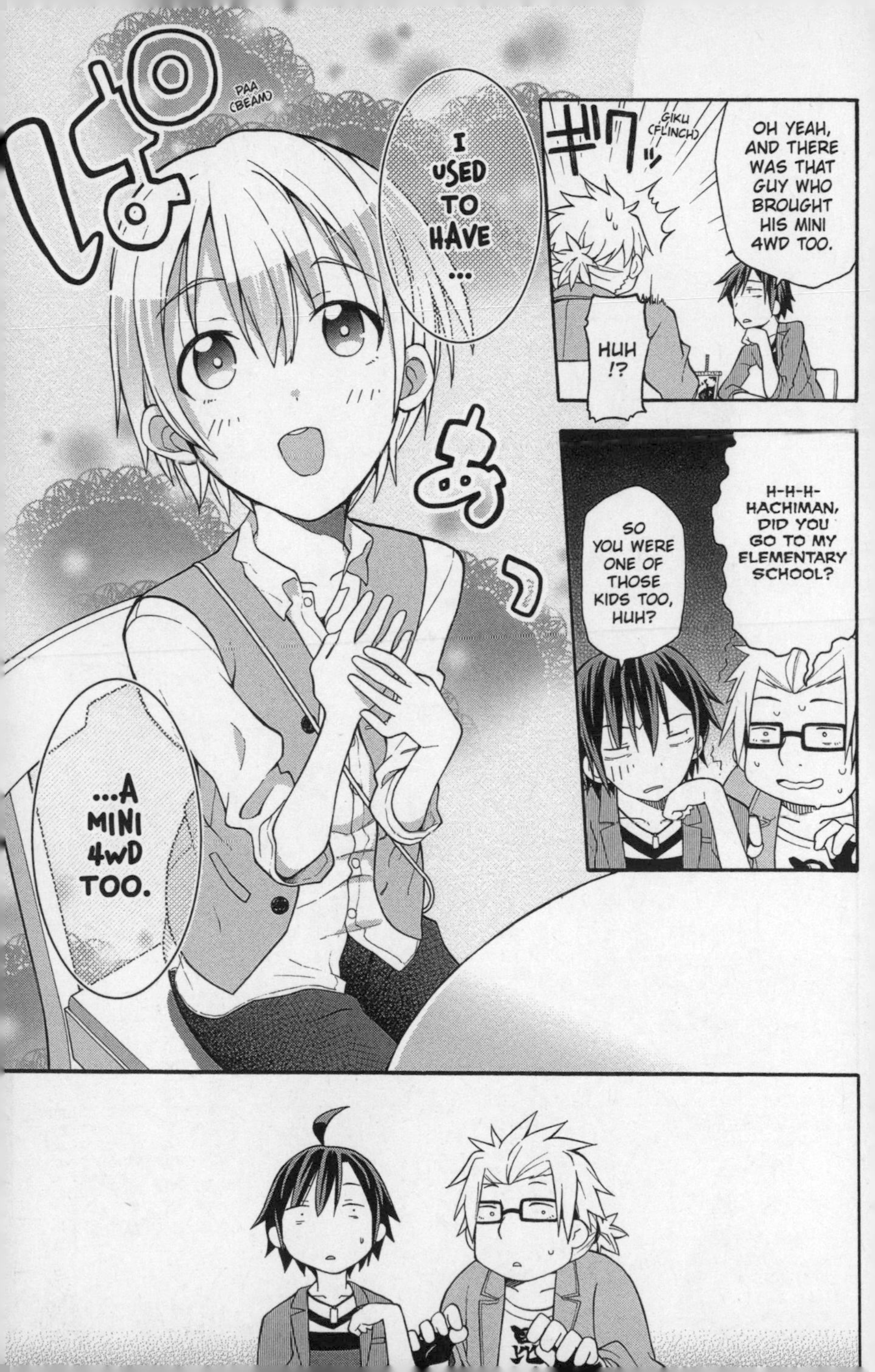
GIKU (FLINCH)
OH YEAH, AND THERE WAS THAT GUY WHO BROUGHT HIS MINI 4WD TOO.
HUH!?
H-H-H-HACHIMAN, DID YOU GO TO MY ELEMENTARY SCHOOL?
SO YOU WERE ONE OF THOSE KIDS TOO, HUH?
PAA (BEAM)
I USED TO HAVE...
...A MINI 4WD TOO.

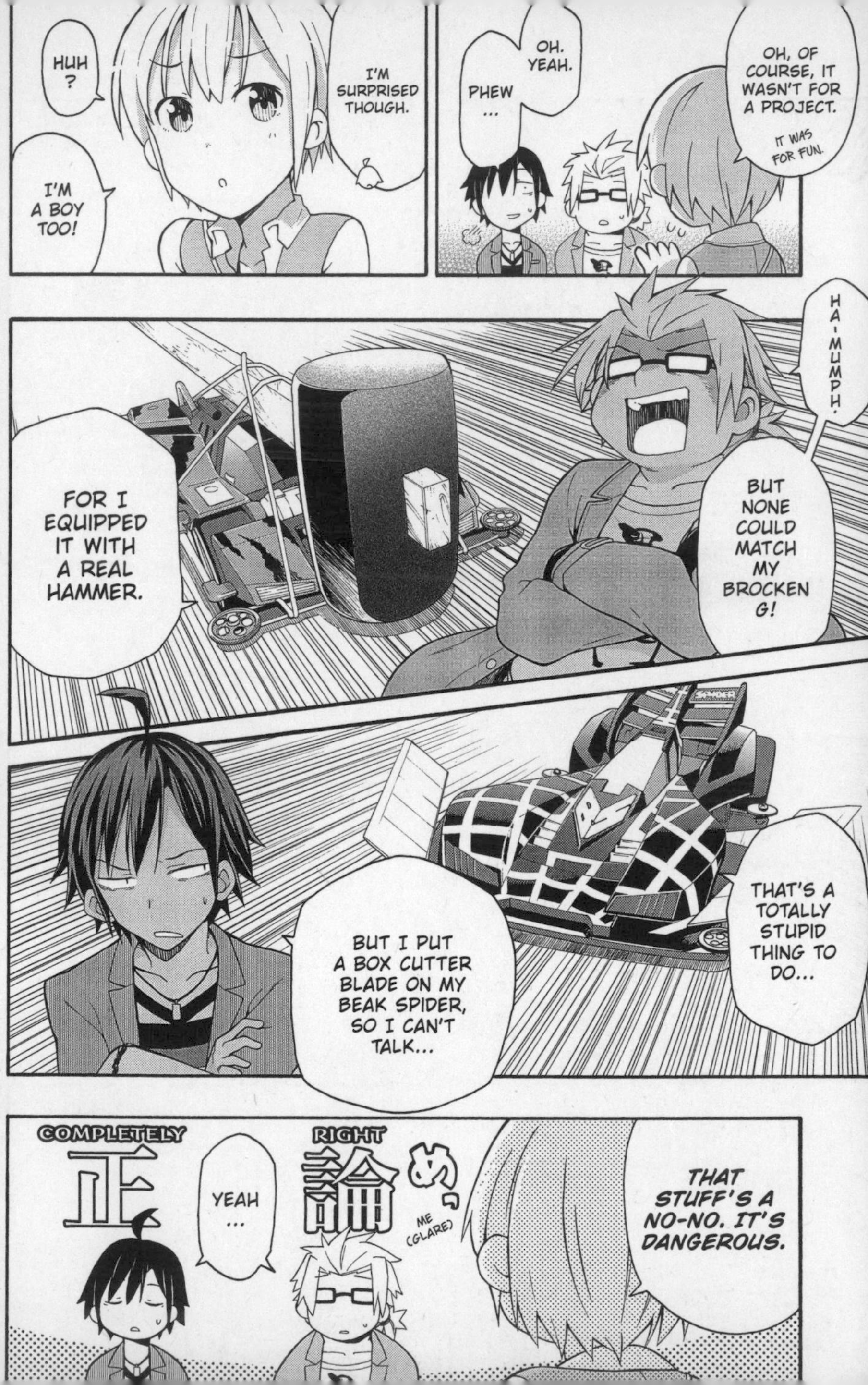
OH, OF COURSE, IT WASN'T FOR A PROJECT.
IT WAS FOR FUN.
OH. YEAH.
PHEW...
I'M SURPRISED THOUGH.
HUH?
I'M A BOY TOO!
HA-MUMPH.
BUT NONE COULD MATCH MY BROCKEN G!
FOR I EQUIPPED IT WITH A REAL HAMMER.
THAT'S A TOTALLY STUPID THING TO DO...
BUT I PUT A BOX CUTTER BLADE ON MY BEAK SPIDER, SO I CAN'T TALK...
THAT STUFF'S A NO-NO. IT'S DANGEROUS.
COMPLETELY RIGHT ME (GLARE)
正論め、
YEAH...

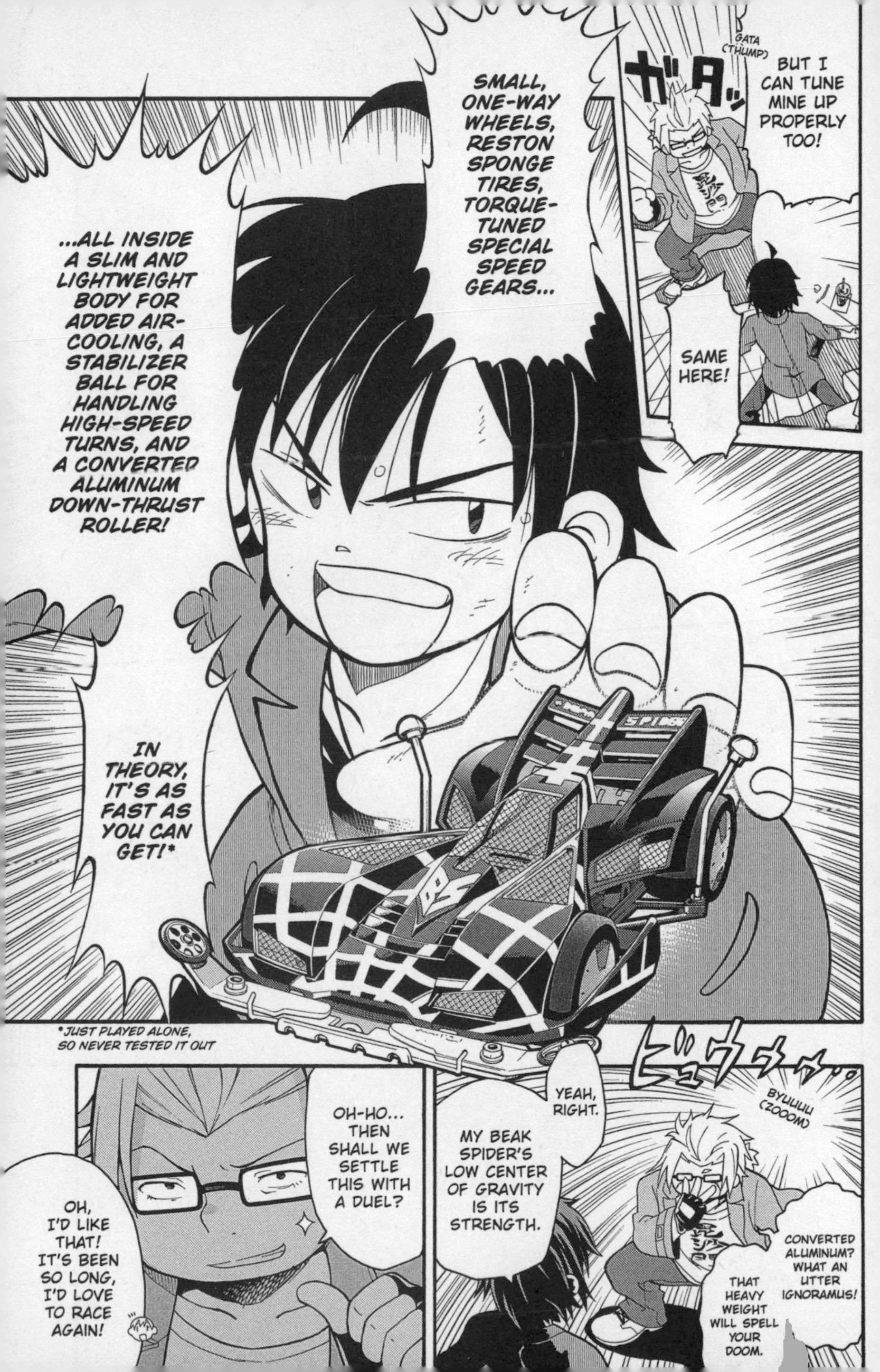
SMALL, ONE-WAY WHEELS, RESTON SPONGE TIRES, TORQUE-TUNED SPECIAL SPEED GEARS...
...ALL INSIDE A SLIM AND LIGHTWEIGHT BODY FOR ADDED AIR-COOLING, A STABILIZER BALL FOR HANDLING HIGH-SPEED TURNS, AND A CONVERTED ALUMINUM DOWN-THRUST ROLLER!
IN THEORY, IT'S AS FAST AS YOU CAN GET!*
ガタッ
GATA (THUMP)
BUT I CAN TUNE MINE UP PROPERLY TOO!
SAME HERE!
*JUST PLAYED ALONE, SO NEVER TESTED IT OUT
BYUUUU (ZOOOM)
YEAH, RIGHT.
MY BEAK SPIDER'S LOW CENTER OF GRAVITY IS ITS STRENGTH.
CONVERTED ALUMINUM? WHAT AN UTTER IGNORAMUS!
THAT HEAVY WEIGHT WILL SPELL YOUR DOOM.
OH-HO... THEN SHALL WE SETTLE THIS WITH A DUEL?
OH, I'D LIKE THAT! IT'S BEEN SO LONG, I'D LOVE TO RACE AGAIN!

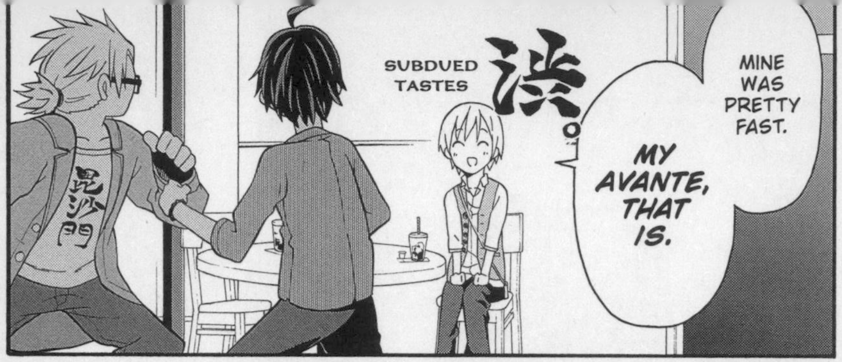
MINE WAS PRETTY FAST.
MY AVANTE, THAT IS.
渋
SUBDUED TASTES
毘沙門

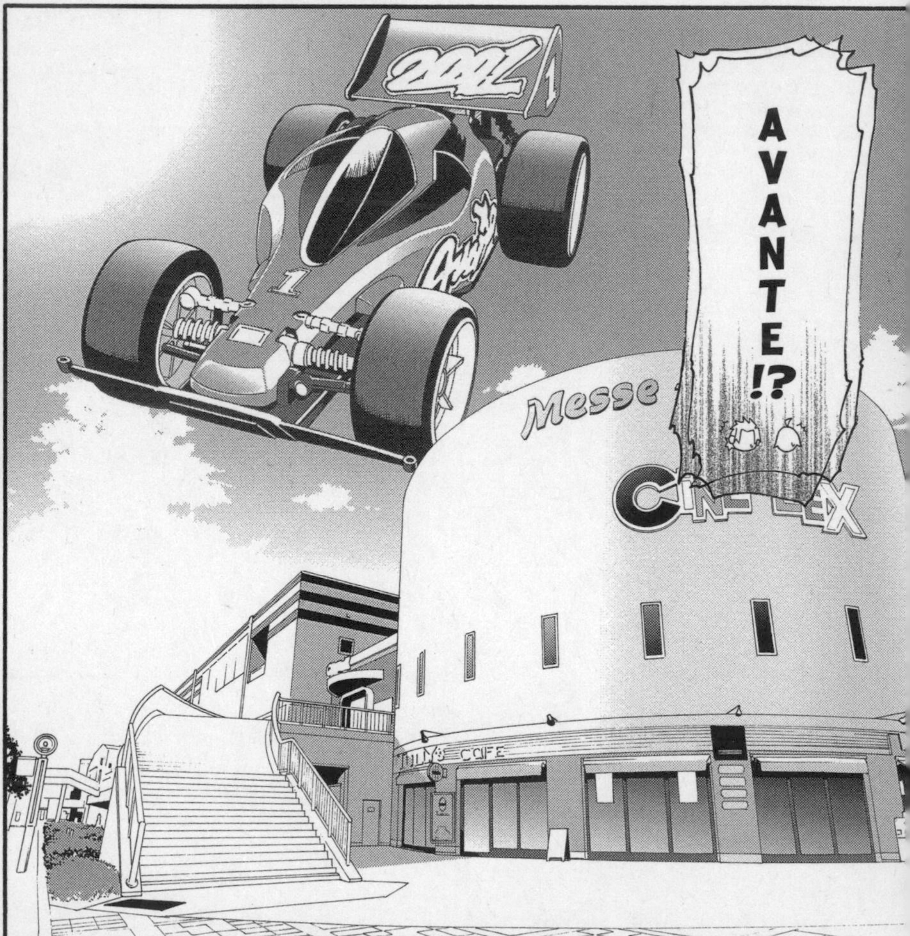
AVANTE!?
Messe

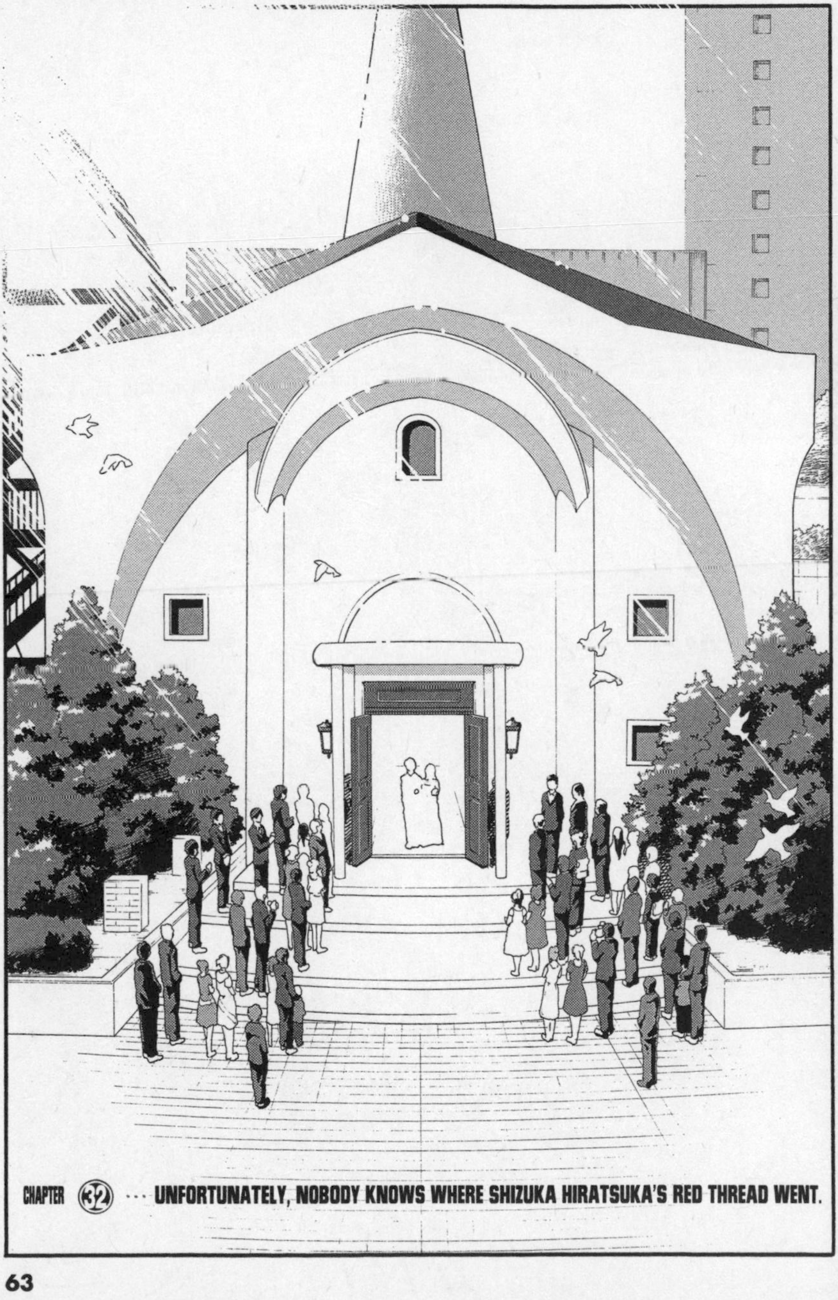
CHAPTER 32 ... UNFORTUNATELY, NOBODY KNOWS WHERE SHIZUKA HIRATSUKA'S RED THREAD WENT.

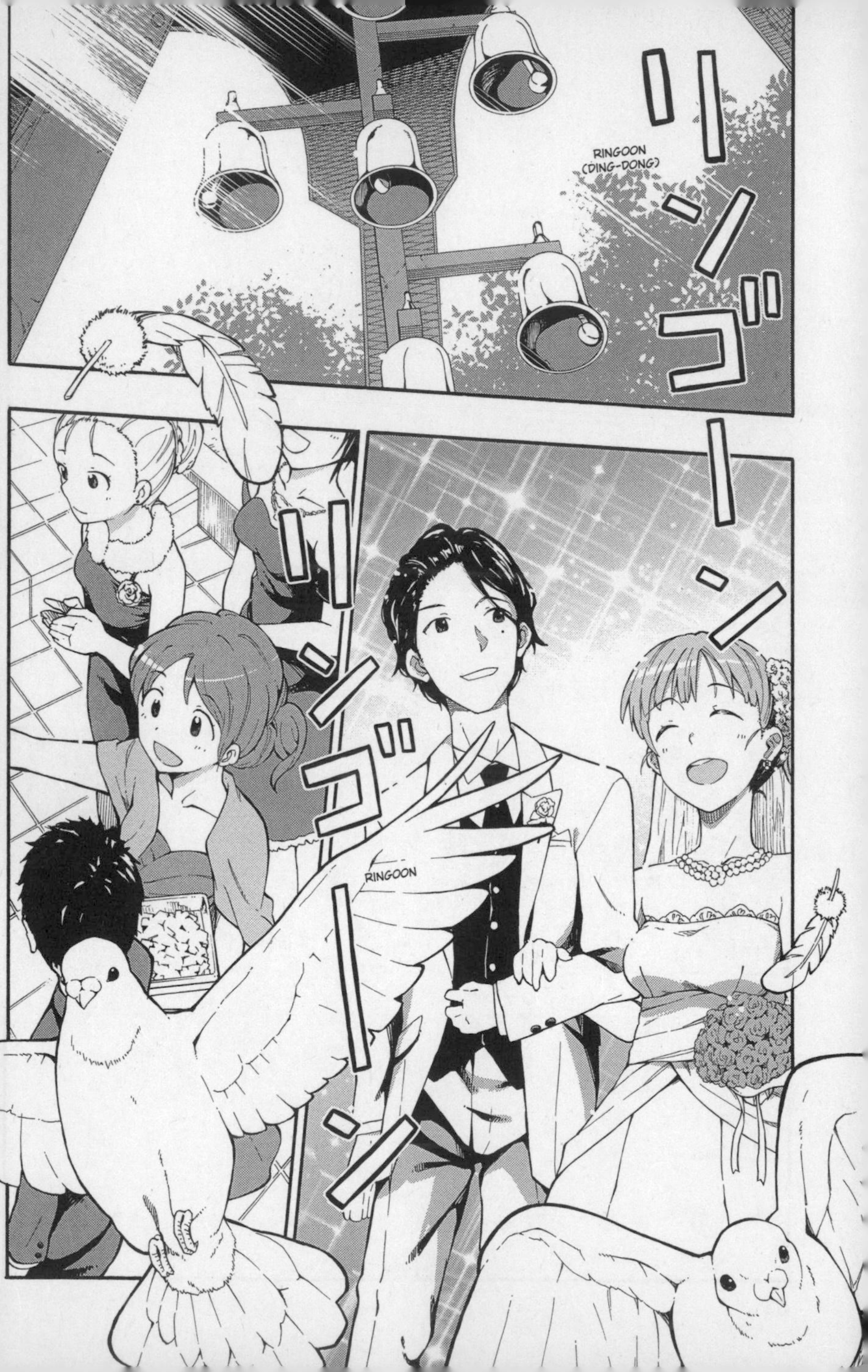
リーンゴーン
RINGOON
(DING-DONG)
リーンゴーン
RINGOON

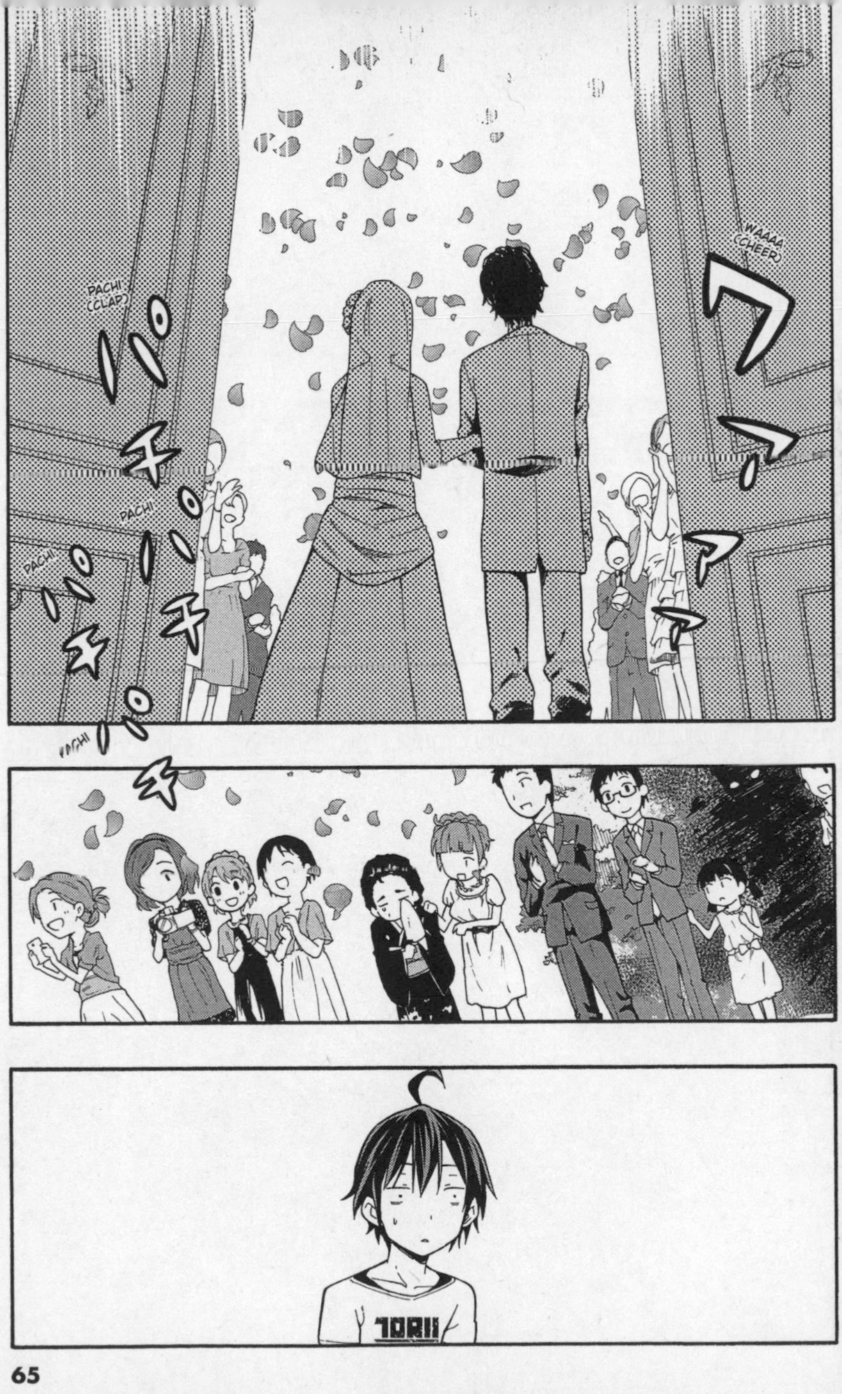
WAAAA (CHEER)
PACHI (CLAP)
PACHI
PACHI
PACHI

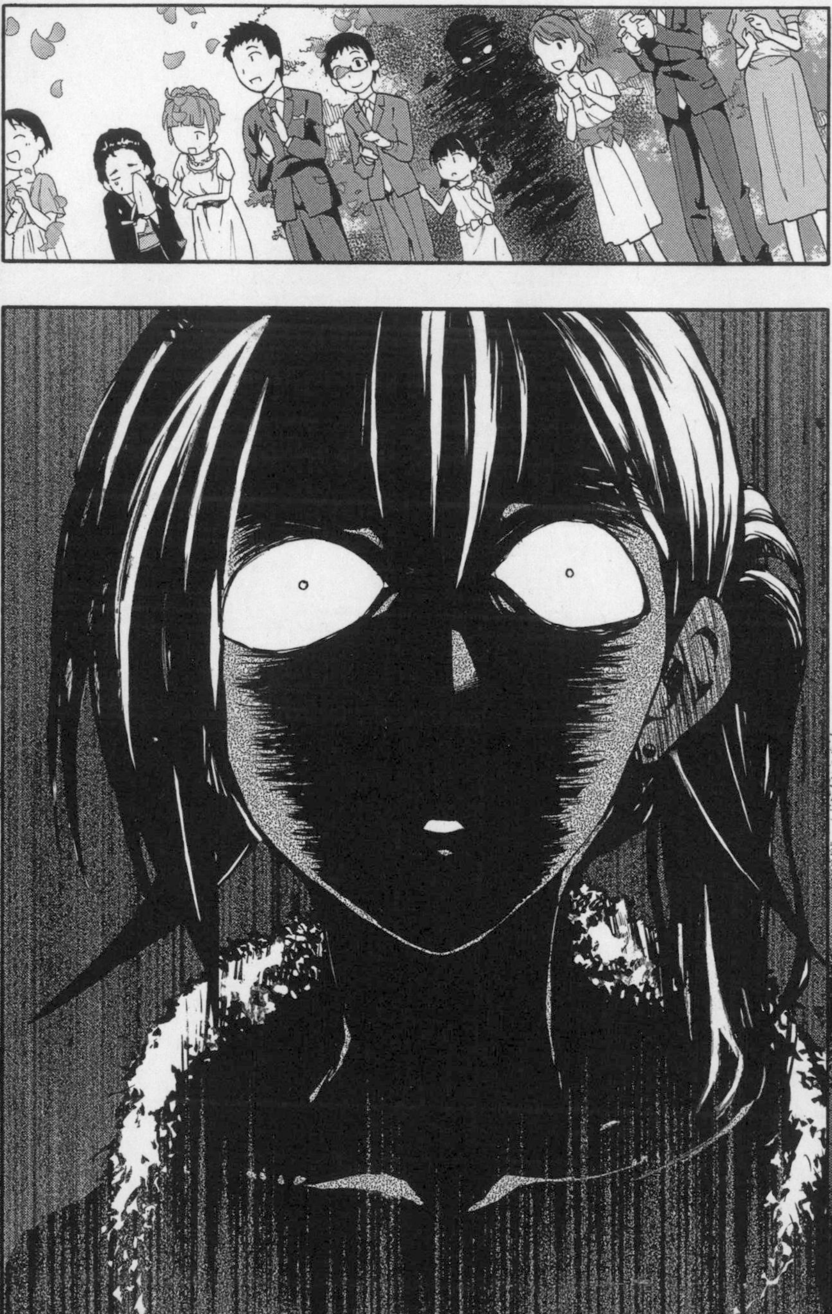

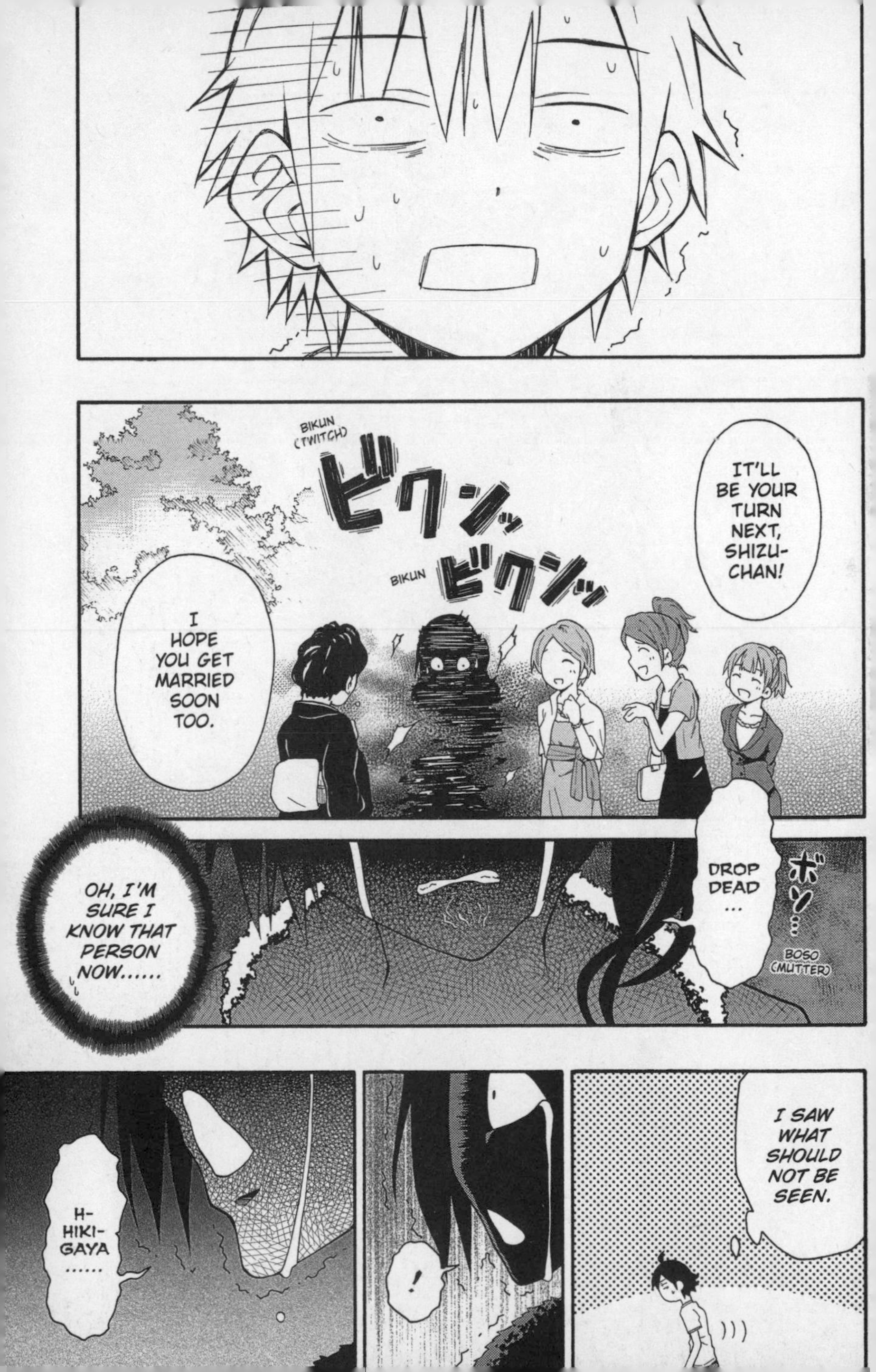
IT'LL BE YOUR TURN NEXT, SHIZU-CHAN!
ビクッ
BIKUN (TWITCH)
ビクッ
BIKUN
I HOPE YOU GET MARRIED SOON TOO.
ボソ…
BOSO (MUTTER)
DROP DEAD …
OH, I'M SURE I KNOW THAT PERSON NOW......
I SAW WHAT SHOULD NOT BE SEEN.
!
H-HIKIGAYA ......

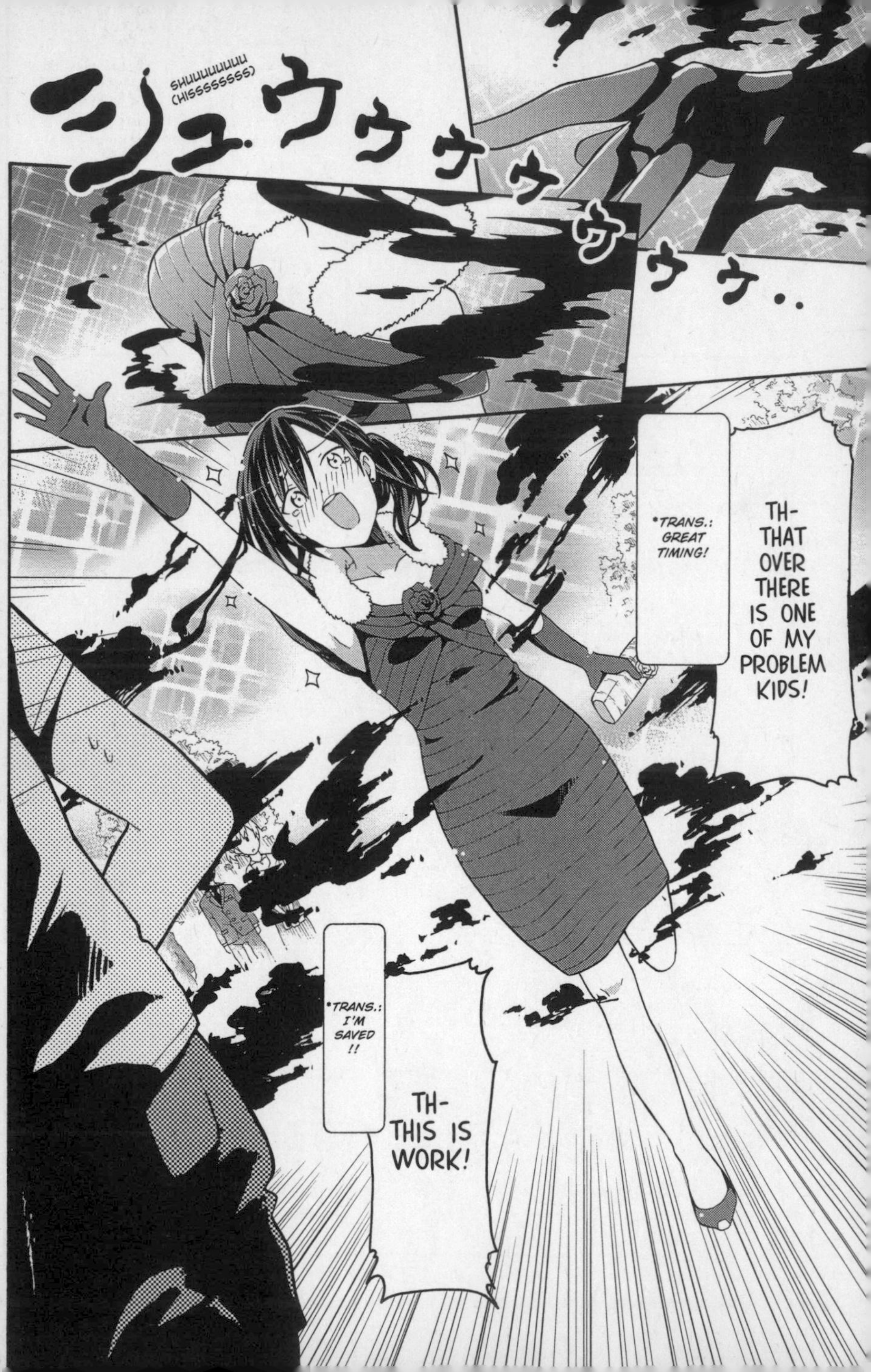
シュウウウウウウウ..
SHUUUUUUUUU (HISSSSSSSS)
TH- THAT OVER THERE IS ONE OF MY PROBLEM KIDS!
*TRANS.: GREAT TIMING!
TH- THIS IS WORK!
*TRANS.: I'M SAVED !!

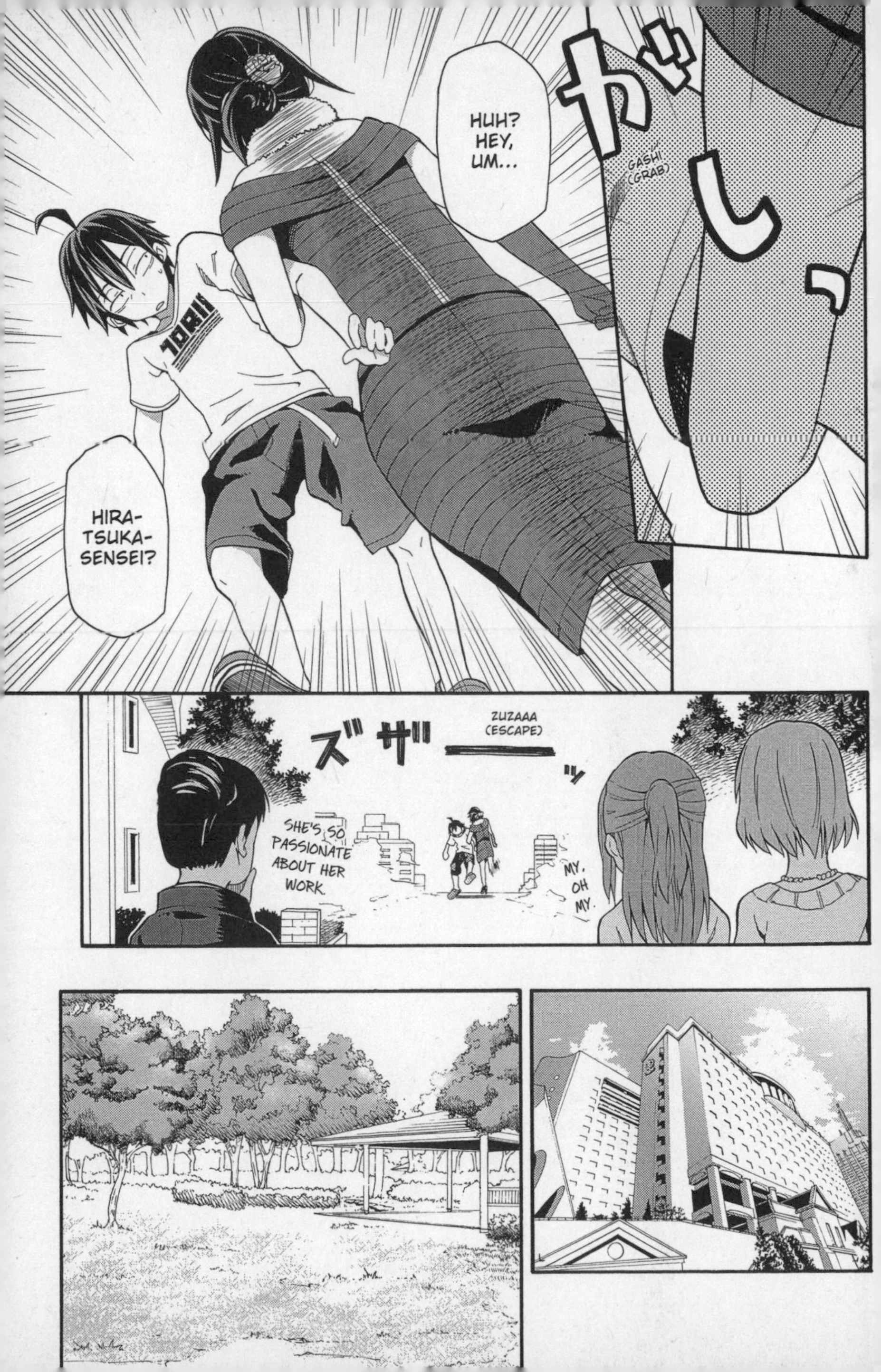
GASHI (GRAB)
HUH? HEY, UM...
HIRA-TSUKA-SENSEI?
ZUZAAA (ESCAPE)
MY, OH MY.
SHE'S SO PASSIONATE ABOUT HER WORK.

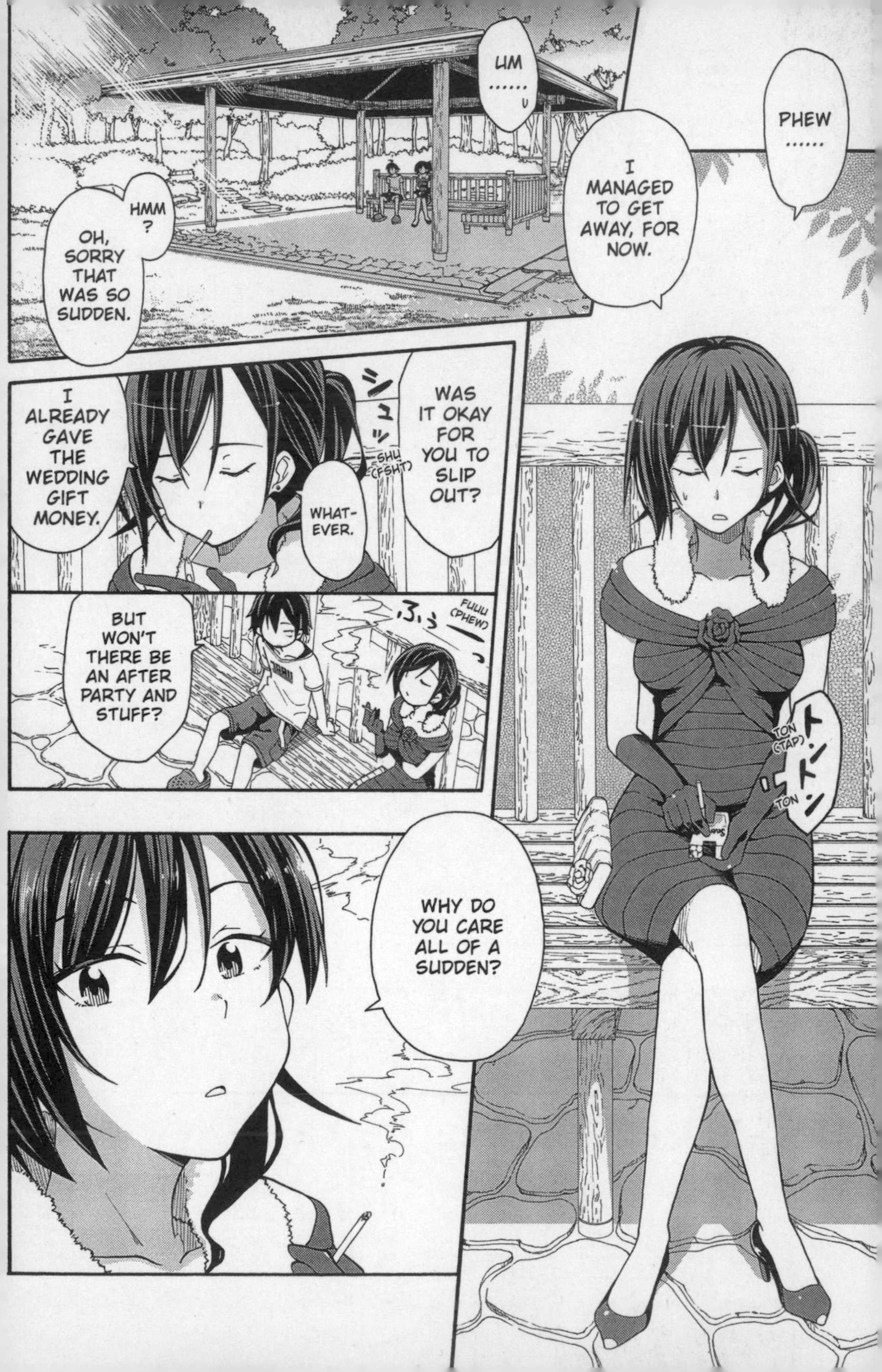
PHEW ......
I MANAGED TO GET AWAY, FOR NOW.
TON (TAP) ト・ン
TON トン
UM ......
HMM? OH, SORRY THAT WAS SO SUDDEN.
WAS IT OKAY FOR YOU TO SLIP OUT?
シュッ SHU (FSHT)
WHAT-EVER.
I ALREADY GAVE THE WEDDING GIFT MONEY.
ふぅ FUUU (PHEW)
BUT WON'T THERE BE AN AFTER PARTY AND STUFF?
WHY DO YOU CARE ALL OF A SUDDEN?

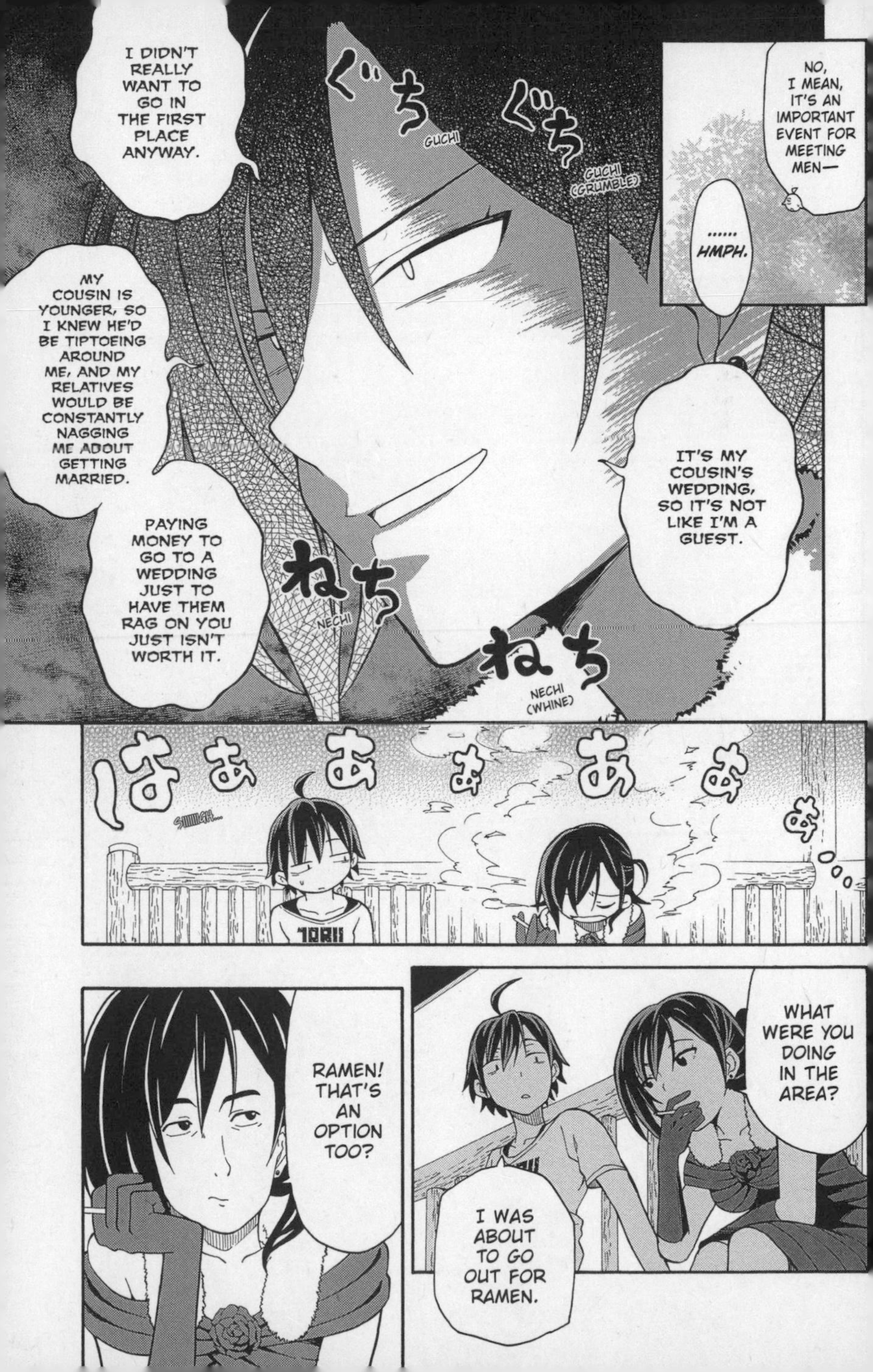
NO, I MEAN, IT'S AN IMPORTANT EVENT FOR MEETING MEN—
...... HMPH.
ぐち ぐち
GUCHI
GUCHI (GRUMBLE)
IT'S MY COUSIN'S WEDDING, SO IT'S NOT LIKE I'M A GUEST.
I DIDN'T REALLY WANT TO GO IN THE FIRST PLACE ANYWAY.
MY COUSIN IS YOUNGER, SO I KNEW HE'D BE TIPTOEING AROUND ME, AND MY RELATIVES WOULD BE CONSTANTLY NAGGING ME ABOUT GETTING MARRIED.
PAYING MONEY TO GO TO A WEDDING JUST TO HAVE THEM RAG ON YOU JUST ISN'T WORTH IT.
ねち
NECHI
ねち
NECHI (WHINE)
はあぁあぁぁ
SIIIIGH...
WHAT WERE YOU DOING IN THE AREA?
I WAS ABOUT TO GO OUT FOR RAMEN.
RAMEN! THAT'S AN OPTION TOO?

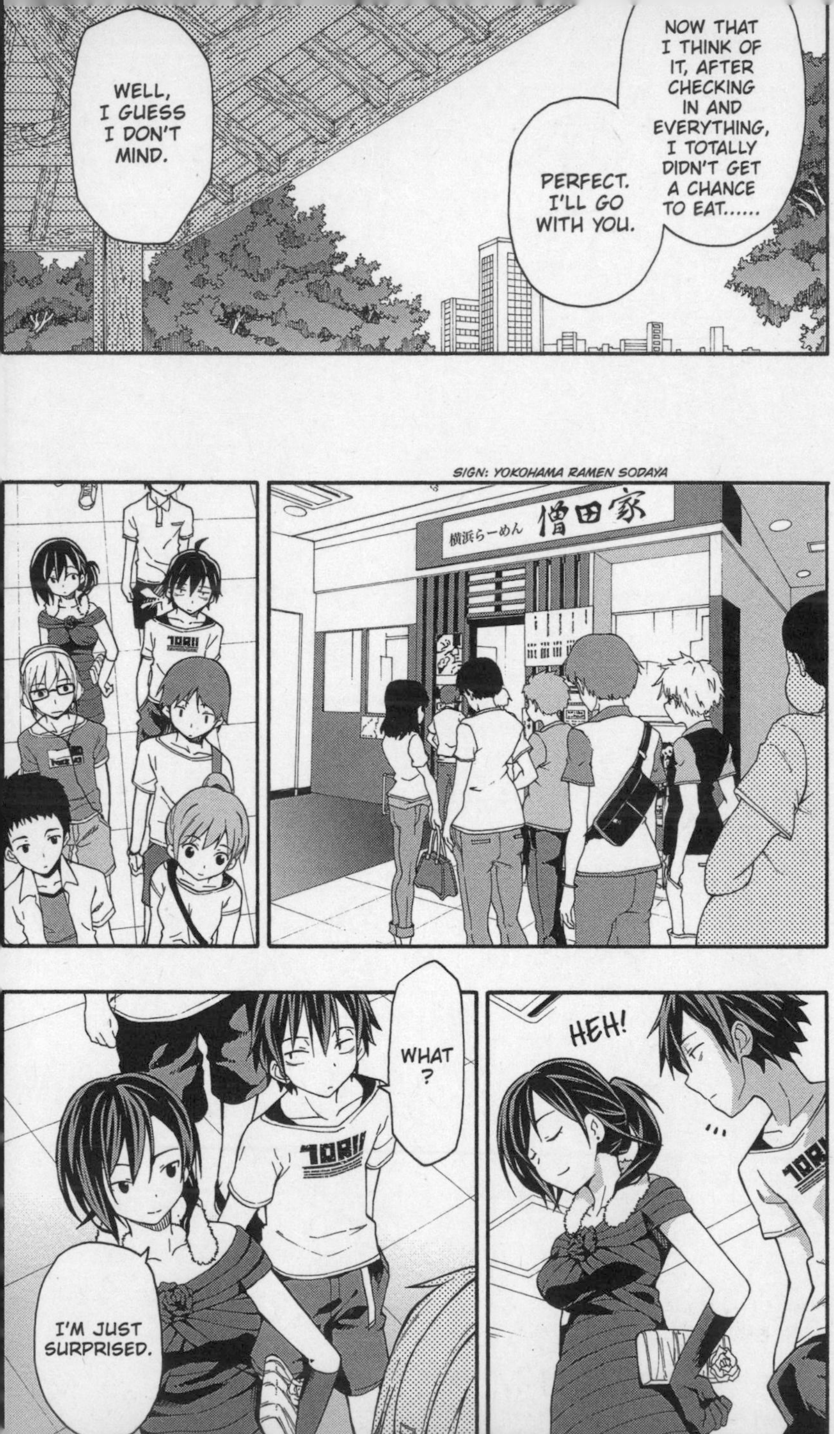
NOW THAT I THINK OF IT, AFTER CHECKING IN AND EVERYTHING, I TOTALLY DIDN'T GET A CHANCE TO EAT......
PERFECT. I'LL GO WITH YOU.
WELL, I GUESS I DON'T MIND.
SIGN: YOKOHAMA RAMEN SODAYA
横浜らーめん 僧田家
HEH!
...
WHAT ?
I'M JUST SURPRISED.

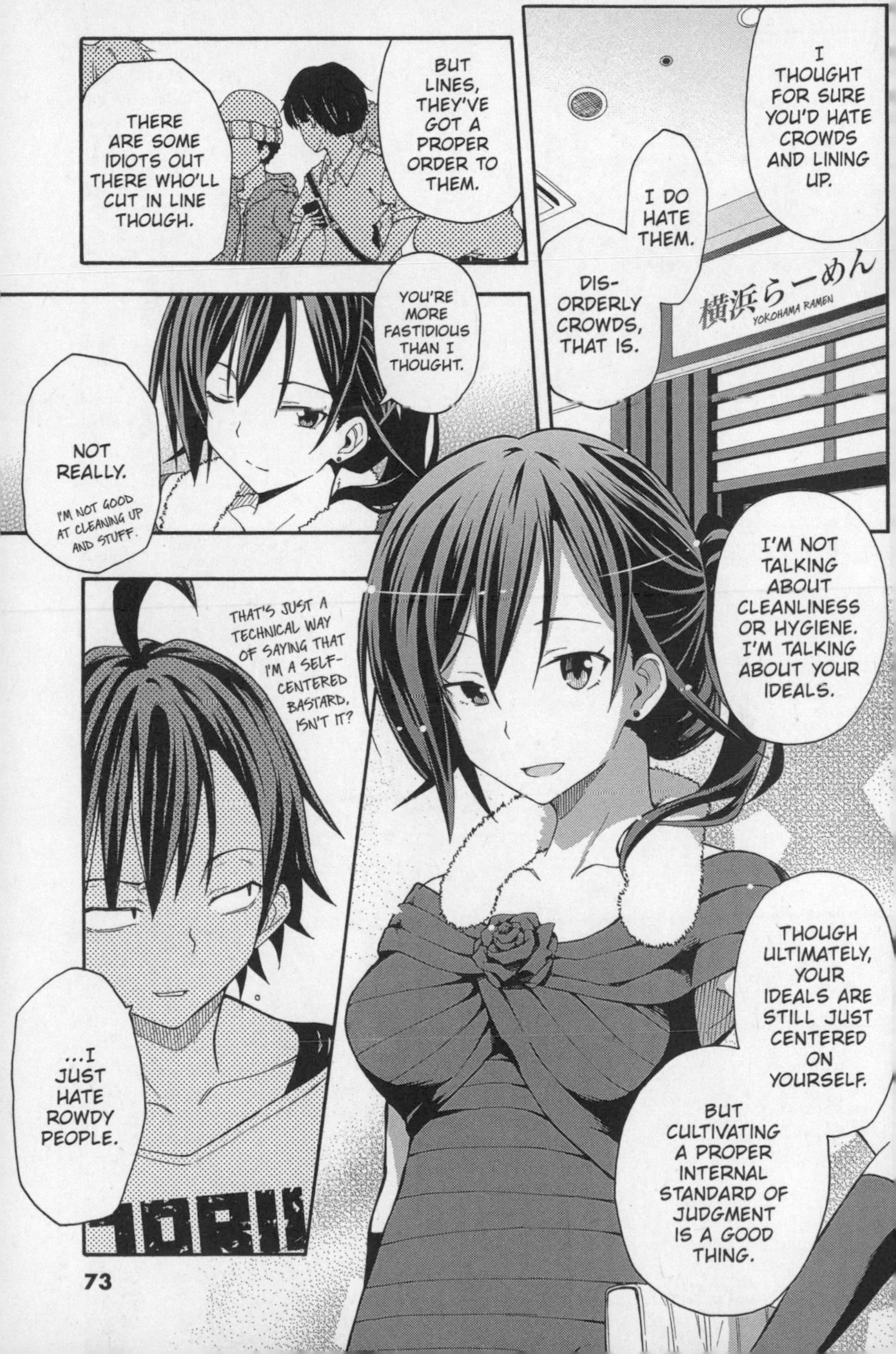
I THOUGHT FOR SURE YOU'D HATE CROWDS AND LINING UP.
I DO HATE THEM.
DIS-ORDERLY CROWDS, THAT IS.
横浜らーめん
YOKOHAMA RAMEN
BUT LINES, THEY'VE GOT A PROPER ORDER TO THEM.
THERE ARE SOME IDIOTS OUT THERE WHO'LL CUT IN LINE THOUGH.
YOU'RE MORE FASTIDIOUS THAN I THOUGHT.
NOT REALLY.
I'M NOT GOOD AT CLEANING UP AND STUFF.
I'M NOT TALKING ABOUT CLEANLINESS OR HYGIENE. I'M TALKING ABOUT YOUR IDEALS.
THOUGH ULTIMATELY, YOUR IDEALS ARE STILL JUST CENTERED ON YOURSELF.
BUT CULTIVATING A PROPER INTERNAL STANDARD OF JUDGMENT IS A GOOD THING.
THAT'S JUST A TECHNICAL WAY OF SAYING THAT I'M A SELF-CENTERED BASTARD, ISN'T IT?
...I JUST HATE ROWDY PEOPLE.

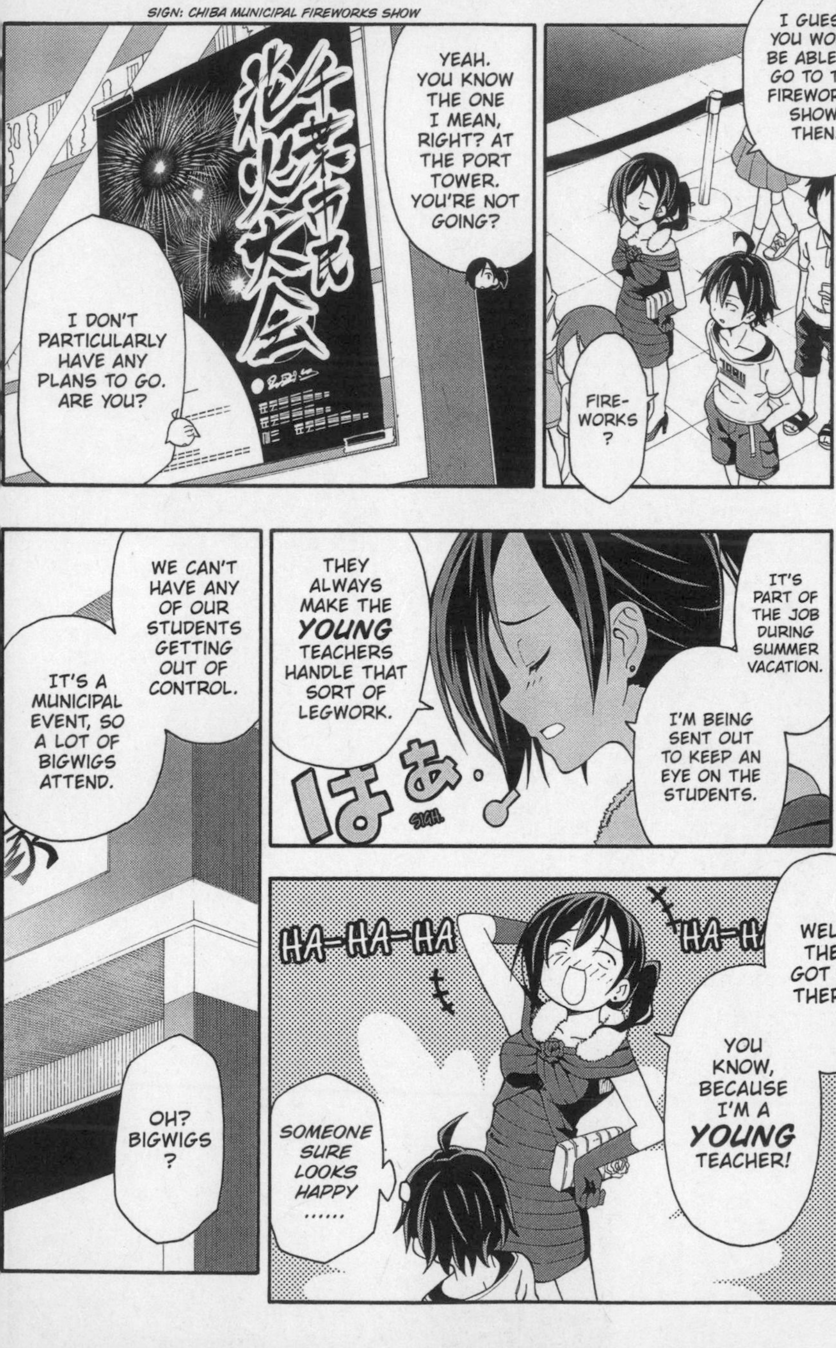
SIGN: CHIBA MUNICIPAL FIREWORKS SHOW
I GUESS YOU WON'T BE ABLE TO GO TO THE FIREWORKS SHOW, THEN.
FIRE-WORKS?
YEAH. YOU KNOW THE ONE I MEAN, RIGHT? AT THE PORT TOWER. YOU'RE NOT GOING?
I DON'T PARTICULARLY HAVE ANY PLANS TO GO. ARE YOU?
IT'S PART OF THE JOB DURING SUMMER VACATION.
I'M BEING SENT OUT TO KEEP AN EYE ON THE STUDENTS.
はあ。
SIGH.
THEY ALWAYS MAKE THE *YOUNG* TEACHERS HANDLE THAT SORT OF LEGWORK.
WELL, THEY GOT ME THERE!
HA-HA-HA
HA-HA
YOU KNOW, BECAUSE I'M A *YOUNG* TEACHER!
SOMEONE SURE LOOKS HAPPY ......
WE CAN'T HAVE ANY OF OUR STUDENTS GETTING OUT OF CONTROL.
IT'S A MUNICIPAL EVENT, SO A LOT OF BIGWIGS ATTEND.
OH? BIGWIGS?

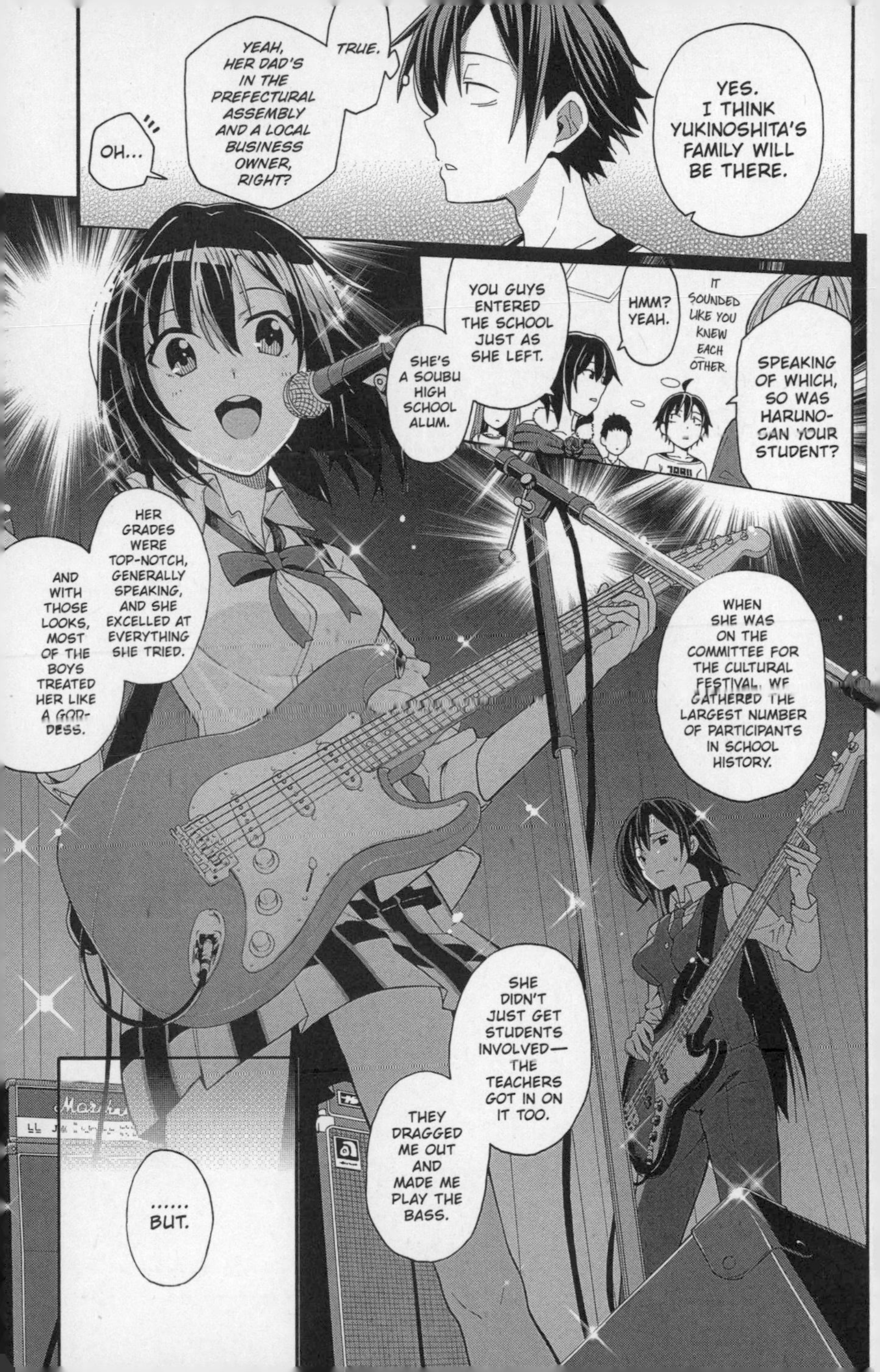
YES. I THINK YUKINOSHITA'S FAMILY WILL BE THERE.
TRUE.
YEAH, HER DAD'S IN THE PREFECTURAL ASSEMBLY AND A LOCAL BUSINESS OWNER, RIGHT?
OH...
SPEAKING OF WHICH, SO WAS HARUNO-SAN YOUR STUDENT?
IT SOUNDED LIKE YOU KNEW EACH OTHER.
HMM? YEAH.
YOU GUYS ENTERED THE SCHOOL JUST AS SHE LEFT.
SHE'S A SOUBU HIGH SCHOOL ALUM.
WHEN SHE WAS ON THE COMMITTEE FOR THE CULTURAL FESTIVAL, WE GATHERED THE LARGEST NUMBER OF PARTICIPANTS IN SCHOOL HISTORY.
HER GRADES WERE TOP-NOTCH, GENERALLY SPEAKING, AND SHE EXCELLED AT EVERYTHING SHE TRIED.
AND WITH THOSE LOOKS, MOST OF THE BOYS TREATED HER LIKE A GOD-DESS.
SHE DIDN'T JUST GET STUDENTS INVOLVED—THE TEACHERS GOT IN ON IT TOO.
THEY DRAGGED ME OUT AND MADE ME PLAY THE BASS.
......BUT.

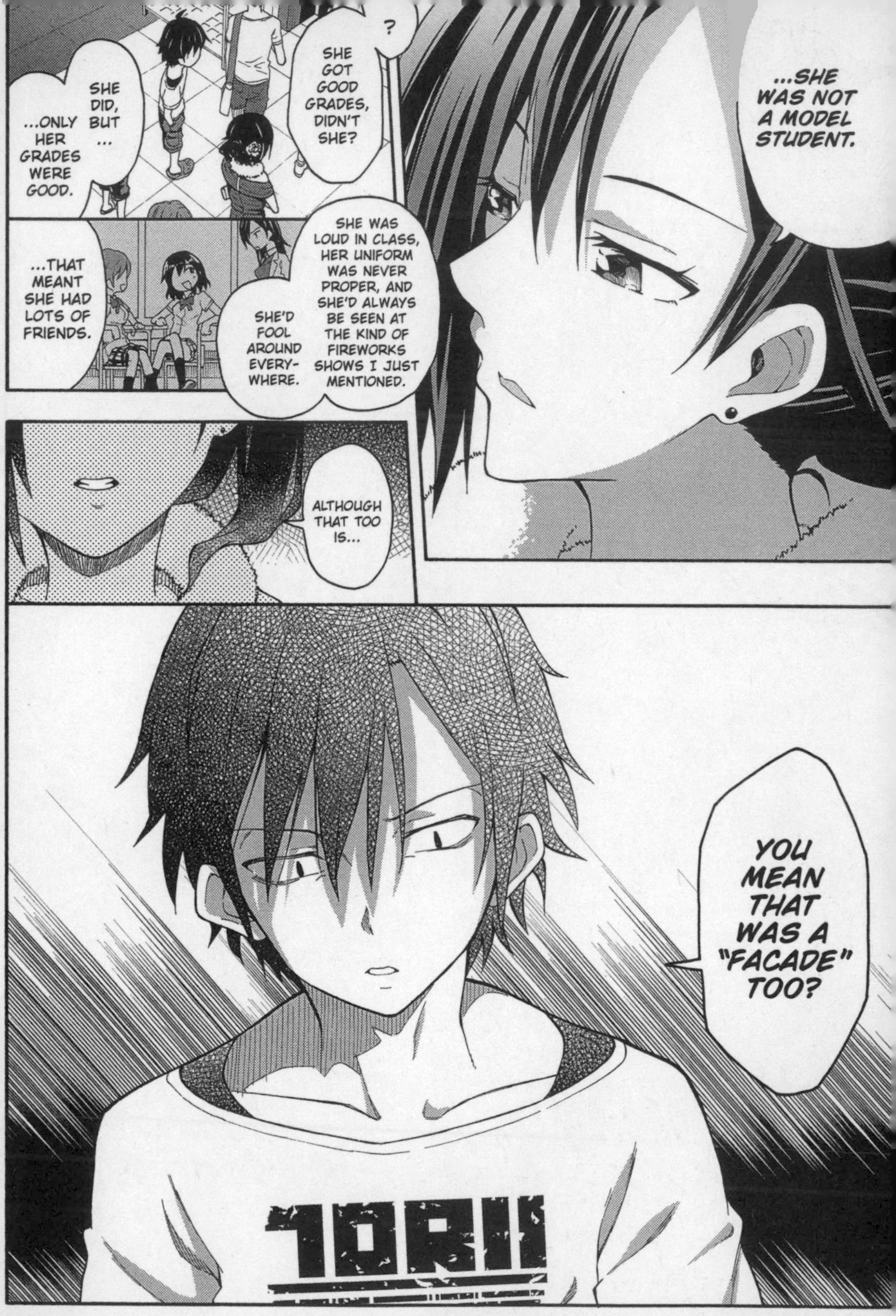
...SHE WAS NOT A MODEL STUDENT.
?
SHE GOT GOOD GRADES, DIDN'T SHE?
SHE DID, BUT ...
...ONLY HER GRADES WERE GOOD.
SHE WAS LOUD IN CLASS, HER UNIFORM WAS NEVER PROPER, AND SHE'D ALWAYS BE SEEN AT THE KIND OF FIREWORKS SHOWS I JUST MENTIONED.
SHE'D FOOL AROUND EVERY-WHERE.
...THAT MEANT SHE HAD LOTS OF FRIENDS.
ALTHOUGH THAT TOO IS...
YOU MEAN THAT WAS A "FACADE" TOO?

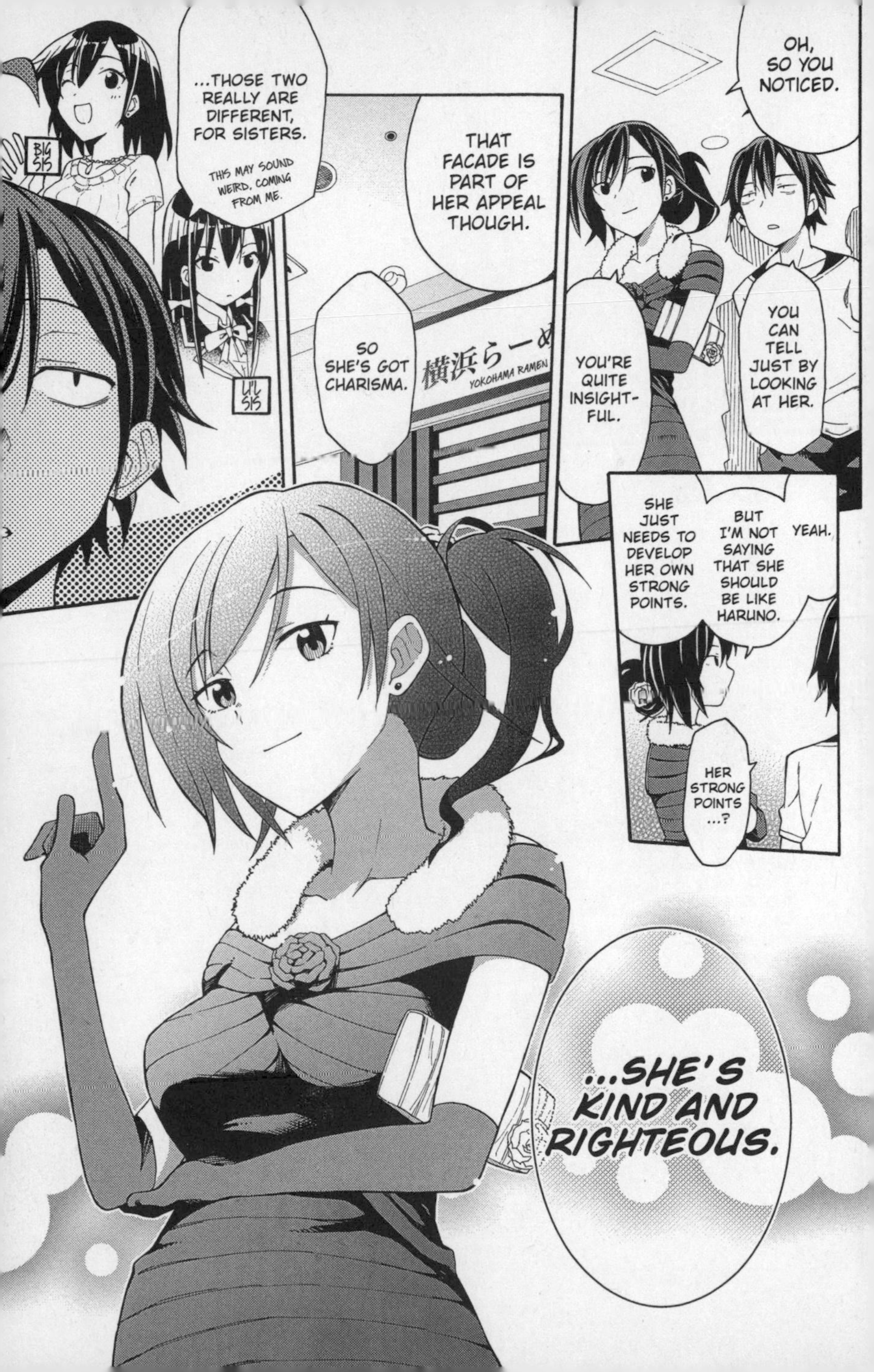
OH, SO YOU NOTICED.
YOU CAN TELL JUST BY LOOKING AT HER.
YOU'RE QUITE INSIGHT-FUL.
THAT FACADE IS PART OF HER APPEAL THOUGH.
SO SHE'S GOT CHARISMA.
横浜らーめ
YOKOHAMA RAMEN
...THOSE TWO REALLY ARE DIFFERENT, FOR SISTERS.
THIS MAY SOUND WEIRD, COMING FROM ME.
BIG SIS
LI'L SIS
YEAH.
BUT I'M NOT SAYING THAT SHE SHOULD BE LIKE HARUNO.
SHE JUST NEEDS TO DEVELOP HER OWN STRONG POINTS.
HER STRONG POINTS ...?
...SHE'S KIND AND RIGHTEOUS.

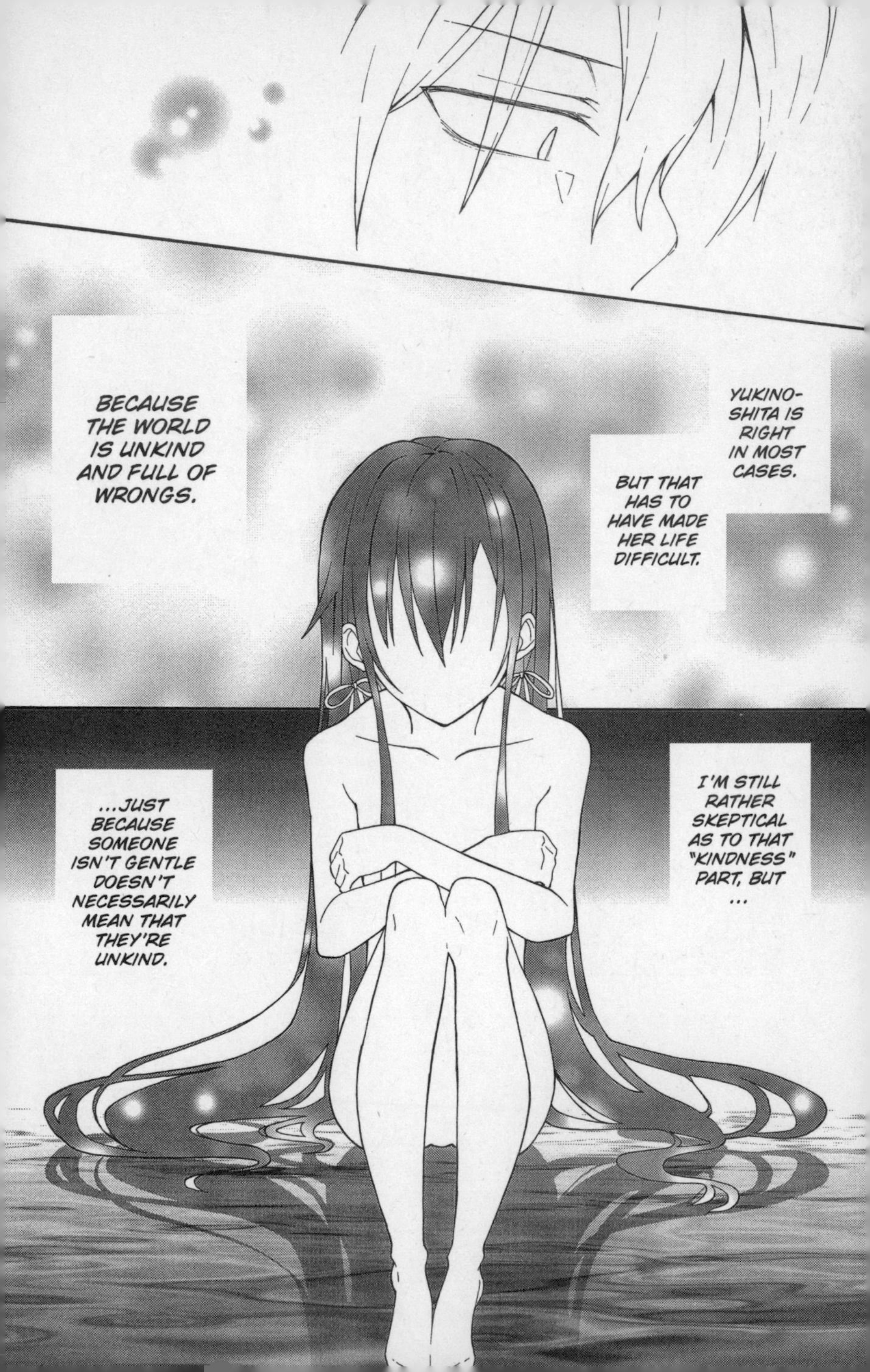
YUKINO-SHITA IS RIGHT IN MOST CASES.
BUT THAT HAS TO HAVE MADE HER LIFE DIFFICULT.
BECAUSE THE WORLD IS UNKIND AND FULL OF WRONGS.
I'M STILL RATHER SKEPTICAL AS TO THAT "KINDNESS" PART, BUT ...
...JUST BECAUSE SOMEONE ISN'T GENTLE DOESN'T NECESSARILY MEAN THAT THEY'RE UNKIND.

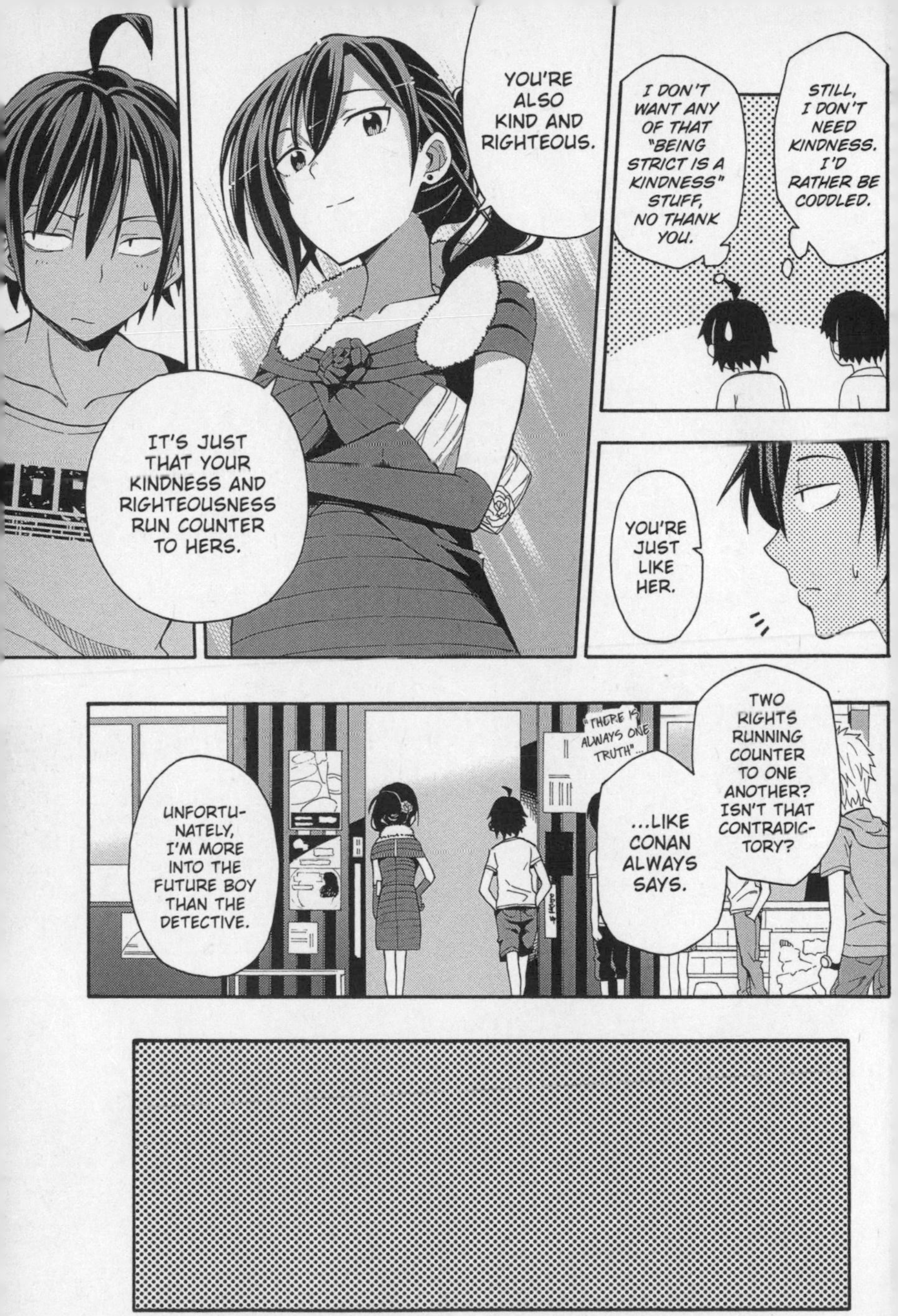
STILL, I DON'T NEED KINDNESS. I'D RATHER BE CODDLED.
I DON'T WANT ANY OF THAT "BEING STRICT IS A KINDNESS" STUFF, NO THANK YOU.
YOU'RE JUST LIKE HER.
YOU'RE ALSO KIND AND RIGHTEOUS.
IT'S JUST THAT YOUR KINDNESS AND RIGHTEOUSNESS RUN COUNTER TO HERS.
TWO RIGHTS RUNNING COUNTER TO ONE ANOTHER? ISN'T THAT CONTRADIC-TORY?
"THERE IS ALWAYS ONE TRUTH"...
...LIKE CONAN ALWAYS SAYS.
UNFORTU-NATELY, I'M MORE INTO THE FUTURE BOY THAN THE DETECTIVE.

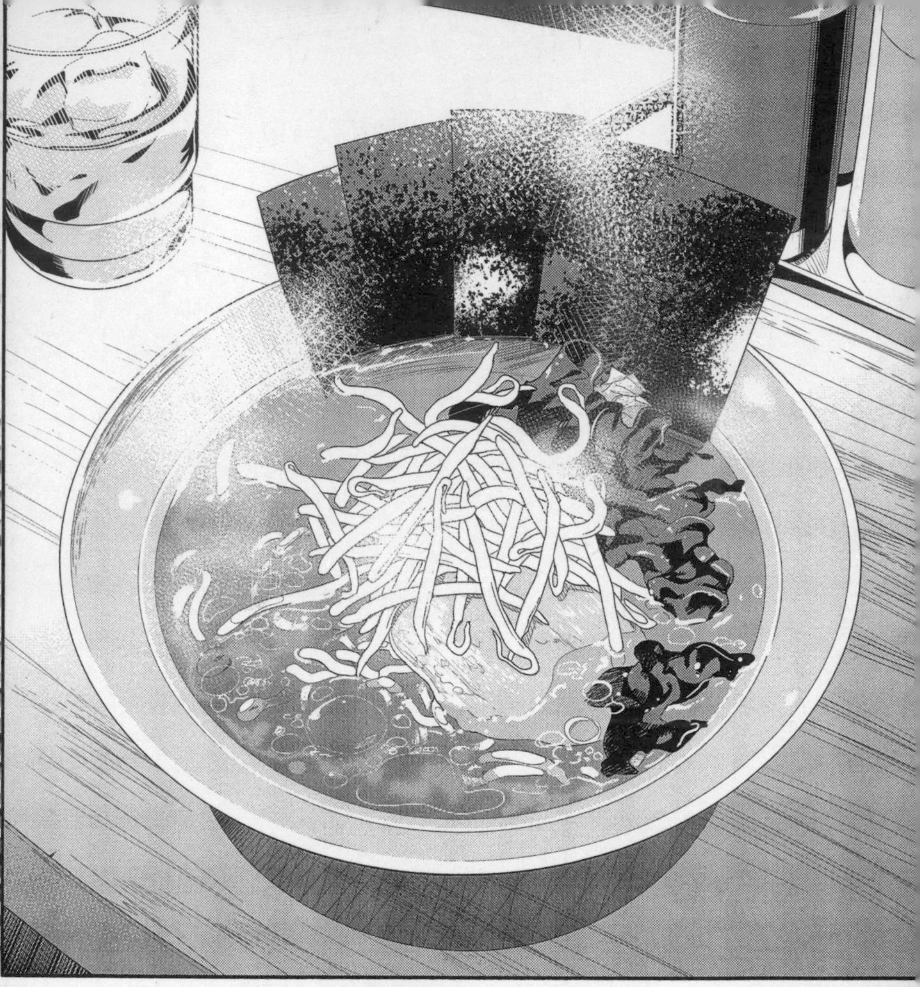
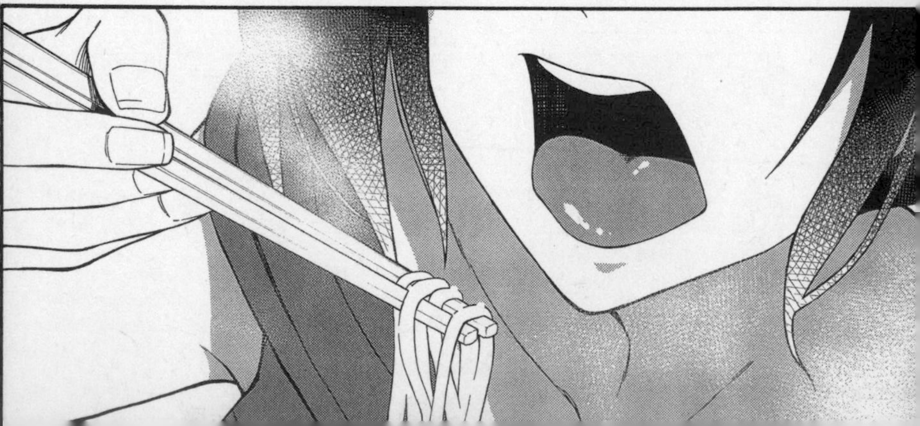

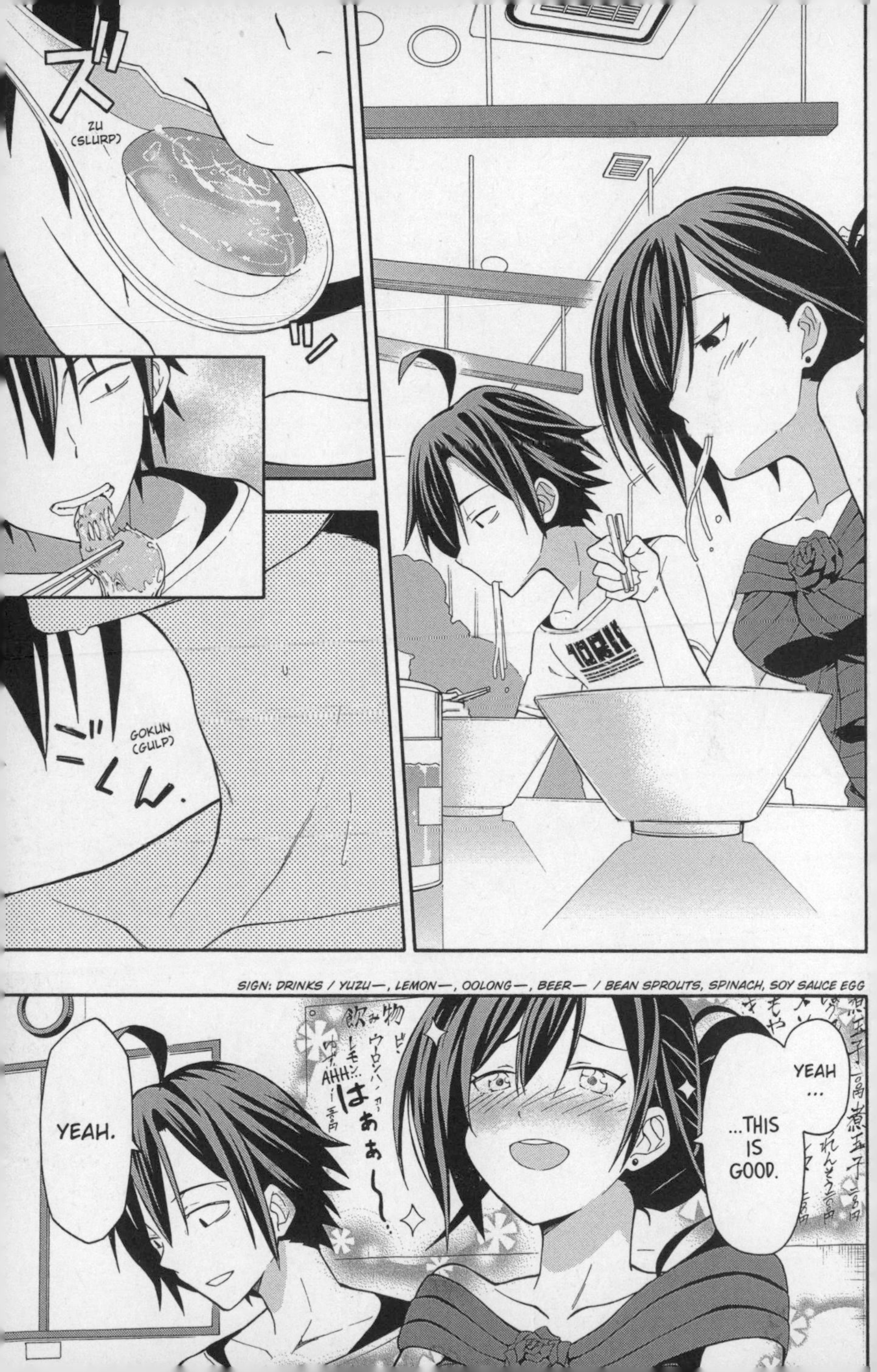
ズ
ZU (SLURP)
ごくん.
GOKUN (GULP)
SIGN: DRINKS / YUZU—, LEMON—, OOLONG—, BEER— / BEAN SPROUTS, SPINACH, SOY SAUCE EGG
YEAH ...
...THIS IS GOOD.
AHHH... はぁぁ~
YEAH.

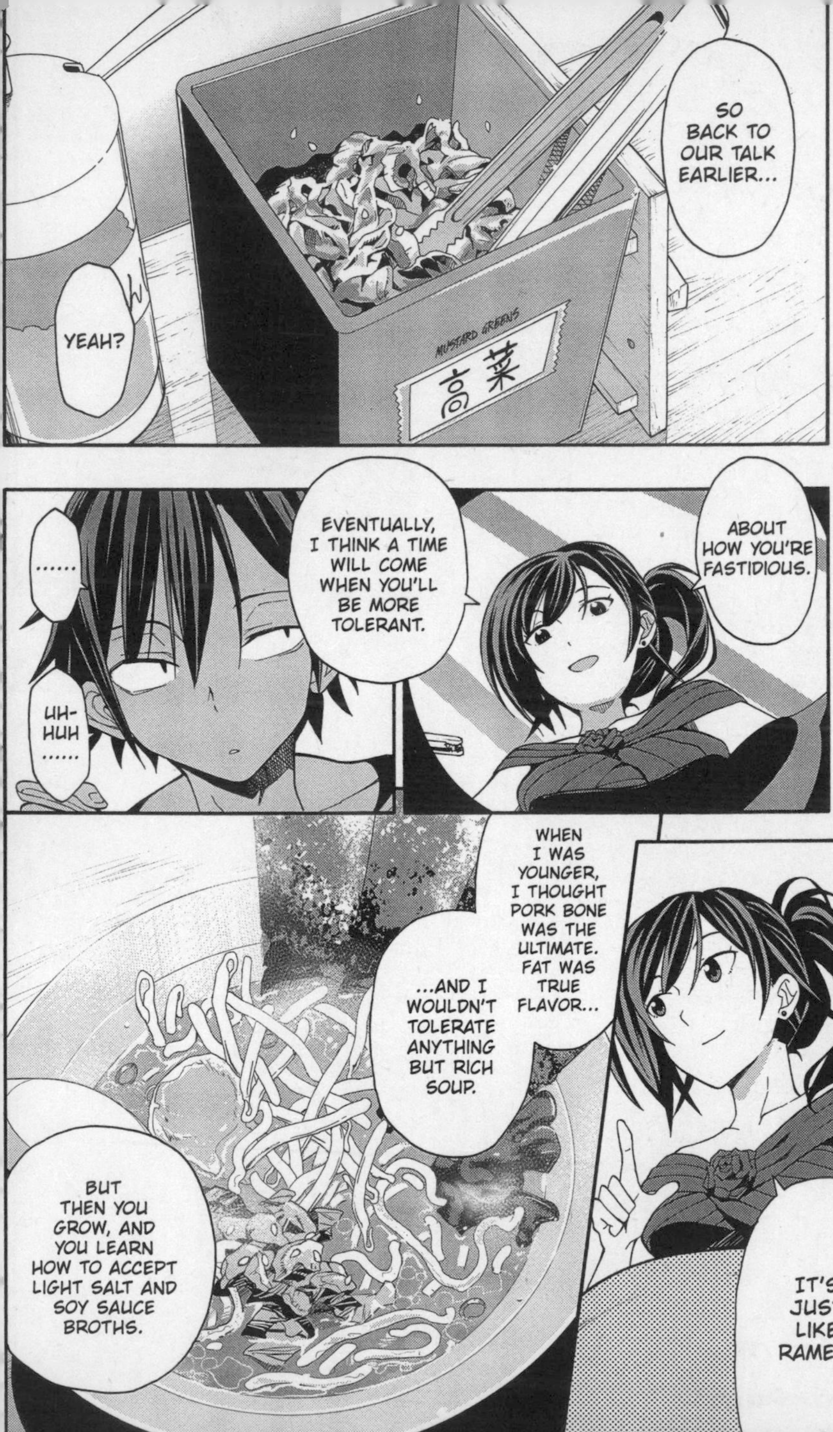
SO BACK TO OUR TALK EARLIER...
YEAH?
MUSTARD GREENS
高菜
ABOUT HOW YOU'RE FASTIDIOUS.
EVENTUALLY, I THINK A TIME WILL COME WHEN YOU'LL BE MORE TOLERANT.
......
UH-HUH ......
IT'S JUST LIKE RAMEN.
WHEN I WAS YOUNGER, I THOUGHT PORK BONE WAS THE ULTIMATE. FAT WAS TRUE FLAVOR...
...AND I WOULDN'T TOLERATE ANYTHING BUT RICH SOUP.
BUT THEN YOU GROW, AND YOU LEARN HOW TO ACCEPT LIGHT SALT AND SOY SAUCE BROTHS.

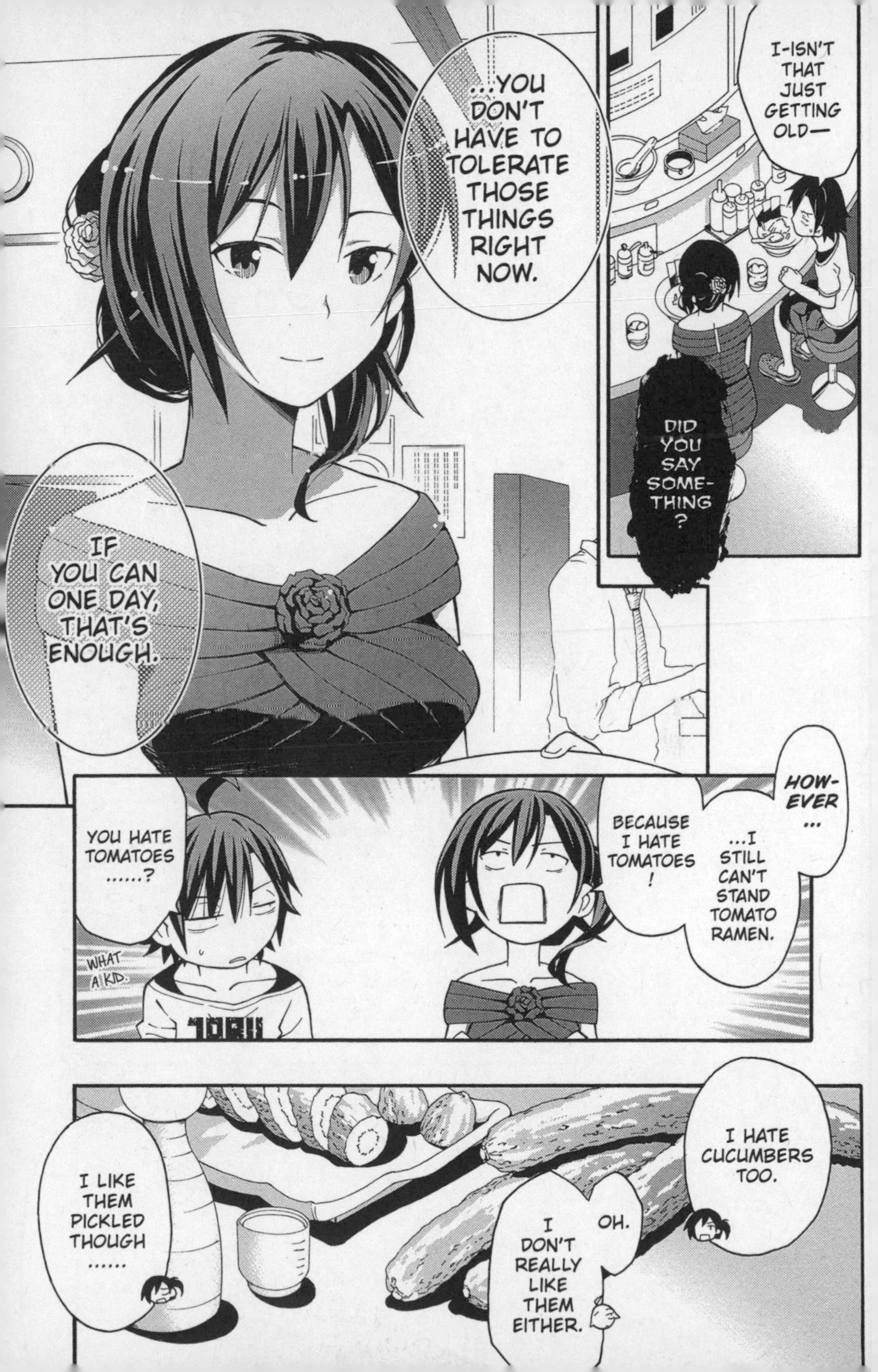
...YOU DON'T HAVE TO TOLERATE THOSE THINGS RIGHT NOW.
IF YOU CAN ONE DAY, THAT'S ENOUGH.
I-ISN'T THAT JUST GETTING OLD—
DID YOU SAY SOMETHING?
HOWEVER...
...I STILL CAN'T STAND TOMATO RAMEN.
BECAUSE I HATE TOMATOES!
YOU HATE TOMATOES......?
WHAT A KID.
I HATE CUCUMBERS TOO.
OH.
I DON'T REALLY LIKE THEM EITHER.
I LIKE THEM PICKLED THOUGH......

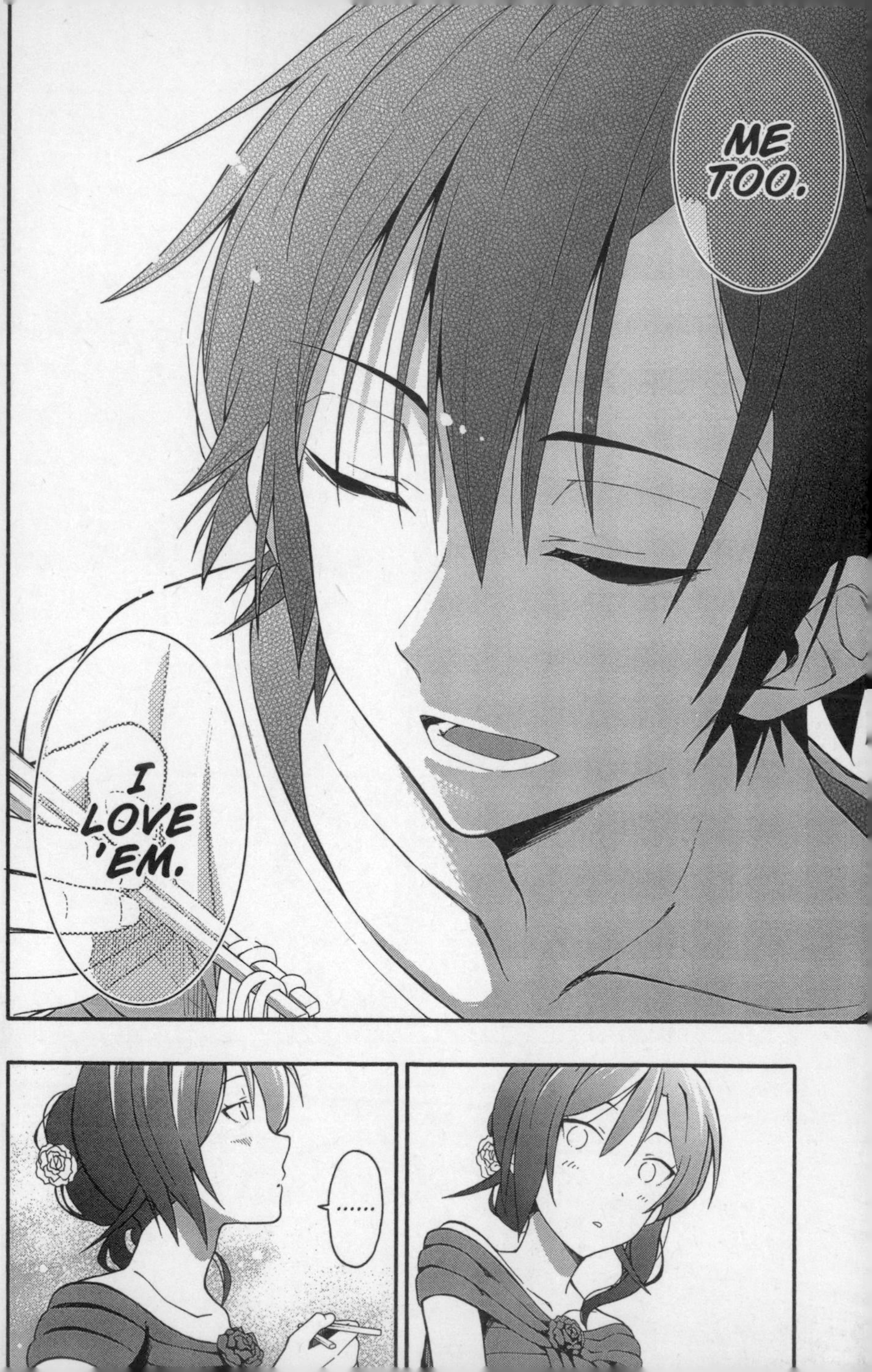
ME TOO.
I LOVE 'EM.
......

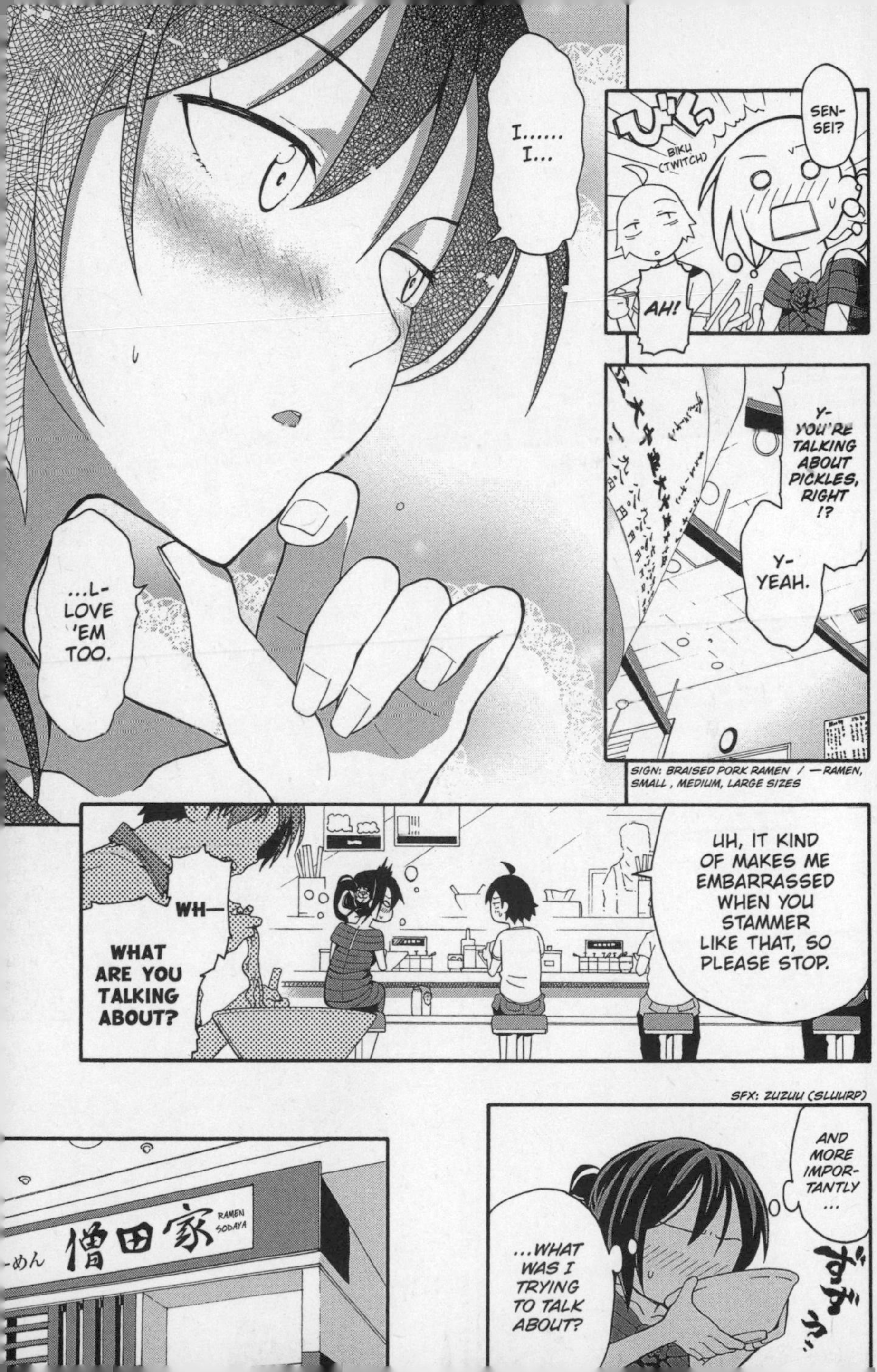
SEN-SEI?
BIKU (TWITCH)
AH!
Y-YOU'RE TALKING ABOUT PICKLES, RIGHT!?
Y-YEAH.
SIGN: BRAISED PORK RAMEN / —RAMEN, SMALL, MEDIUM, LARGE SIZES
I...... I...
...L-LOVE 'EM TOO.
UH, IT KIND OF MAKES ME EMBARRASSED WHEN YOU STAMMER LIKE THAT, SO PLEASE STOP.
WH—
WHAT ARE YOU TALKING ABOUT?
SFX: ZUZUU (SLUURP)
AND MORE IMPOR-TANTLY ...
...WHAT WAS I TRYING TO TALK ABOUT?
僧田家
RAMEN SODAYA
ーめん

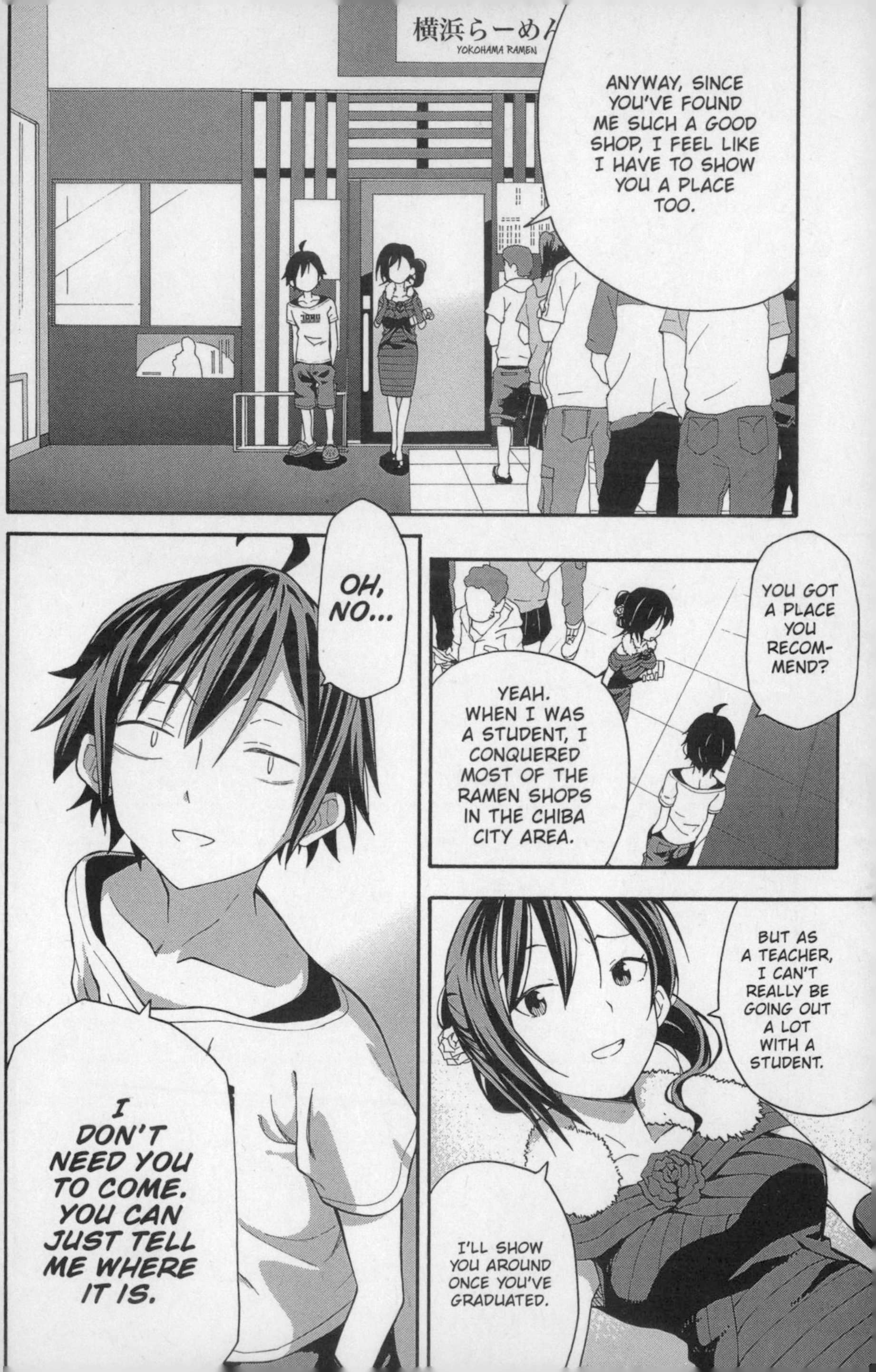

横浜らーめ
YOKOHAMA RAMEN
ANYWAY, SINCE YOU'VE FOUND ME SUCH A GOOD SHOP, I FEEL LIKE I HAVE TO SHOW YOU A PLACE TOO.
YOU GOT A PLACE YOU RECOMMEND?
YEAH. WHEN I WAS A STUDENT, I CONQUERED MOST OF THE RAMEN SHOPS IN THE CHIBA CITY AREA.
BUT AS A TEACHER, I CAN'T REALLY BE GOING OUT A LOT WITH A STUDENT.
I'LL SHOW YOU AROUND ONCE YOU'VE GRADUATED.
OH, NO...
I DON'T NEED YOU TO COME. YOU CAN JUST TELL ME WHERE IT IS.

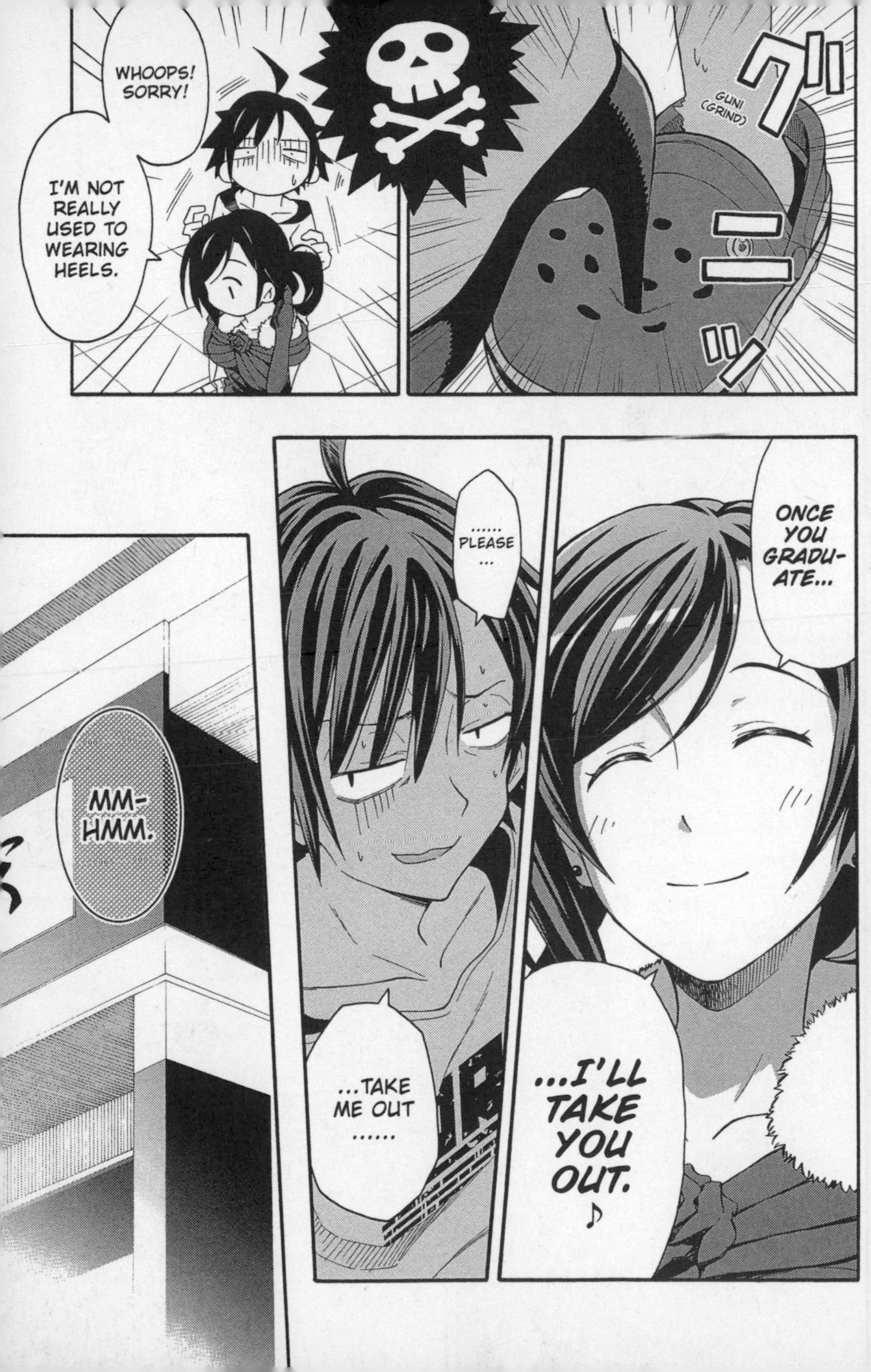
GUNI (GRIND)
WHOOPS! SORRY!
I'M NOT REALLY USED TO WEARING HEELS.
ONCE YOU GRADUATE...
...I'LL TAKE YOU OUT. ♪
......PLEASE...
...TAKE ME OUT......
MM-HMM.

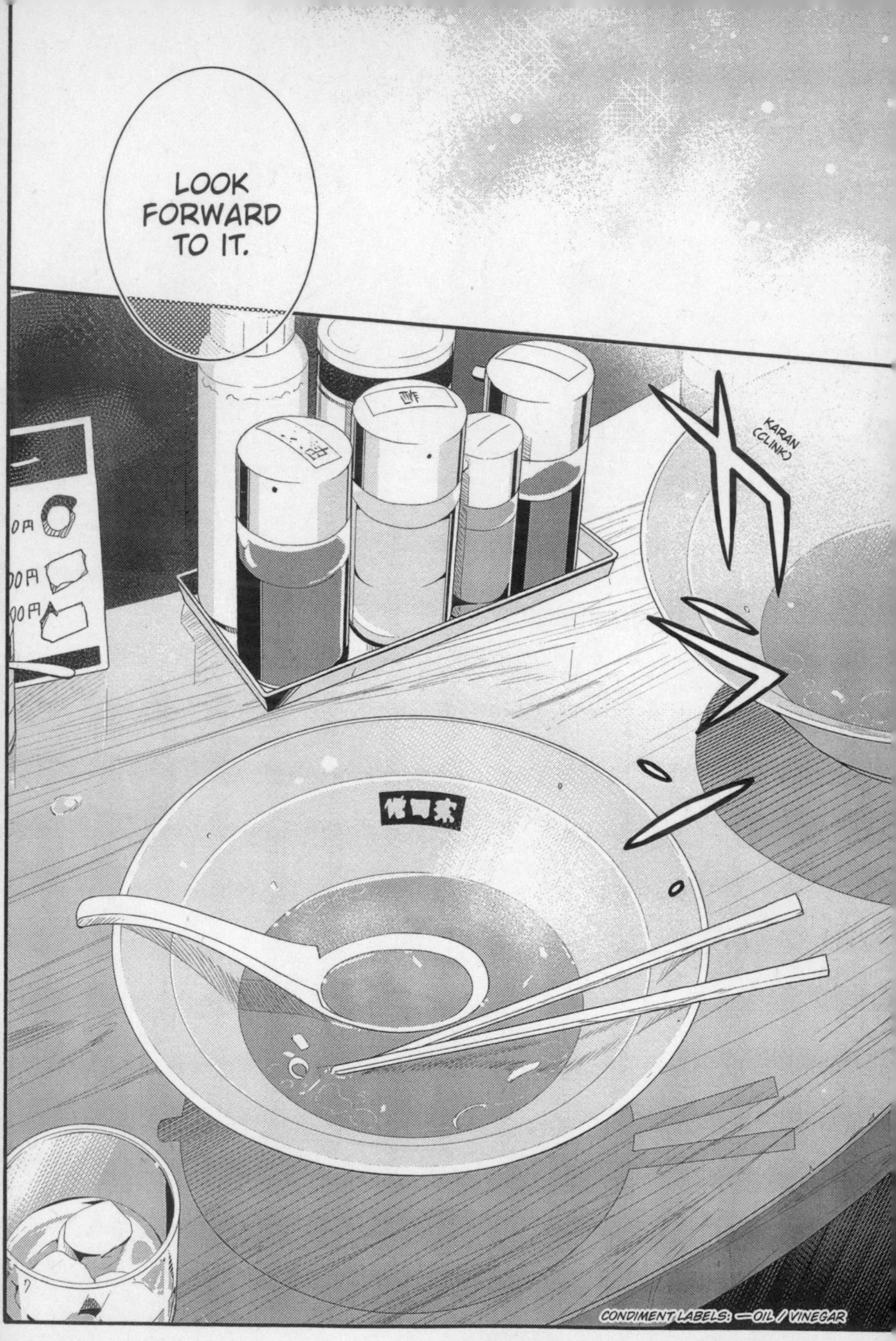
LOOK FORWARD TO IT.
KARAN (CLINK)
CONDIMENT LABELS: —OIL / VINEGAR

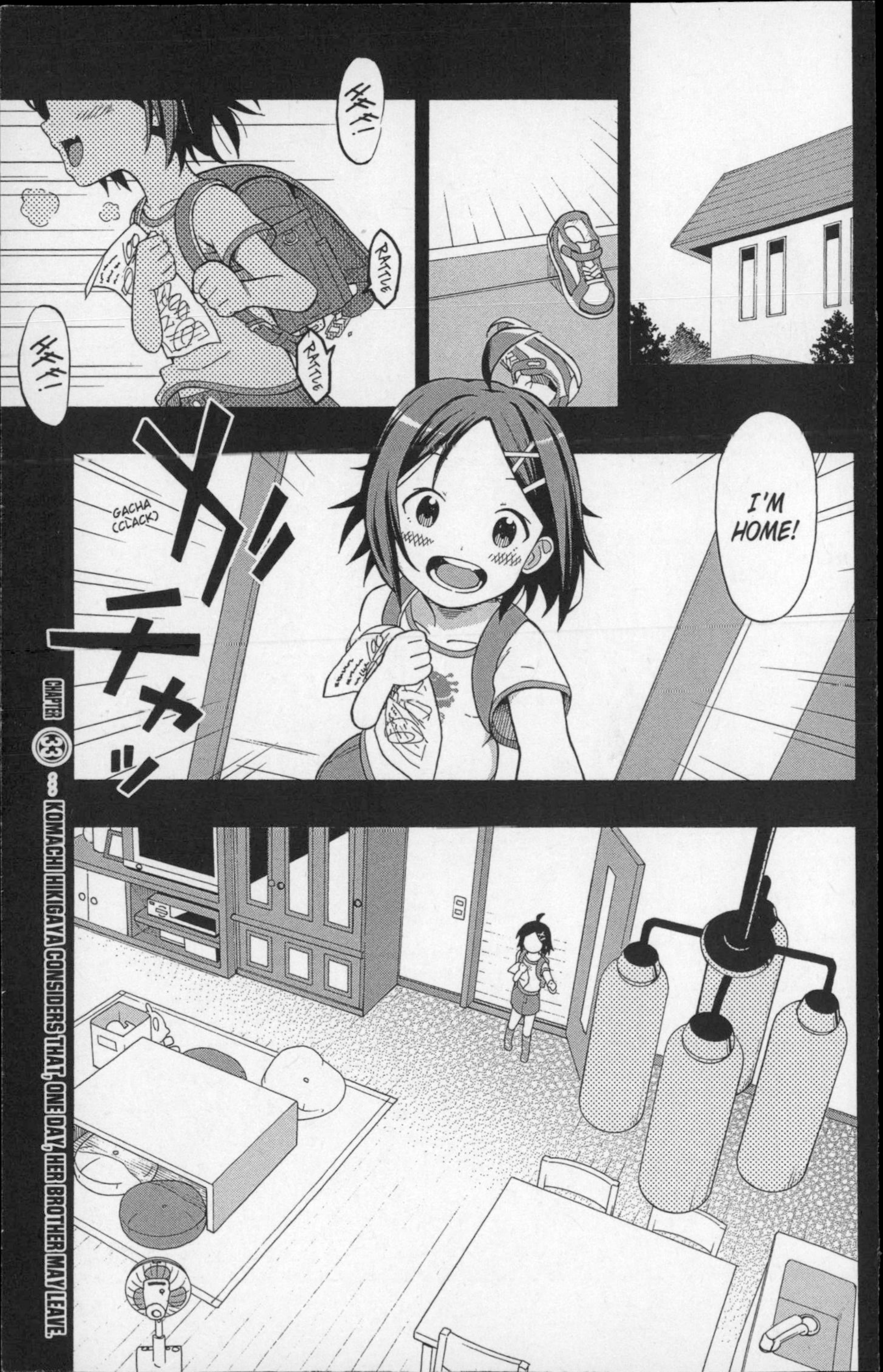
HFFF!
RATTLE
RATTLE
HFFF!
I'M HOME!
GACHA (CLACK)
CHAPTER 33 ... KOMACHI HIKIGAYA CONSIDERS THAT, ONE DAY, HER BROTHER MAY LEAVE.

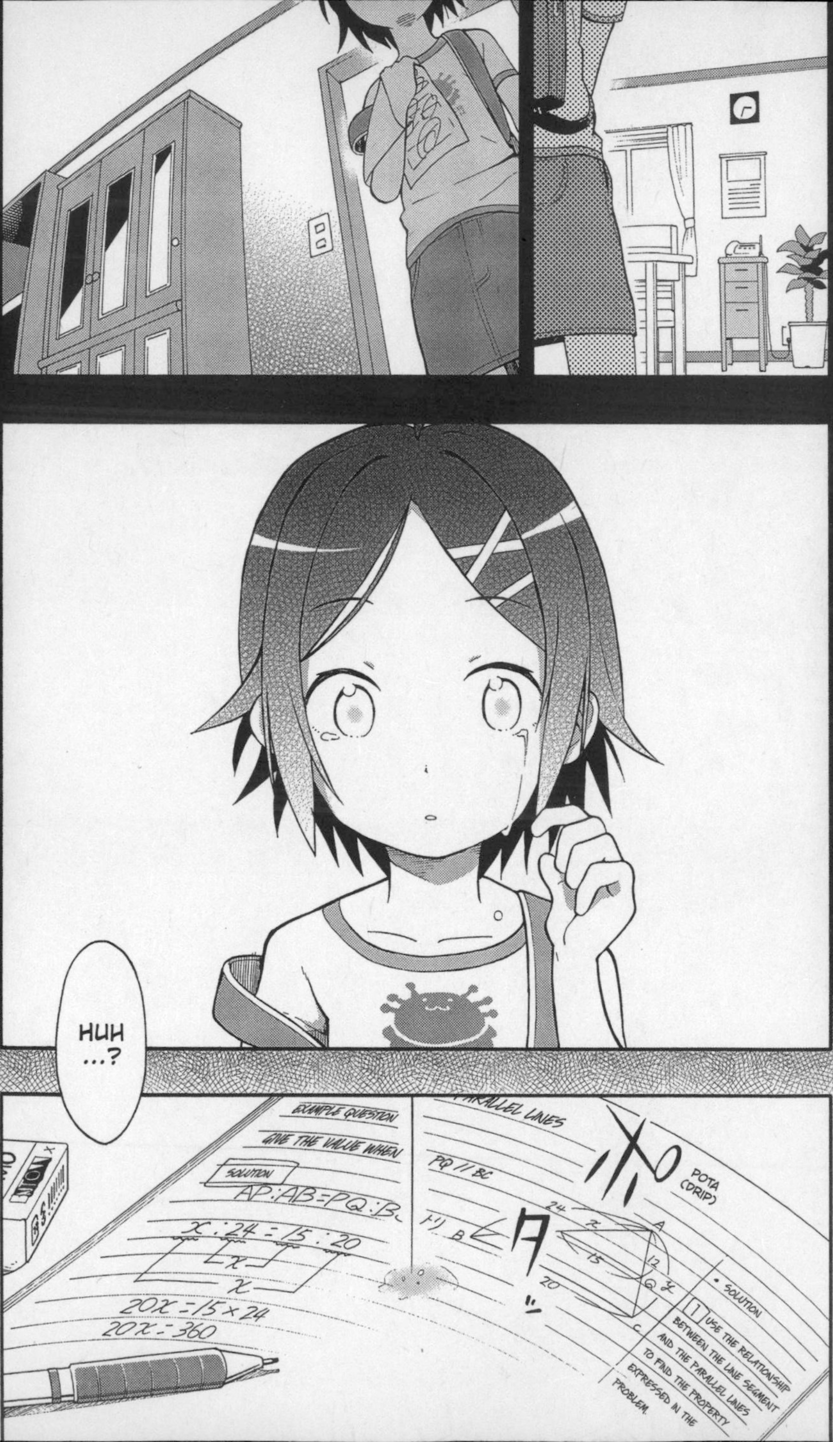
HUH ...?
POTA (DRIP)
PARALLEL LINES
PQ // BC
• SOLUTION
1 USE THE RELATIONSHIP BETWEEN THE LINE SEGMENT AND THE PARALLEL LINES TO FIND THE PROPERTY EXPRESSED IN THE PROBLEM.
EXAMPLE QUESTION
GIVE THE VALUE WHEN
SOLUTION
AP:AB=PQ:B
x:24=15:20
20x=15×24
20x=360

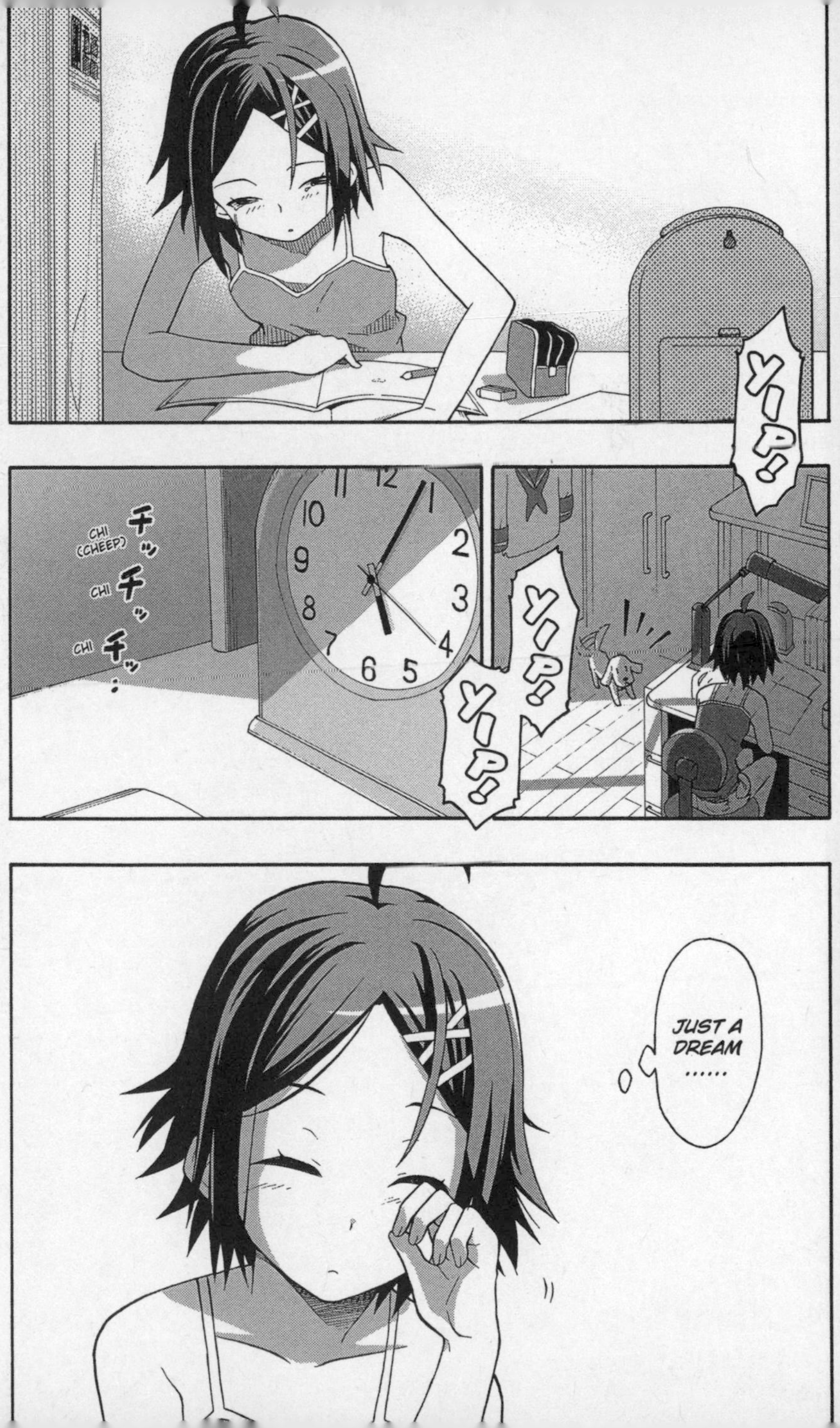
YIP!
YIP!
YIP!
チッ
CHI (CHEEP)
チッ
CHI
チッ…
CHI
JUST A DREAM ......

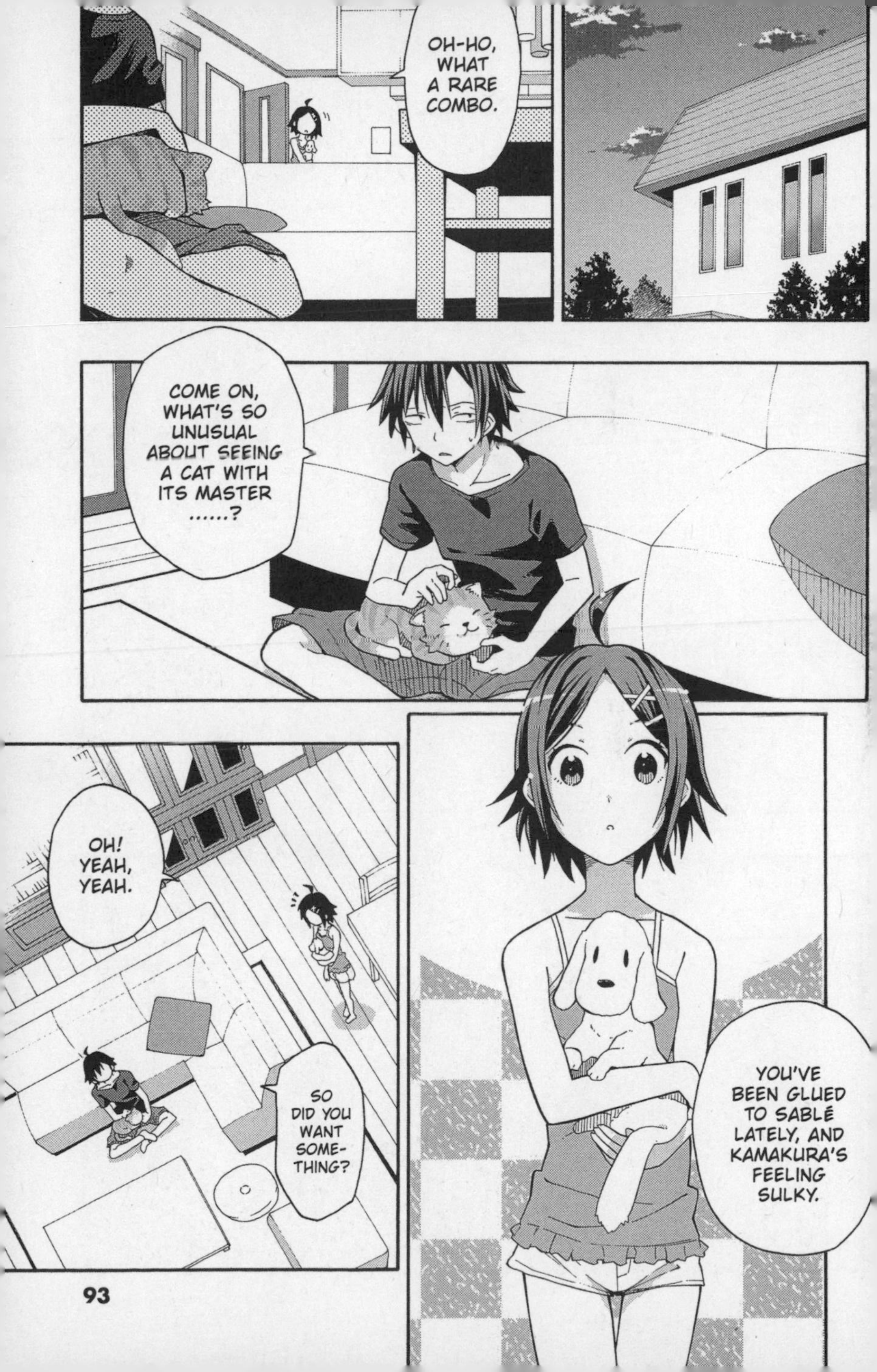
OH-HO, WHAT A RARE COMBO.
COME ON, WHAT'S SO UNUSUAL ABOUT SEEING A CAT WITH ITS MASTER ......?
YOU'VE BEEN GLUED TO SABLÉ LATELY, AND KAMAKURA'S FEELING SULKY.
OH! YEAH, YEAH.
SO DID YOU WANT SOME-THING?

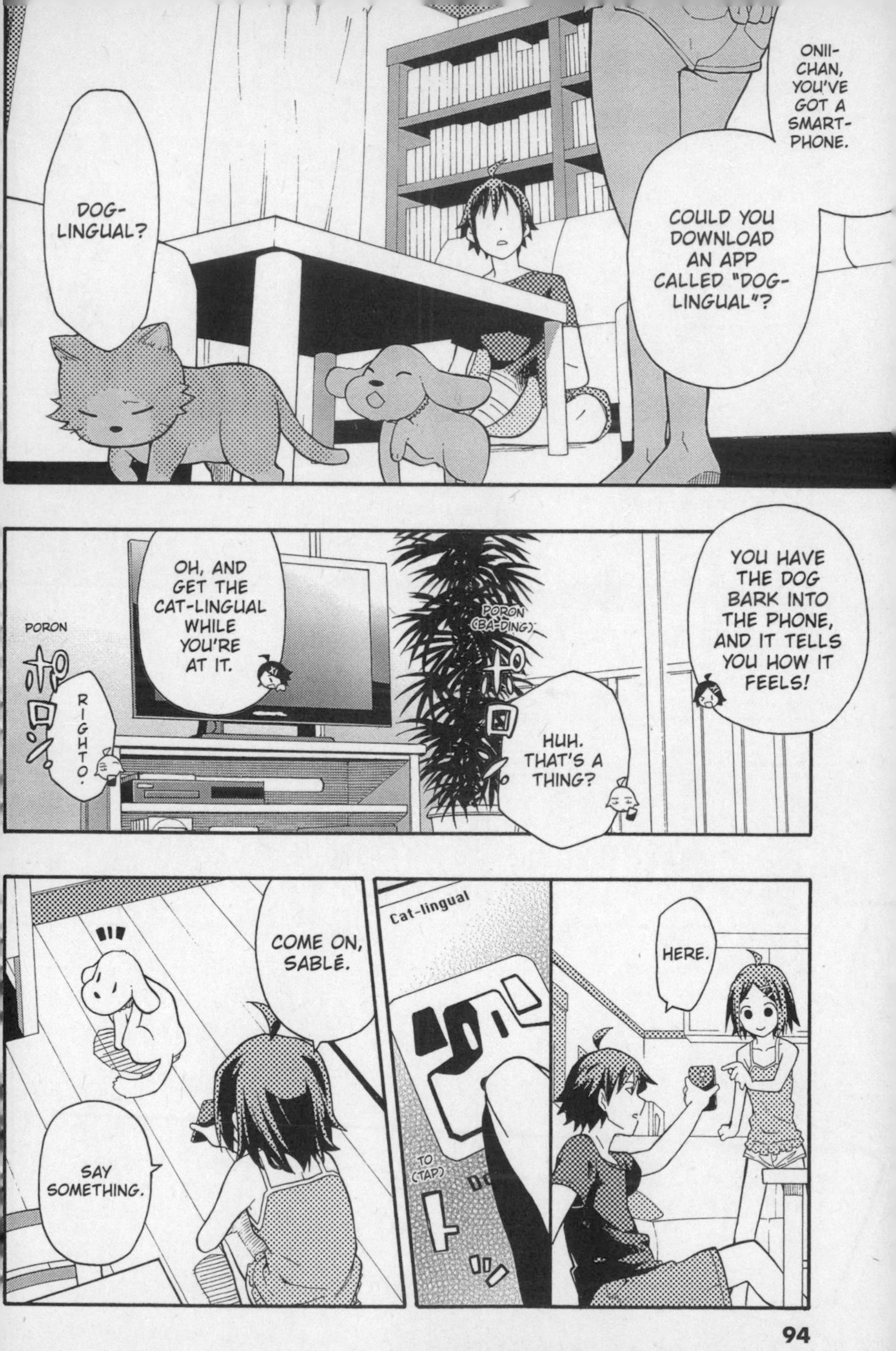
ONII-CHAN, YOU'VE GOT A SMART-PHONE.
COULD YOU DOWNLOAD AN APP CALLED "DOG-LINGUAL"?
DOG-LINGUAL?
YOU HAVE THE DOG BARK INTO THE PHONE, AND IT TELLS YOU HOW IT FEELS!
PORON (BA-DING)
HUH. THAT'S A THING?
OH, AND GET THE CAT-LINGUAL WHILE YOU'RE AT IT.
PORON
RIGHTO.
HERE.
Cat-lingual
TO (TAP)
COME ON, SABLÉ.
SAY SOMETHING.

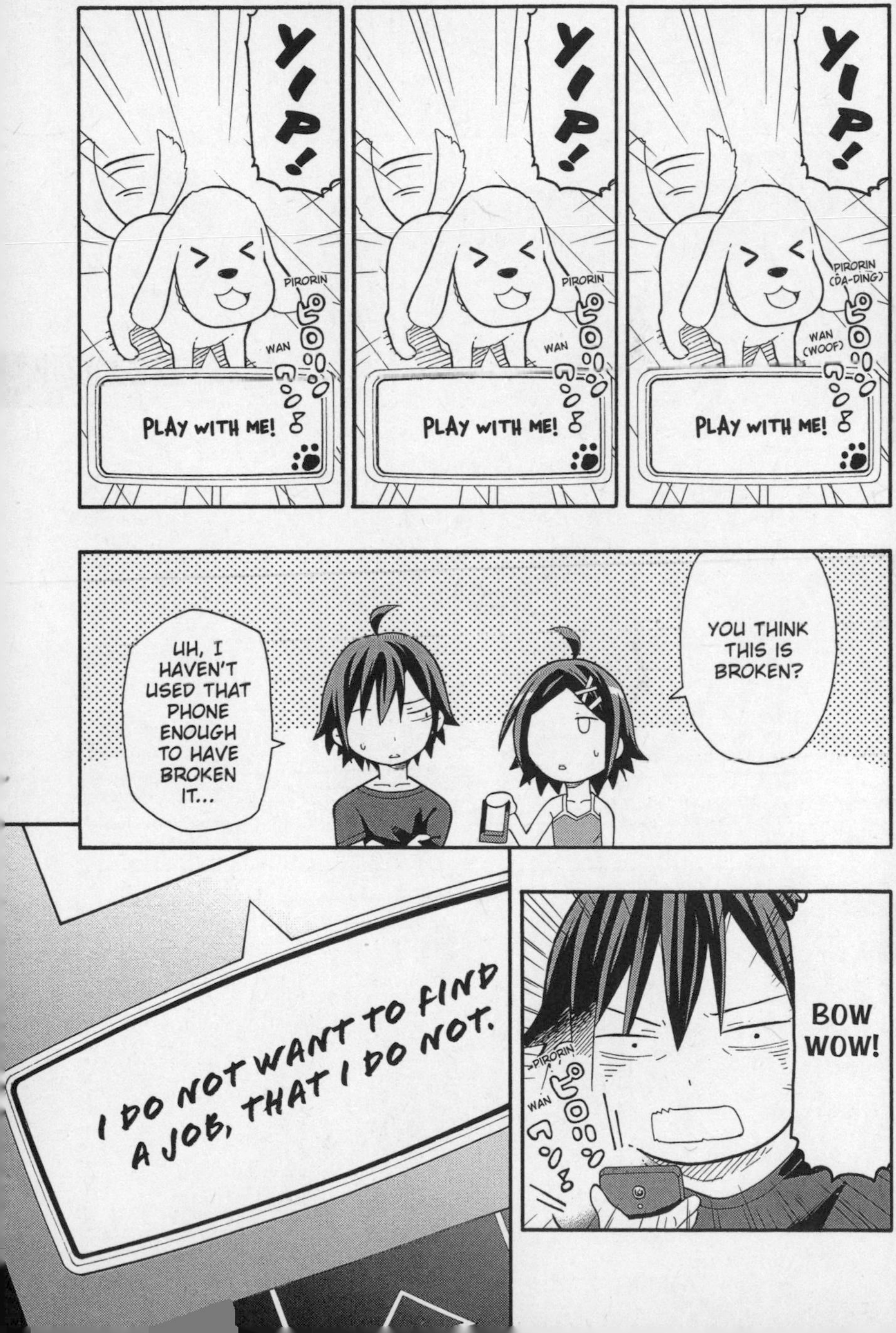
YIP!
PIRORIN (DA-DING)
WAN (WOOF)
PLAY WITH ME!
YIP!
PIRORIN
WAN
PLAY WITH ME!
YIP!
PIRORIN
WAN
PLAY WITH ME!
YOU THINK THIS IS BROKEN?
UH, I HAVEN'T USED THAT PHONE ENOUGH TO HAVE BROKEN IT...
BOW WOW!
PIRORIN
WAN
I DO NOT WANT TO FIND A JOB, THAT I DO NOT.

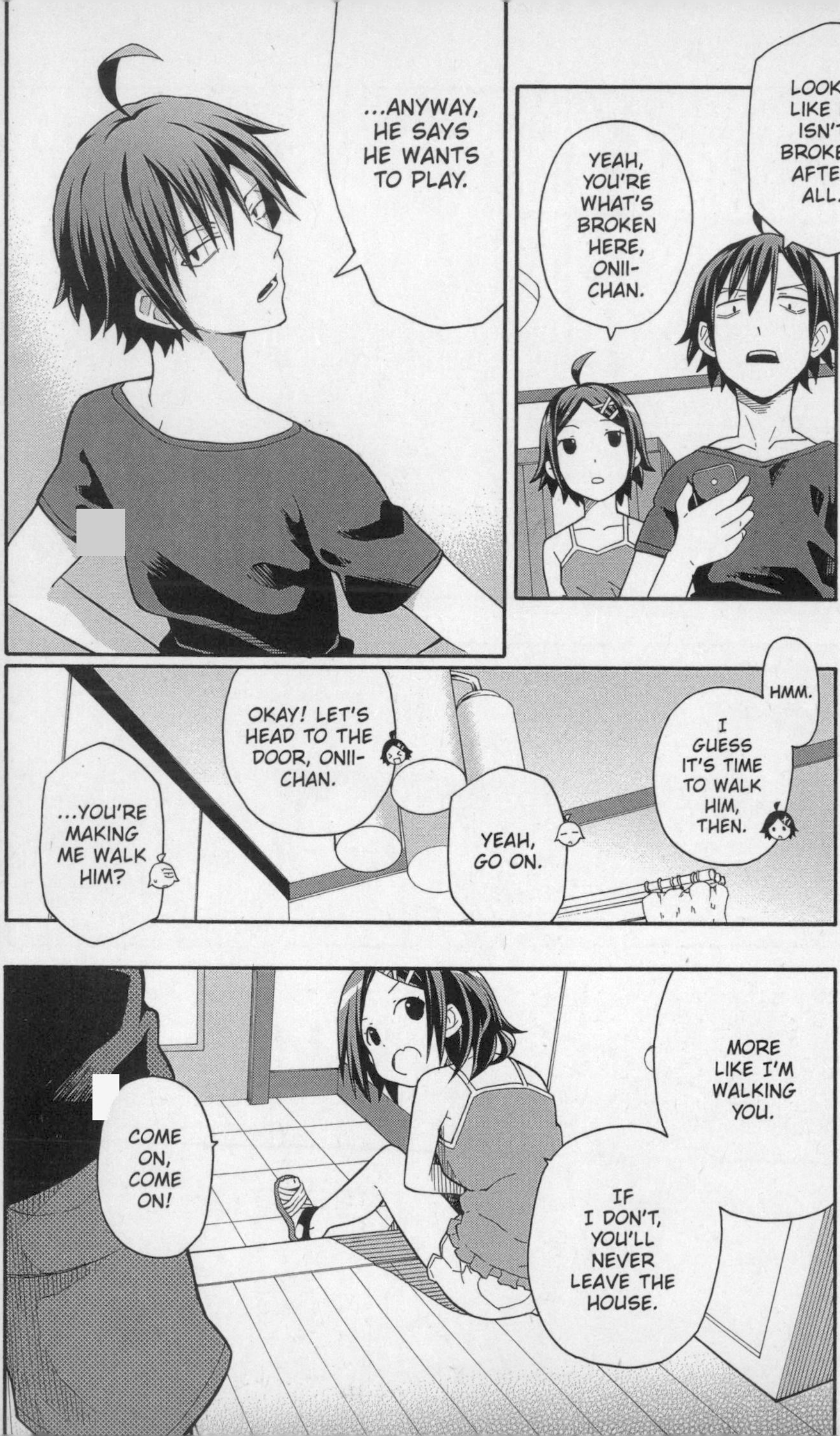
LOOKS LIKE IT ISN'T BROKEN, AFTER ALL.
YEAH, YOU'RE WHAT'S BROKEN HERE, ONII-CHAN.
...ANYWAY, HE SAYS HE WANTS TO PLAY.
HMM.
I GUESS IT'S TIME TO WALK HIM, THEN.
YEAH, GO ON.
OKAY! LET'S HEAD TO THE DOOR, ONII-CHAN.
...YOU'RE MAKING ME WALK HIM?
MORE LIKE I'M WALKING YOU.
IF I DON'T, YOU'LL NEVER LEAVE THE HOUSE.
COME ON, COME ON!

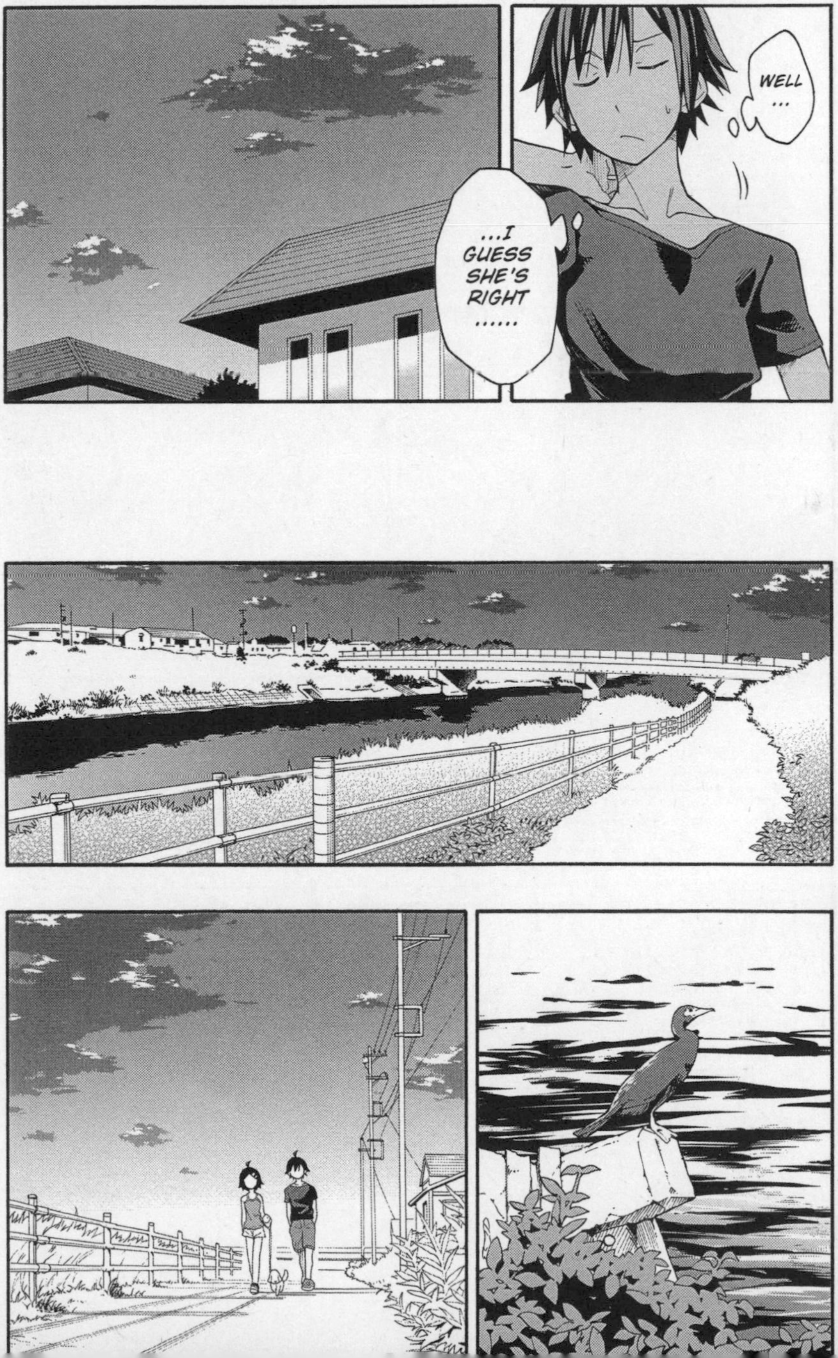
WELL ...
...I GUESS SHE'S RIGHT ......

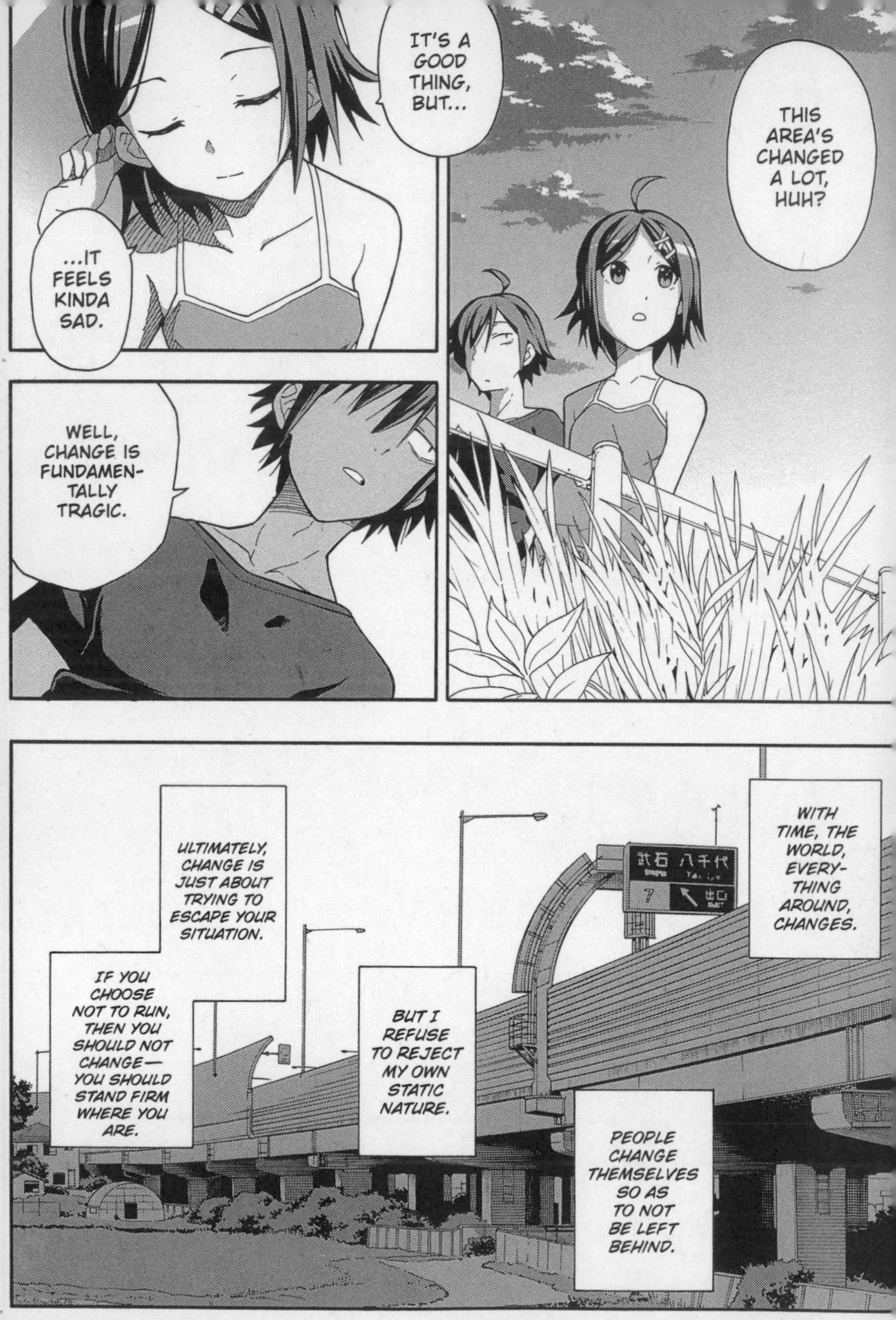
THIS AREA'S CHANGED A LOT, HUH?
IT'S A GOOD THING, BUT...
...IT FEELS KINDA SAD.
WELL, CHANGE IS FUNDAMENTALLY TRAGIC.
WITH TIME, THE WORLD, EVERYTHING AROUND, CHANGES.
PEOPLE CHANGE THEMSELVES SO AS TO NOT BE LEFT BEHIND.
ULTIMATELY, CHANGE IS JUST ABOUT TRYING TO ESCAPE YOUR SITUATION.
IF YOU CHOOSE NOT TO RUN, THEN YOU SHOULD NOT CHANGE—YOU SHOULD STAND FIRM WHERE YOU ARE.
BUT I REFUSE TO REJECT MY OWN STATIC NATURE.

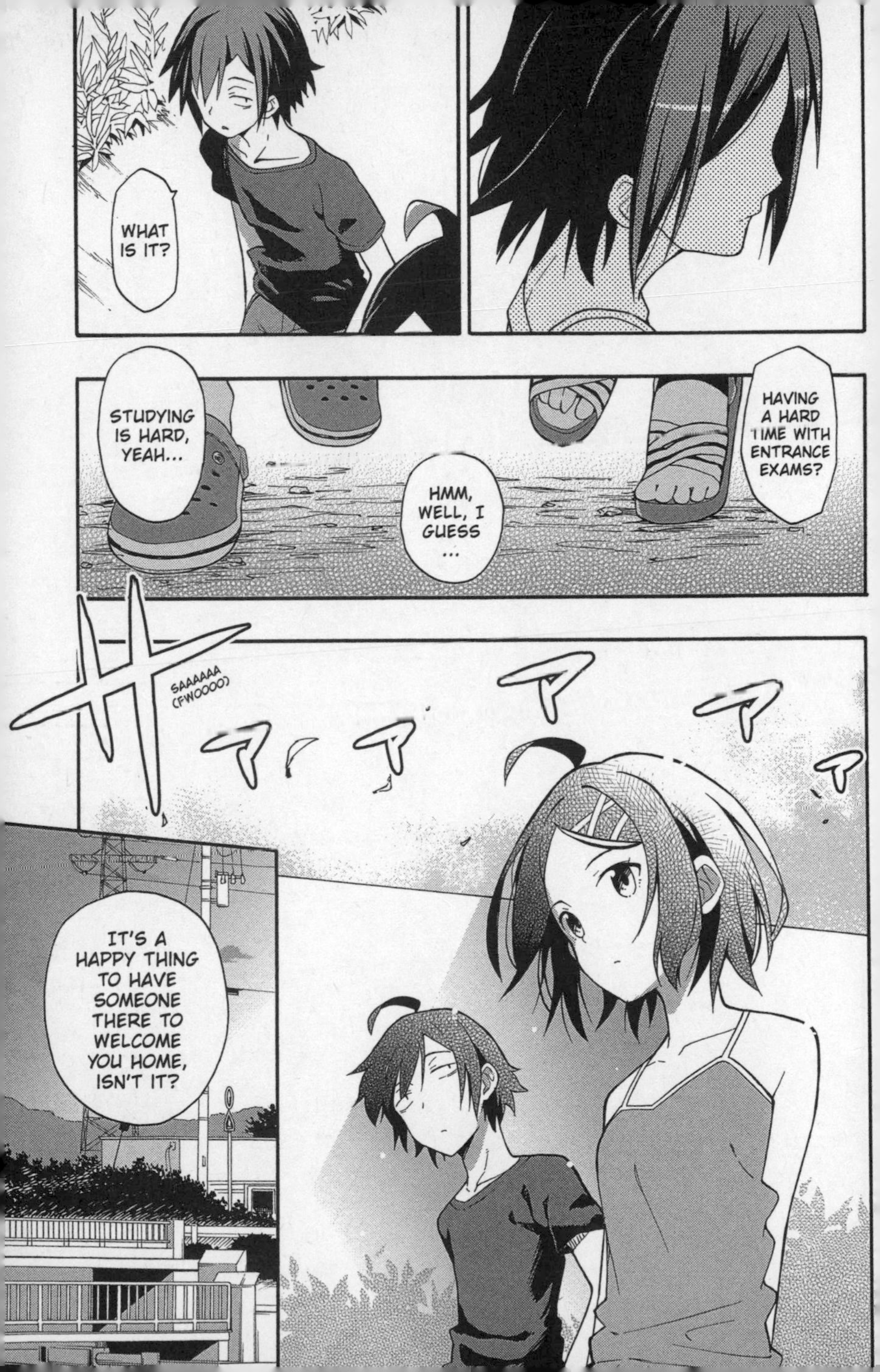
WHAT IS IT?
HAVING A HARD TIME WITH ENTRANCE EXAMS?
HMM, WELL, I GUESS ...
STUDYING IS HARD, YEAH...
SAAAAAA (FWOOOO)
IT'S A HAPPY THING TO HAVE SOMEONE THERE TO WELCOME YOU HOME, ISN'T IT?

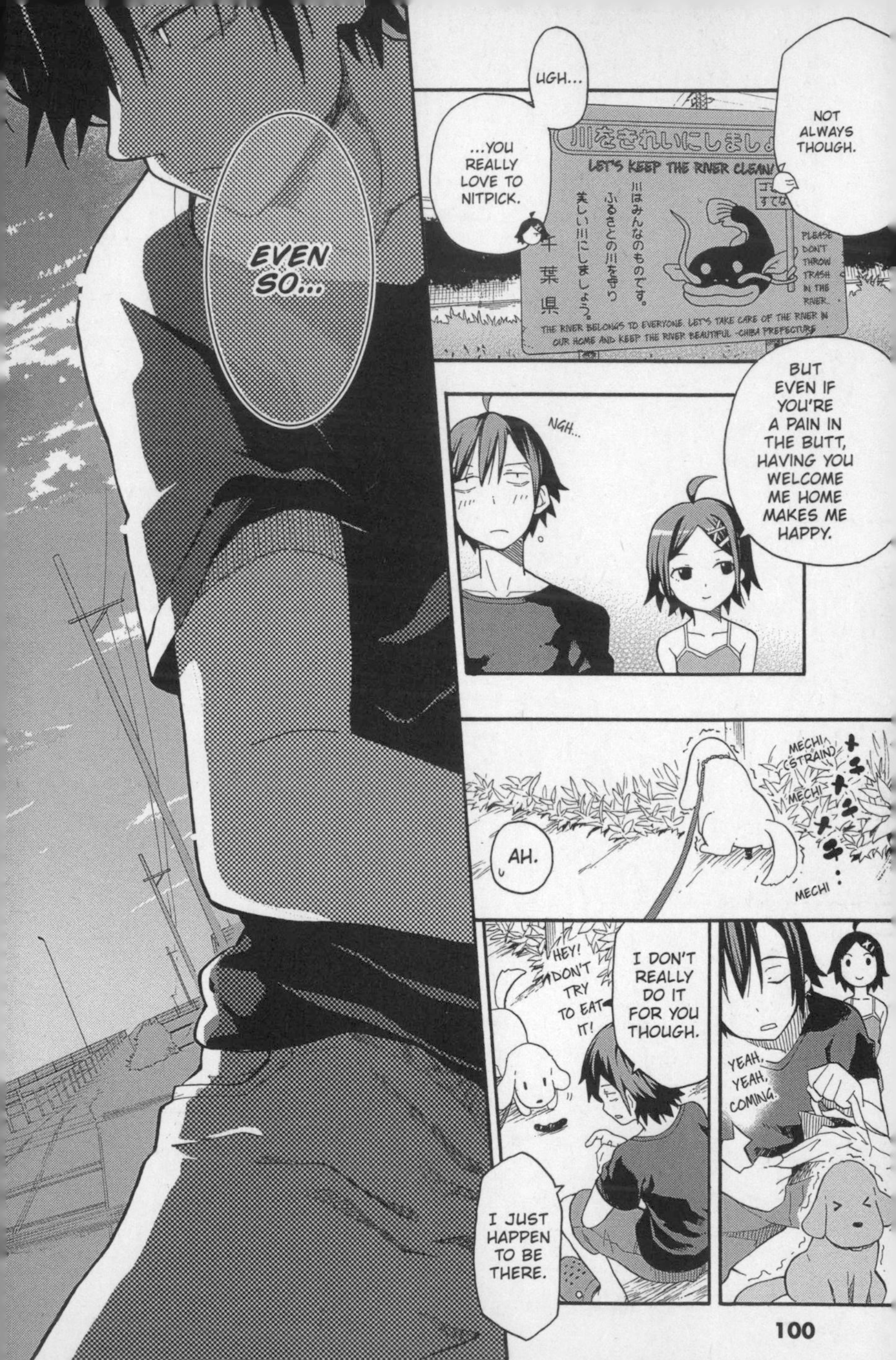
NOT ALWAYS THOUGH.
UGH...
...YOU REALLY LOVE TO NITPICK.
川をきれいにしましょ
LET'S KEEP THE RIVER CLEAN!
川はみんなのものです。
ふるさとの川を守り
美しい川にしましょう。
千葉県
PLEASE DON'T THROW TRASH IN THE RIVER.
THE RIVER BELONGS TO EVERYONE. LET'S TAKE CARE OF THE RIVER IN OUR HOME AND KEEP THE RIVER BEAUTIFUL -CHIBA PREFECTURE
BUT EVEN IF YOU'RE A PAIN IN THE BUTT, HAVING YOU WELCOME ME HOME MAKES ME HAPPY.
NGH...
MECHI (STRAIN)
MECHI
MECHI
AH.
YEAH, YEAH, COMING.
I DON'T REALLY DO IT FOR YOU THOUGH.
HEY! DON'T TRY TO EAT IT!
I JUST HAPPEN TO BE THERE.
EVEN SO...

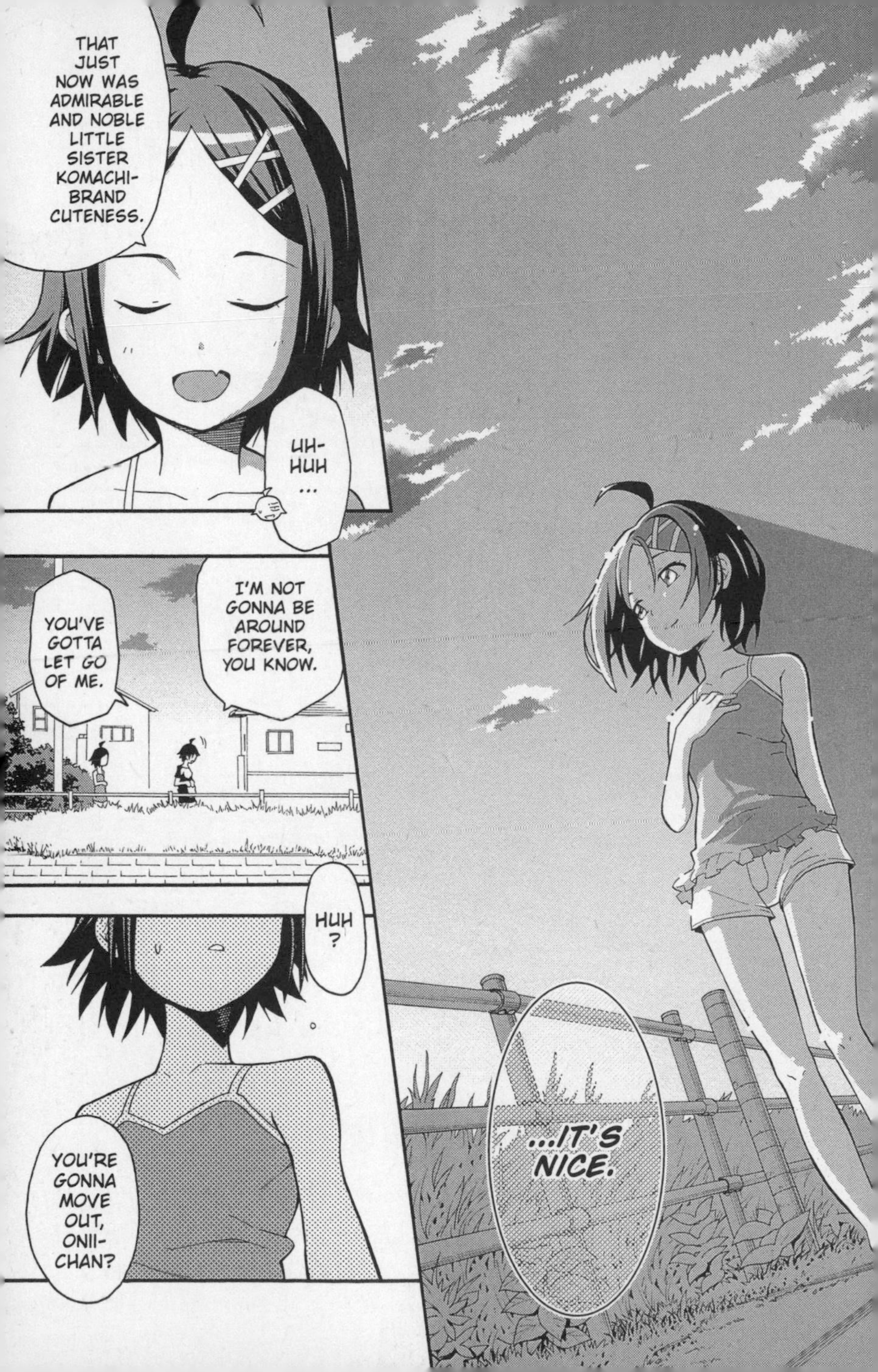
...IT'S NICE.
THAT JUST NOW WAS ADMIRABLE AND NOBLE LITTLE SISTER KOMACHI-BRAND CUTENESS.
UH-HUH ...
I'M NOT GONNA BE AROUND FOREVER, YOU KNOW.
YOU'VE GOTTA LET GO OF ME.
HUH?
YOU'RE GONNA MOVE OUT, ONII-CHAN?

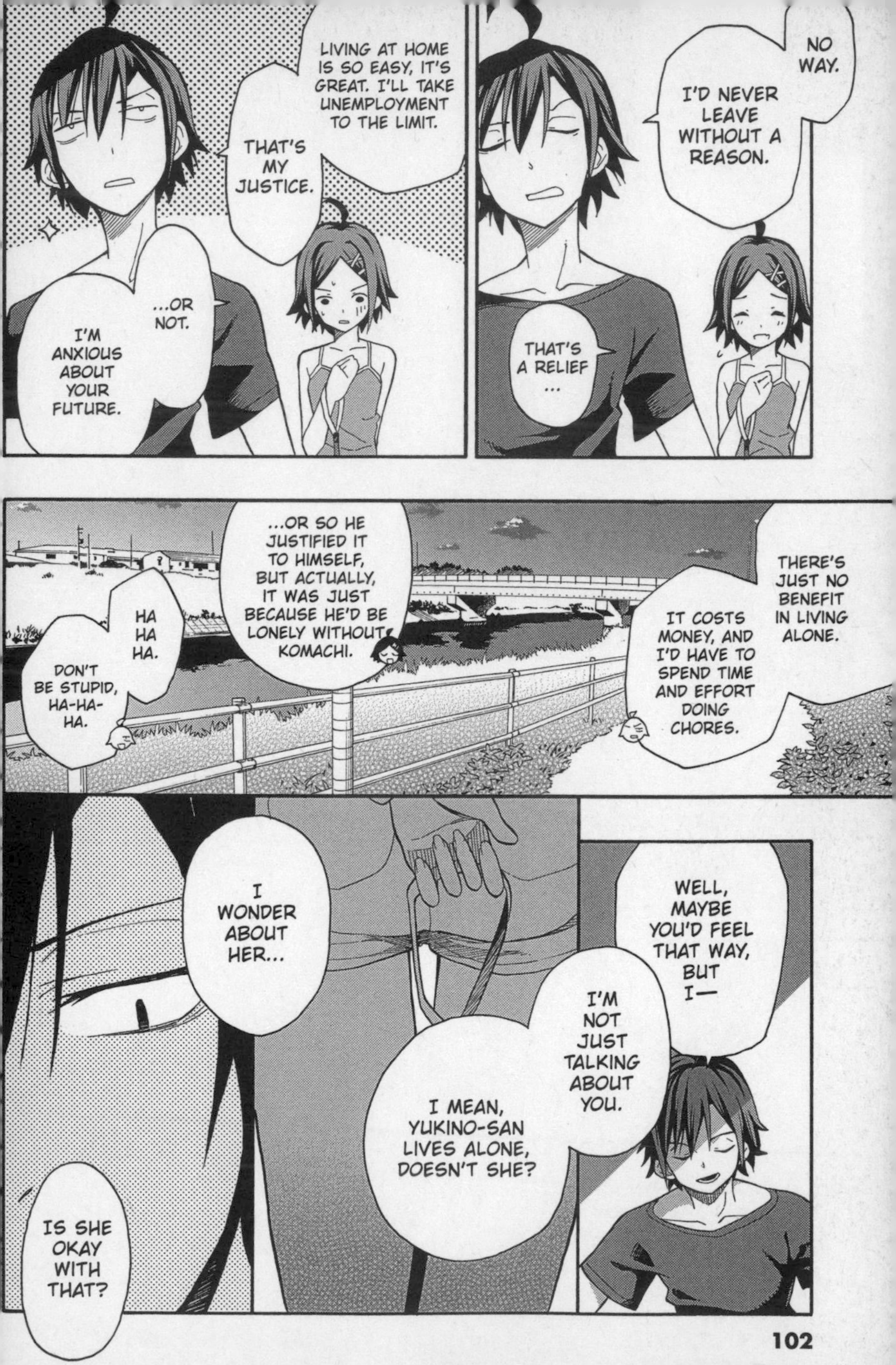
NO WAY.
I'D NEVER LEAVE WITHOUT A REASON.
THAT'S A RELIEF ...
LIVING AT HOME IS SO EASY, IT'S GREAT. I'LL TAKE UNEMPLOYMENT TO THE LIMIT.
THAT'S MY JUSTICE.
...OR NOT.
I'M ANXIOUS ABOUT YOUR FUTURE.
THERE'S JUST NO BENEFIT IN LIVING ALONE.
IT COSTS MONEY, AND I'D HAVE TO SPEND TIME AND EFFORT DOING CHORES.
...OR SO HE JUSTIFIED IT TO HIMSELF, BUT ACTUALLY, IT WAS JUST BECAUSE HE'D BE LONELY WITHOUT KOMACHI.
HA HA HA.
DON'T BE STUPID, HA-HA-HA.
WELL, MAYBE YOU'D FEEL THAT WAY, BUT I—
I'M NOT JUST TALKING ABOUT YOU.
I MEAN, YUKINO-SAN LIVES ALONE, DOESN'T SHE?
I WONDER ABOUT HER...
IS SHE OKAY WITH THAT?

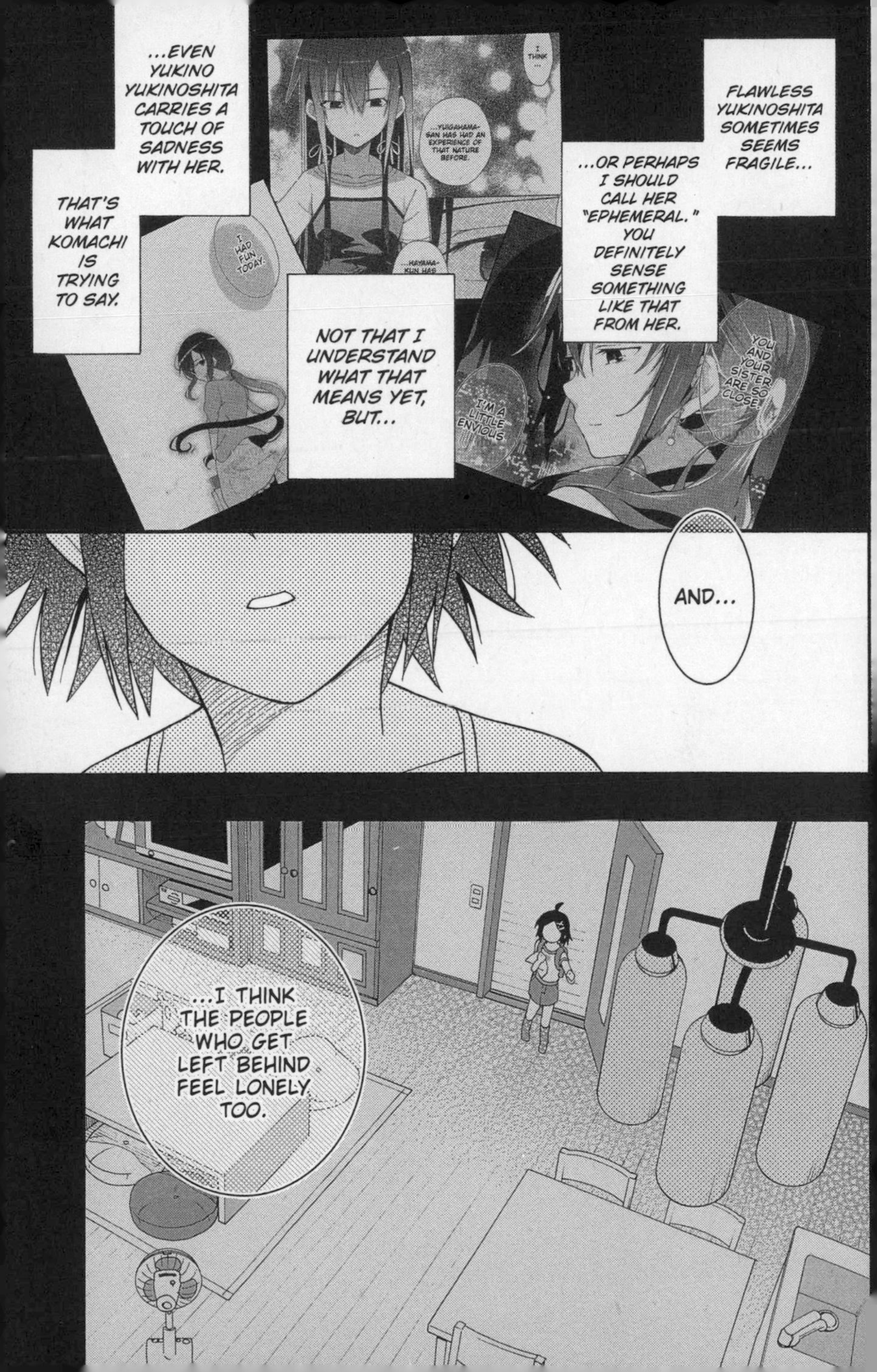
FLAWLESS YUKINOSHITA SOMETIMES SEEMS FRAGILE...
...OR PERHAPS I SHOULD CALL HER "EPHEMERAL." YOU DEFINITELY SENSE SOMETHING LIKE THAT FROM HER.
YOU AND YOUR SISTER ARE SO CLOSE.
I'M A LITTLE ENVIOUS.
I THINK...
...YUIGAHAMA-SAN HAS HAD AN EXPERIENCE OF THAT NATURE BEFORE.
...EVEN YUKINO YUKINOSHITA CARRIES A TOUCH OF SADNESS WITH HER.
THAT'S WHAT KOMACHI IS TRYING TO SAY.
I HAD FUN TODAY.
-HAYAMA-KUN HAS
NOT THAT I UNDERSTAND WHAT THAT MEANS YET, BUT...
AND...
...I THINK THE PEOPLE WHO GET LEFT BEHIND FEEL LONELY TOO.

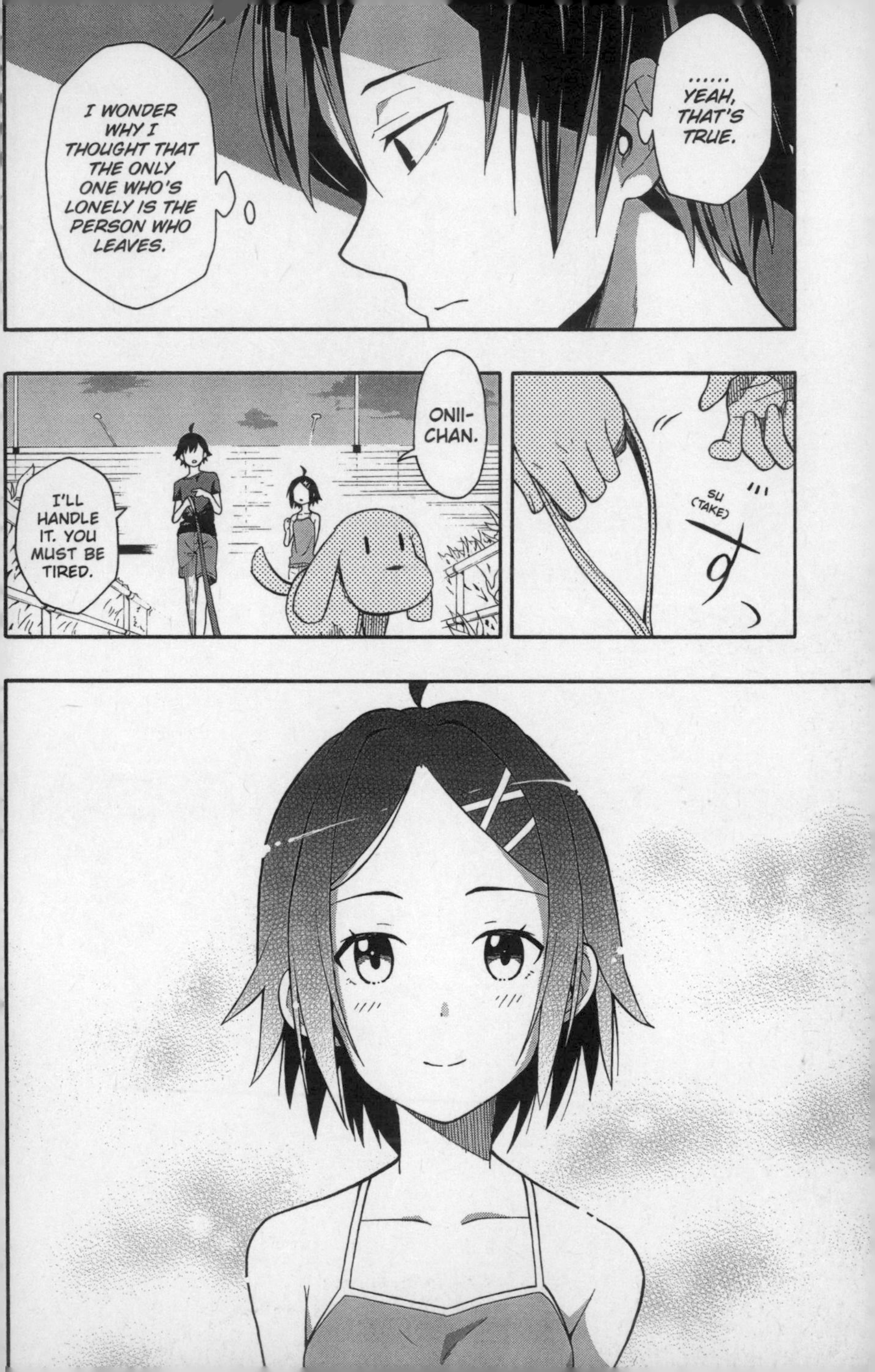
......
YEAH, THAT'S TRUE.
I WONDER WHY I THOUGHT THAT THE ONLY ONE WHO'S LONELY IS THE PERSON WHO LEAVES.
SU (TAKE)
ONII-CHAN.
I'LL HANDLE IT. YOU MUST BE TIRED.

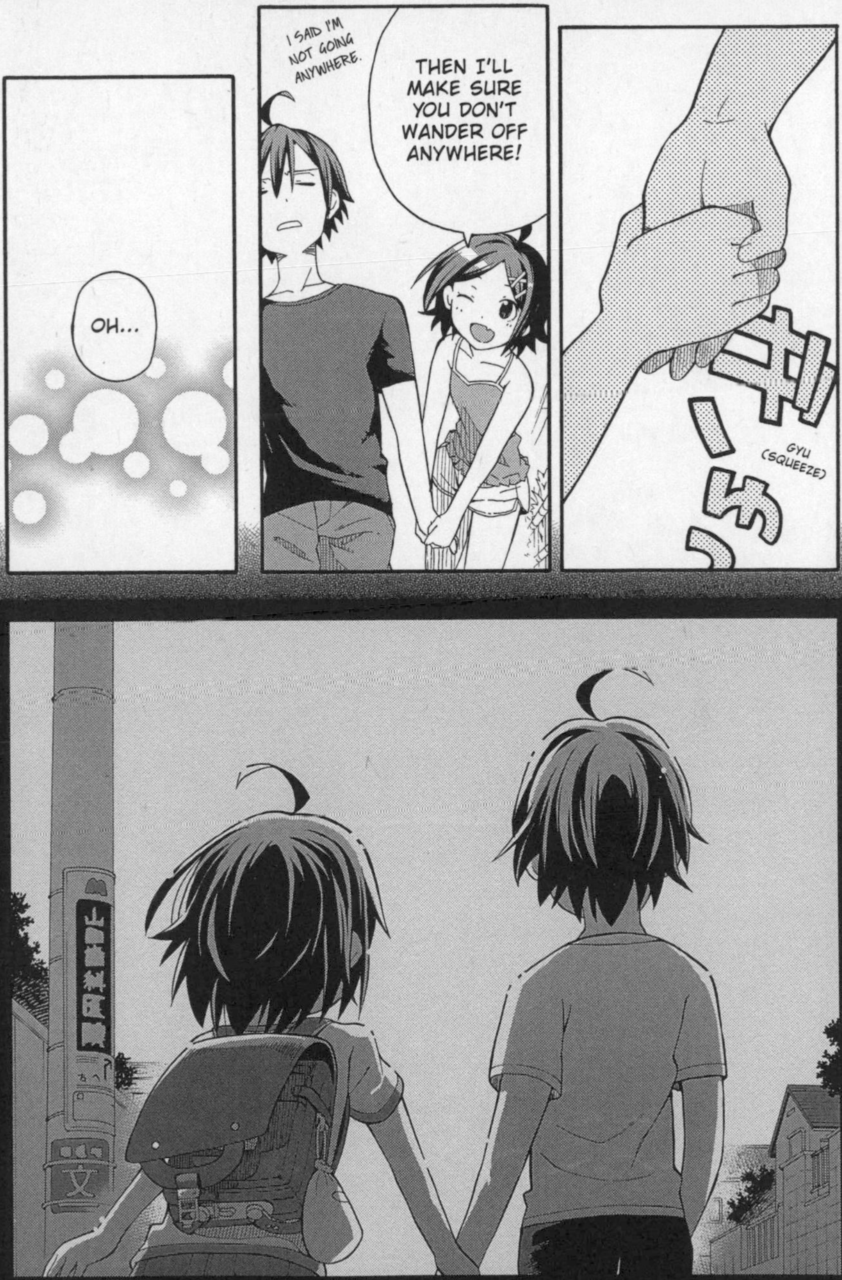
GYU (SQUEEZE)
THEN I'LL MAKE SURE YOU DON'T WANDER OFF ANYWHERE!
I SAID I'M NOT GOING ANYWHERE.
OH...

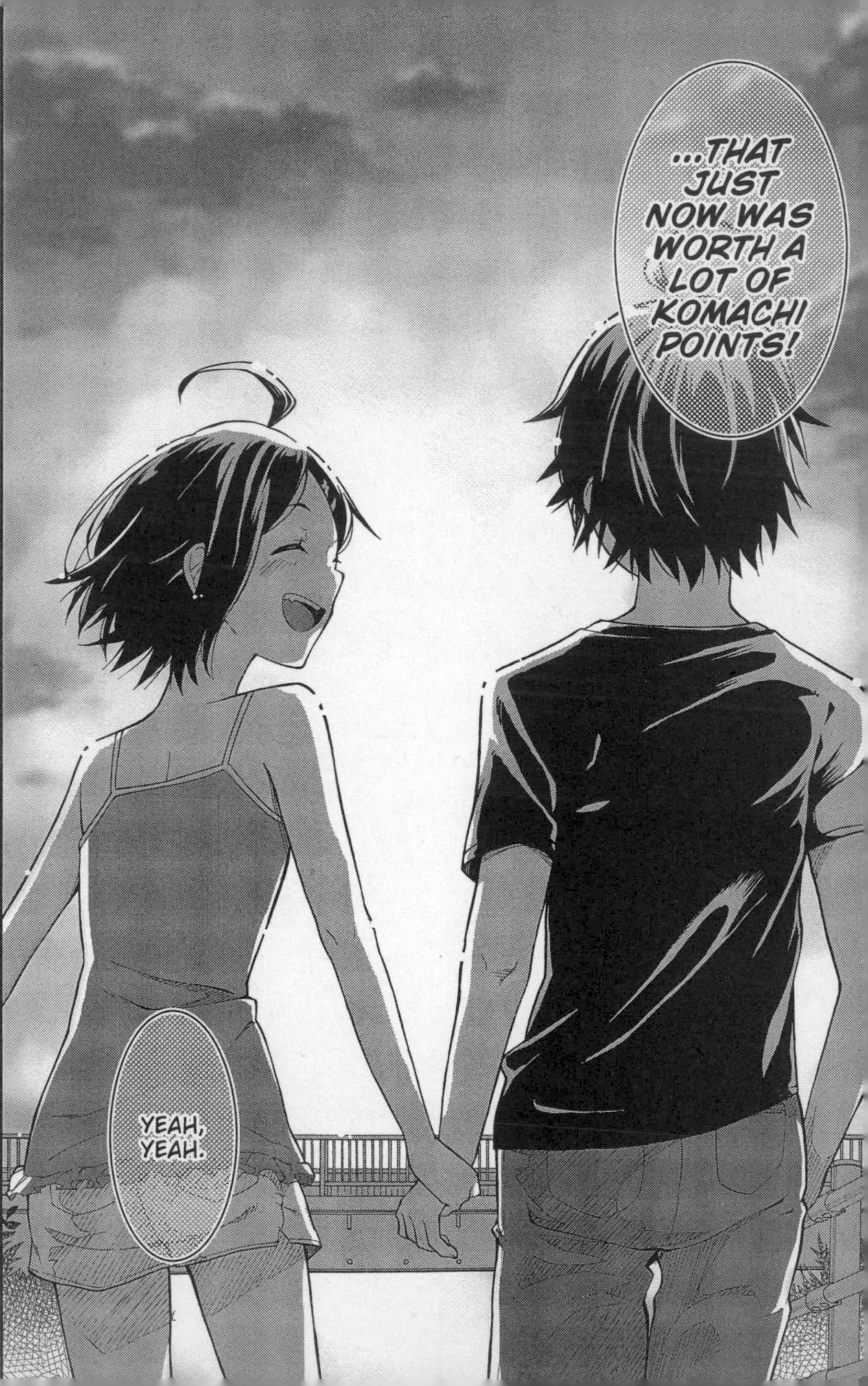
...THAT JUST NOW WAS WORTH A LOT OF KOMACHI POINTS!
YEAH, YEAH.

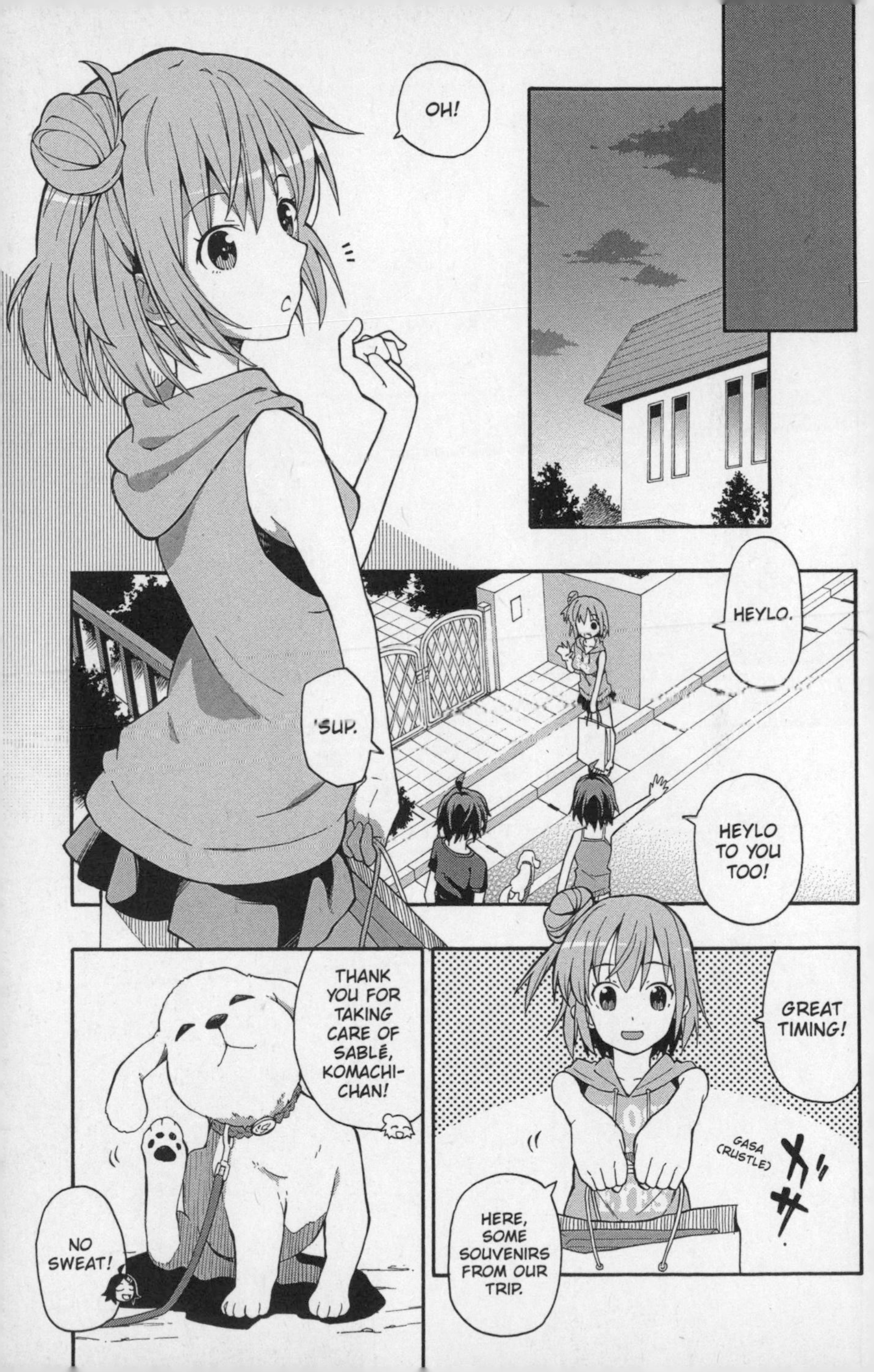
OH!
HEYLO.
HEYLO TO YOU TOO!
'SUP.
GREAT TIMING!
GASA (RUSTLE)
HERE, SOME SOUVENIRS FROM OUR TRIP.
THANK YOU FOR TAKING CARE OF SABLÉ, KOMACHI-CHAN!
NO SWEAT!

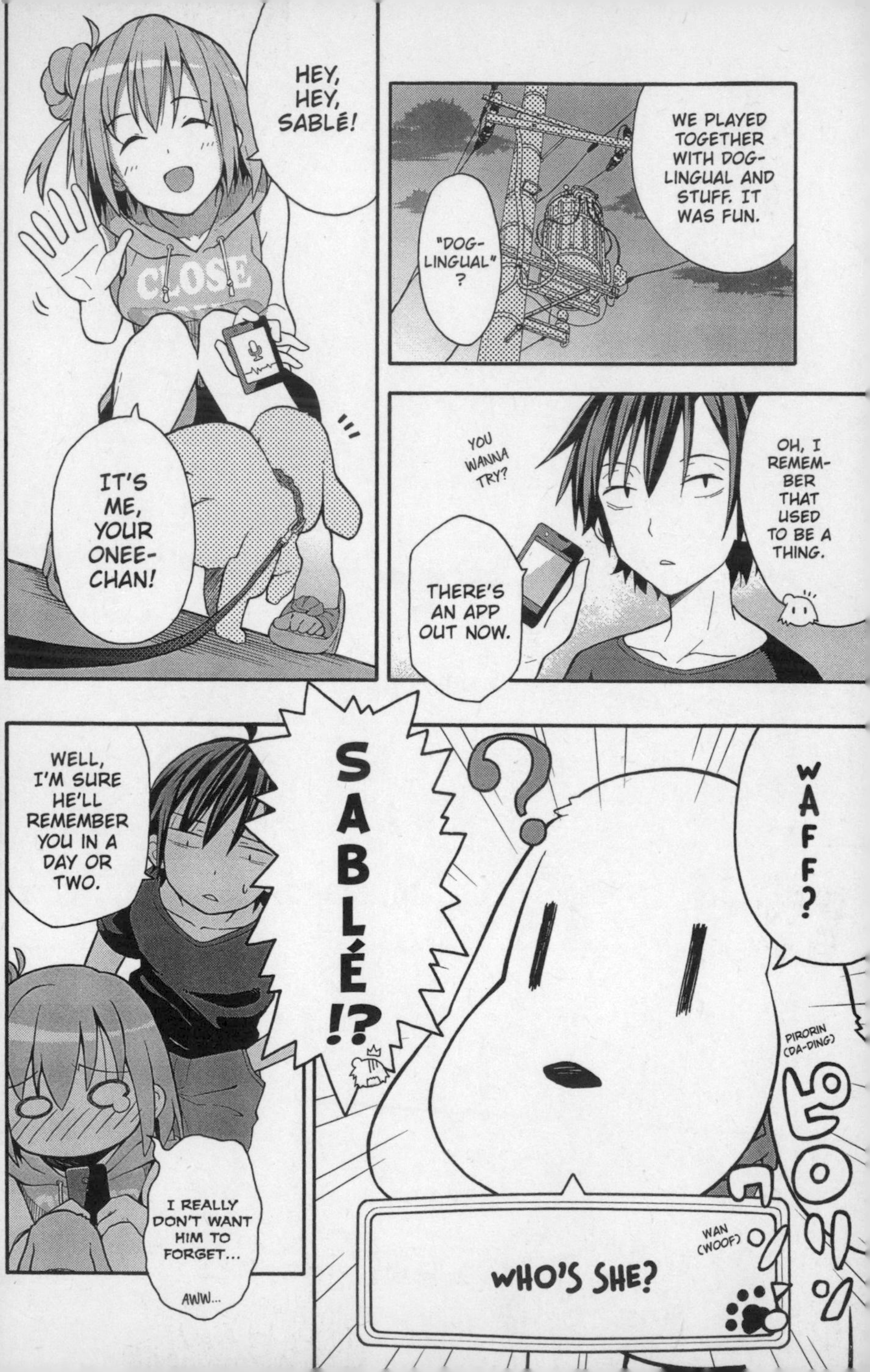
WE PLAYED TOGETHER WITH DOG-LINGUAL AND STUFF. IT WAS FUN.
"DOG-LINGUAL"?
OH, I REMEMBER THAT USED TO BE A THING.
YOU WANNA TRY?
THERE'S AN APP OUT NOW.
HEY, HEY, SABLÉ!
IT'S ME, YOUR ONEE-CHAN!
WAFF?
PIRORIN (DA-DING)
WAN (WOOF)
WHO'S SHE?
SABLÉ!?
WELL, I'M SURE HE'LL REMEMBER YOU IN A DAY OR TWO.
I REALLY DON'T WANT HIM TO FORGET...
AWW...

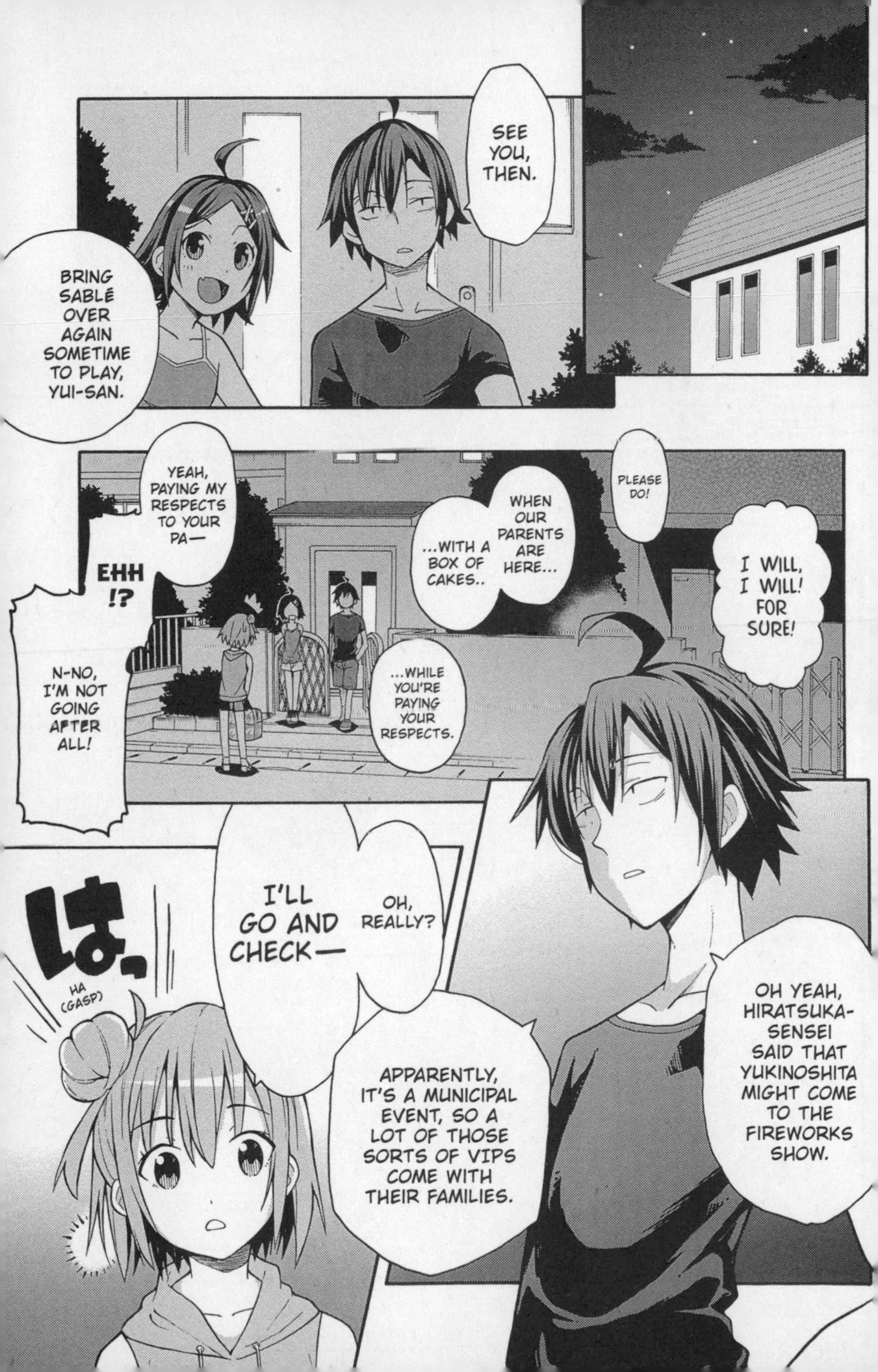
SEE YOU, THEN.
BRING SABLÉ OVER AGAIN SOMETIME TO PLAY, YUI-SAN.
I WILL, I WILL! FOR SURE!
PLEASE DO!
WHEN OUR PARENTS ARE HERE...
...WITH A BOX OF CAKES..
...WHILE YOU'RE PAYING YOUR RESPECTS.
YEAH, PAYING MY RESPECTS TO YOUR PA—
EHH !?
N-NO, I'M NOT GOING AFTER ALL!
OH YEAH, HIRATSUKA-SENSEI SAID THAT YUKINOSHITA MIGHT COME TO THE FIREWORKS SHOW.
APPARENTLY, IT'S A MUNICIPAL EVENT, SO A LOT OF THOSE SORTS OF VIPS COME WITH THEIR FAMILIES.
OH, REALLY?
I'LL GO AND CHECK—
はっ
HA (GASP)

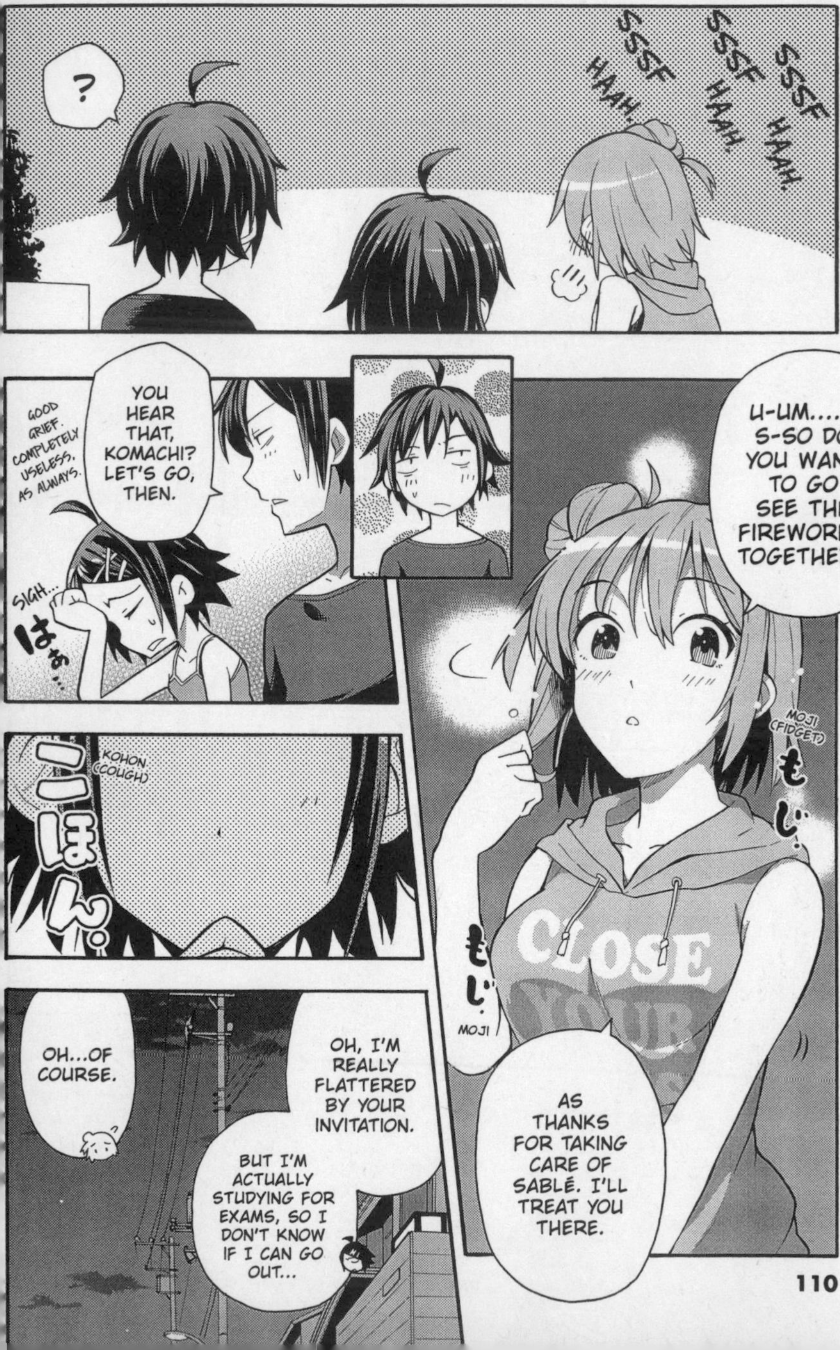
SSSF HAAAH.
SSSF HAAAH.
SSSF HAAAH.
?
U-UM...... S-SO DO YOU WANT TO GO SEE THE FIREWORKS TOGETHER?
MOJI (FIDGET)
もじ。
もじ。
MOJI
AS THANKS FOR TAKING CARE OF SABLÉ. I'LL TREAT YOU THERE.
YOU HEAR THAT, KOMACHI? LET'S GO, THEN.
GOOD GRIEF. COMPLETELY USELESS, AS ALWAYS.
SIGH...
はぁ…
こほん。
KOHON (COUGH)
OH, I'M REALLY FLATTERED BY YOUR INVITATION.
BUT I'M ACTUALLY STUDYING FOR EXAMS, SO I DON'T KNOW IF I CAN GO OUT...
OH...OF COURSE.

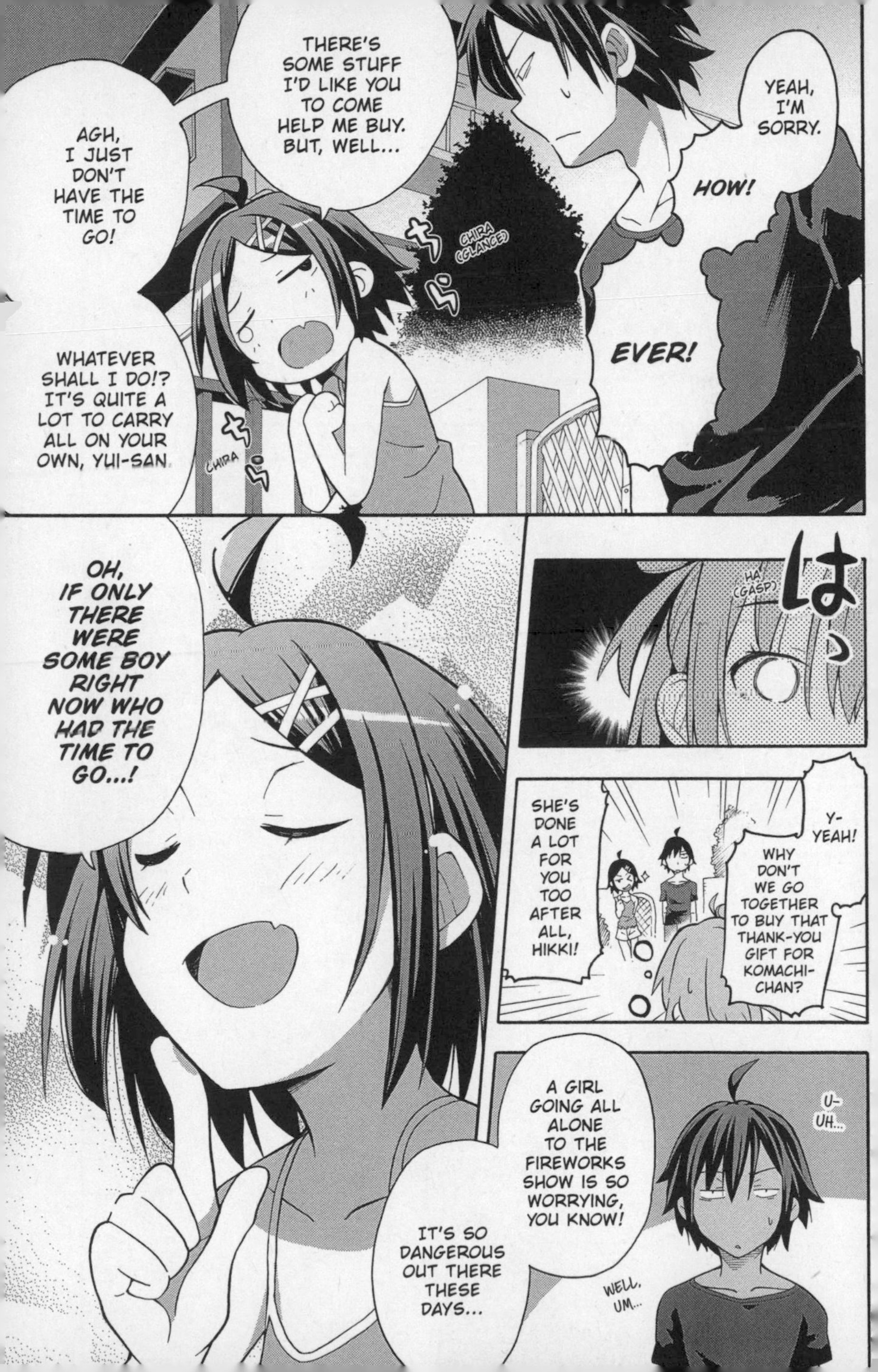
YEAH, I'M SORRY.
THERE'S SOME STUFF I'D LIKE YOU TO COME HELP ME BUY. BUT, WELL...
HOW!
AGH, I JUST DON'T HAVE THE TIME TO GO!
CHIRA (GLANCE)
EVER!
WHATEVER SHALL I DO!? IT'S QUITE A LOT TO CARRY ALL ON YOUR OWN, YUI-SAN.
CHIRA
HA (GASP)
Y-YEAH! WHY DON'T WE GO TOGETHER TO BUY THAT THANK-YOU GIFT FOR KOMACHI-CHAN?
SHE'S DONE A LOT FOR YOU TOO AFTER ALL, HIKKI!
U-UH...
A GIRL GOING ALL ALONE TO THE FIREWORKS SHOW IS SO WORRYING, YOU KNOW!
WELL, UM...
IT'S SO DANGEROUS OUT THERE THESE DAYS...
OH, IF ONLY THERE WERE SOME BOY RIGHT NOW WHO HAD THE TIME TO GO...!

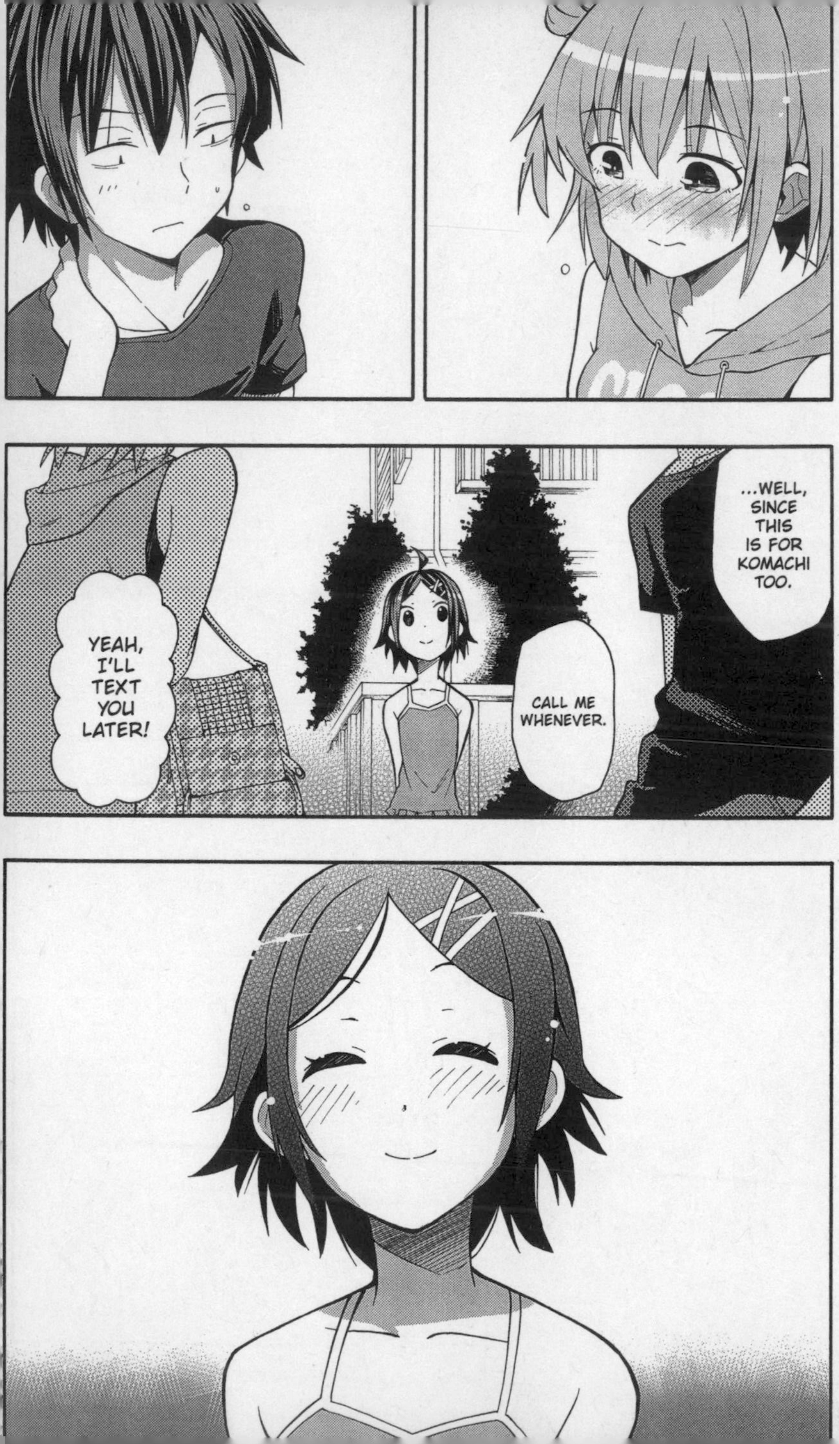
...WELL, SINCE THIS IS FOR KOMACHI TOO.
CALL ME WHENEVER.
YEAH, I'LL TEXT YOU LATER!

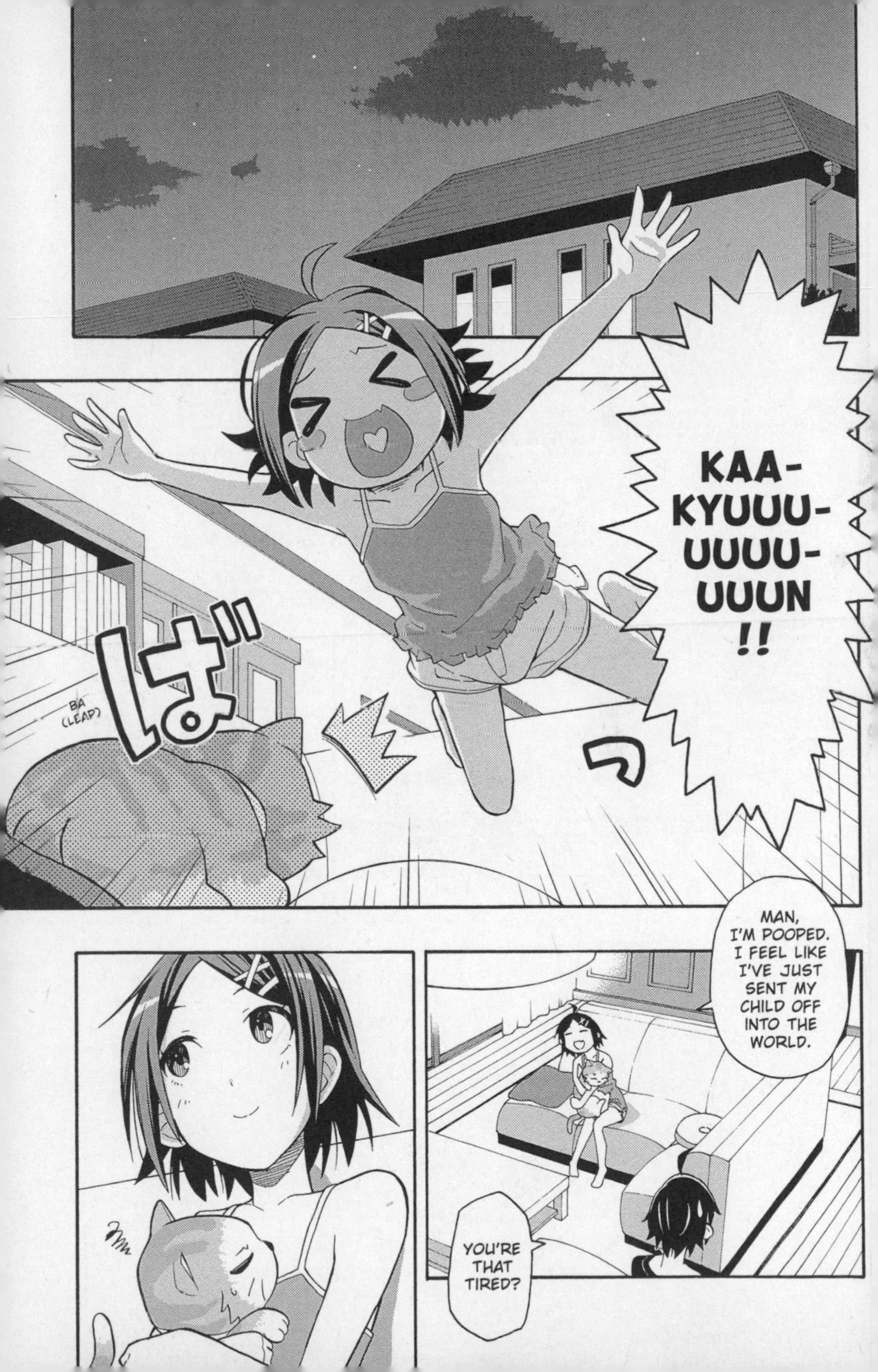
KAA-KYUUU-UUUU-UUUN!!
ば
BA (LEAP)
MAN, I'M POOPED. I FEEL LIKE I'VE JUST SENT MY CHILD OFF INTO THE WORLD.
YOU'RE THAT TIRED?

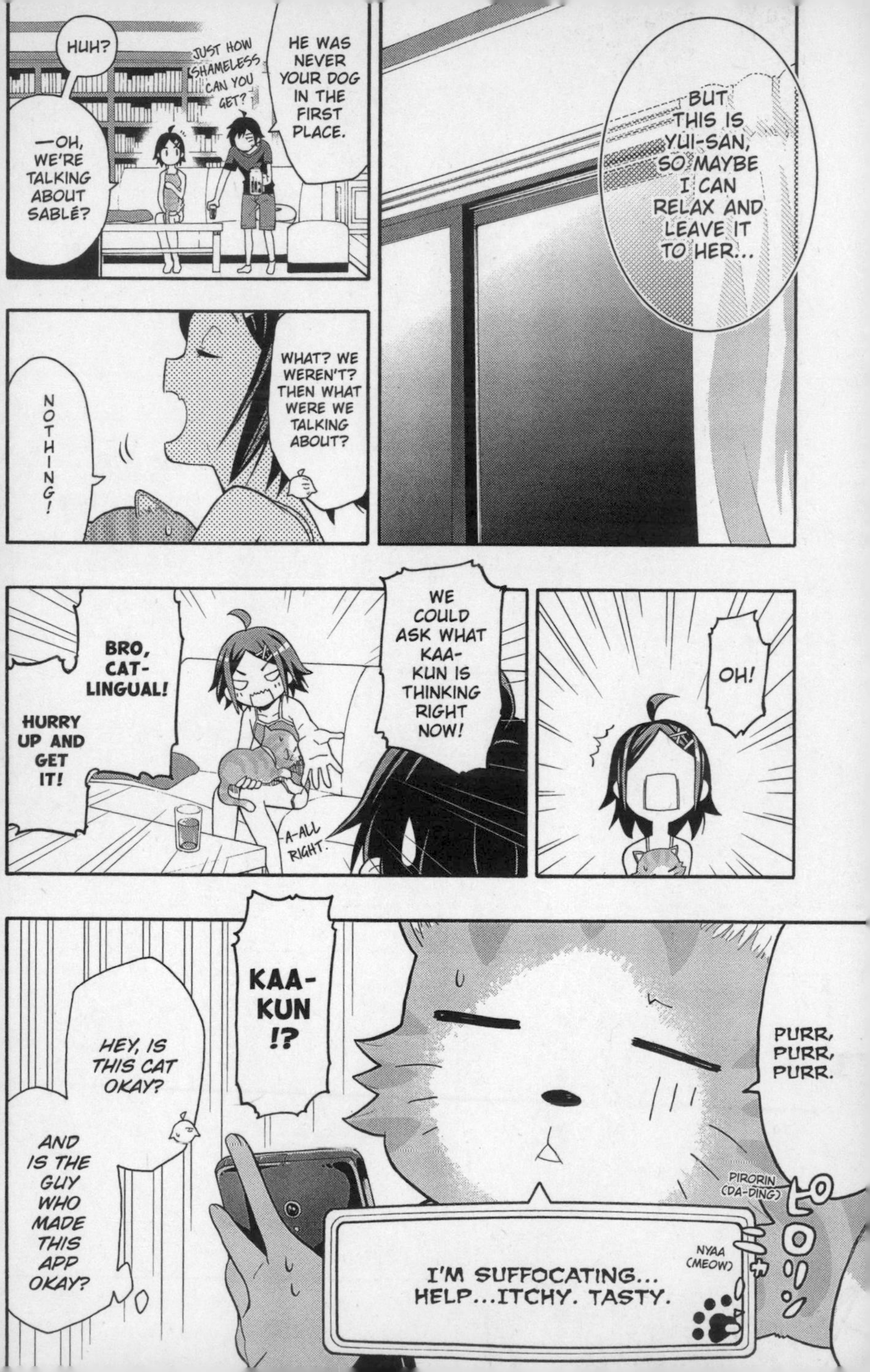
BUT THIS IS YUI-SAN, SO MAYBE I CAN RELAX AND LEAVE IT TO HER...
HE WAS NEVER YOUR DOG IN THE FIRST PLACE.
JUST HOW SHAMELESS CAN YOU GET?
HUH?
—OH, WE'RE TALKING ABOUT SABLÉ?
WHAT? WE WEREN'T? THEN WHAT WERE WE TALKING ABOUT?
NOTHING!
OH!
WE COULD ASK WHAT KAA-KUN IS THINKING RIGHT NOW!
BRO, CAT-LINGUAL!
HURRY UP AND GET IT!
A-ALL RIGHT.
PURR, PURR, PURR.
PIRORIN (DA-DING)
KAA-KUN!?
HEY, IS THIS CAT OKAY?
NYAA (MEOW)
I'M SUFFOCATING... HELP...ITCHY. TASTY.
AND IS THE GUY WHO MADE THIS APP OKAY?

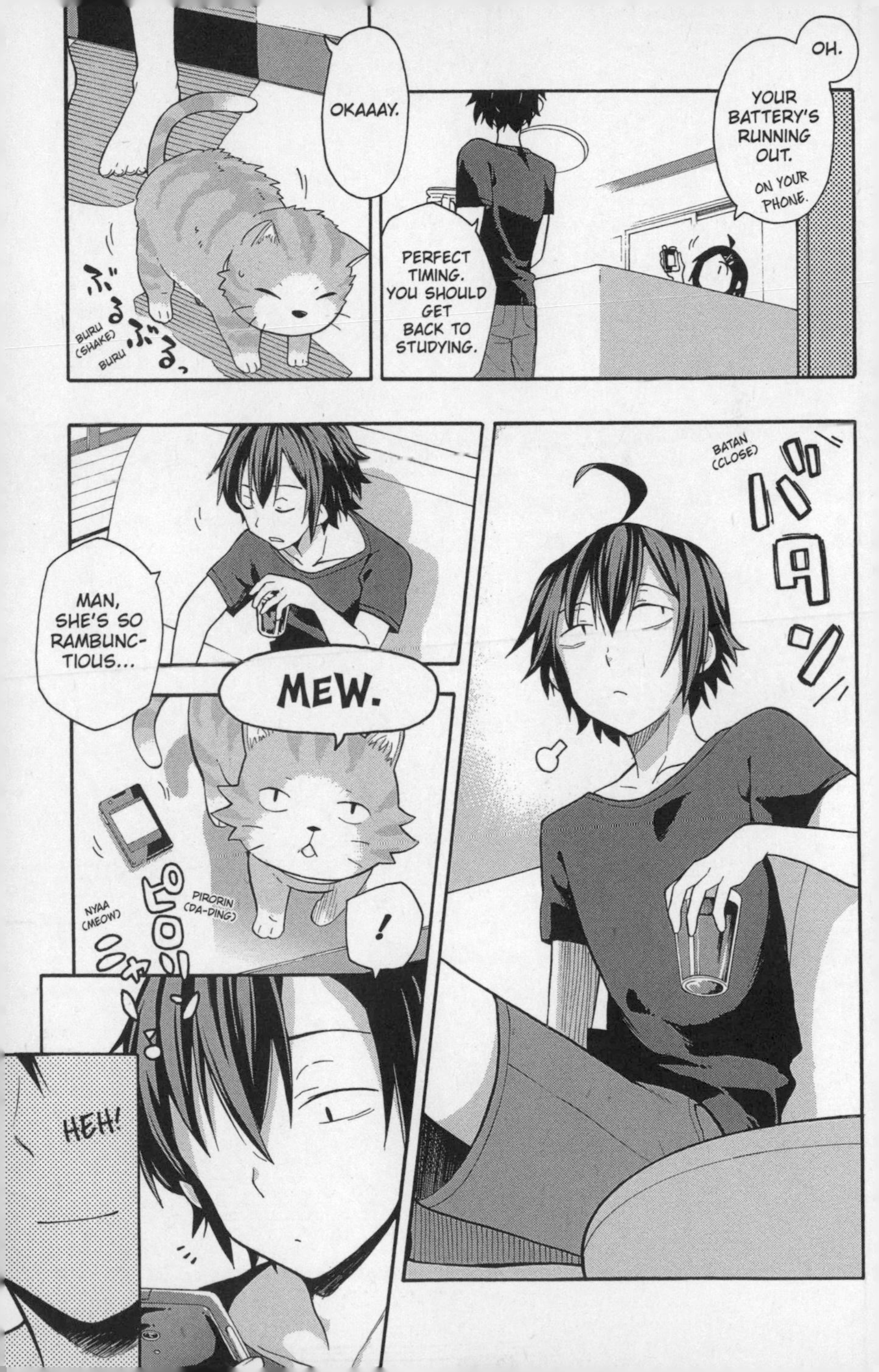
OH.
YOUR BATTERY'S RUNNING OUT.
ON YOUR PHONE.
PERFECT TIMING. YOU SHOULD GET BACK TO STUDYING.
OKAAAY.
ぶる
BURU (SHAKE)
ぶるっ
BURU
BATAN (CLOSE)
バタン
MAN, SHE'S SO RAMBUNC-TIOUS...
MEW.
PIRORIN (DA-DING)
ピロリン
NYAA (MEOW)
にゃ
!
HEH!

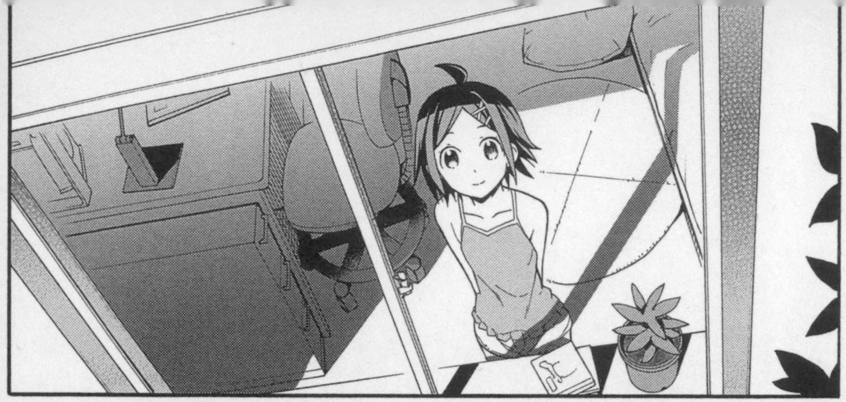

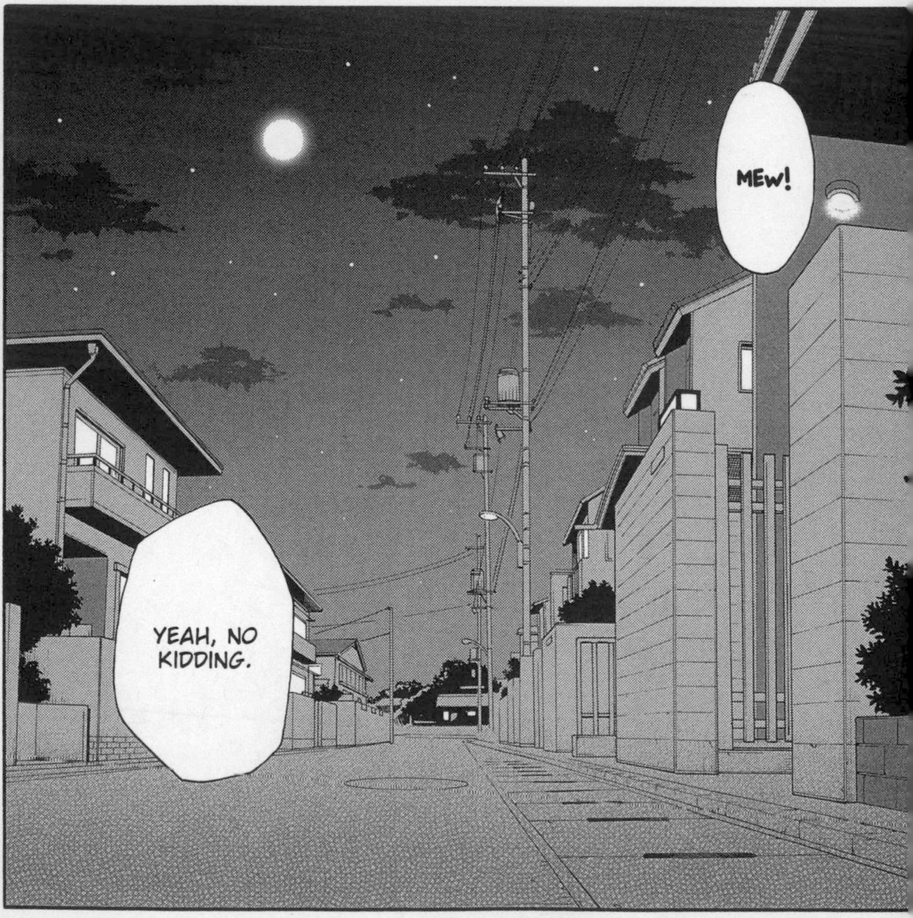
MEW!
YEAH, NO KIDDING.

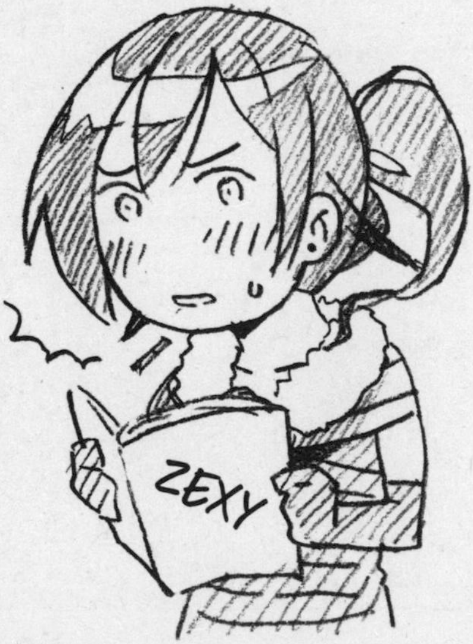
ZEXY

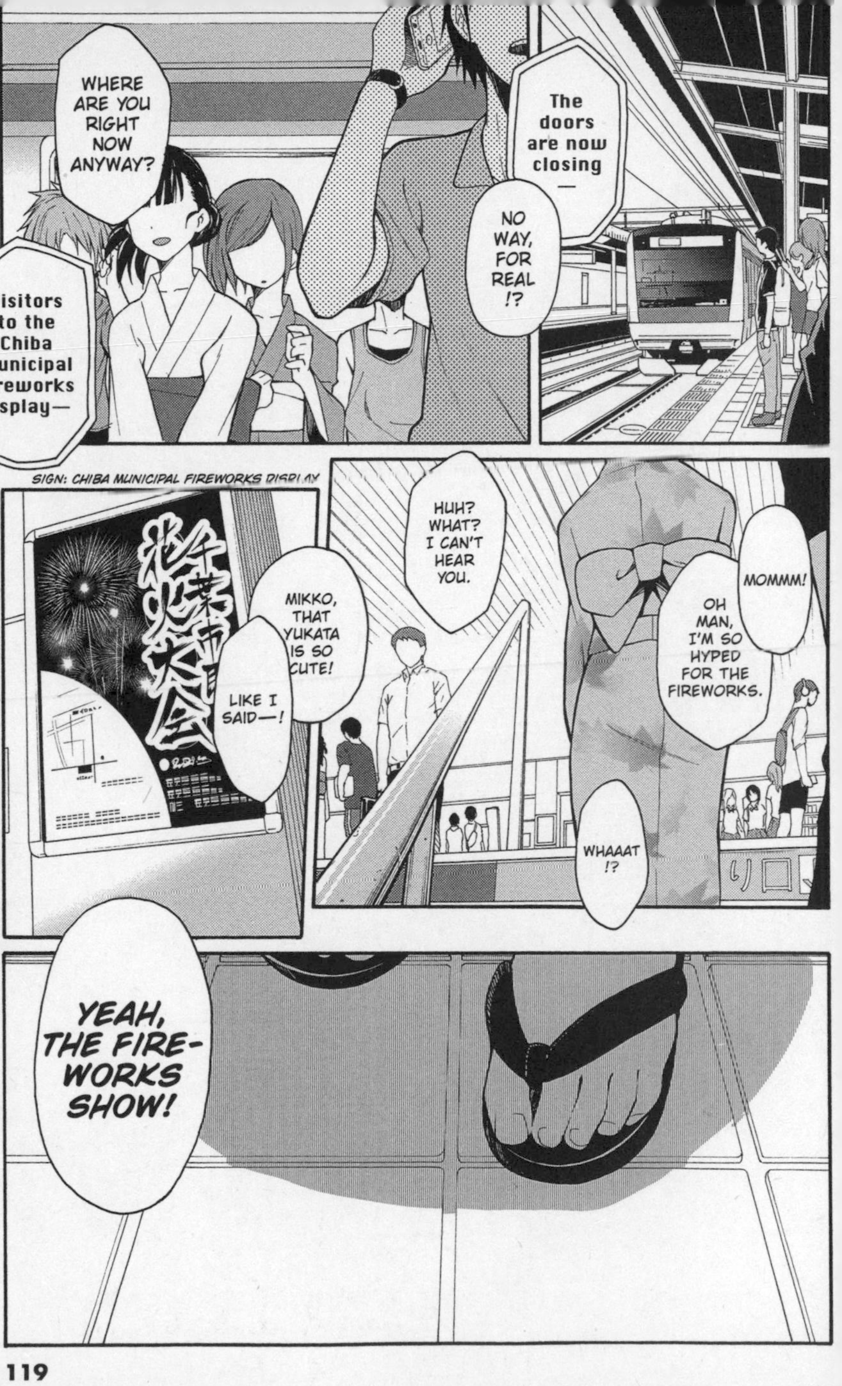
The doors are now closing—
NO WAY, FOR REAL!?
WHERE ARE YOU RIGHT NOW ANYWAY?
Visitors to the Chiba Municipal Fireworks Display—
MOMMM!
OH MAN, I'M SO HYPED FOR THE FIREWORKS.
WHAAAT!?
HUH? WHAT? I CAN'T HEAR YOU.
MIKKO, THAT YUKATA IS SO CUTE!
LIKE I SAID—!
SIGN: CHIBA MUNICIPAL FIREWORKS DISPLAY
YEAH, THE FIRE-WORKS SHOW!

CHAPTER 34 ... AND SO YUI YUIGAHAMA DISAPPEARS INTO THE THRONG.

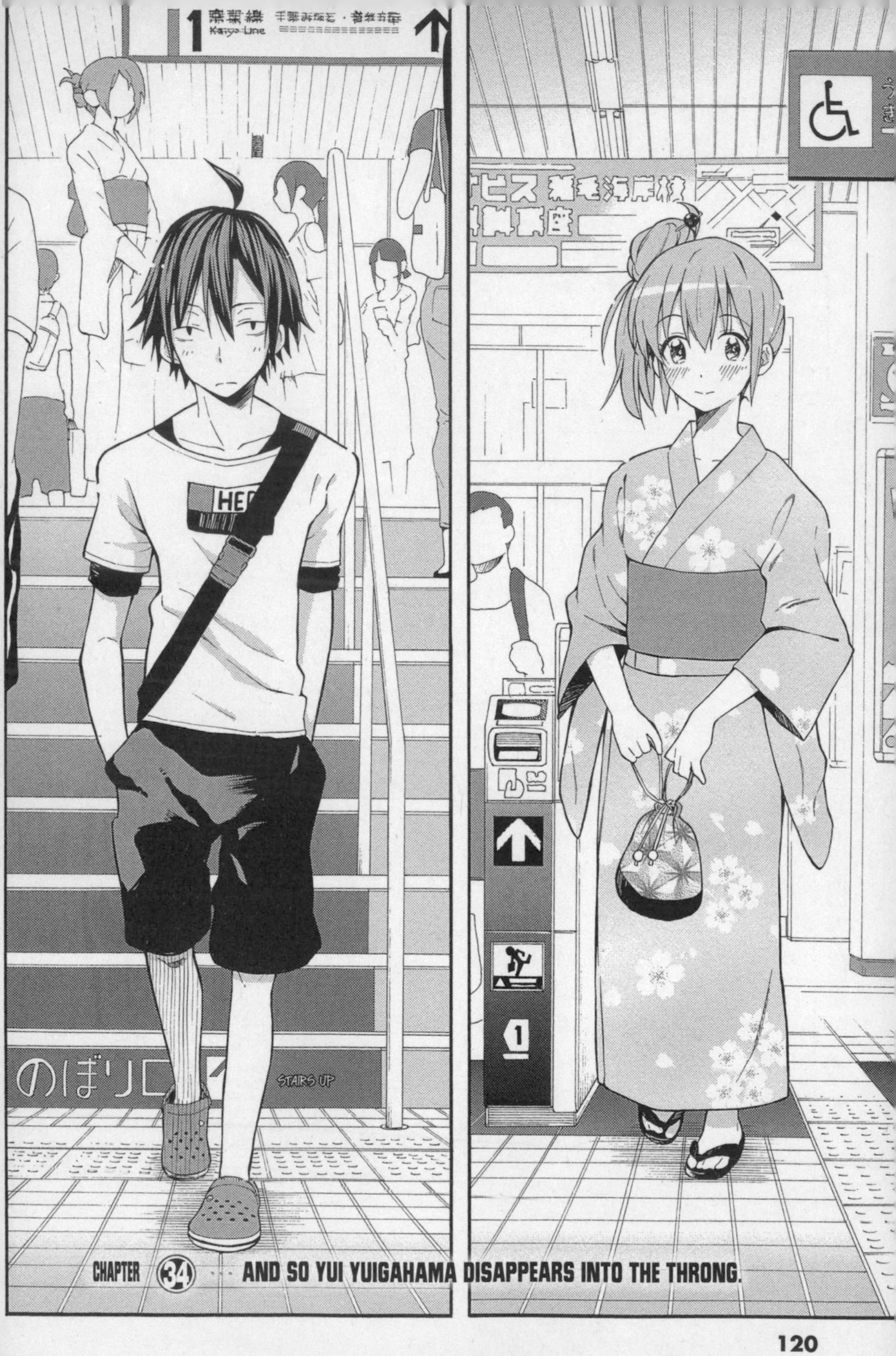
のぼり口
STAIRS UP

CHAPTER 34 ... AND SO YUI YUIGAHAMA DISAPPEARS INTO THE THRONG.

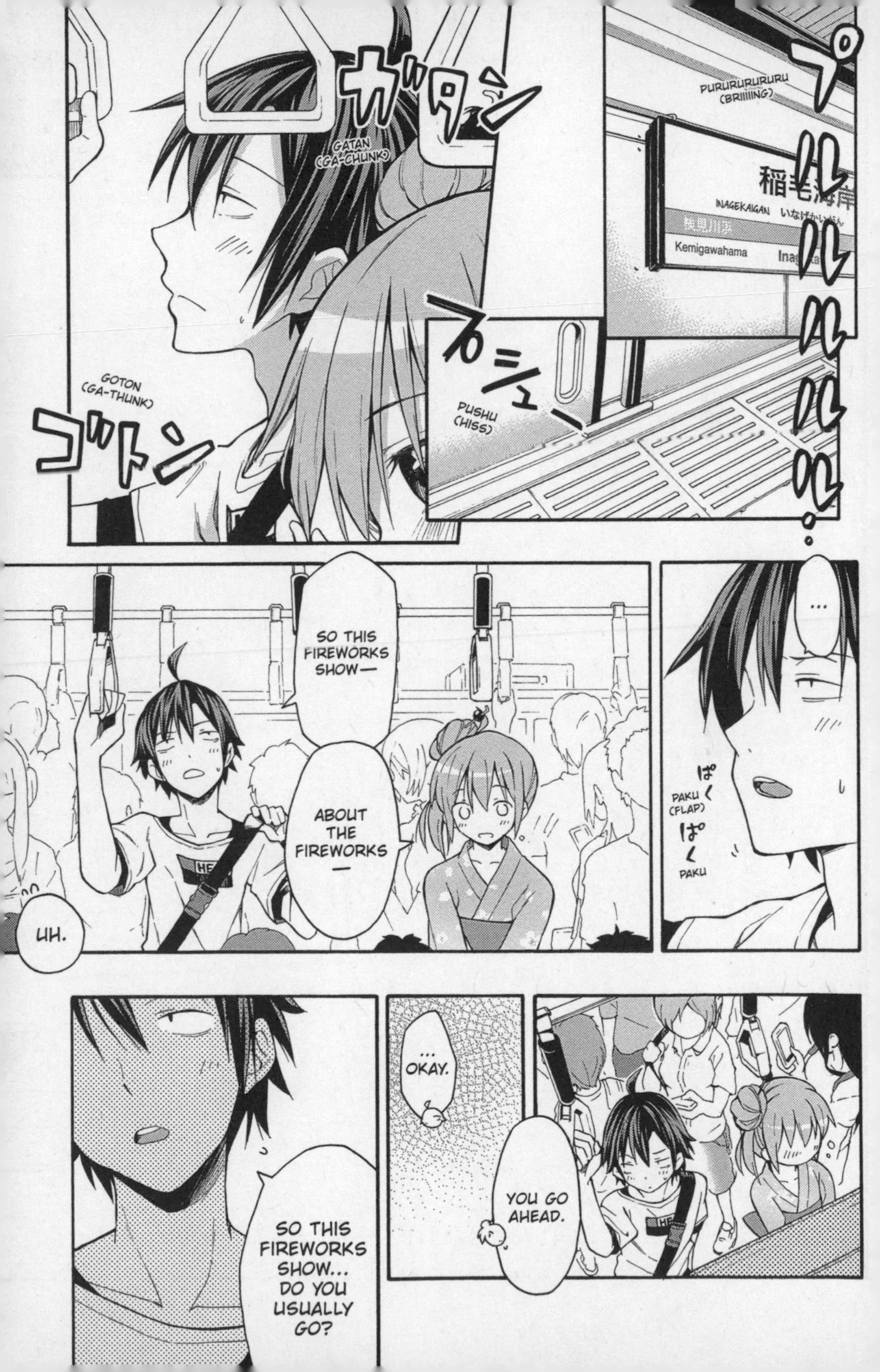
Pururururururu
(Briiiiing)
稲毛海岸
INAGEKAIGAN
Kemigawahama
Pushu
(Hiss)
Gatan
(Ga-chunk)
Goton
(Ga-thunk)
...
ぱく
Paku
(Flap)
ぱく
Paku
So this fireworks show—
About the fireworks—
Uh.
You go ahead.
...Okay.
So this fireworks show... do you usually go?

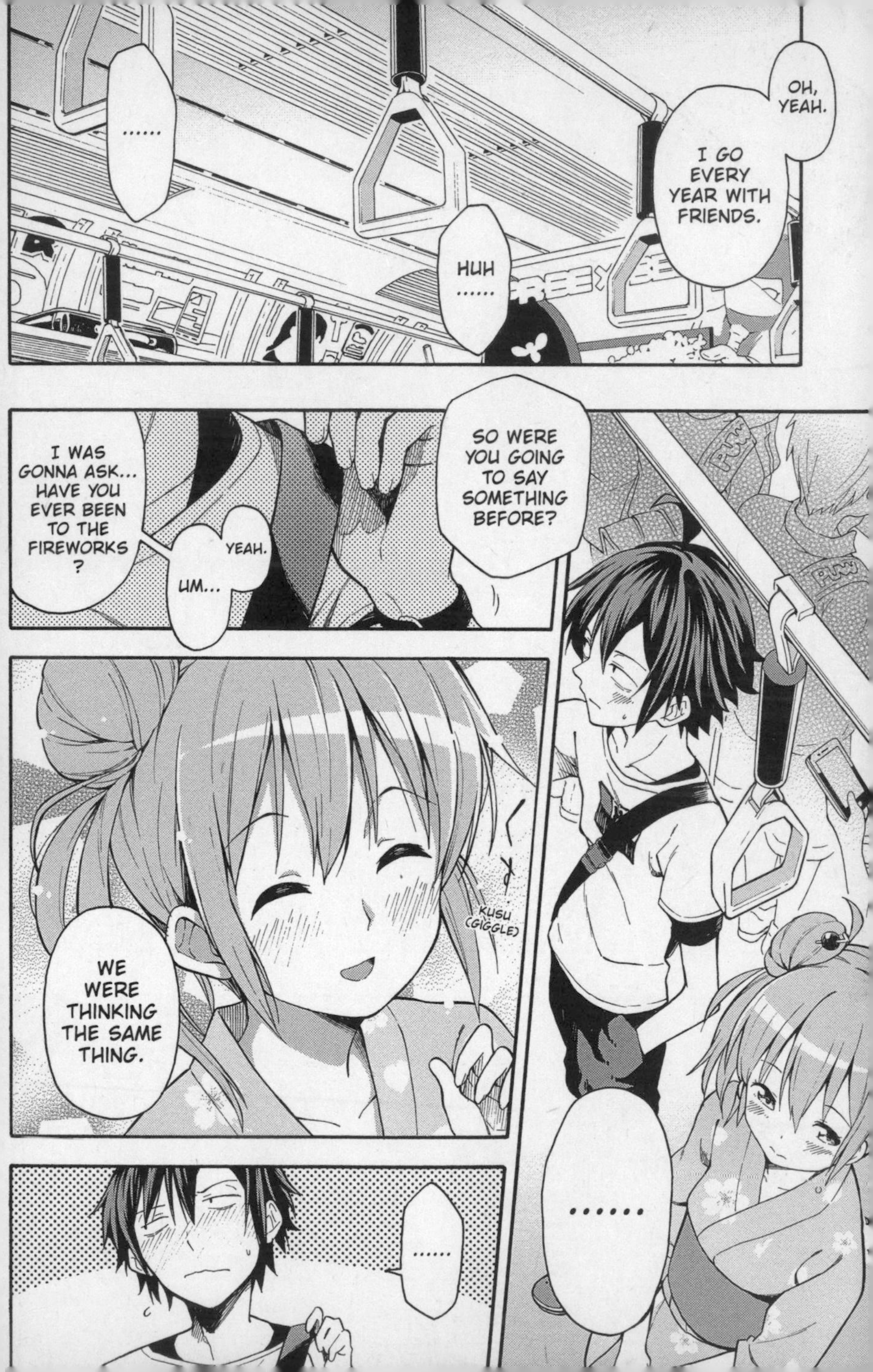
OH, YEAH.
I GO EVERY YEAR WITH FRIENDS.
HUH ......
......
SO WERE YOU GOING TO SAY SOMETHING BEFORE?
......
YEAH.
UM...
I WAS GONNA ASK... HAVE YOU EVER BEEN TO THE FIREWORKS?
KUSU (GIGGLE)
WE WERE THINKING THE SAME THING.
......

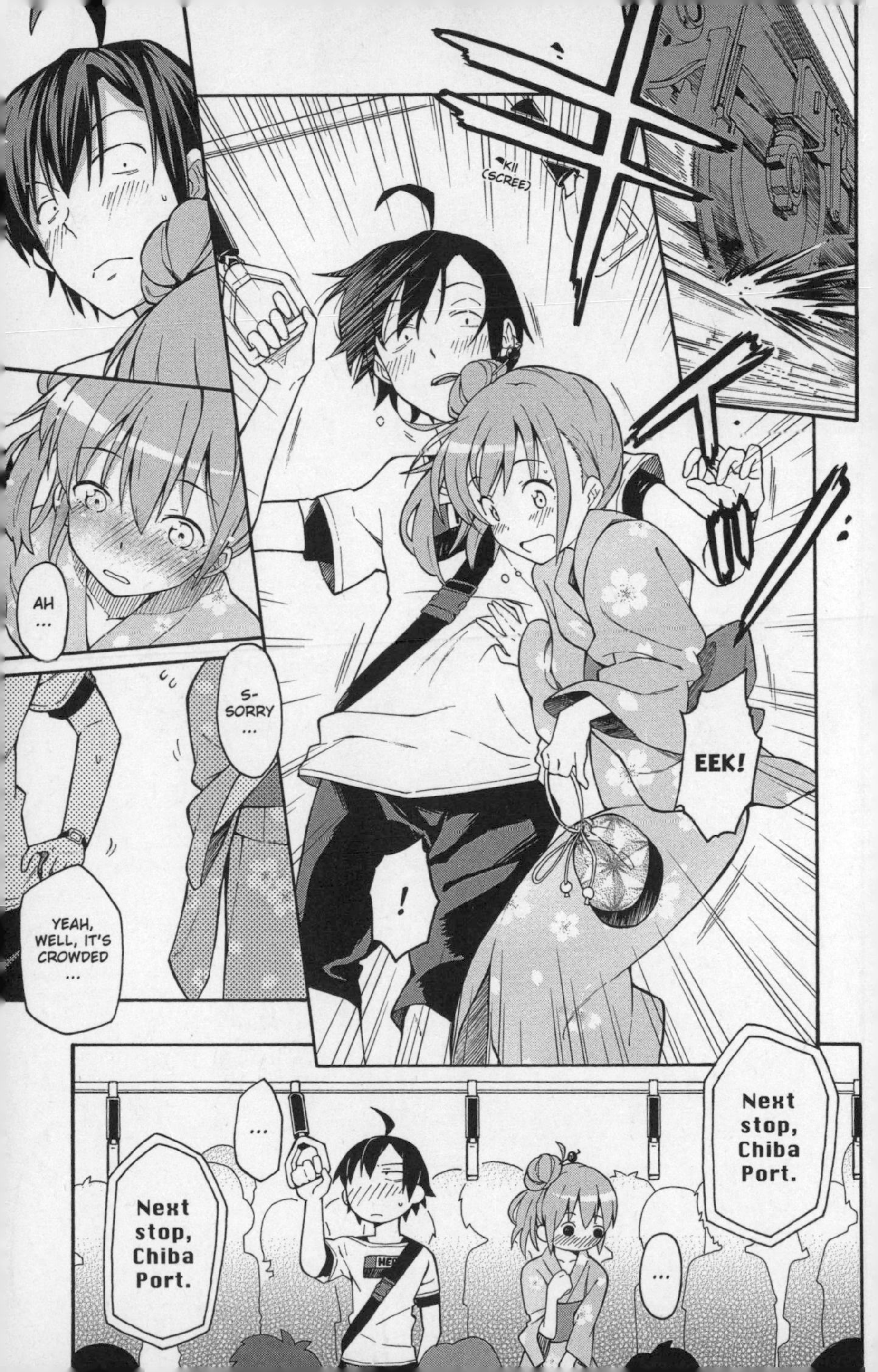
KII
(SCREE)
EEK!
!
AH ...
S-SORRY ...
YEAH, WELL, IT'S CROWDED ...
Next stop, Chiba Port.
...
...
Next stop, Chiba Port.

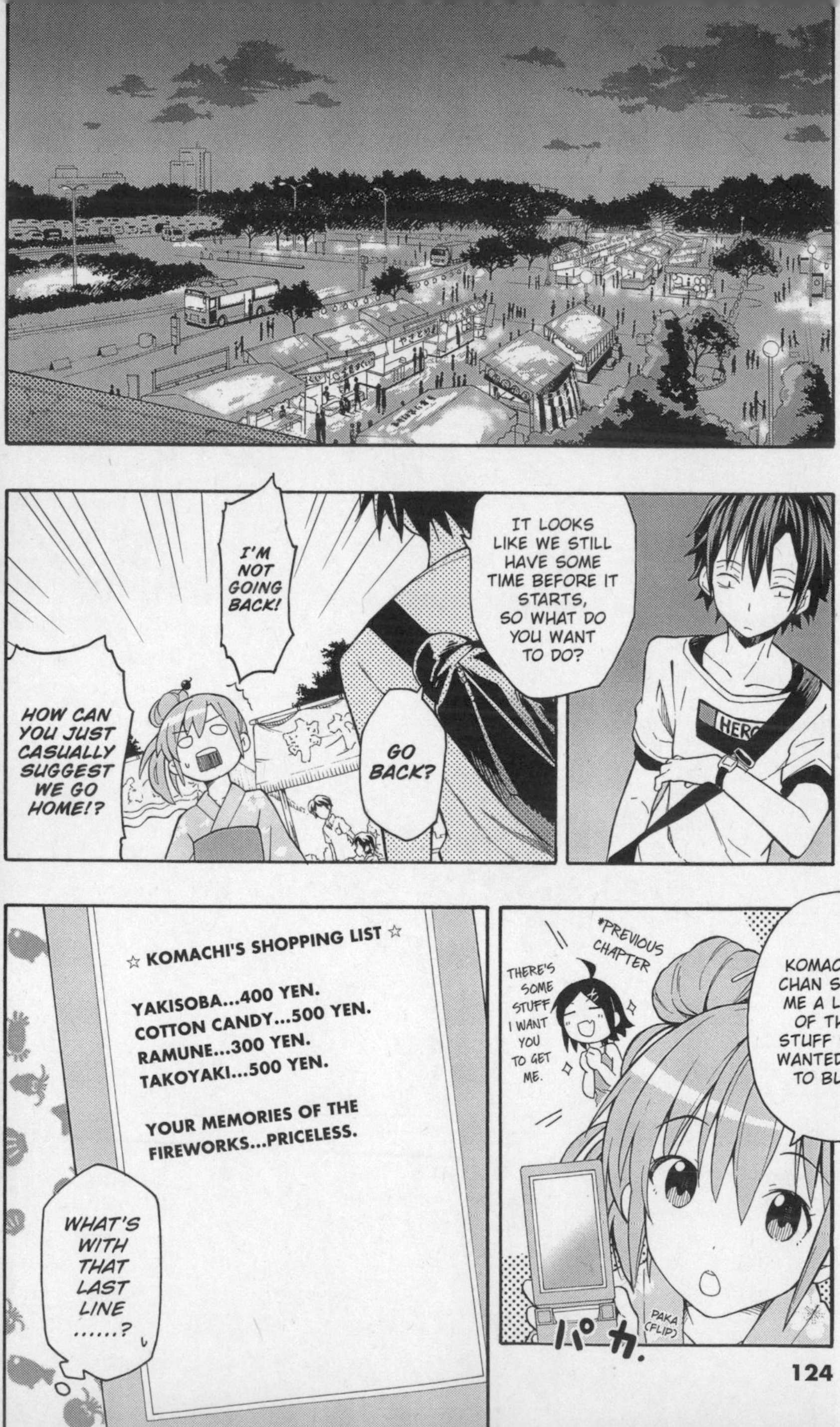

IT LOOKS LIKE WE STILL HAVE SOME TIME BEFORE IT STARTS, SO WHAT DO YOU WANT TO DO?
HERO
GO BACK?
I'M NOT GOING BACK!
HOW CAN YOU JUST CASUALLY SUGGEST WE GO HOME!?
KOMACHI-CHAN SENT ME A LIST OF THE STUFF SHE WANTED US TO BUY.
*PREVIOUS CHAPTER
THERE'S SOME STUFF I WANT YOU TO GET ME.
PAKA (FLIP)
パカ
☆ KOMACHI'S SHOPPING LIST ☆
YAKISOBA...400 YEN.
COTTON CANDY...500 YEN.
RAMUNE...300 YEN.
TAKOYAKI...500 YEN.
YOUR MEMORIES OF THE FIREWORKS...PRICELESS.
WHAT'S WITH THAT LAST LINE ......?

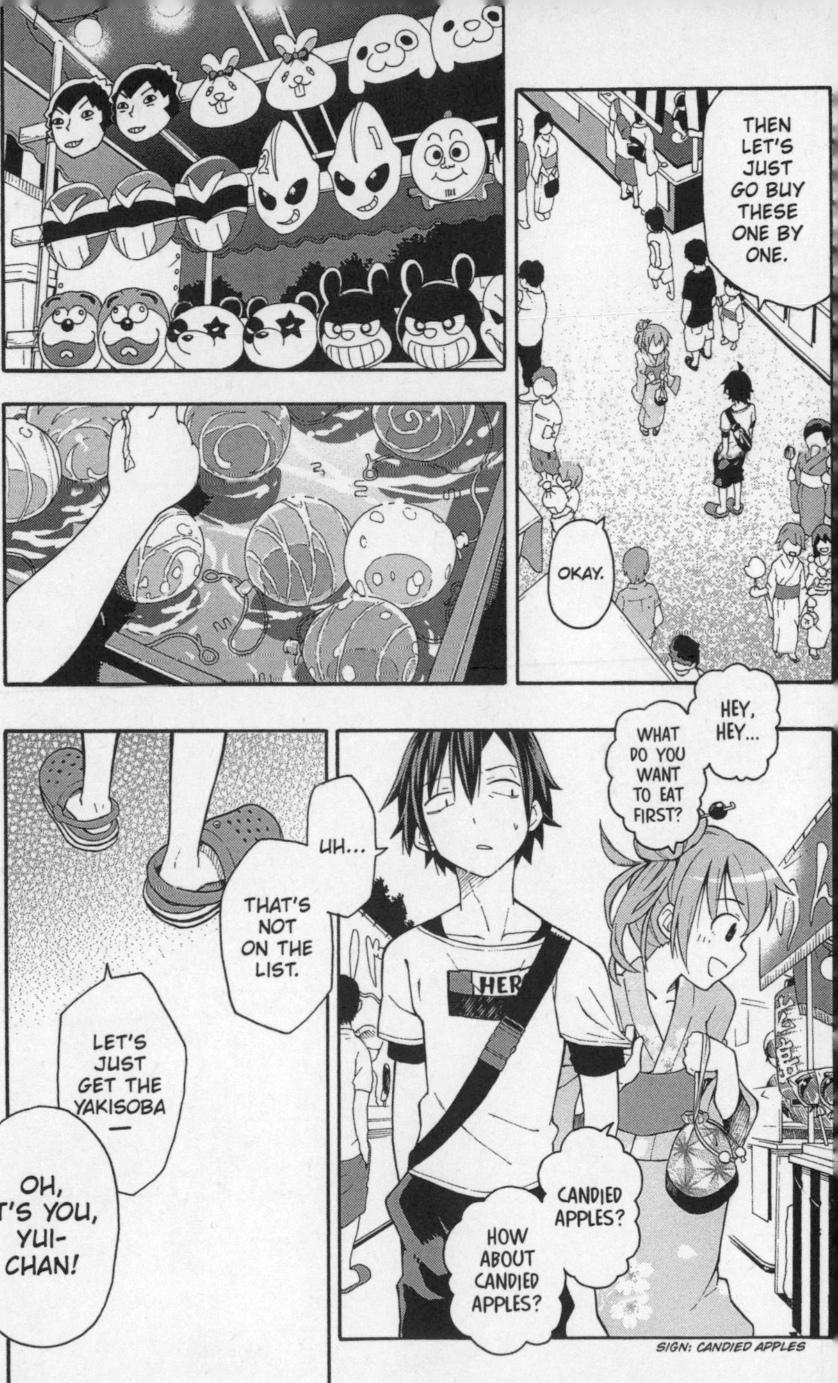
THEN LET'S JUST GO BUY THESE ONE BY ONE.
OKAY.
HEY, HEY...
WHAT DO YOU WANT TO EAT FIRST?
CANDIED APPLES?
HOW ABOUT CANDIED APPLES?
UH...
THAT'S NOT ON THE LIST.
LET'S JUST GET THE YAKISOBA—
OH, IT'S YOU, YUI-CHAN!
SIGN: CANDIED APPLES

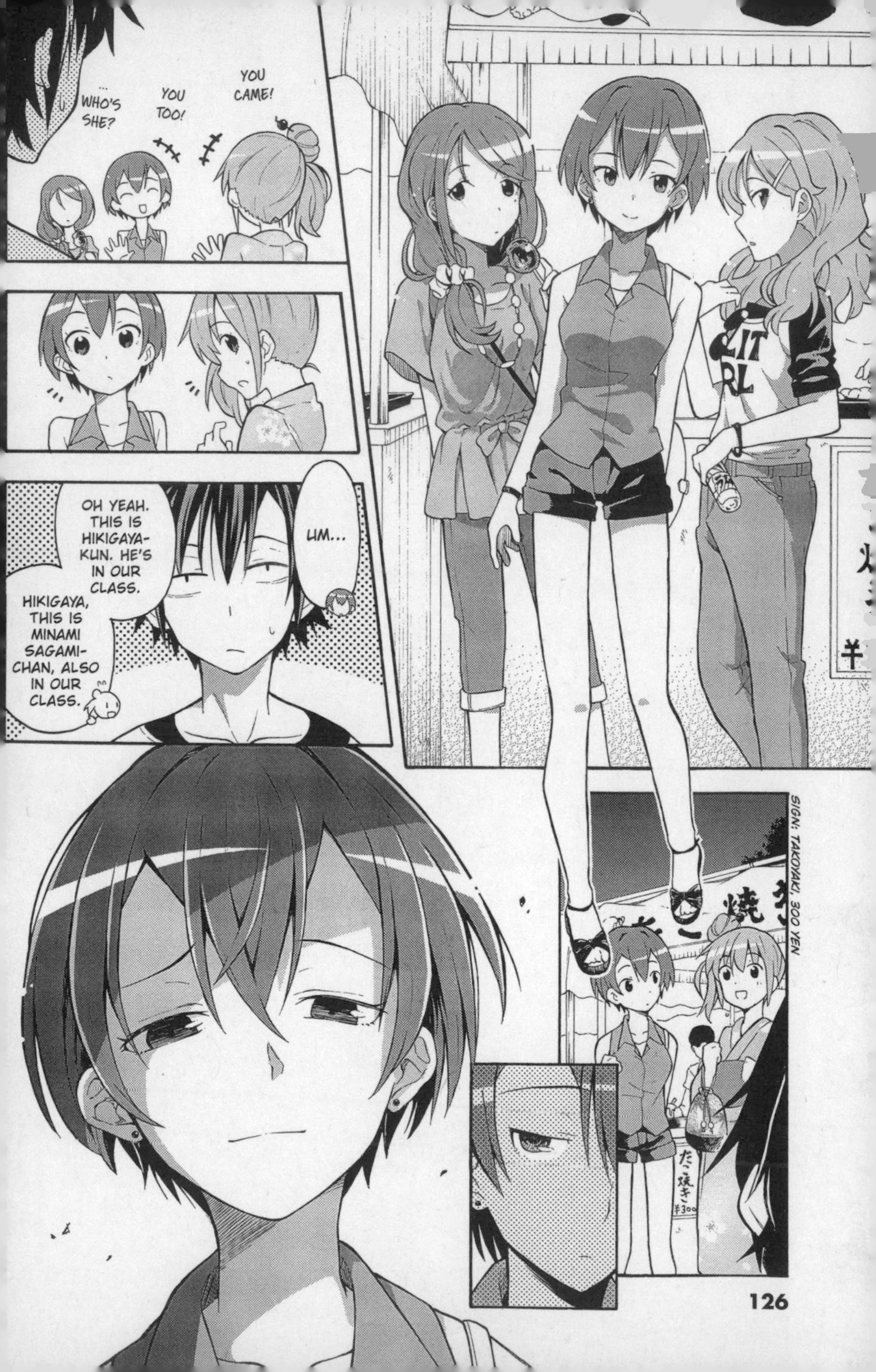
YOU CAME!
YOU TOO!
... WHO'S SHE?
UM...
OH YEAH. THIS IS HIKIGAYA-KUN. HE'S IN OUR CLASS.
HIKIGAYA, THIS IS MINAMI SAGAMI-CHAN, ALSO IN OUR CLASS.
SIGN: TAKOYAKI, 300 YEN
たこ焼き ¥300

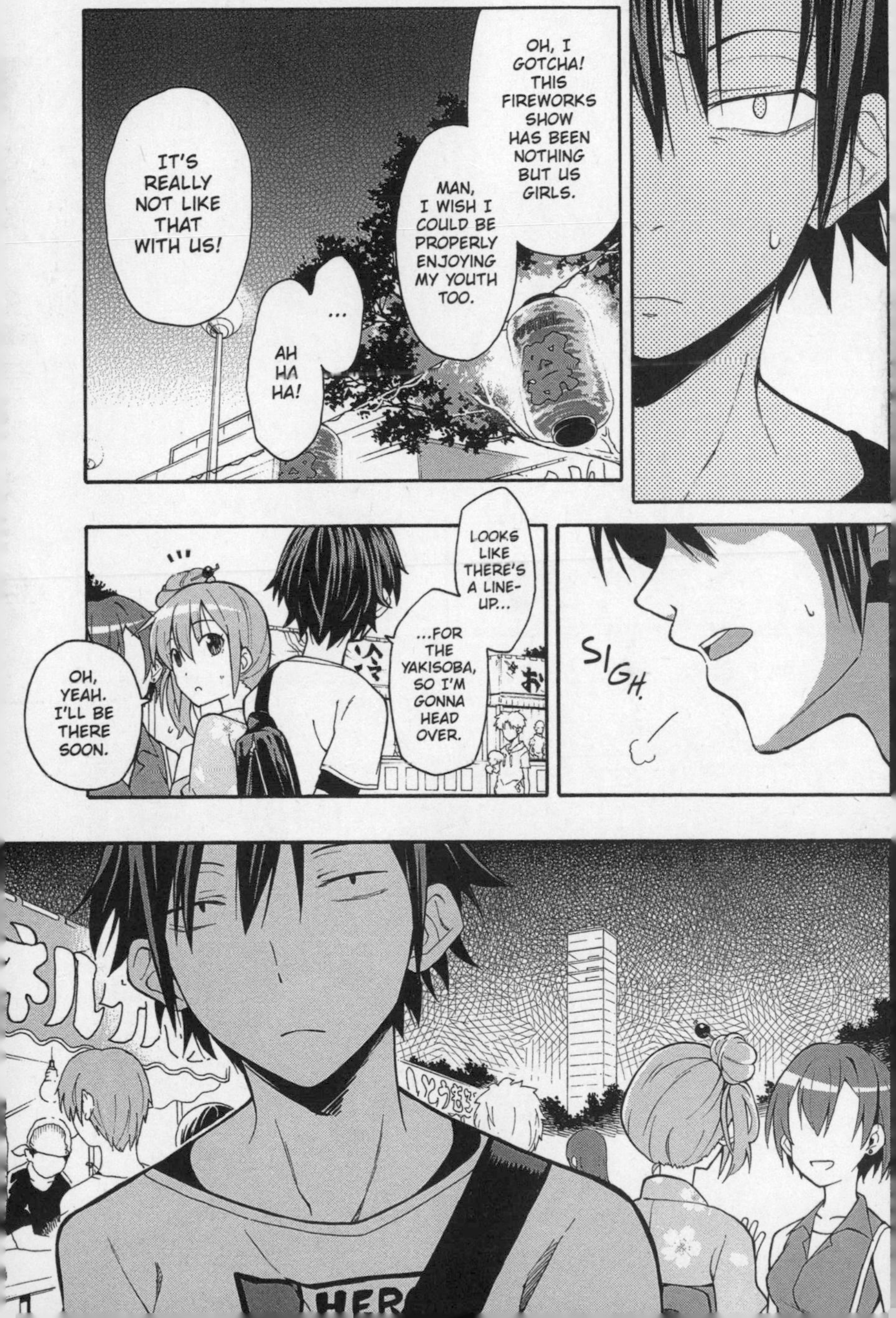
OH, I GOTCHA! THIS FIREWORKS SHOW HAS BEEN NOTHING BUT US GIRLS.
MAN, I WISH I COULD BE PROPERLY ENJOYING MY YOUTH TOO.
...
AH HA HA!
IT'S REALLY NOT LIKE THAT WITH US!
SIGH.
LOOKS LIKE THERE'S A LINE-UP...
...FOR THE YAKISOBA, SO I'M GONNA HEAD OVER.
OH, YEAH. I'LL BE THERE SOON.

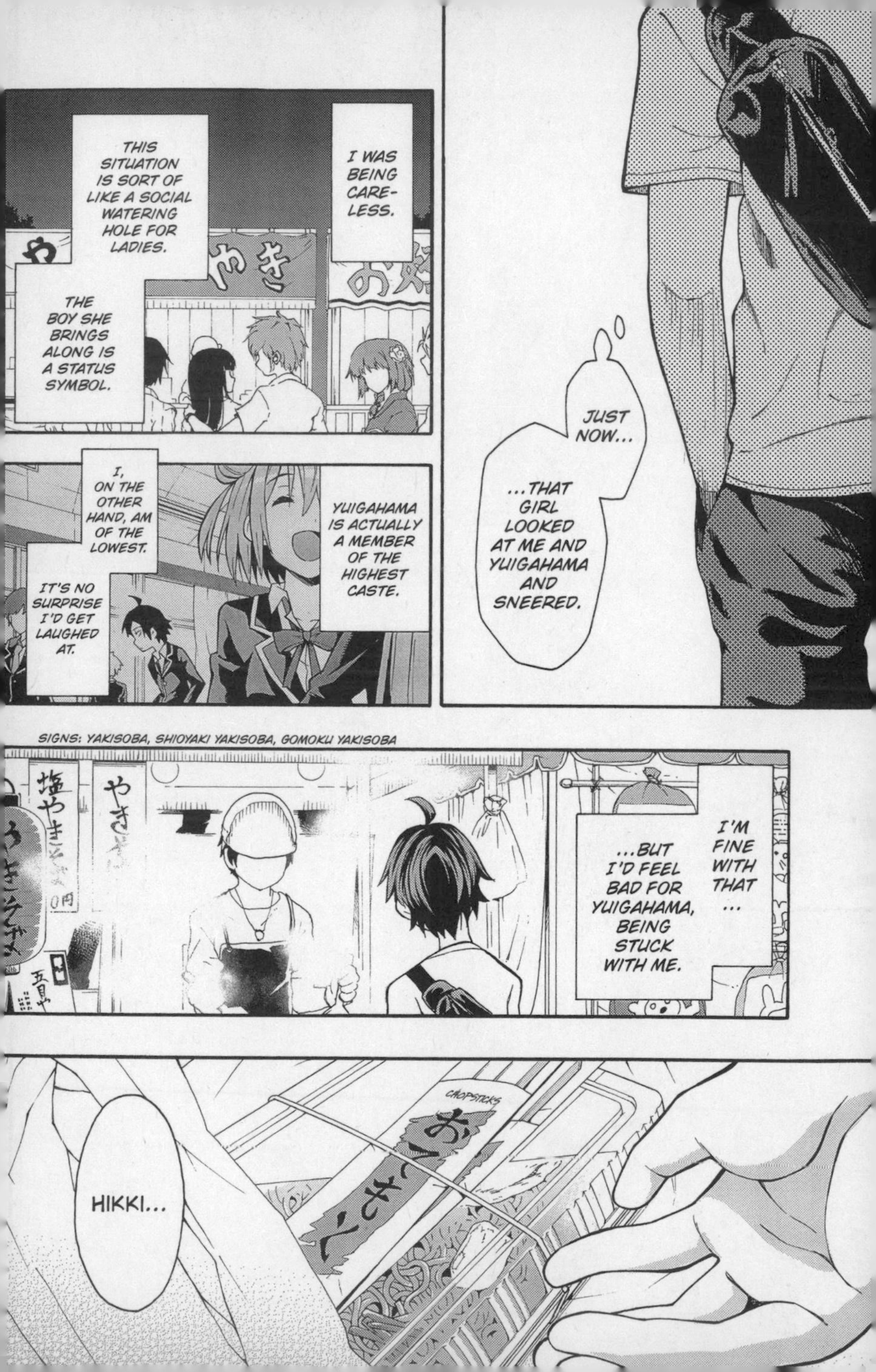
JUST NOW...
...THAT GIRL LOOKED AT ME AND YUIGAHAMA AND SNEERED.
I WAS BEING CARE-LESS.
THIS SITUATION IS SORT OF LIKE A SOCIAL WATERING HOLE FOR LADIES.
THE BOY SHE BRINGS ALONG IS A STATUS SYMBOL.
YUIGAHAMA IS ACTUALLY A MEMBER OF THE HIGHEST CASTE.
I, ON THE OTHER HAND, AM OF THE LOWEST.
IT'S NO SURPRISE I'D GET LAUGHED AT.
SIGNS: YAKISOBA, SHIOYAKI YAKISOBA, GOMOKU YAKISOBA
I'M FINE WITH THAT...
...BUT I'D FEEL BAD FOR YUIGAHAMA, BEING STUCK WITH ME.
CHOPSTICKS
HIKKI...

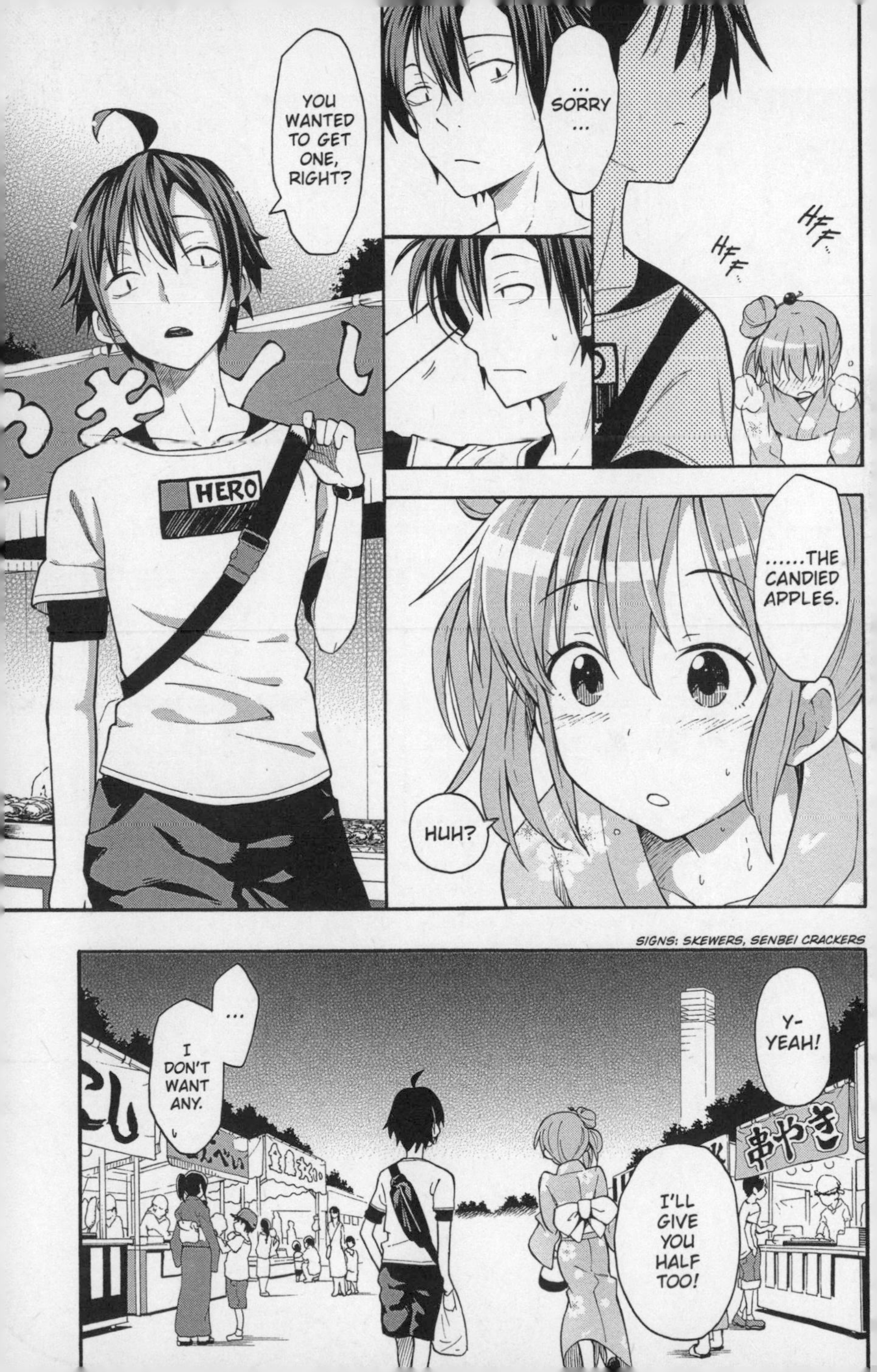
... SORRY ...
HFF HFF
......THE CANDIED APPLES.
HUH?
YOU WANTED TO GET ONE, RIGHT?
SIGNS: SKEWERS, SENBEI CRACKERS
Y-YEAH!
I'LL GIVE YOU HALF TOO!
... I DON'T WANT ANY.

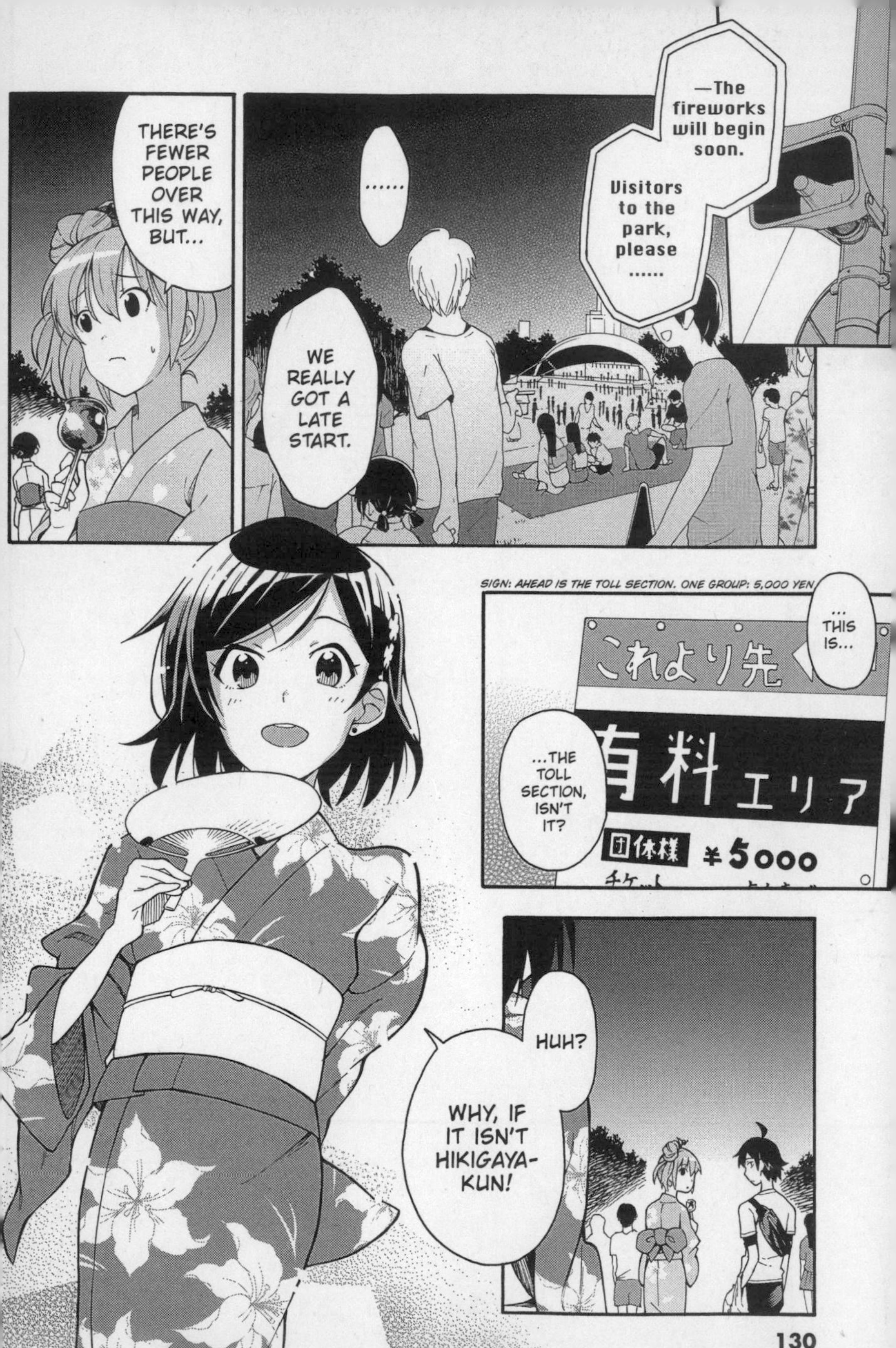
—The fireworks will begin soon.
Visitors to the park, please ......
......
WE REALLY GOT A LATE START.
THERE'S FEWER PEOPLE OVER THIS WAY, BUT...
SIGN: AHEAD IS THE TOLL SECTION. ONE GROUP: 5,000 YEN
... THIS IS...
これより先
有料エリア
団体様 ¥5000
...THE TOLL SECTION, ISN'T IT?
HUH?
WHY, IF IT ISN'T HIKIGAYA-KUN!

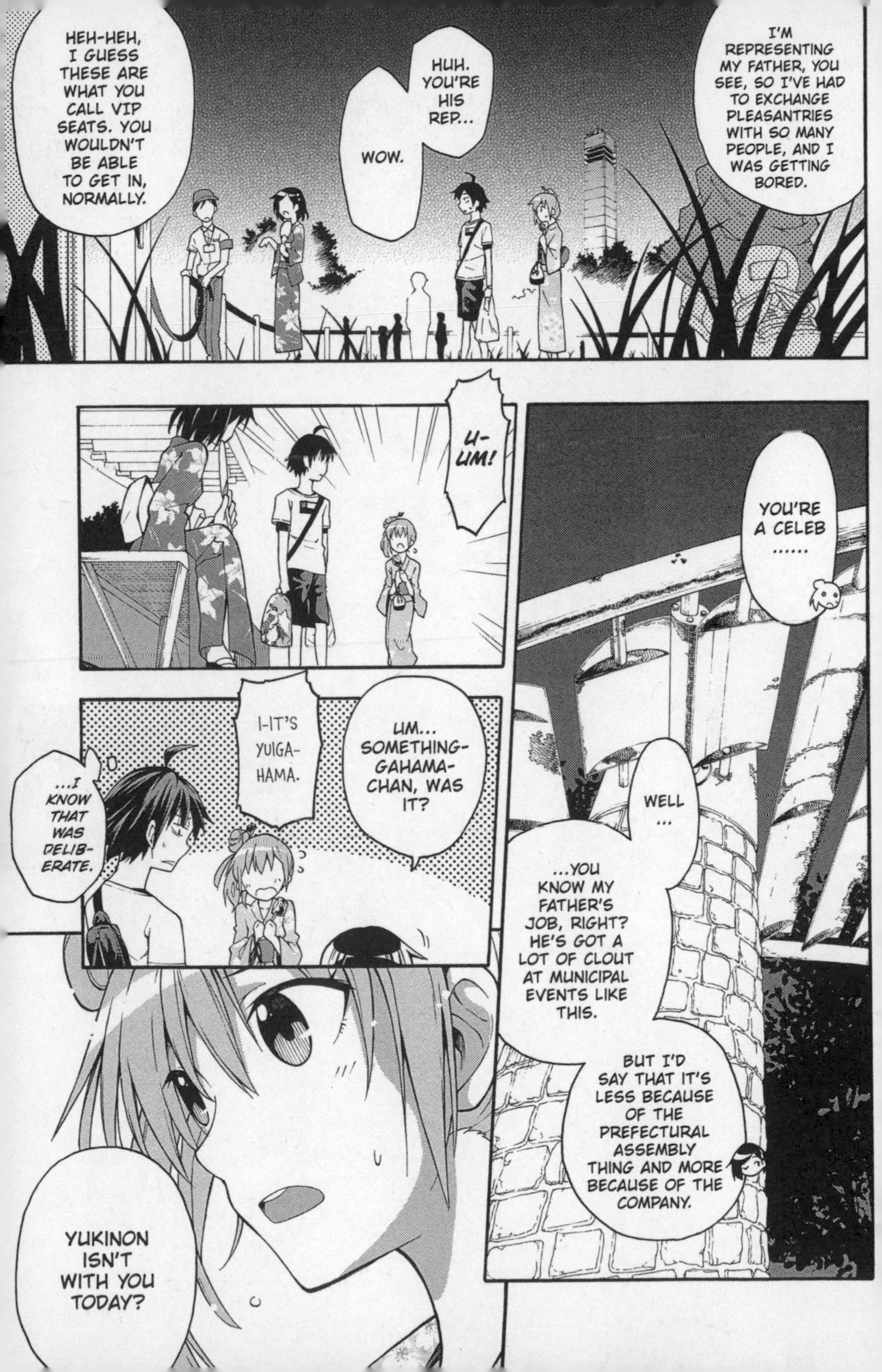
I'M REPRESENTING MY FATHER, YOU SEE, SO I'VE HAD TO EXCHANGE PLEASANTRIES WITH SO MANY PEOPLE, AND I WAS GETTING BORED.
HUH. YOU'RE HIS REP...
WOW.
HEH-HEH, I GUESS THESE ARE WHAT YOU CALL VIP SEATS. YOU WOULDN'T BE ABLE TO GET IN, NORMALLY.
YOU'RE A CELEB ......
WELL ...
...YOU KNOW MY FATHER'S JOB, RIGHT? HE'S GOT A LOT OF CLOUT AT MUNICIPAL EVENTS LIKE THIS.
BUT I'D SAY THAT IT'S LESS BECAUSE OF THE PREFECTURAL ASSEMBLY THING AND MORE BECAUSE OF THE COMPANY.
U-UM!
UM... SOMETHING-GAHAMA-CHAN, WAS IT?
I-IT'S YUIGA-HAMA.
...I KNOW THAT WAS DELIB-ERATE.
YUKINON ISN'T WITH YOU TODAY?

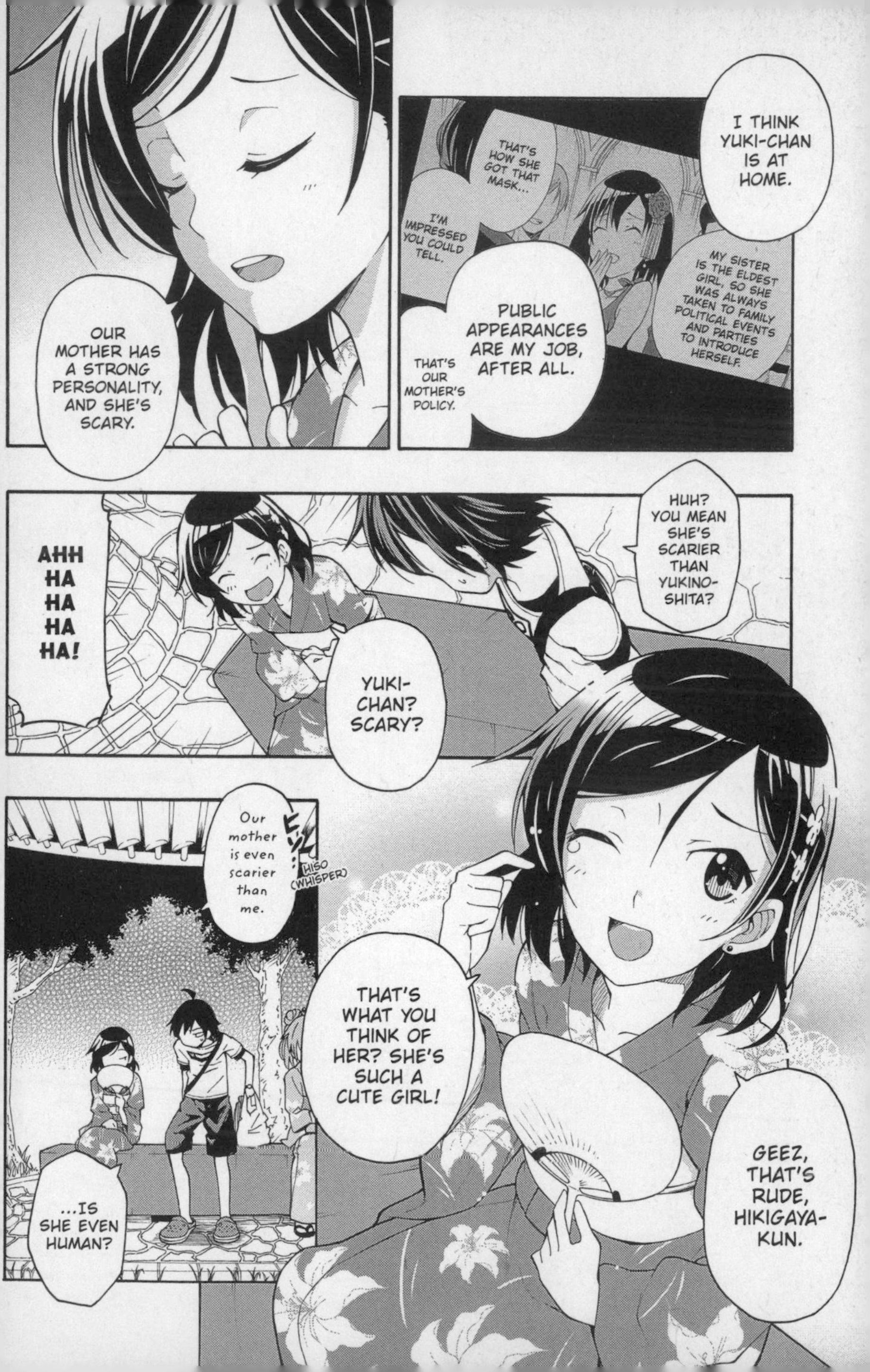
I THINK YUKI-CHAN IS AT HOME.
MY SISTER IS THE ELDEST GIRL, SO SHE WAS ALWAYS TAKEN TO FAMILY POLITICAL EVENTS AND PARTIES TO INTRODUCE HERSELF.
THAT'S HOW SHE GOT THAT MASK...
I'M IMPRESSED YOU COULD TELL.
PUBLIC APPEARANCES ARE MY JOB, AFTER ALL.
THAT'S OUR MOTHER'S POLICY.
OUR MOTHER HAS A STRONG PERSONALITY, AND SHE'S SCARY.
HUH? YOU MEAN SHE'S SCARIER THAN YUKINO-SHITA?
YUKI-CHAN? SCARY?
AHHH HA HA HA HA!
THAT'S WHAT YOU THINK OF HER? SHE'S SUCH A CUTE GIRL!
GEEZ, THAT'S RUDE, HIKIGAYA-KUN.
Our mother is even scarier than me.
HISO (WHISPER)
...IS SHE EVEN HUMAN?

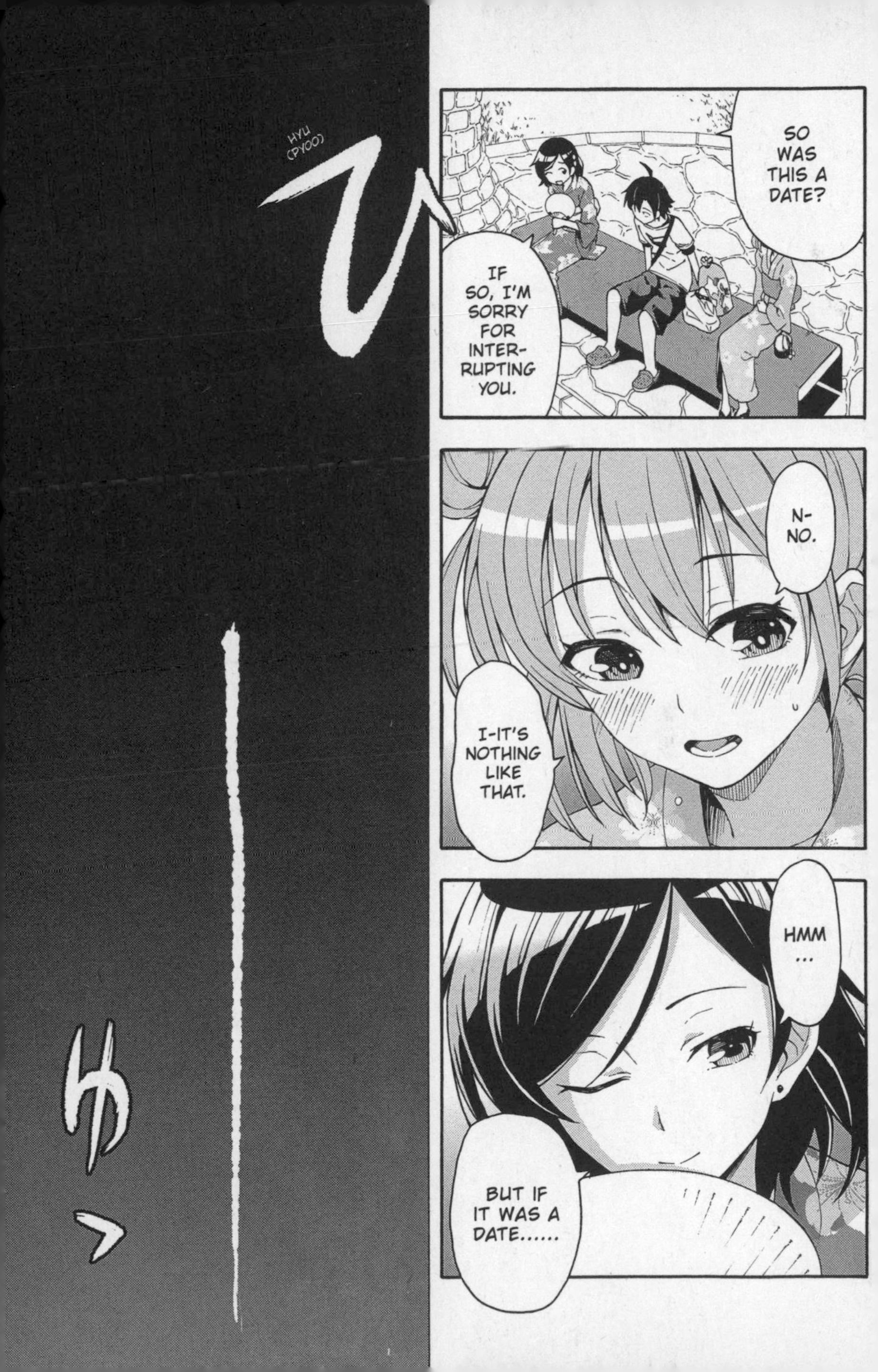
SO WAS THIS A DATE?
IF SO, I'M SORRY FOR INTER-RUPTING YOU.
N-NO.
I-IT'S NOTHING LIKE THAT.
HMM...
BUT IF IT WAS A DATE......
HYU (PYOO)

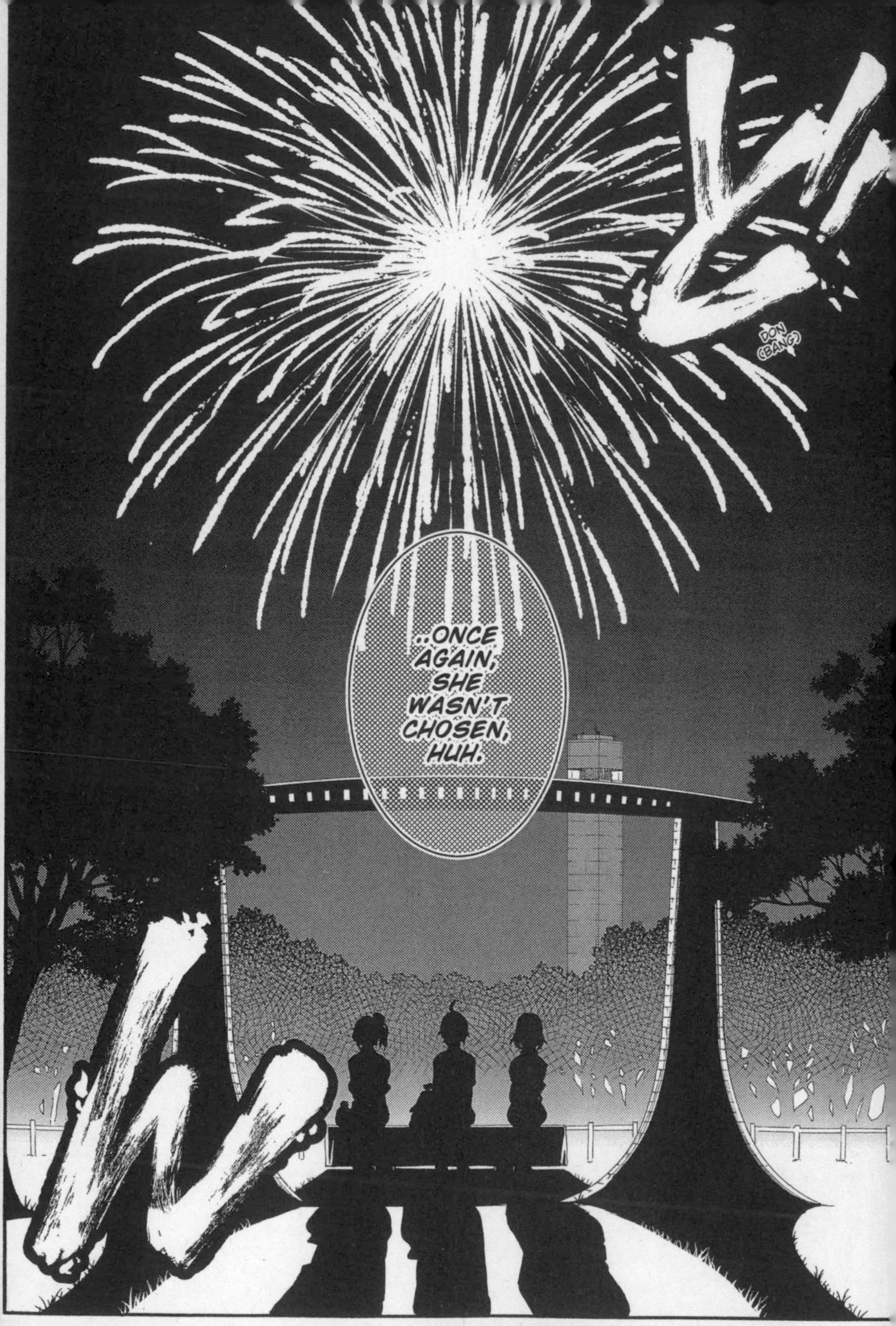
DON (BANG)
..ONCE AGAIN, SHE WASN'T CHOSEN, HUH.

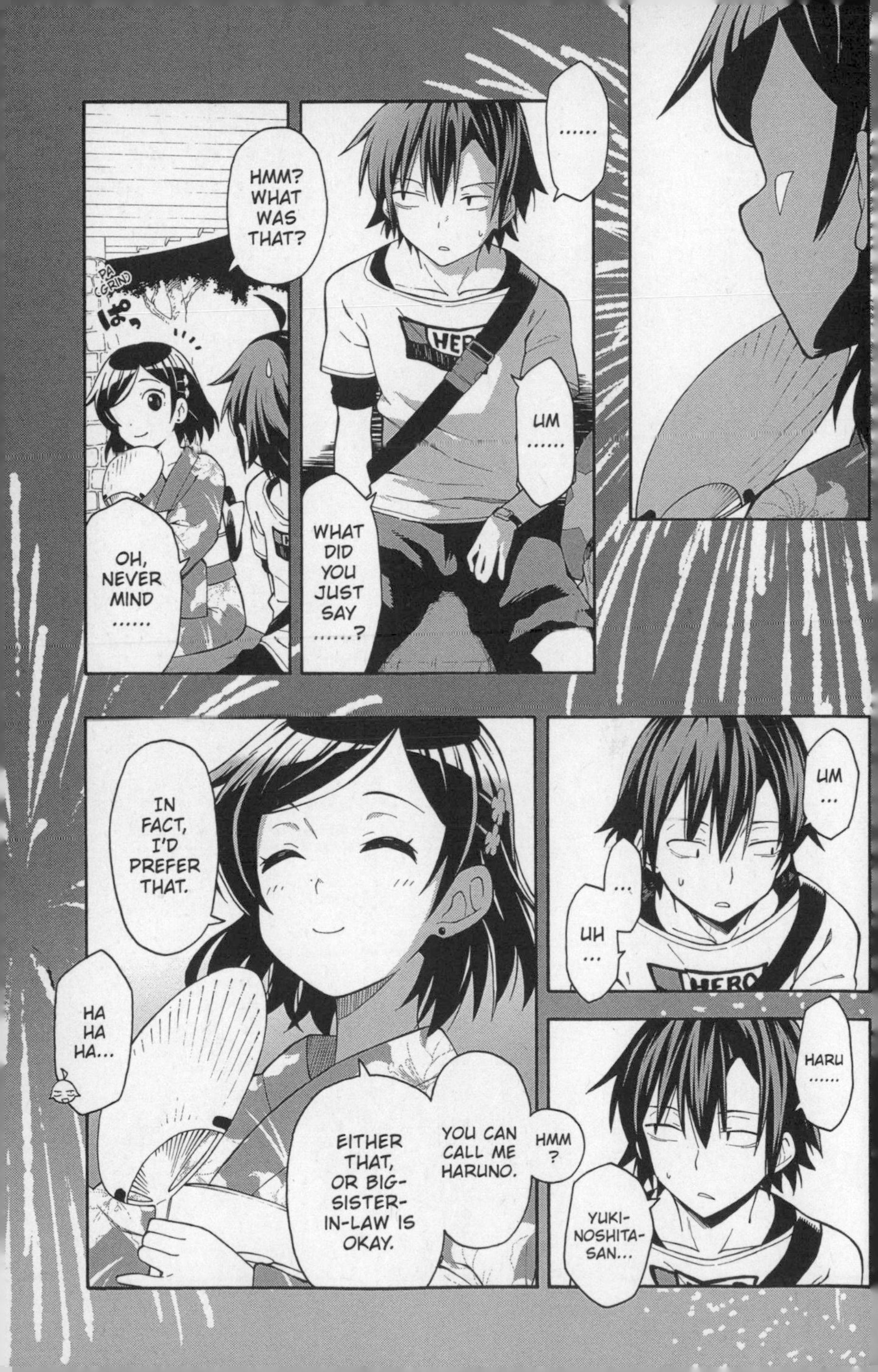
......
UM ......
WHAT DID YOU JUST SAY ......?
HMM? WHAT WAS THAT?
PA (GRIN)
ぱっ
OH, NEVER MIND ......
UM ...
... UH ...
HARU ......
YUKI-NOSHITA-SAN...
HMM ?
YOU CAN CALL ME HARUNO.
EITHER THAT, OR BIG-SISTER-IN-LAW IS OKAY.
IN FACT, I'D PREFER THAT.
HA HA HA...

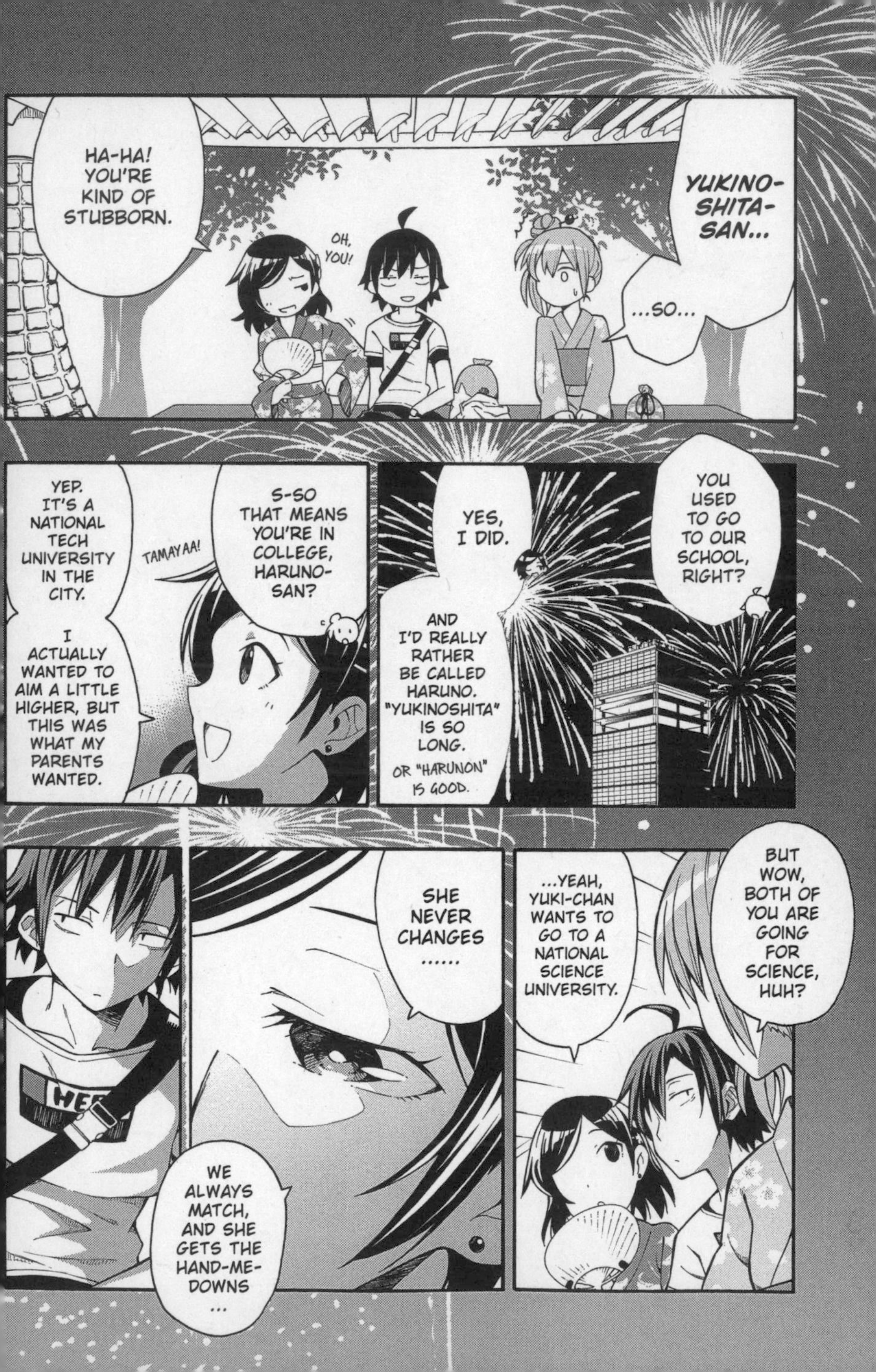
YUKINO-SHITA-SAN...
...SO...
HA-HA! YOU'RE KIND OF STUBBORN.
OH, YOU!
YOU USED TO GO TO OUR SCHOOL, RIGHT?
YES, I DID.
AND I'D REALLY RATHER BE CALLED HARUNO. "YUKINOSHITA" IS SO LONG.
OR "HARUNON" IS GOOD.
S-SO THAT MEANS YOU'RE IN COLLEGE, HARUNO-SAN?
TAMAYAA!
YEP. IT'S A NATIONAL TECH UNIVERSITY IN THE CITY.
I ACTUALLY WANTED TO AIM A LITTLE HIGHER, BUT THIS WAS WHAT MY PARENTS WANTED.
BUT WOW, BOTH OF YOU ARE GOING FOR SCIENCE, HUH?
...YEAH, YUKI-CHAN WANTS TO GO TO A NATIONAL SCIENCE UNIVERSITY.
SHE NEVER CHANGES ......
WE ALWAYS MATCH, AND SHE GETS THE HAND-ME-DOWNS ...

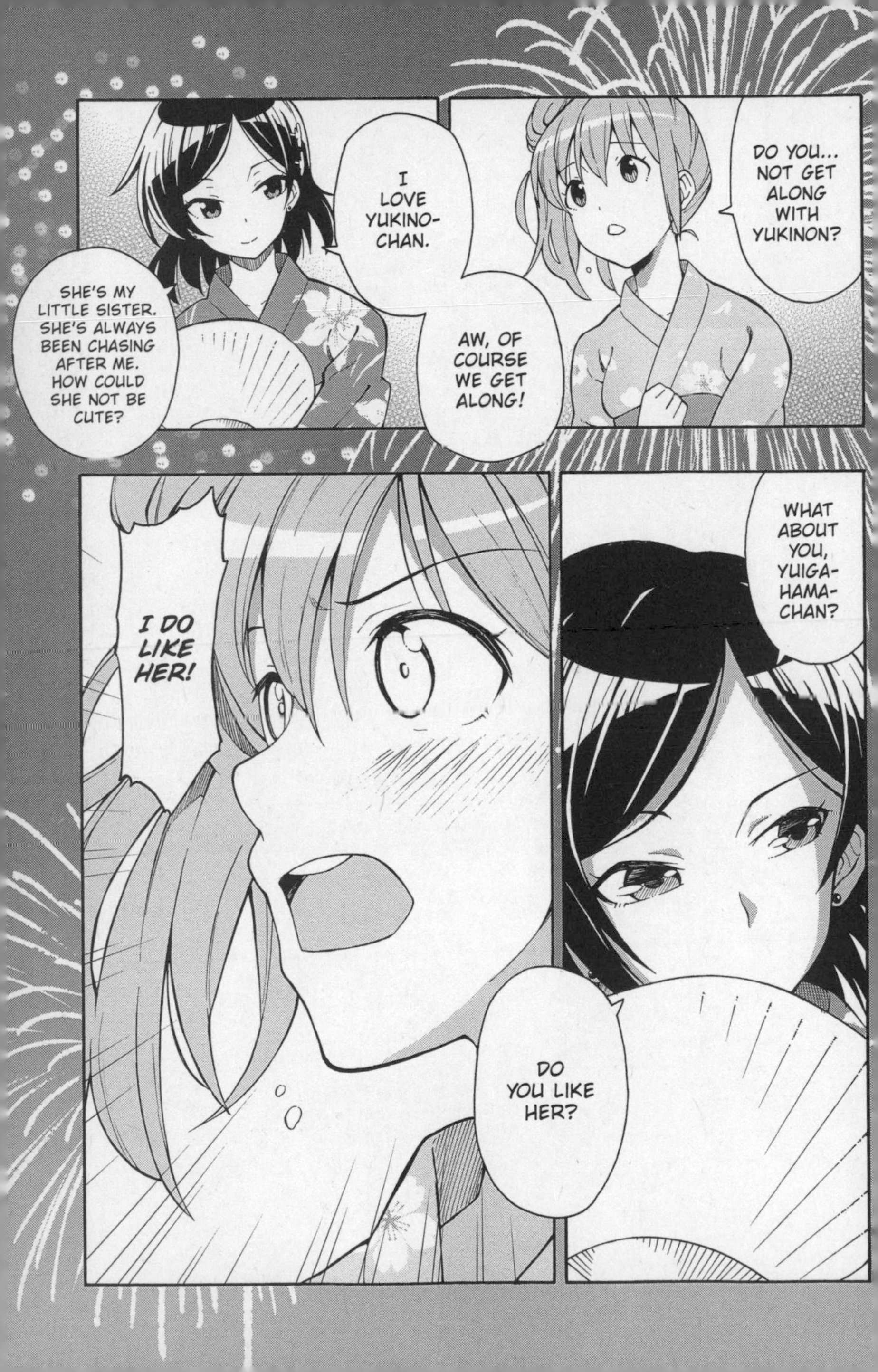
DO YOU... NOT GET ALONG WITH YUKINON?
AW, OF COURSE WE GET ALONG!
I LOVE YUKINO-CHAN.
SHE'S MY LITTLE SISTER. SHE'S ALWAYS BEEN CHASING AFTER ME. HOW COULD SHE NOT BE CUTE?
WHAT ABOUT YOU, YUIGA-HAMA-CHAN?
DO YOU LIKE HER?
I DO LIKE HER!

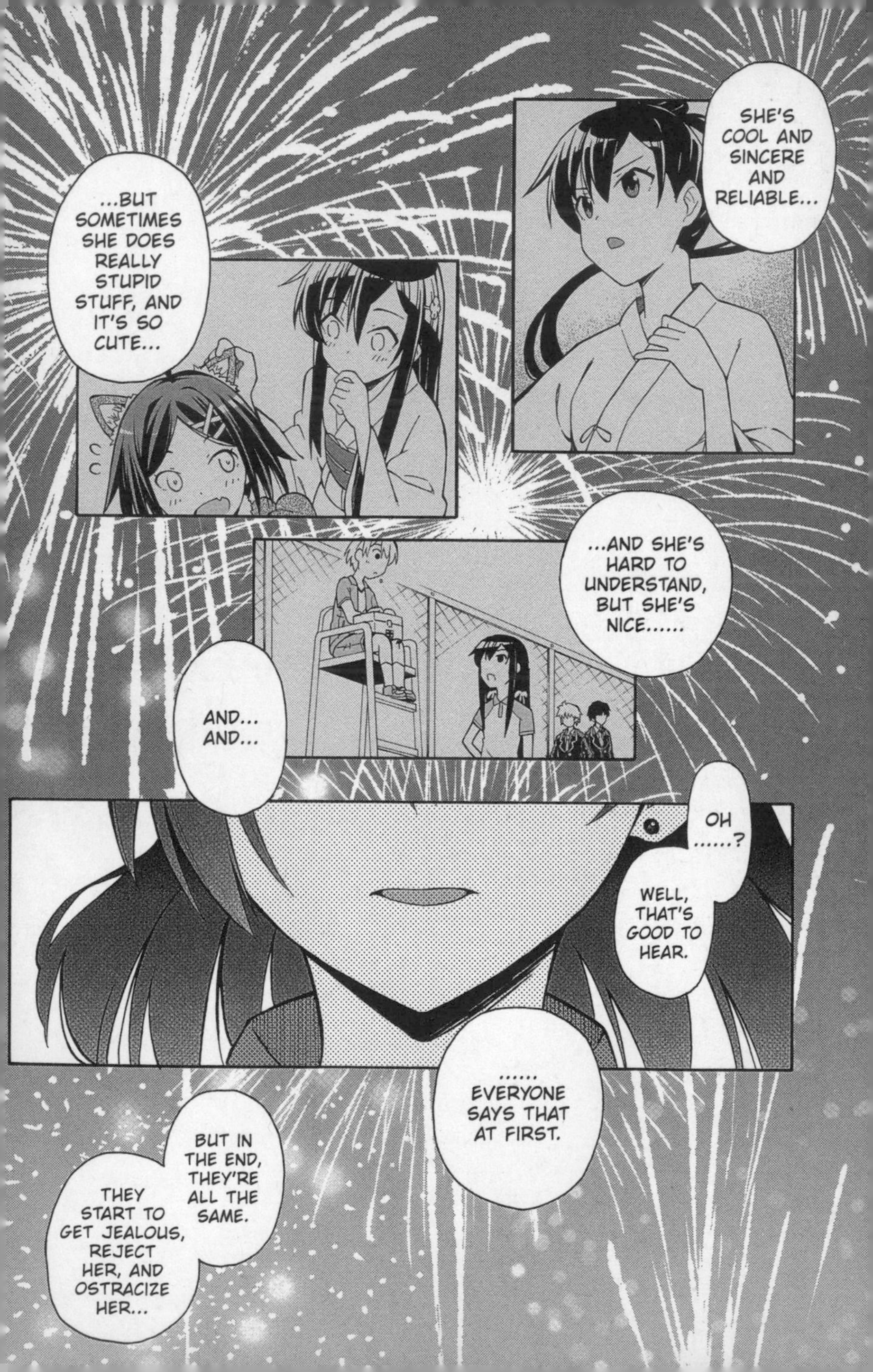
SHE'S COOL AND SINCERE AND RELIABLE...
...BUT SOMETIMES SHE DOES REALLY STUPID STUFF, AND IT'S SO CUTE...
...AND SHE'S HARD TO UNDERSTAND, BUT SHE'S NICE......
AND... AND...
OH ......?
WELL, THAT'S GOOD TO HEAR.
...... EVERYONE SAYS THAT AT FIRST.
BUT IN THE END, THEY'RE ALL THE SAME.
THEY START TO GET JEALOUS, REJECT HER, AND OSTRACIZE HER...

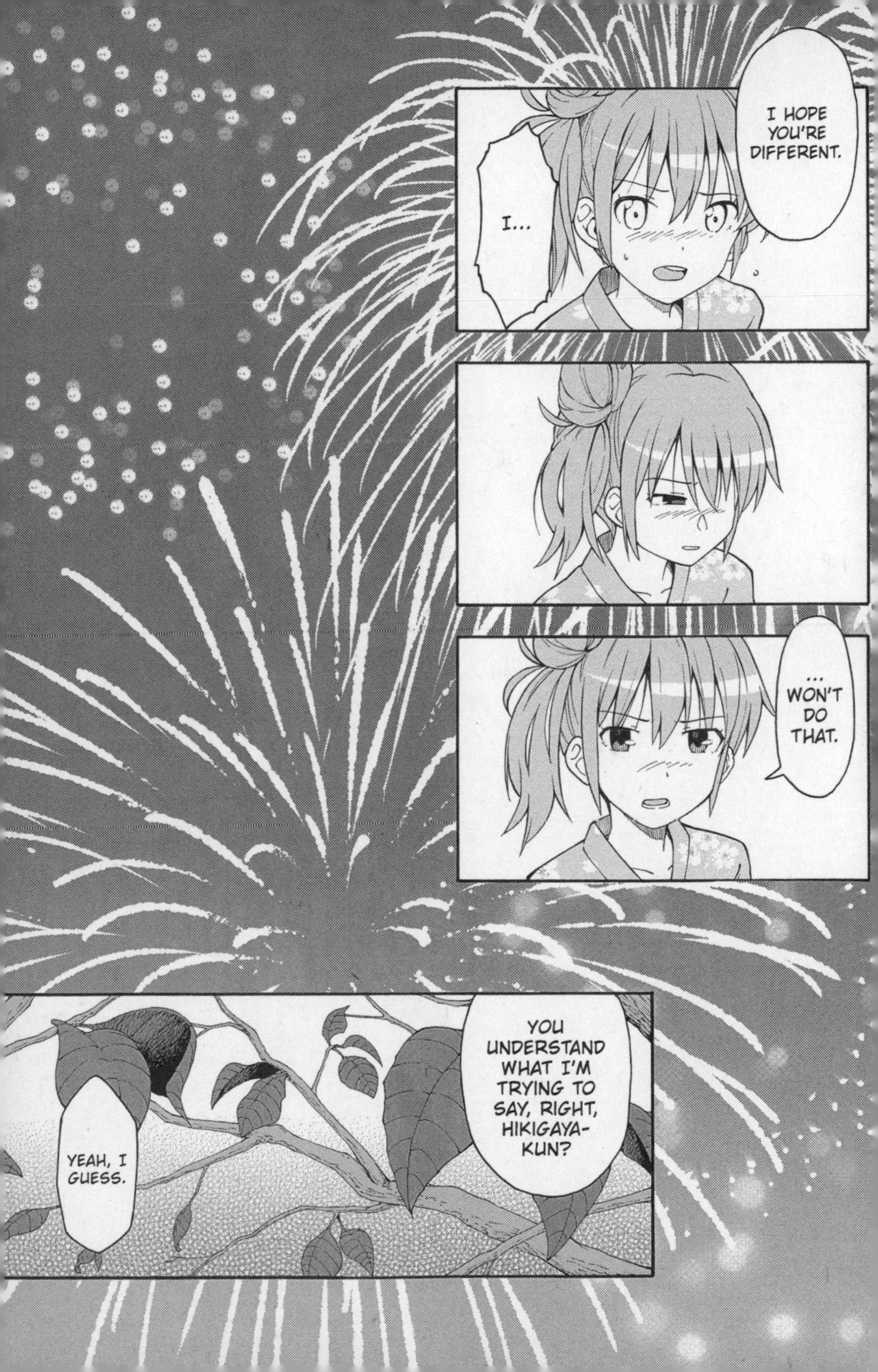
I HOPE YOU'RE DIFFERENT.
I...
... WON'T DO THAT.
YOU UNDERSTAND WHAT I'M TRYING TO SAY, RIGHT, HIKIGAYA-KUN?
YEAH, I GUESS.

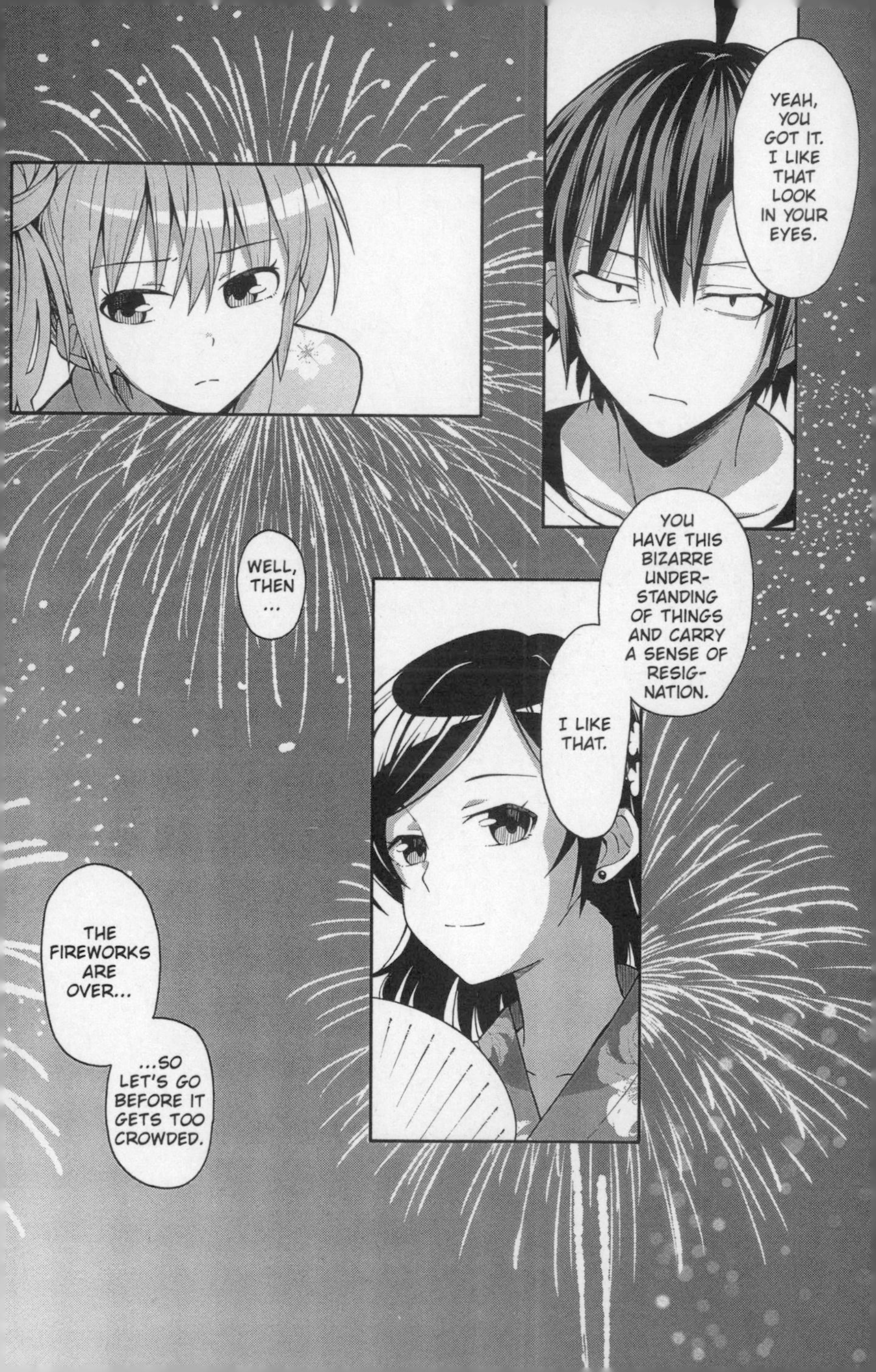
YEAH, YOU GOT IT. I LIKE THAT LOOK IN YOUR EYES.
YOU HAVE THIS BIZARRE UNDER-STANDING OF THINGS AND CARRY A SENSE OF RESIG-NATION.
I LIKE THAT.
WELL, THEN ...
THE FIREWORKS ARE OVER...
...SO LET'S GO BEFORE IT GETS TOO CROWDED.

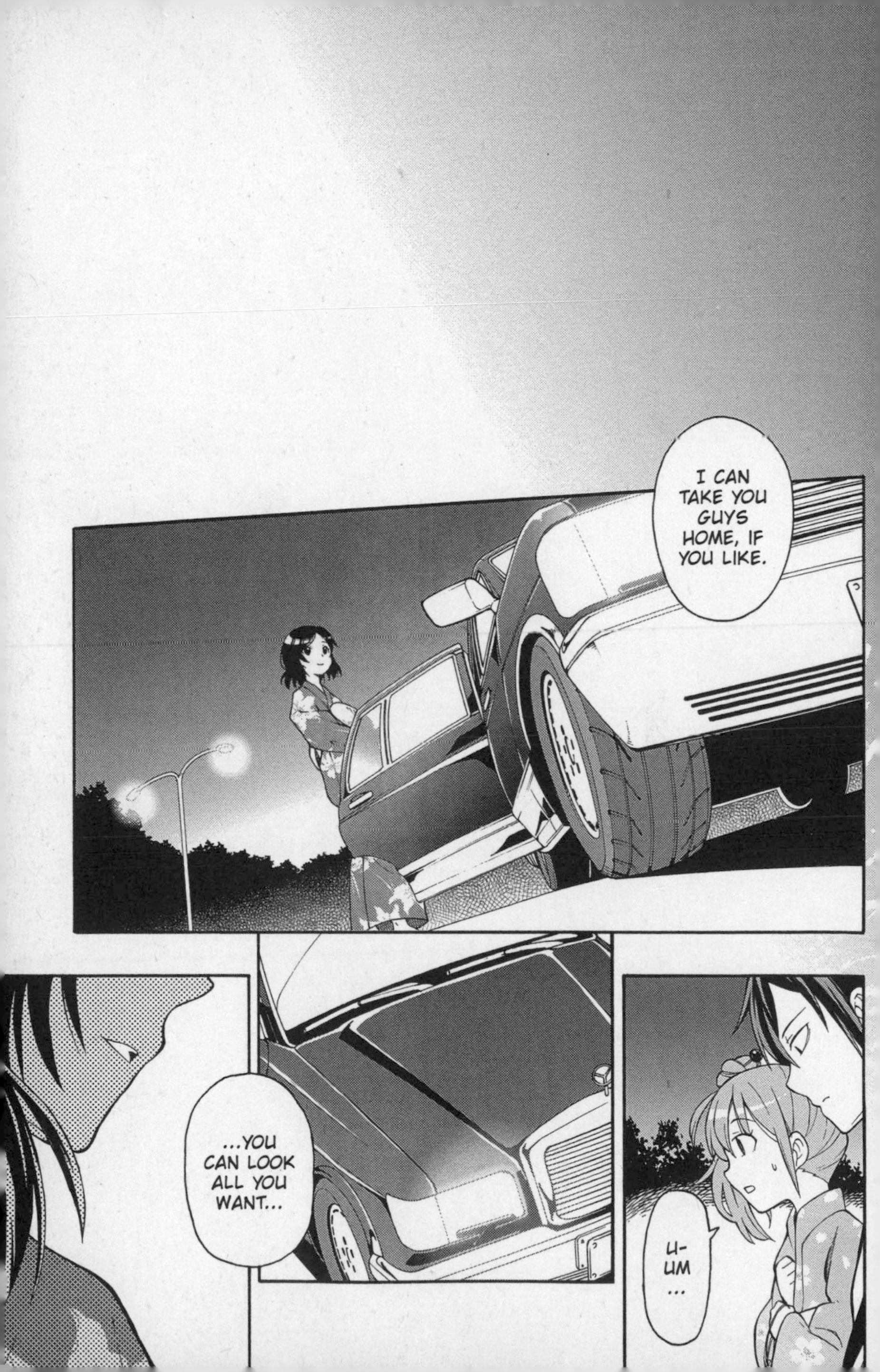
I CAN TAKE YOU GUYS HOME, IF YOU LIKE.
U-UM ...
...YOU CAN LOOK ALL YOU WANT...

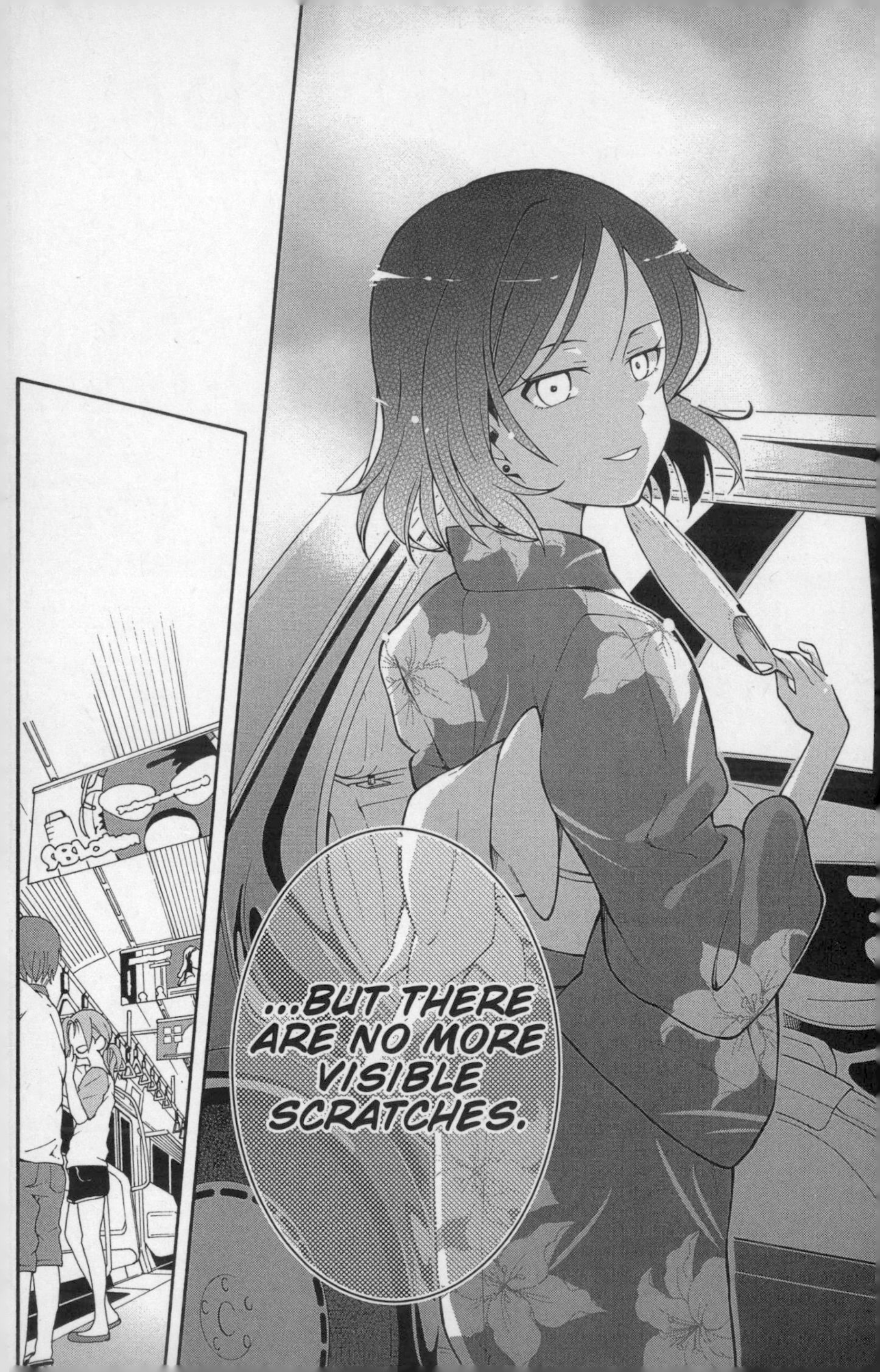
...BUT THERE ARE NO MORE VISIBLE SCRATCHES.

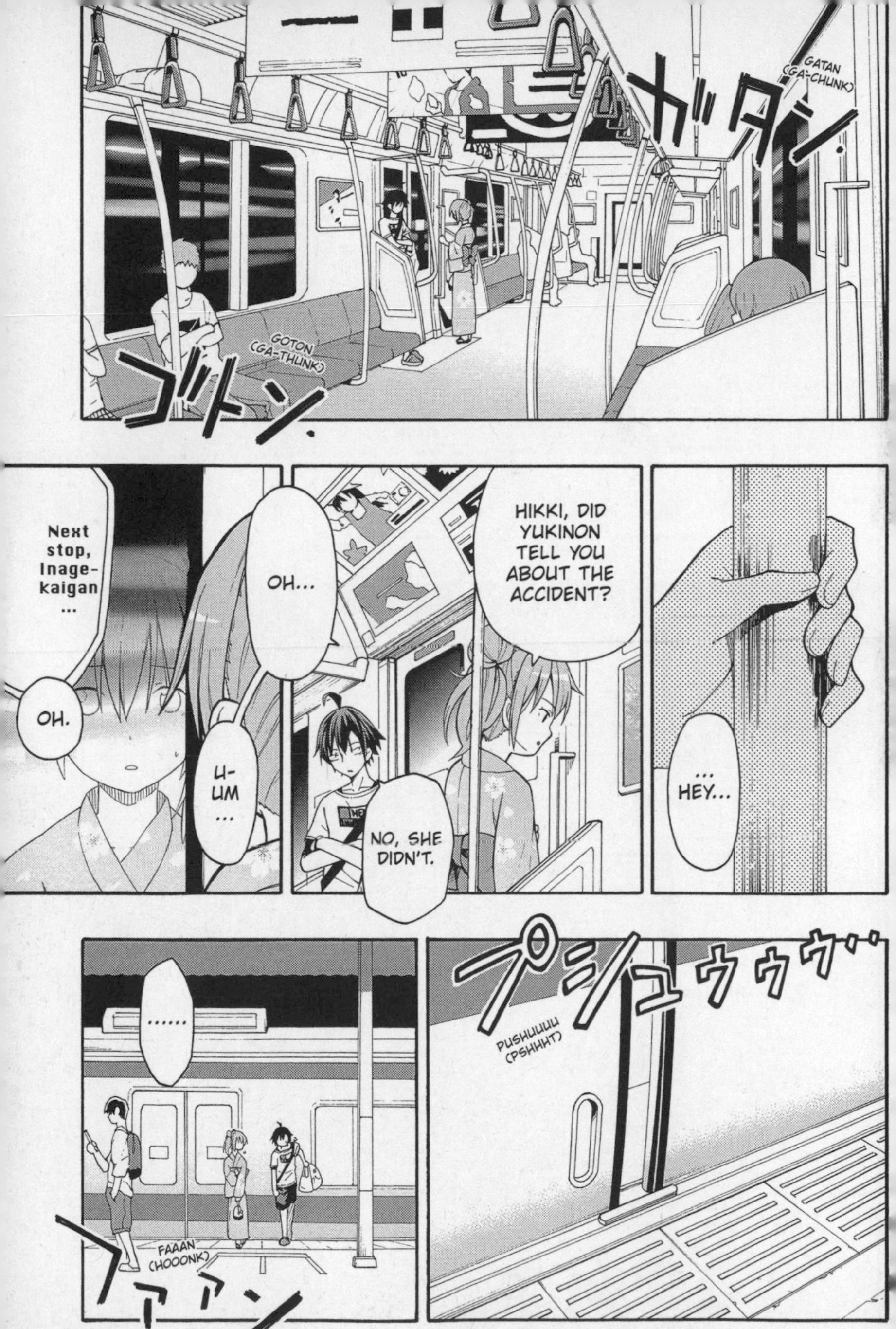
GATAN (GA-CHUNK)
GOTON (GA-CHUNK)
... HEY...
HIKKI, DID YUKINON TELL YOU ABOUT THE ACCIDENT?
NO, SHE DIDN'T.
U-UM...
OH...
Next stop, Inage-kaigan...
OH.
PUSHUUUU (PSHHHT)
......
FAAAN (HOOONK)

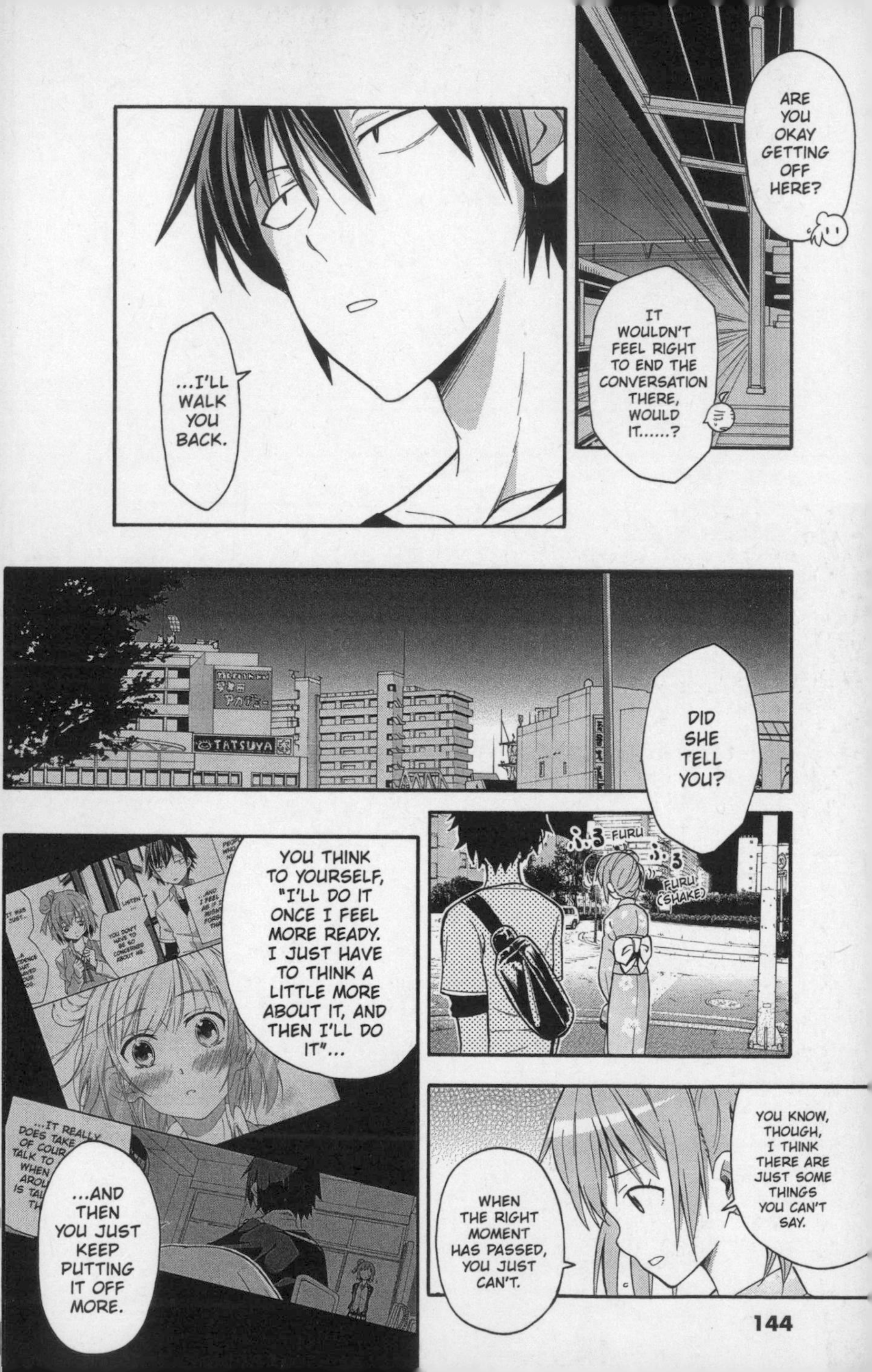
ARE YOU OKAY GETTING OFF HERE?
IT WOULDN'T FEEL RIGHT TO END THE CONVERSATION THERE, WOULD IT......?
...I'LL WALK YOU BACK.
TATSUYA
DID SHE TELL YOU?
FURU FURU (SHAKE)
YOU KNOW, THOUGH, I THINK THERE ARE JUST SOME THINGS YOU CAN'T SAY.
WHEN THE RIGHT MOMENT HAS PASSED, YOU JUST CAN'T.
YOU THINK TO YOURSELF, "I'LL DO IT ONCE I FEEL MORE READY. I JUST HAVE TO THINK A LITTLE MORE ABOUT IT, AND THEN I'LL DO IT"...
...AND THEN YOU JUST KEEP PUTTING IT OFF MORE.

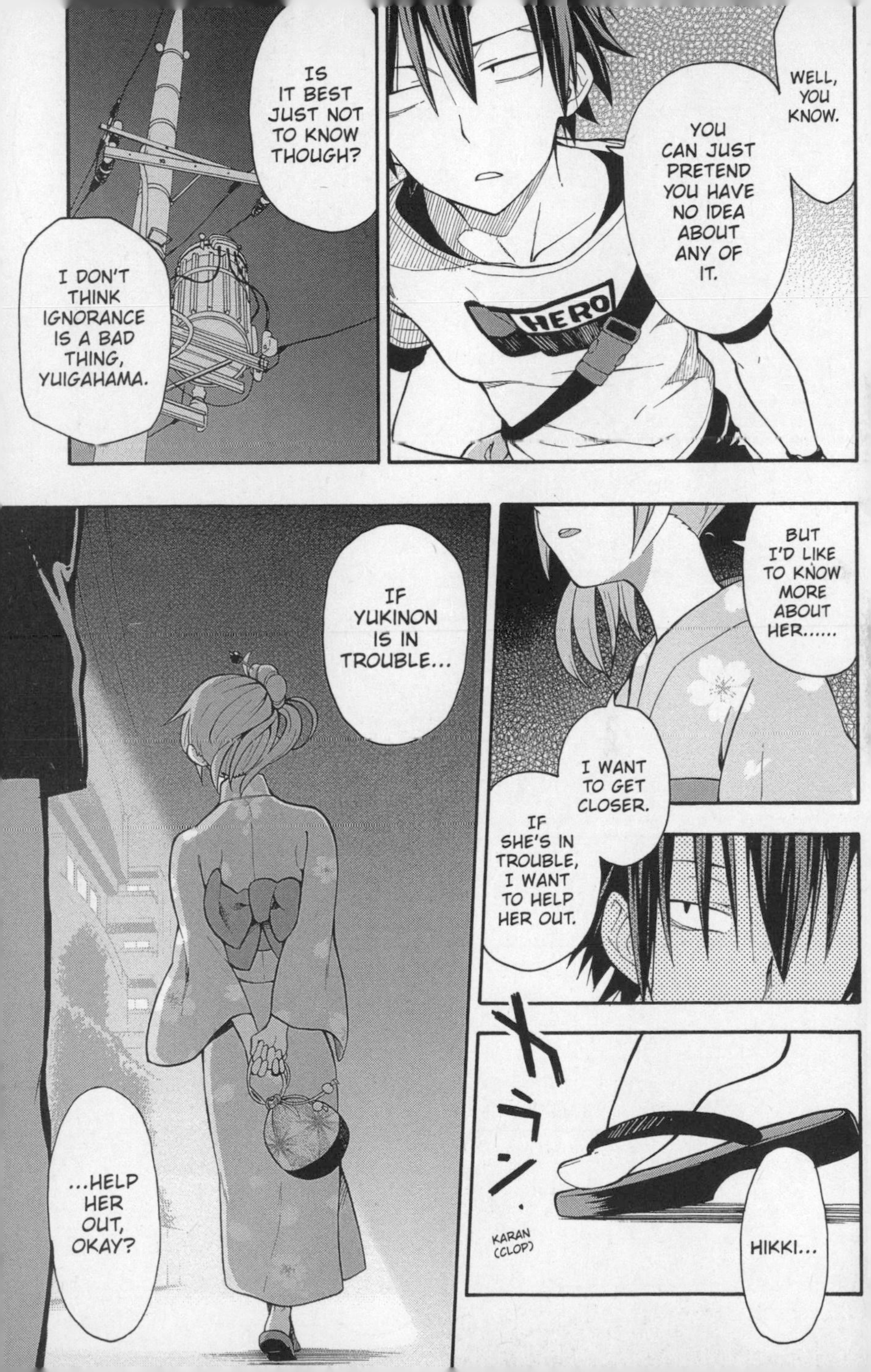
WELL, YOU KNOW.
YOU CAN JUST PRETEND YOU HAVE NO IDEA ABOUT ANY OF IT.
HERO
IS IT BEST JUST NOT TO KNOW THOUGH?
I DON'T THINK IGNORANCE IS A BAD THING, YUIGAHAMA.
BUT I'D LIKE TO KNOW MORE ABOUT HER......
I WANT TO GET CLOSER.
IF SHE'S IN TROUBLE, I WANT TO HELP HER OUT.
HIKKI...
KARAN (CLOP)
IF YUKINON IS IN TROUBLE...
...HELP HER OUT, OKAY?

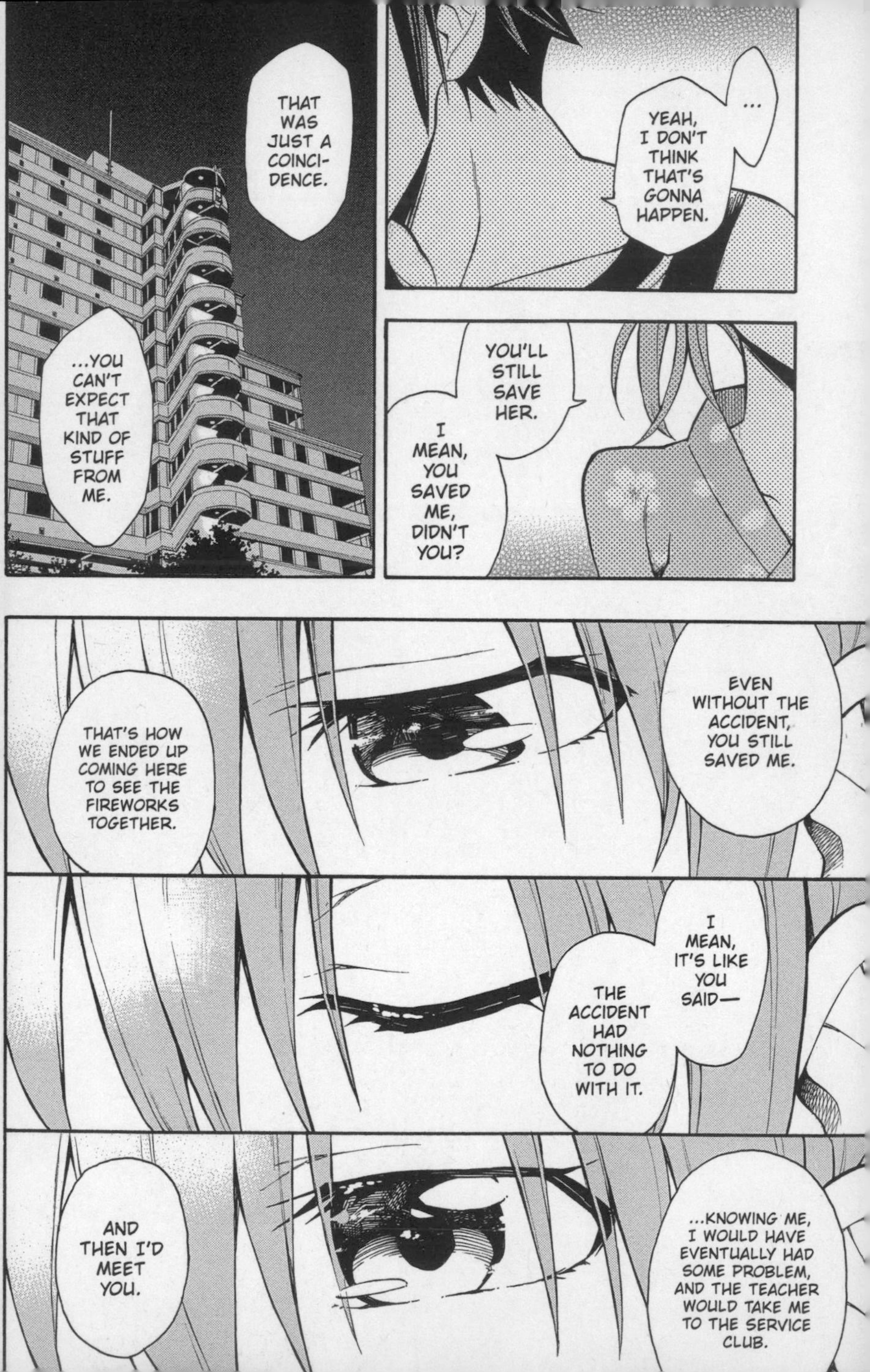
...
YEAH, I DON'T THINK THAT'S GONNA HAPPEN.
YOU'LL STILL SAVE HER.
I MEAN, YOU SAVED ME, DIDN'T YOU?
THAT WAS JUST A COINCIDENCE.
...YOU CAN'T EXPECT THAT KIND OF STUFF FROM ME.
EVEN WITHOUT THE ACCIDENT, YOU STILL SAVED ME.
THAT'S HOW WE ENDED UP COMING HERE TO SEE THE FIREWORKS TOGETHER.
I MEAN, IT'S LIKE YOU SAID—
THE ACCIDENT HAD NOTHING TO DO WITH IT.
...KNOWING ME, I WOULD HAVE EVENTUALLY HAD SOME PROBLEM, AND THE TEACHER WOULD TAKE ME TO THE SERVICE CLUB.
AND THEN I'D MEET YOU.

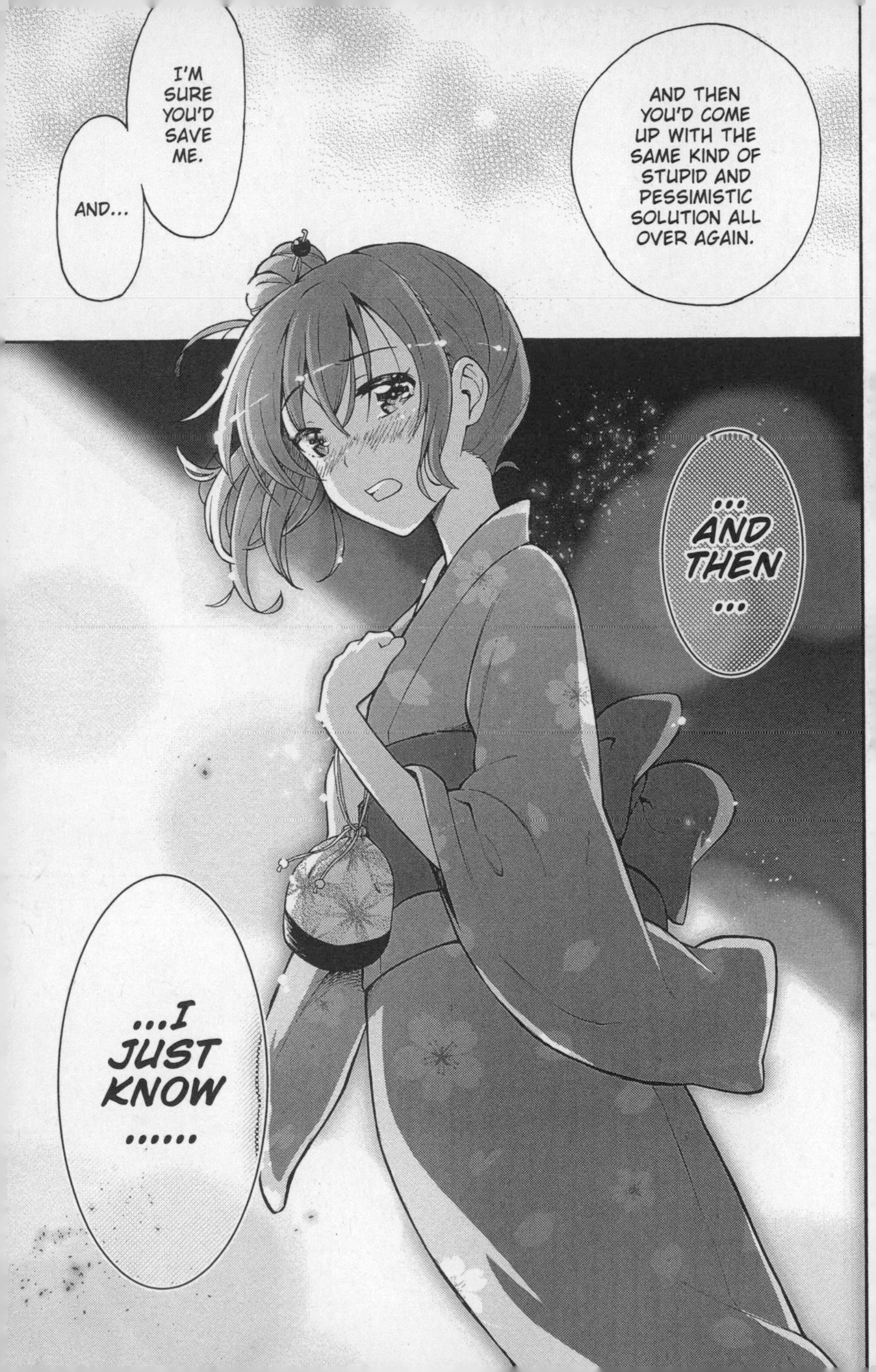
AND THEN YOU'D COME UP WITH THE SAME KIND OF STUPID AND PESSIMISTIC SOLUTION ALL OVER AGAIN.
I'M SURE YOU'D SAVE ME.
AND...
...AND THEN...
...I JUST KNOW......

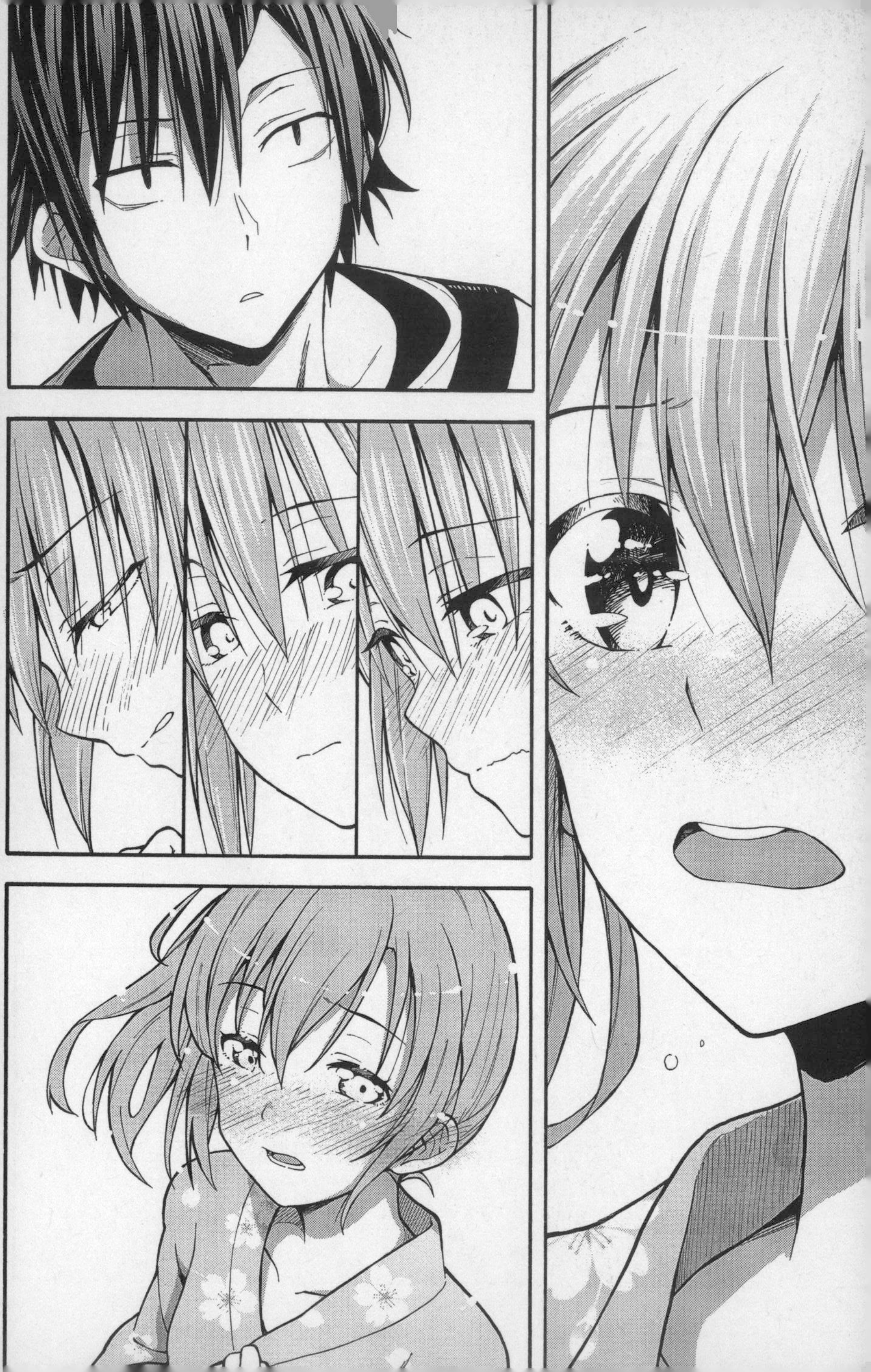

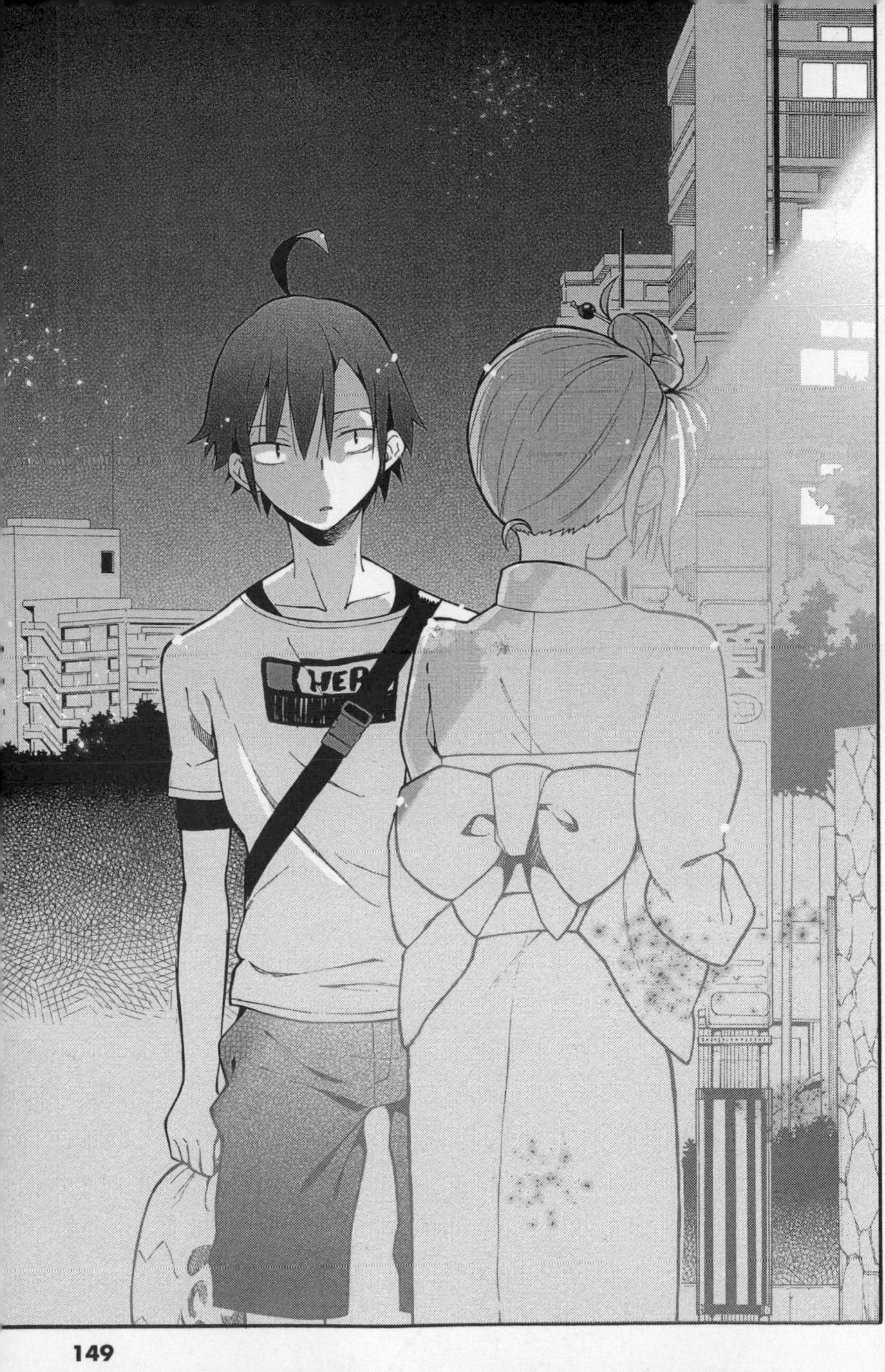
HER

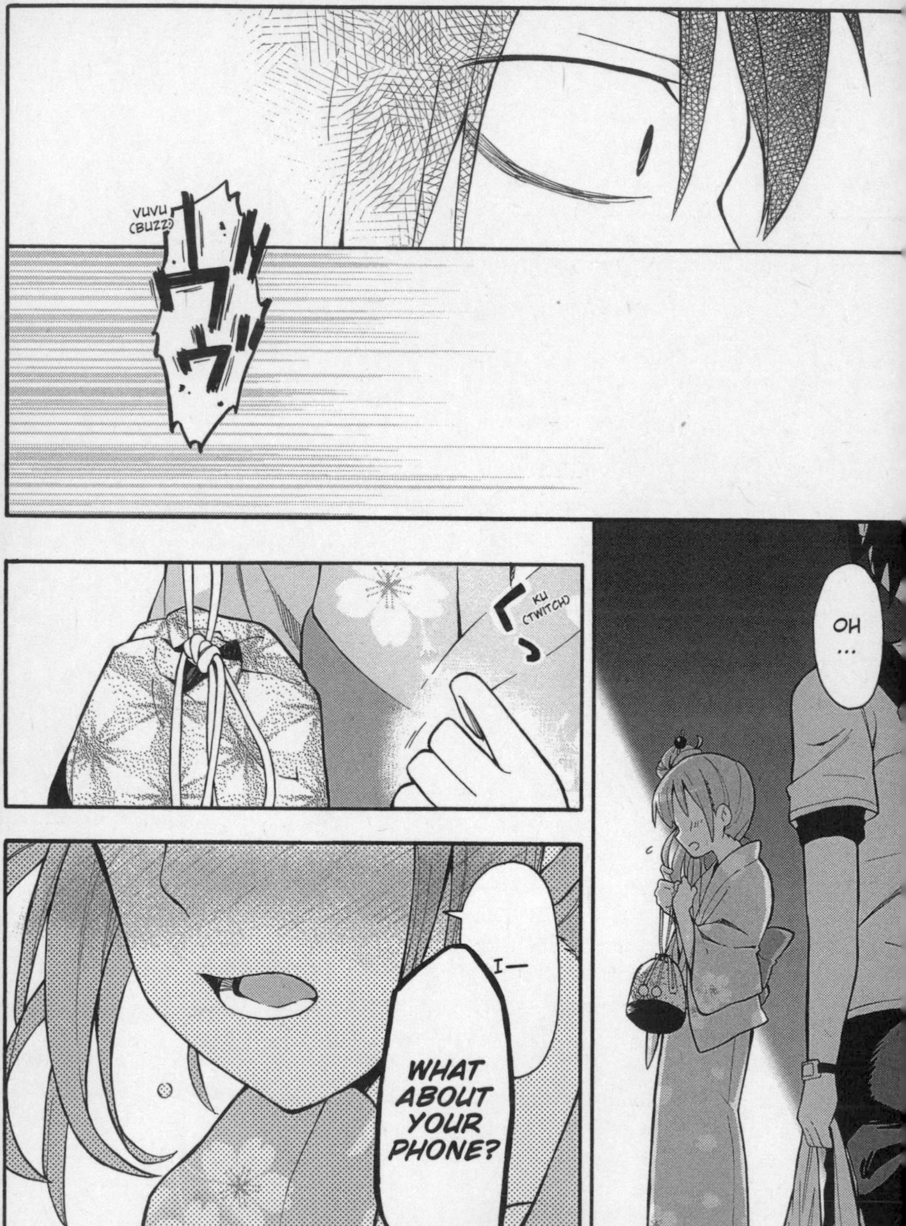
VUVU (BUZZ)
OH ...
KU (TWITCH)
I—
WHAT ABOUT YOUR PHONE?

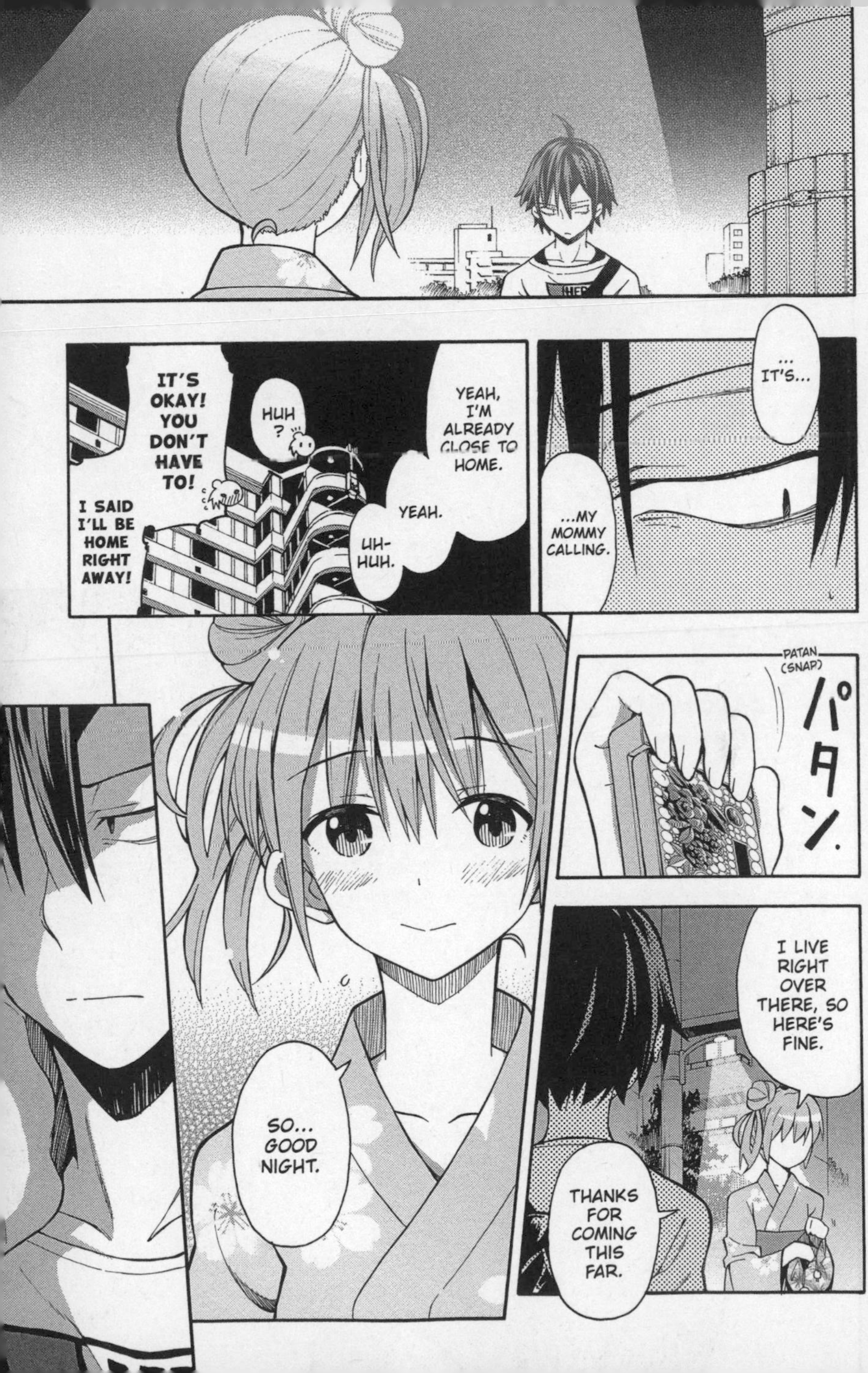

... IT'S...
...MY MOMMY CALLING.
YEAH, I'M ALREADY CLOSE TO HOME.
YEAH.
UH-HUH.
HUH?
IT'S OKAY! YOU DON'T HAVE TO!
I SAID I'LL BE HOME RIGHT AWAY!
PATAN (SNAP)
パタン.
I LIVE RIGHT OVER THERE, SO HERE'S FINE.
THANKS FOR COMING THIS FAR.
SO... GOOD NIGHT.

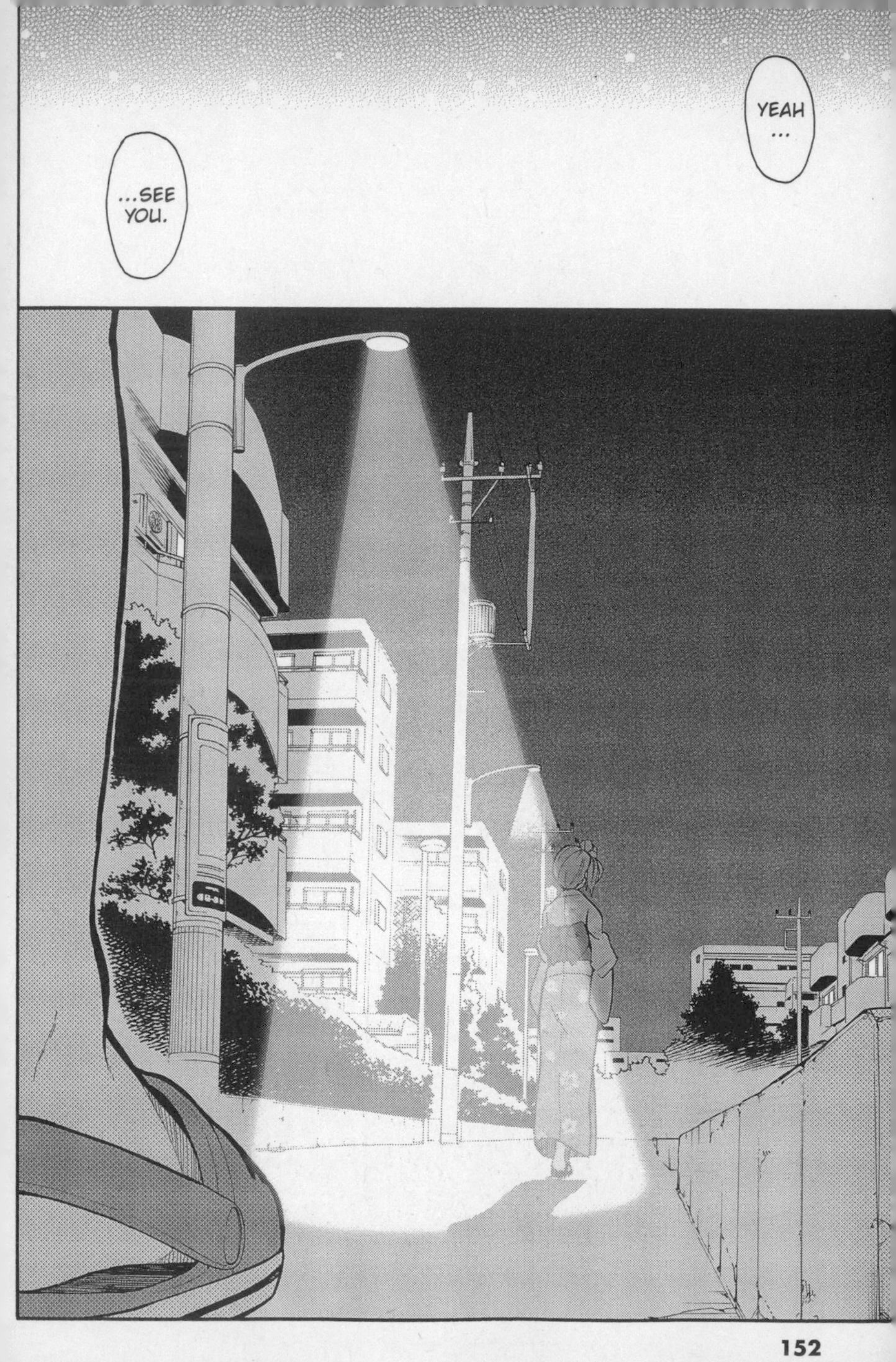
YEAH ...
...SEE YOU.

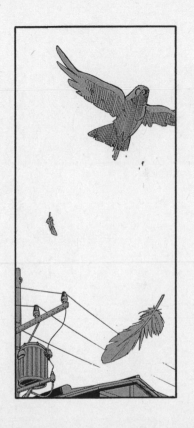

CHAPTER 35

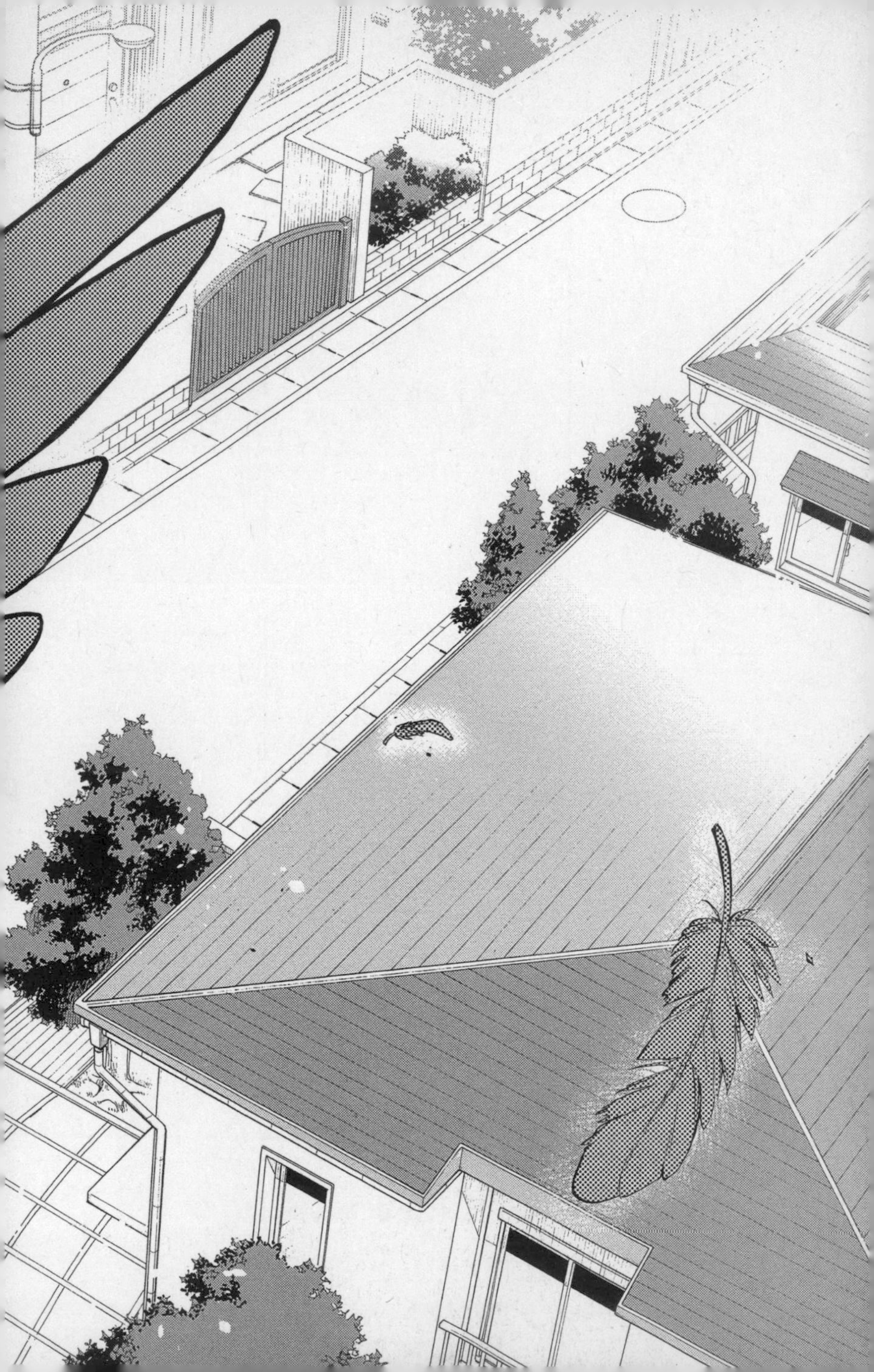

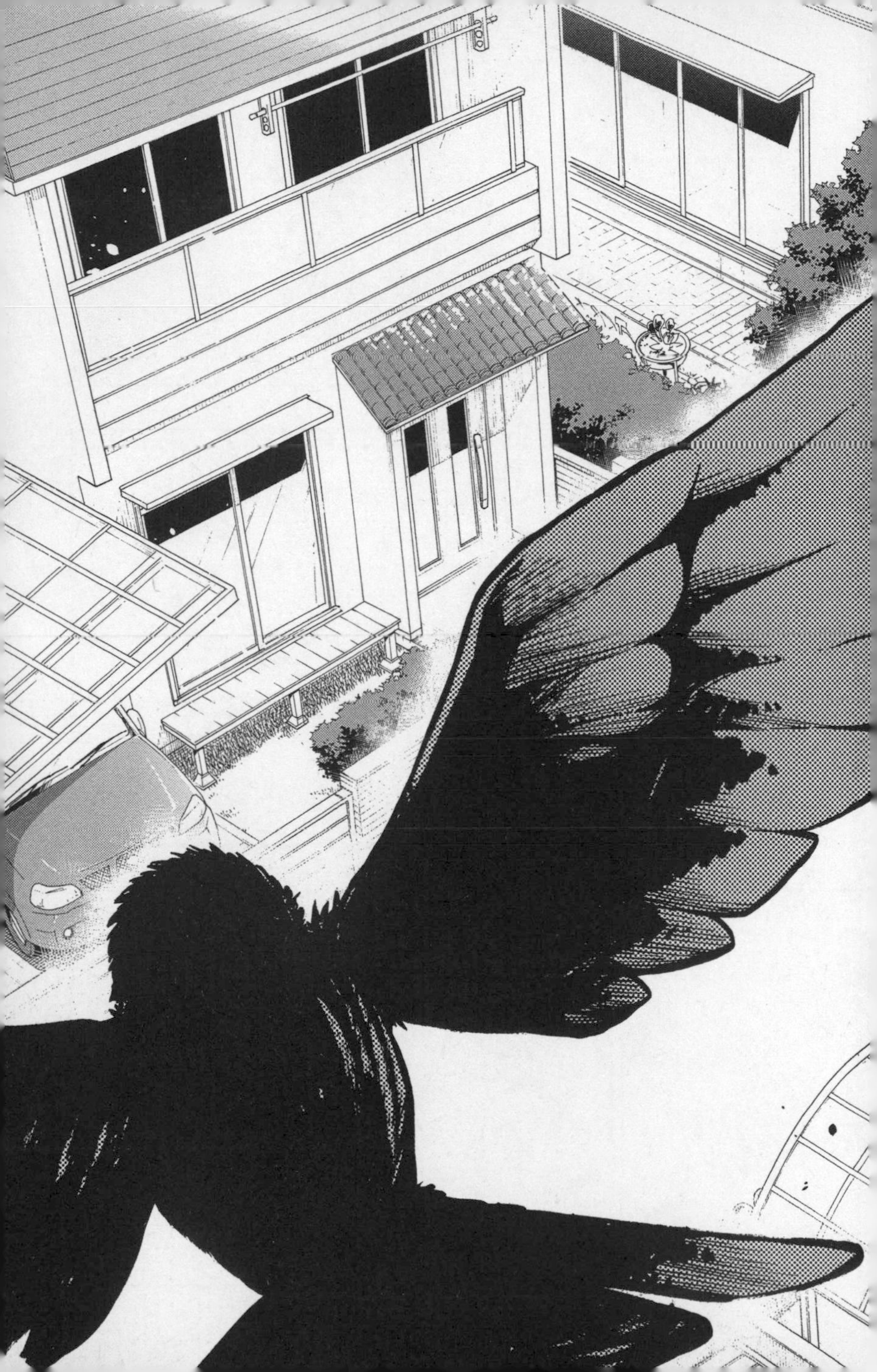

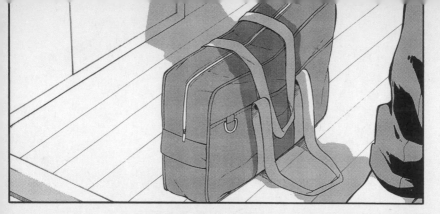

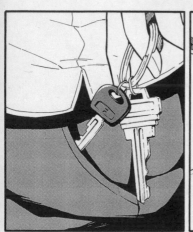

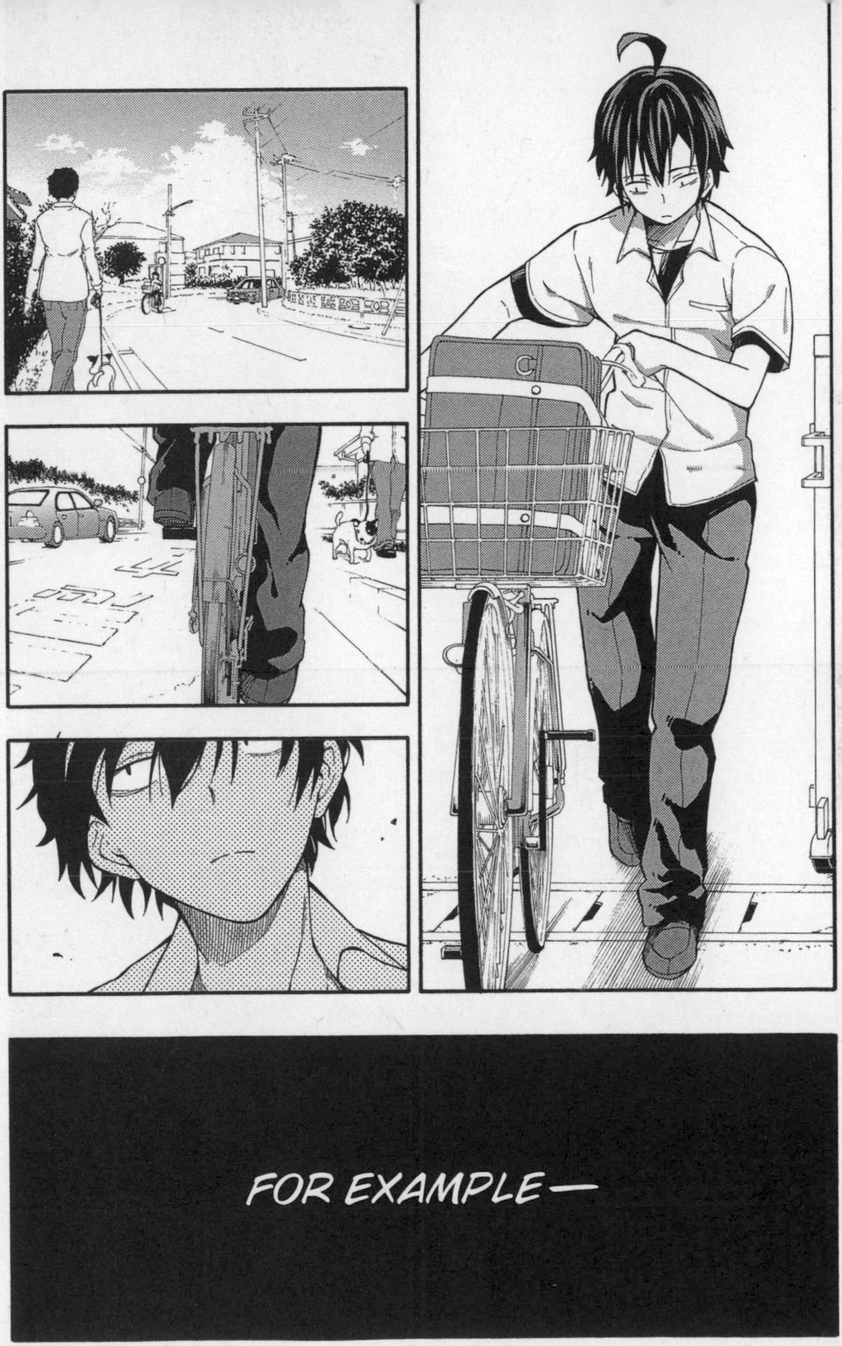
FOR EXAMPLE—

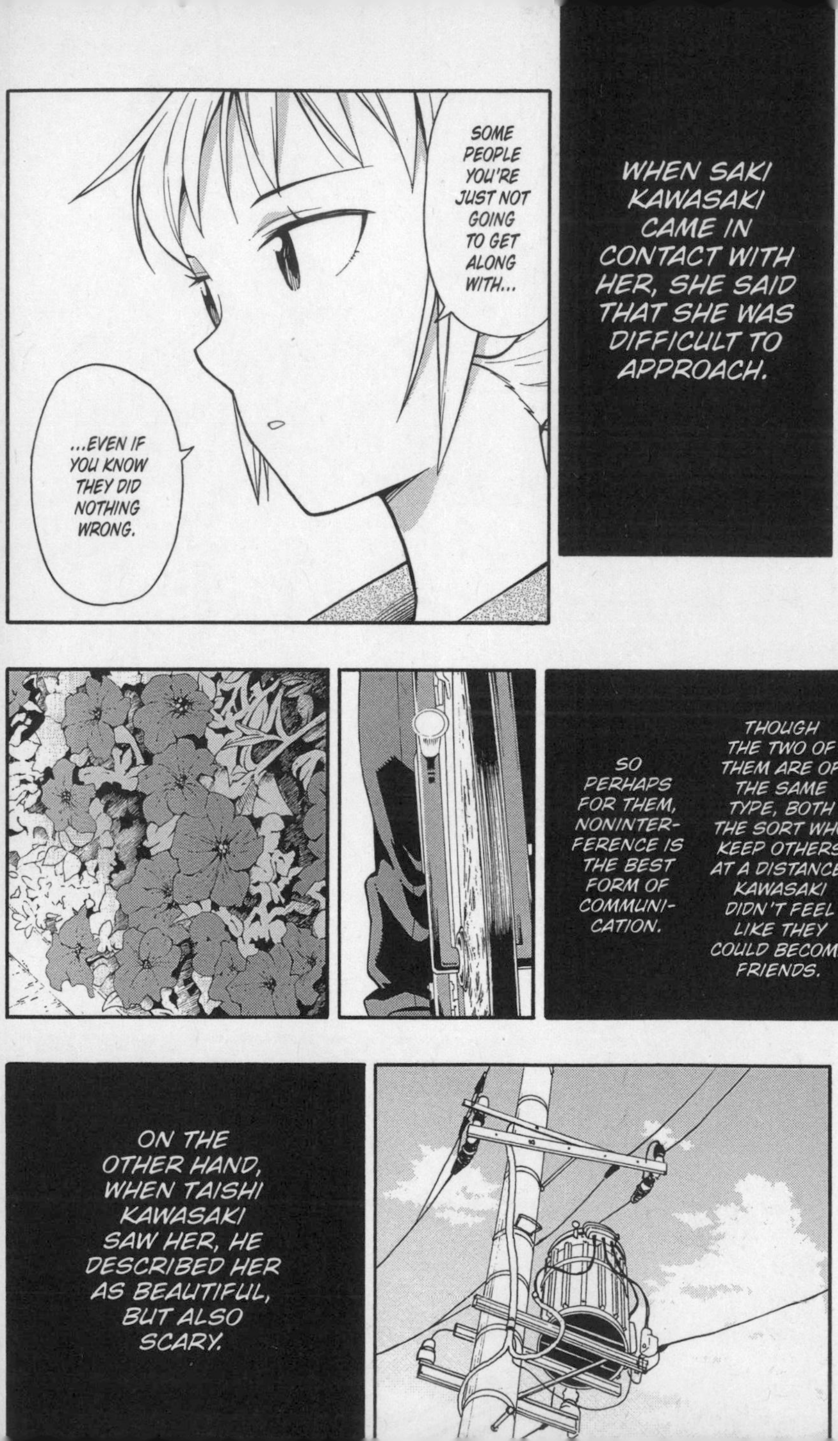
WHEN SAKI KAWASAKI CAME IN CONTACT WITH HER, SHE SAID THAT SHE WAS DIFFICULT TO APPROACH.
SOME PEOPLE YOU'RE JUST NOT GOING TO GET ALONG WITH...
...EVEN IF YOU KNOW THEY DID NOTHING WRONG.
THOUGH THE TWO OF THEM ARE OF THE SAME TYPE, BOTH THE SORT WHO KEEP OTHERS AT A DISTANCE, KAWASAKI DIDN'T FEEL LIKE THEY COULD BECOME FRIENDS.
SO PERHAPS FOR THEM, NONINTERFERENCE IS THE BEST FORM OF COMMUNICATION.
ON THE OTHER HAND, WHEN TAISHI KAWASAKI SAW HER, HE DESCRIBED HER AS BEAUTIFUL, BUT ALSO SCARY.

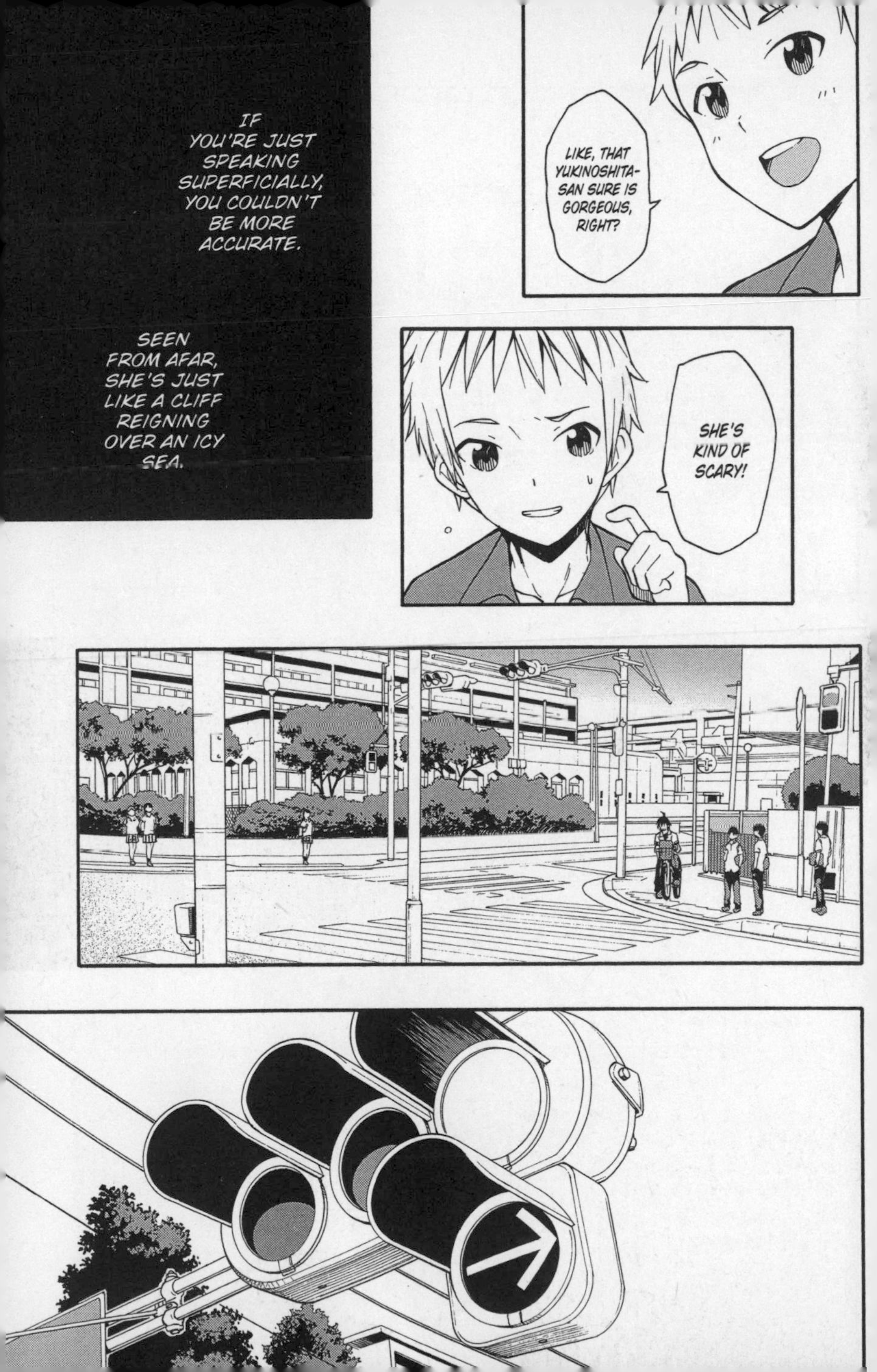
LIKE, THAT YUKINOSHITA-SAN SURE IS GORGEOUS, RIGHT?
SHE'S KIND OF SCARY!
IF YOU'RE JUST SPEAKING SUPERFICIALLY, YOU COULDN'T BE MORE ACCURATE.
SEEN FROM AFAR, SHE'S JUST LIKE A CLIFF REIGNING OVER AN ICY SEA.

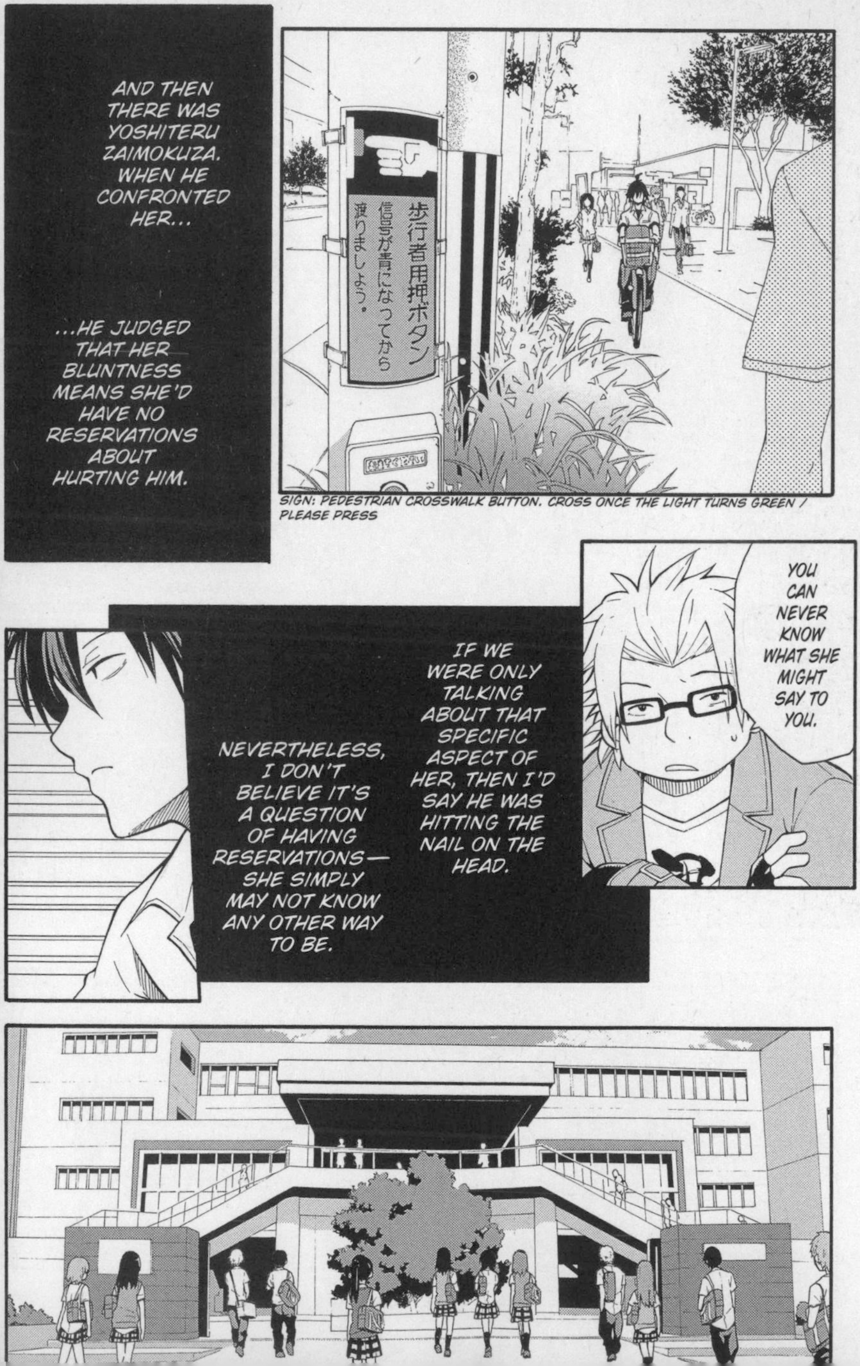
歩行者用押ボタン
信号が青になってから
渡りましょう。
SIGN: PEDESTRIAN CROSSWALK BUTTON. CROSS ONCE THE LIGHT TURNS GREEN / PLEASE PRESS
AND THEN THERE WAS YOSHITERU ZAIMOKUZA. WHEN HE CONFRONTED HER...
...HE JUDGED THAT HER BLUNTNESS MEANS SHE'D HAVE NO RESERVATIONS ABOUT HURTING HIM.
YOU CAN NEVER KNOW WHAT SHE MIGHT SAY TO YOU.
IF WE WERE ONLY TALKING ABOUT THAT SPECIFIC ASPECT OF HER, THEN I'D SAY HE WAS HITTING THE NAIL ON THE HEAD.
NEVERTHELESS, I DON'T BELIEVE IT'S A QUESTION OF HAVING RESERVATIONS—SHE SIMPLY MAY NOT KNOW ANY OTHER WAY TO BE.

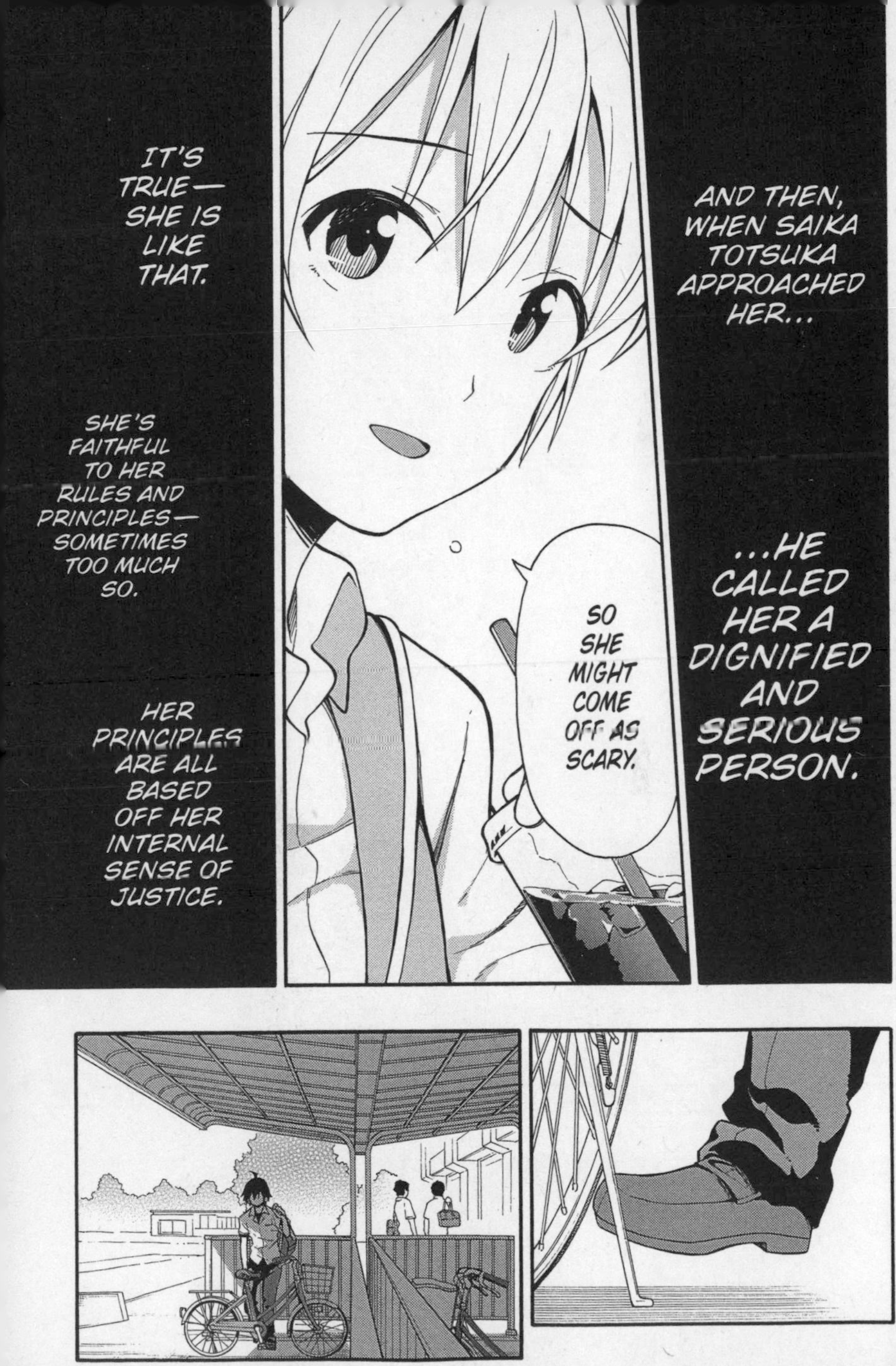
AND THEN, WHEN SAIKA TOTSUKA APPROACHED HER...
...HE CALLED HER A DIGNIFIED AND SERIOUS PERSON.
SO SHE MIGHT COME OFF AS SCARY.
IT'S TRUE—SHE IS LIKE THAT.
SHE'S FAITHFUL TO HER RULES AND PRINCIPLES—SOMETIMES TOO MUCH SO.
HER PRINCIPLES ARE ALL BASED OFF HER INTERNAL SENSE OF JUSTICE.

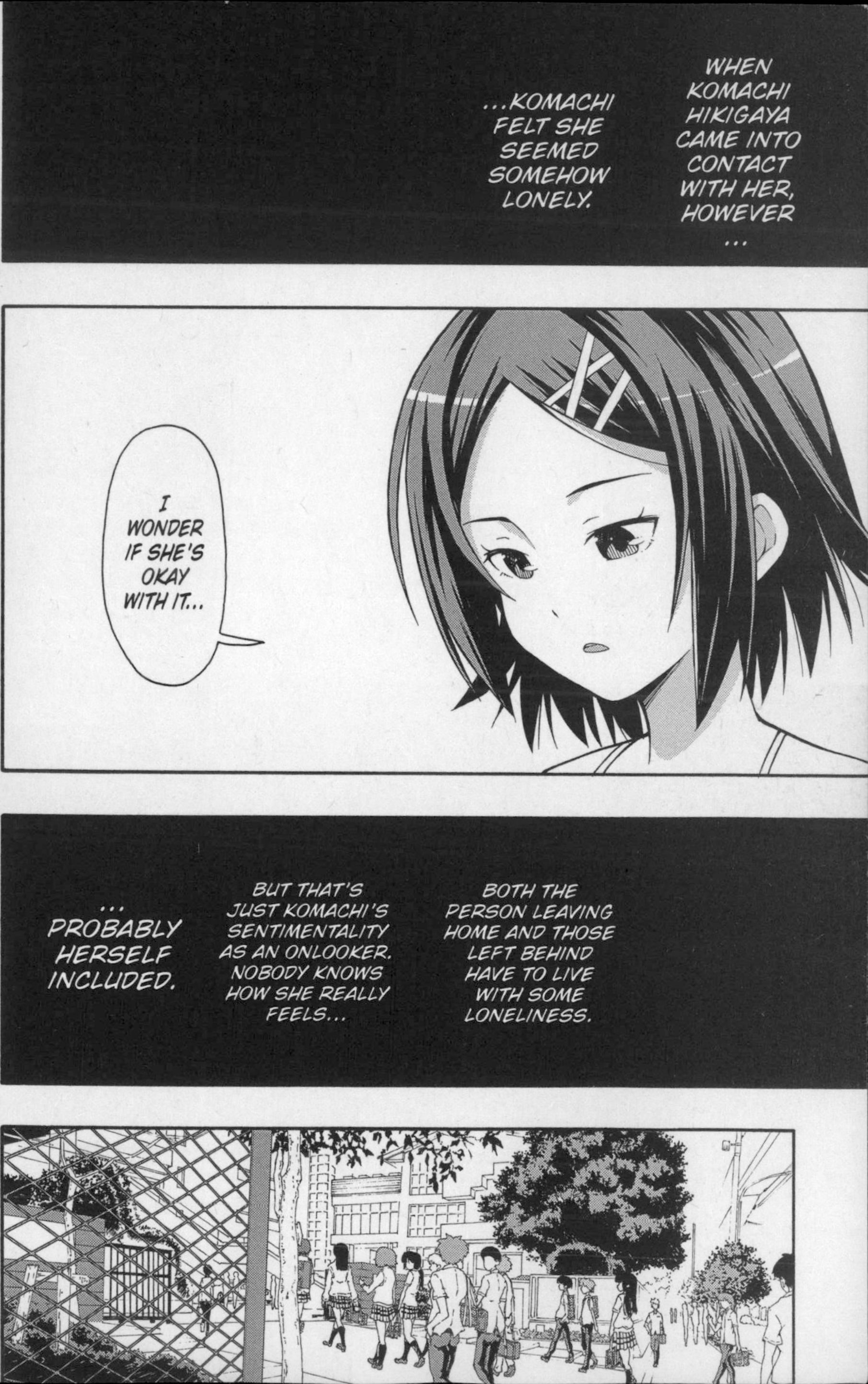
WHEN KOMACHI HIKIGAYA CAME INTO CONTACT WITH HER, HOWEVER...
...KOMACHI FELT SHE SEEMED SOMEHOW LONELY.
I WONDER IF SHE'S OKAY WITH IT...
BOTH THE PERSON LEAVING HOME AND THOSE LEFT BEHIND HAVE TO LIVE WITH SOME LONELINESS.
BUT THAT'S JUST KOMACHI'S SENTIMENTALITY AS AN ONLOOKER. NOBODY KNOWS HOW SHE REALLY FEELS...
...PROBABLY HERSELF INCLUDED.

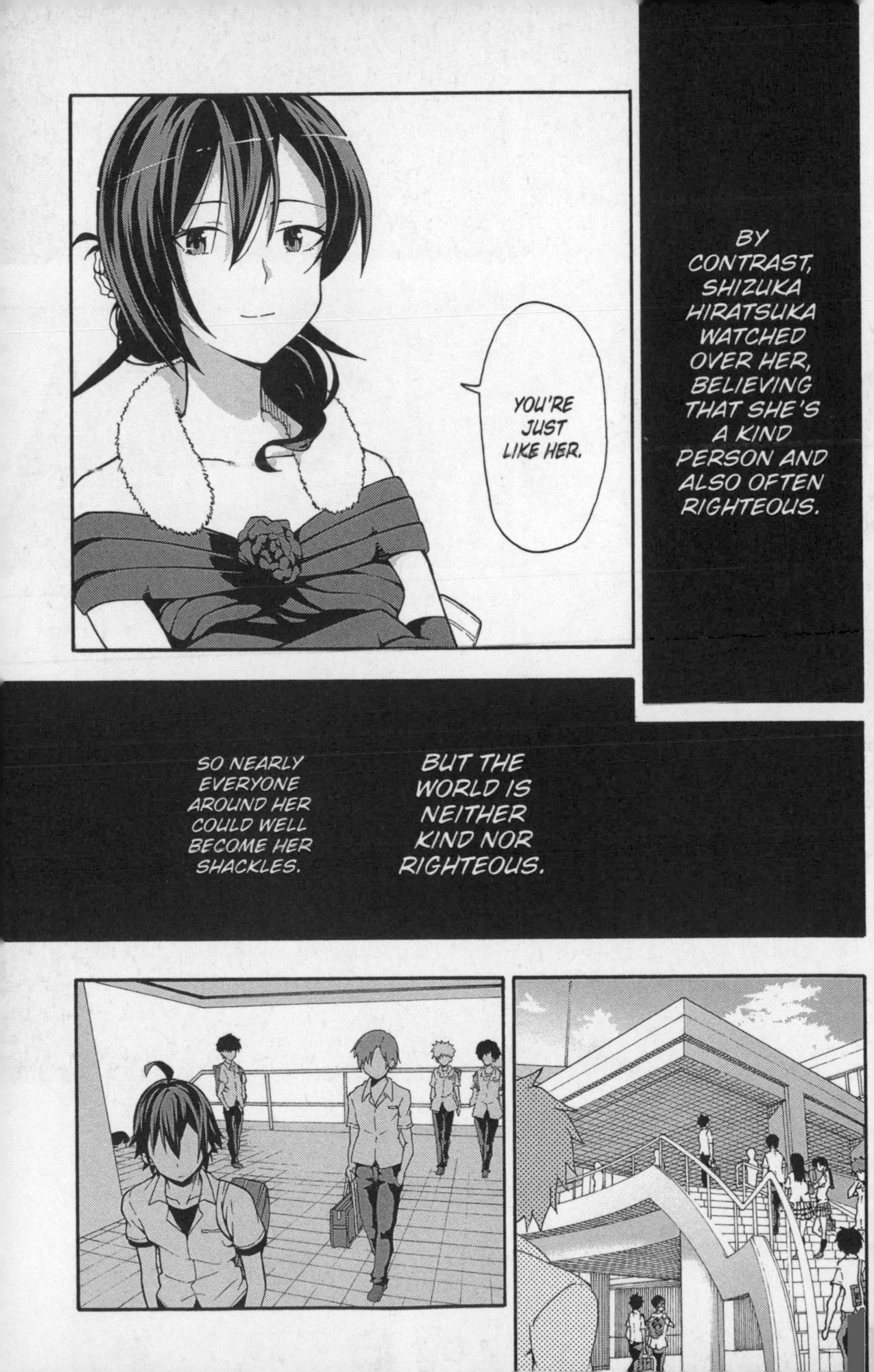
BY CONTRAST, SHIZUKA HIRATSUKA WATCHED OVER HER, BELIEVING THAT SHE'S A KIND PERSON AND ALSO OFTEN RIGHTEOUS.
YOU'RE JUST LIKE HER.
BUT THE WORLD IS NEITHER KIND NOR RIGHTEOUS.
SO NEARLY EVERYONE AROUND HER COULD WELL BECOME HER SHACKLES.

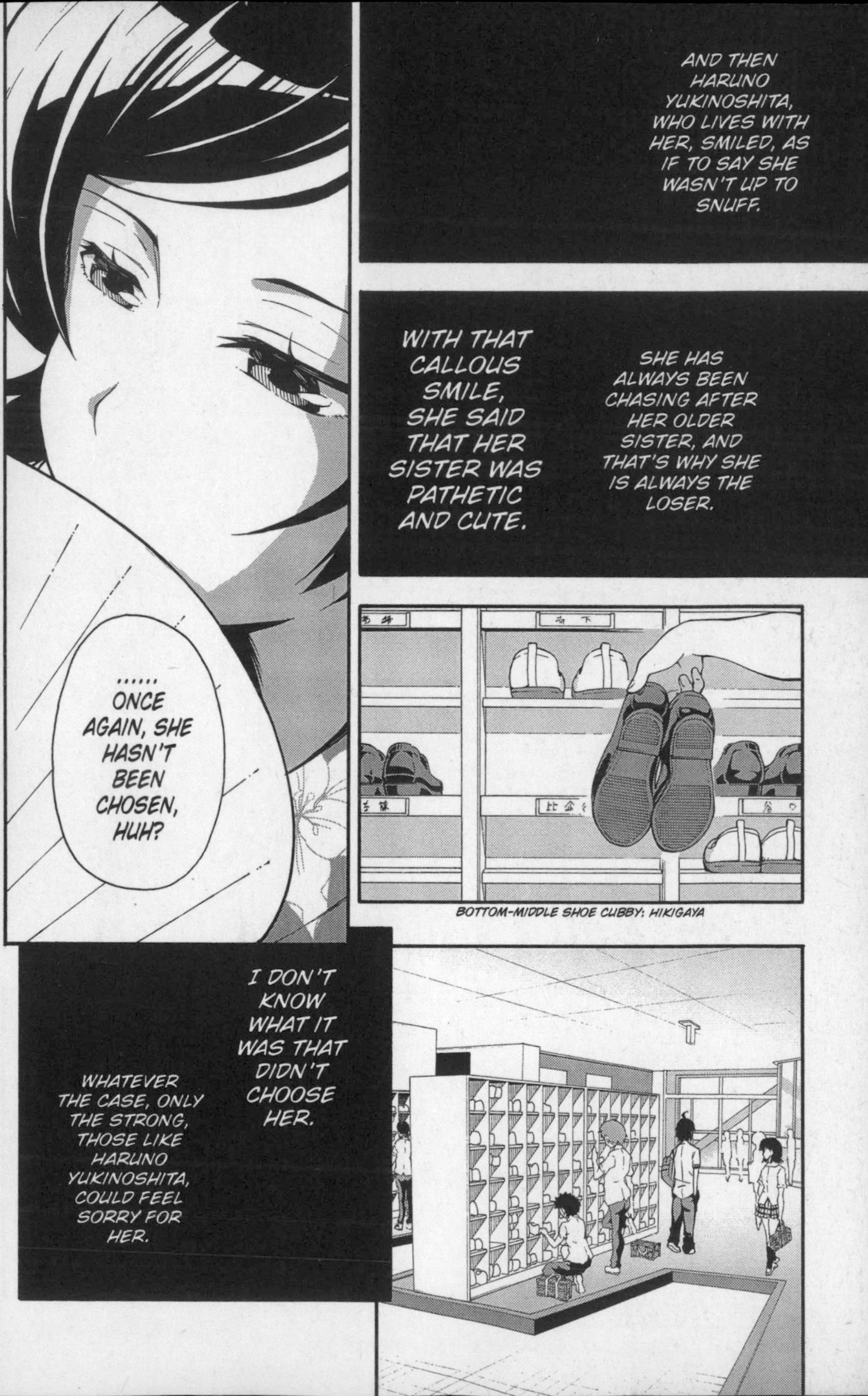
AND THEN HARUNO YUKINOSHITA, WHO LIVES WITH HER, SMILED, AS IF TO SAY SHE WASN'T UP TO SNUFF.
SHE HAS ALWAYS BEEN CHASING AFTER HER OLDER SISTER, AND THAT'S WHY SHE IS ALWAYS THE LOSER.
WITH THAT CALLOUS SMILE, SHE SAID THAT HER SISTER WAS PATHETIC AND CUTE.
BOTTOM-MIDDLE SHOE CUBBY: HIKIGAYA
...... ONCE AGAIN, SHE HASN'T BEEN CHOSEN, HUH?
I DON'T KNOW WHAT IT WAS THAT DIDN'T CHOOSE HER.
WHATEVER THE CASE, ONLY THE STRONG, THOSE LIKE HARUNO YUKINOSHITA, COULD FEEL SORRY FOR HER.

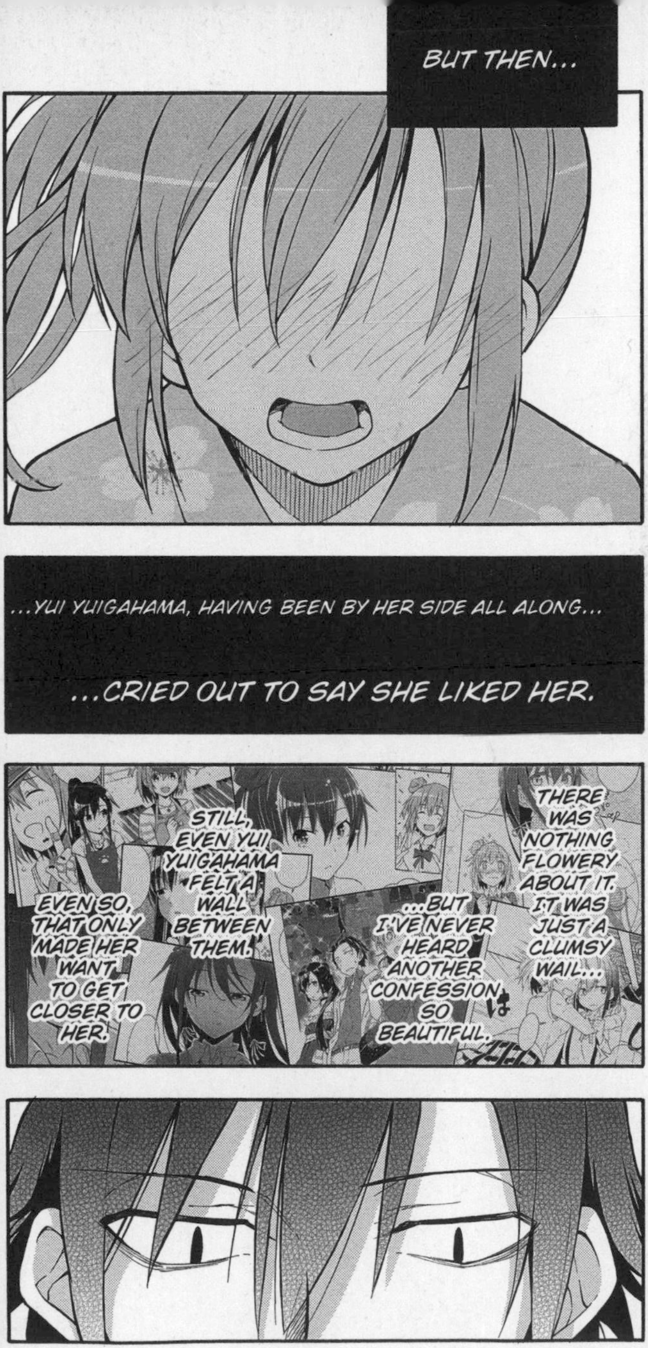
BUT THEN...
...YUI YUIGAHAMA, HAVING BEEN BY HER SIDE ALL ALONG...
...CRIED OUT TO SAY SHE LIKED HER.
THERE WAS NOTHING FLOWERY ABOUT IT. IT WAS JUST A CLUMSY WAIL...
...BUT I'VE NEVER HEARD ANOTHER CONFESSION SO BEAUTIFUL.
STILL, EVEN YUI YUIGAHAMA FELT A WALL BETWEEN THEM.
EVEN SO, THAT ONLY MADE HER WANT TO GET CLOSER TO HER.

AND AS FOR HACHIMAN HIKIGAYA...

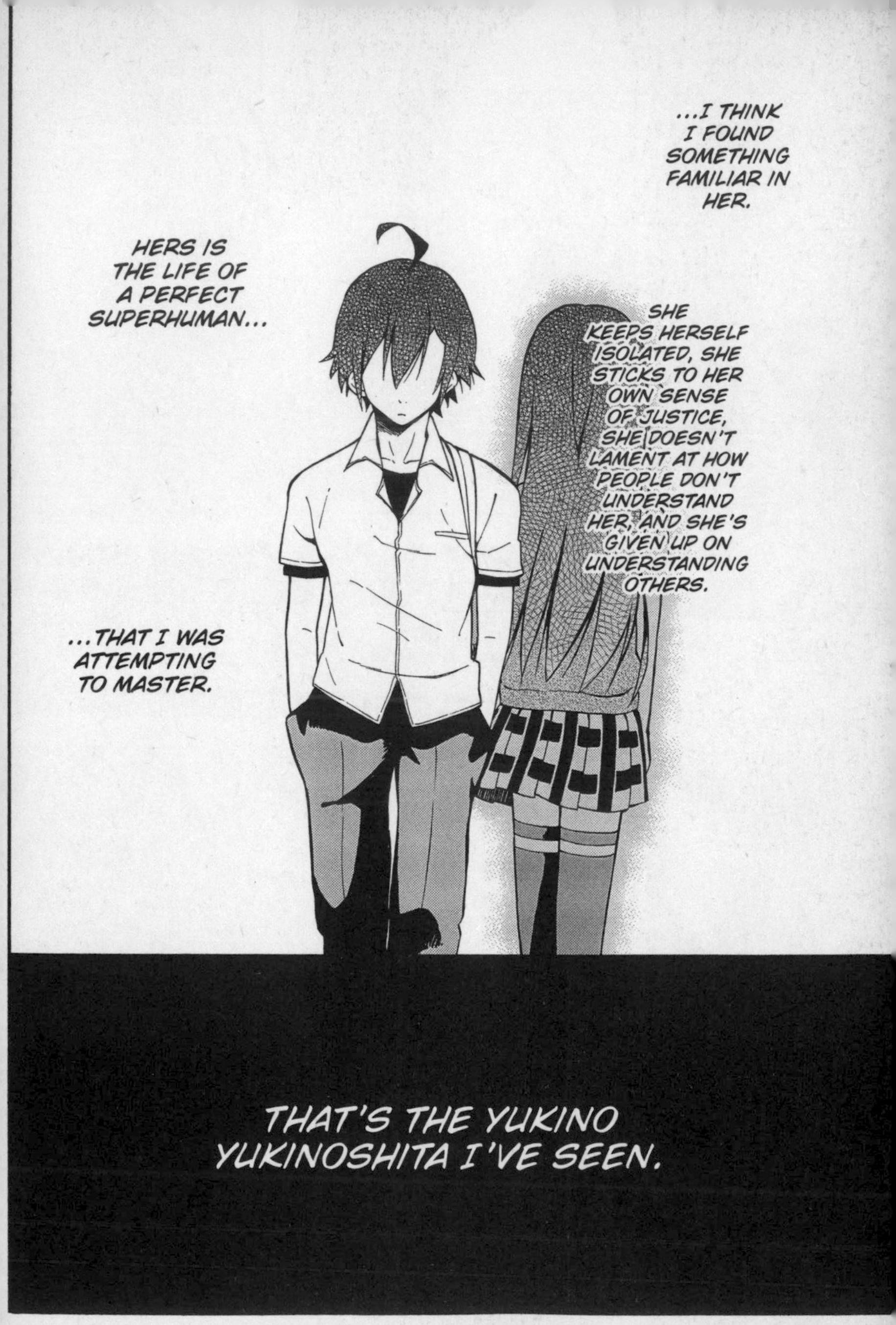
...I THINK I FOUND SOMETHING FAMILIAR IN HER.
SHE KEEPS HERSELF ISOLATED, SHE STICKS TO HER OWN SENSE OF JUSTICE, SHE DOESN'T LAMENT AT HOW PEOPLE DON'T UNDERSTAND HER, AND SHE'S GIVEN UP ON UNDERSTANDING OTHERS.
HERS IS THE LIFE OF A PERFECT SUPERHUMAN...
...THAT I WAS ATTEMPTING TO MASTER.
THAT'S THE YUKINO YUKINOSHITA I'VE SEEN.

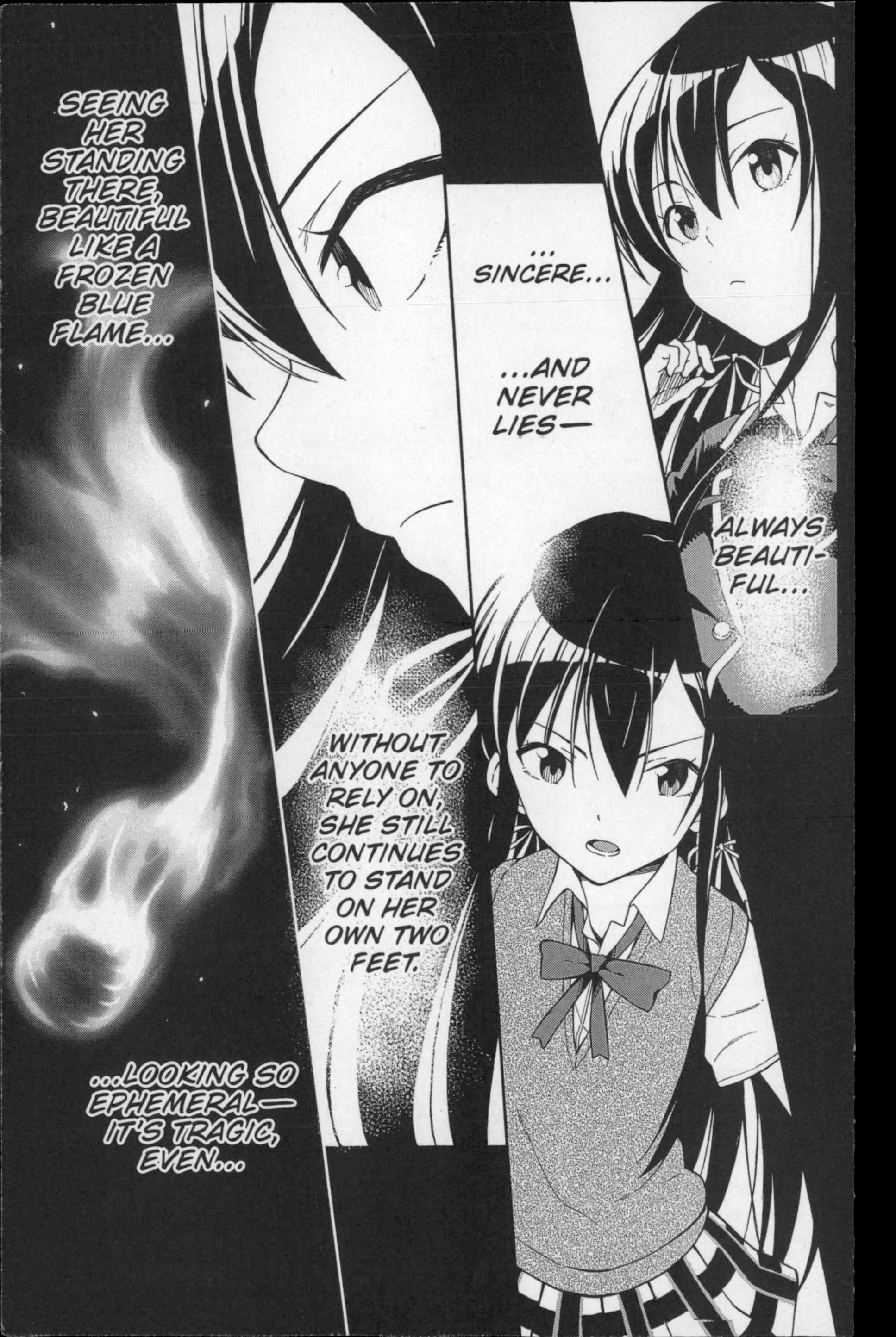
...SINCERE...
...AND NEVER LIES—
ALWAYS BEAUTIFUL...
WITHOUT ANYONE TO RELY ON, SHE STILL CONTINUES TO STAND ON HER OWN TWO FEET.
SEEING HER STANDING THERE, BEAUTIFUL LIKE A FROZEN BLUE FLAME...
...LOOKING SO EPHEMERAL—IT'S TRAGIC, EVEN...

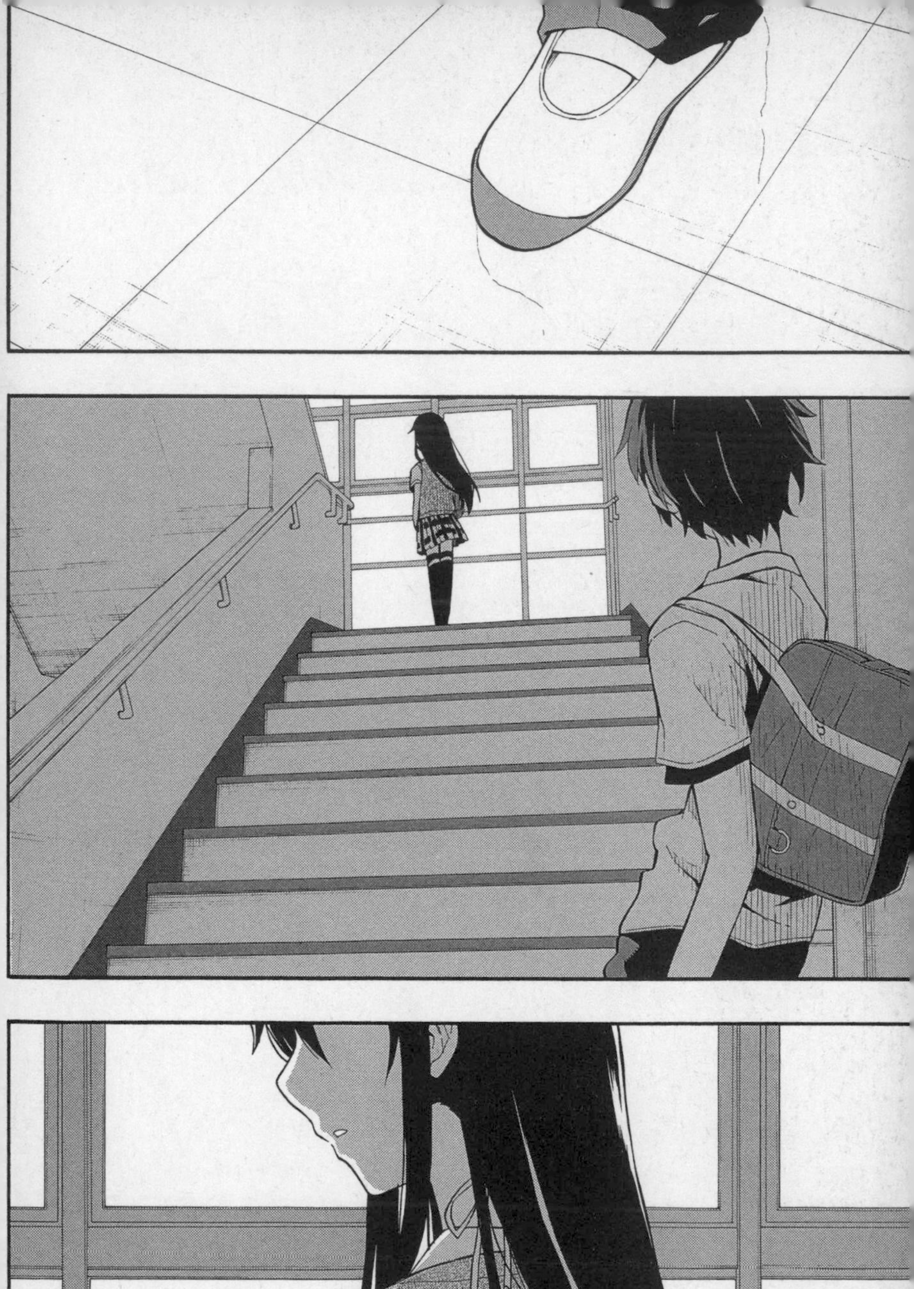

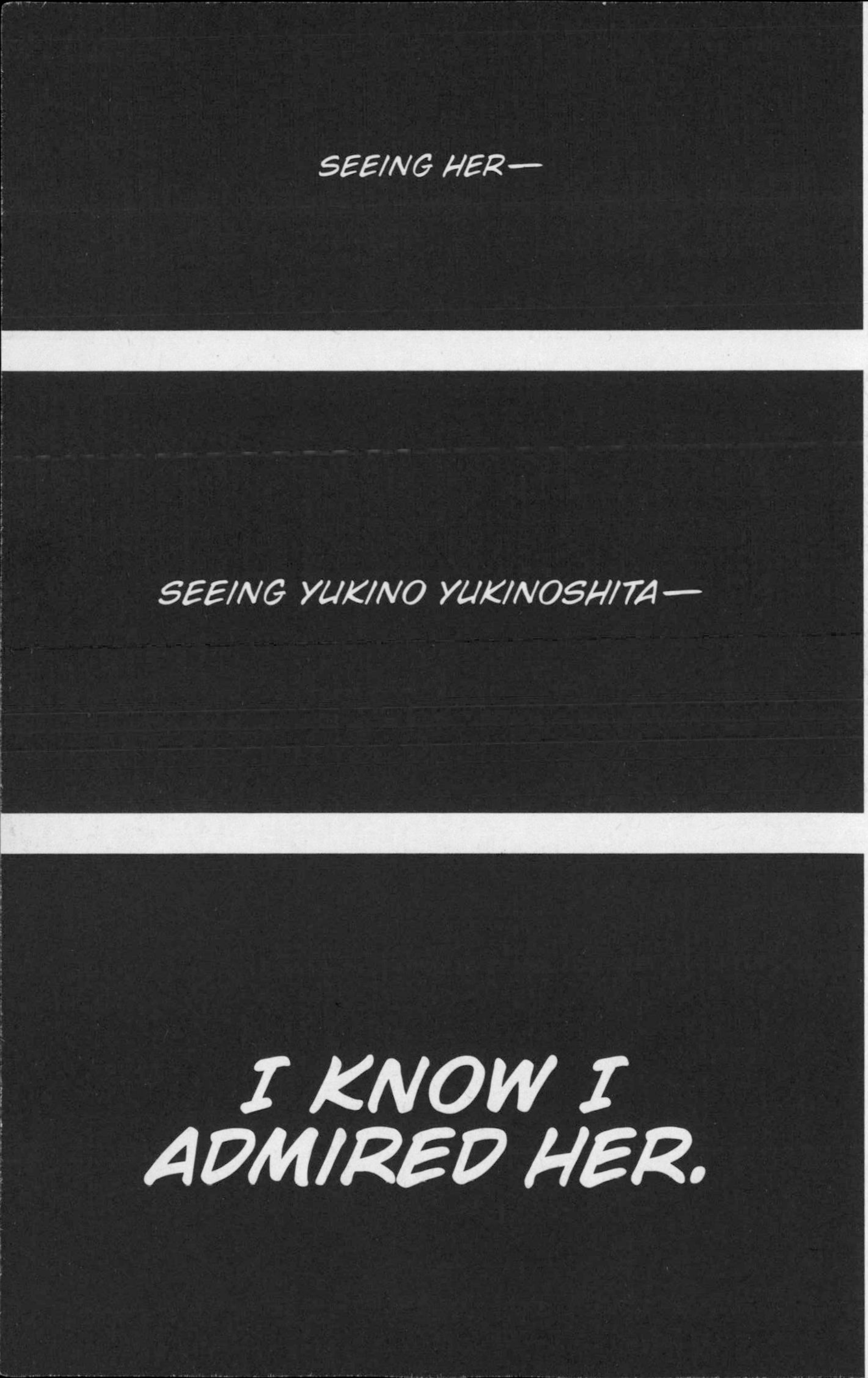
SEEING HER—
SEEING YUKINO YUKINOSHITA—
I KNOW I ADMIRED HER.

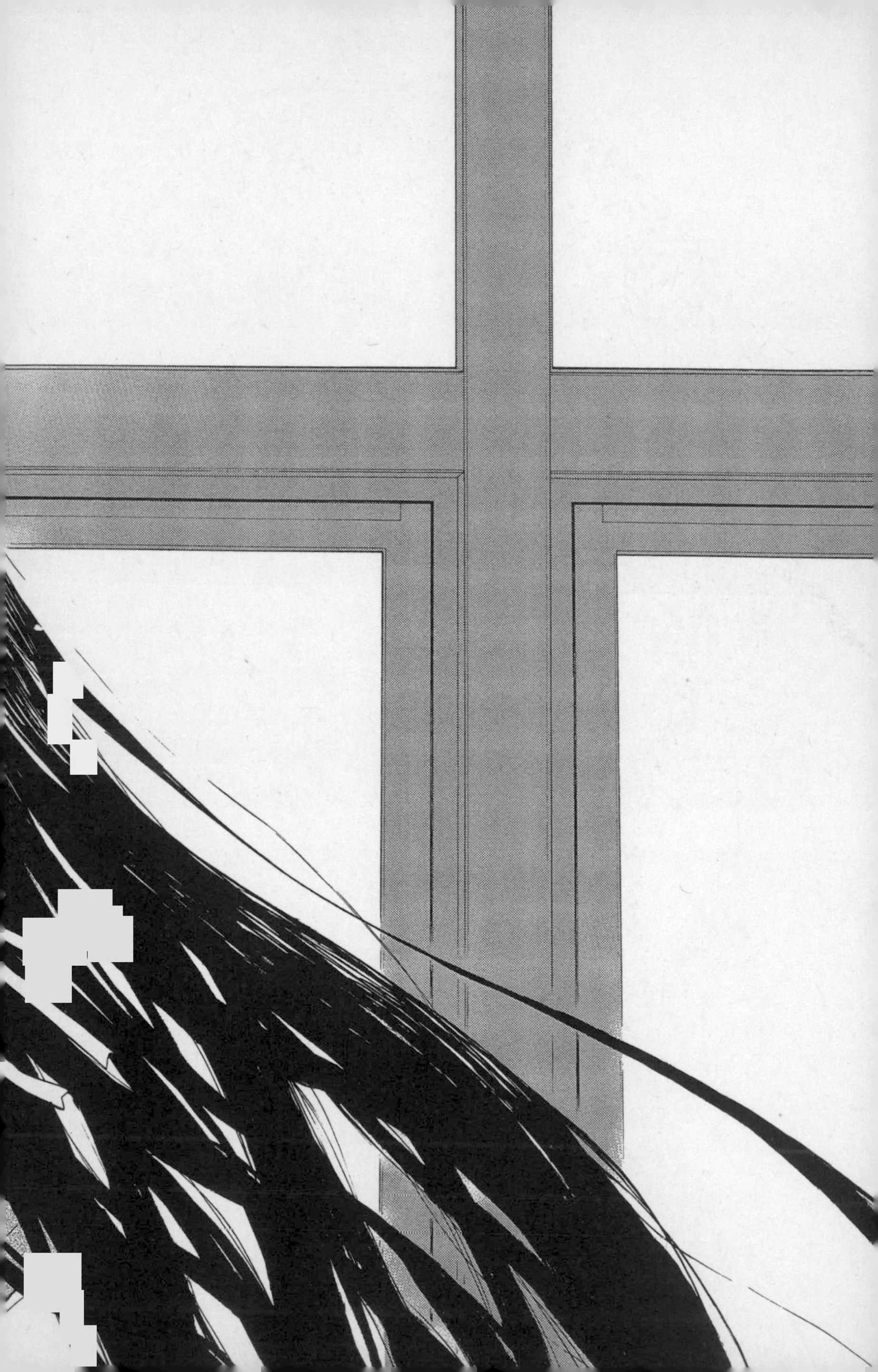

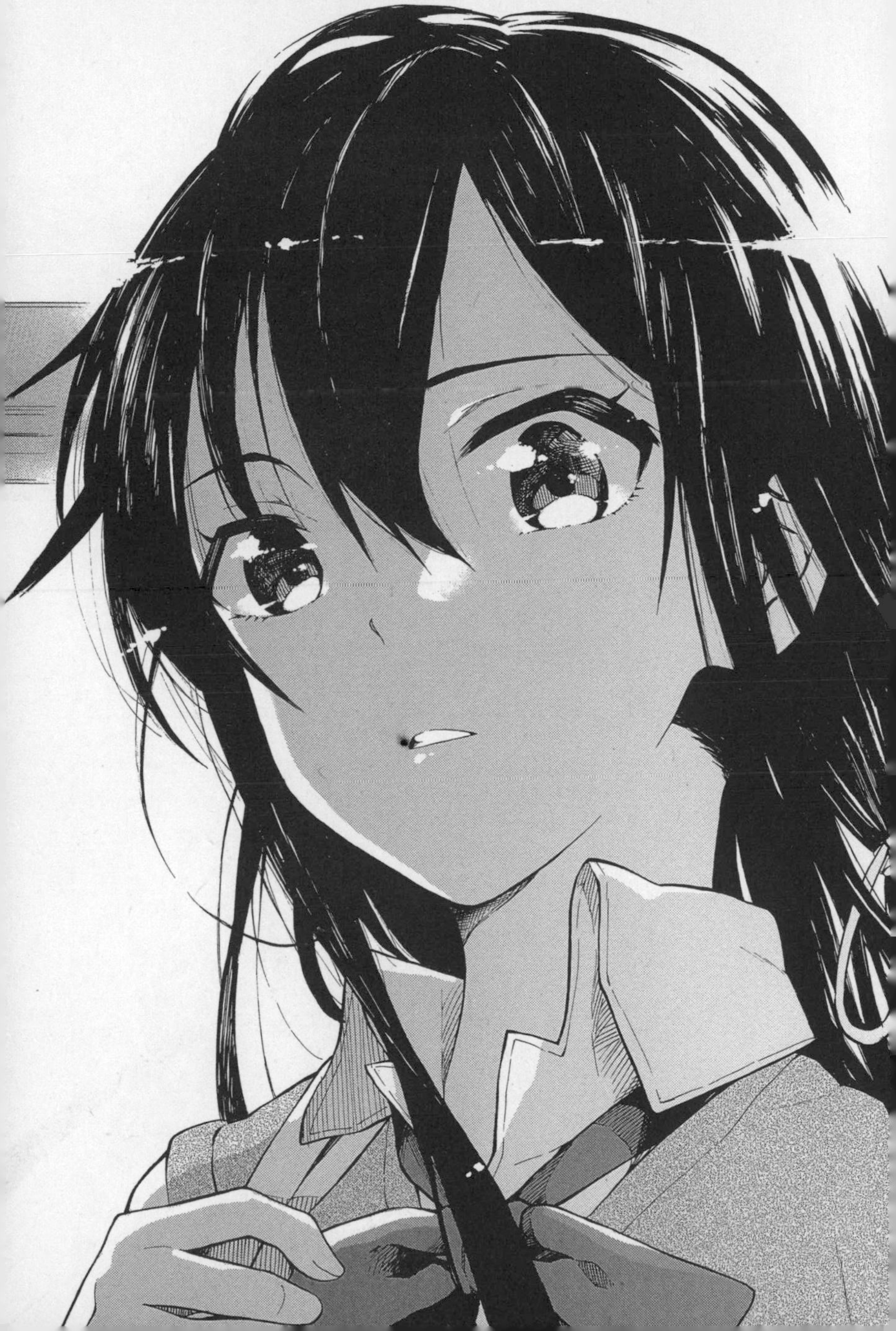

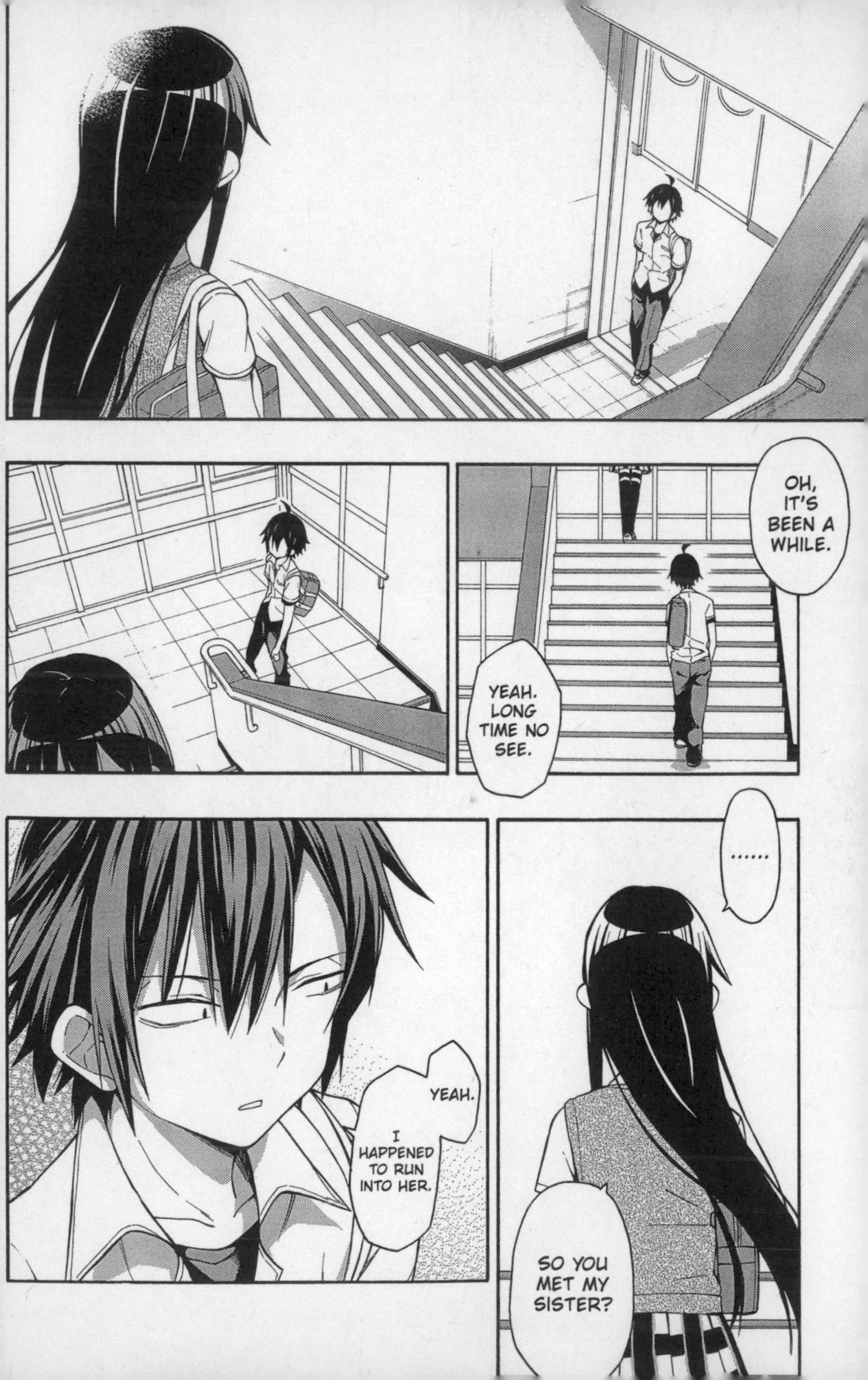
OH, IT'S BEEN A WHILE.
YEAH. LONG TIME NO SEE.
......
SO YOU MET MY SISTER?
YEAH.
I HAPPENED TO RUN INTO HER.

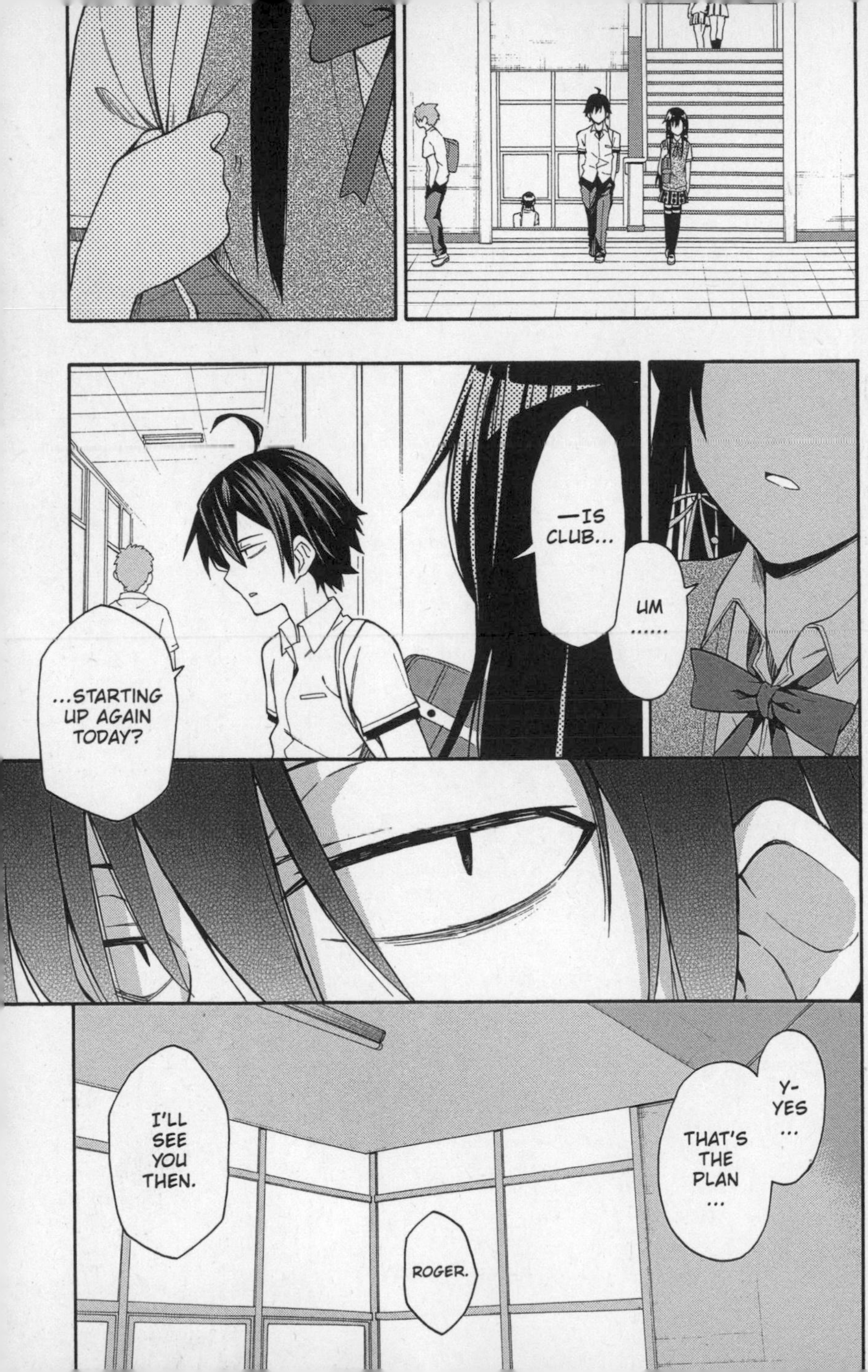
UM ......
—IS CLUB...
...STARTING UP AGAIN TODAY?
Y-YES ... THAT'S THE PLAN ...
ROGER.
I'LL SEE YOU THEN.

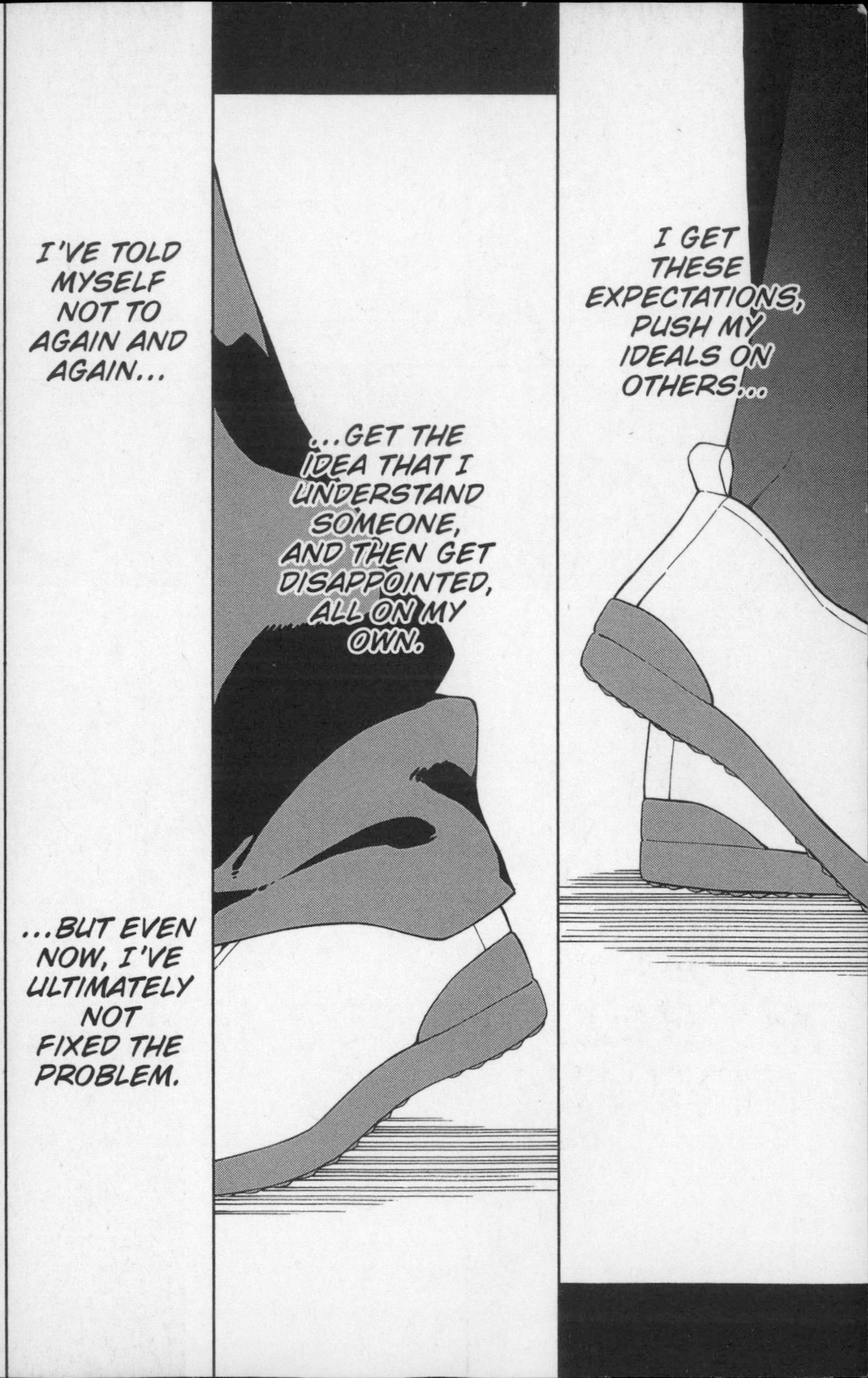
I GET THESE EXPECTATIONS, PUSH MY IDEALS ON OTHERS...
...GET THE IDEA THAT I UNDERSTAND SOMEONE, AND THEN GET DISAPPOINTED, ALL ON MY OWN.
I'VE TOLD MYSELF NOT TO AGAIN AND AGAIN...
...BUT EVEN NOW, I'VE ULTIMATELY NOT FIXED THE PROBLEM.

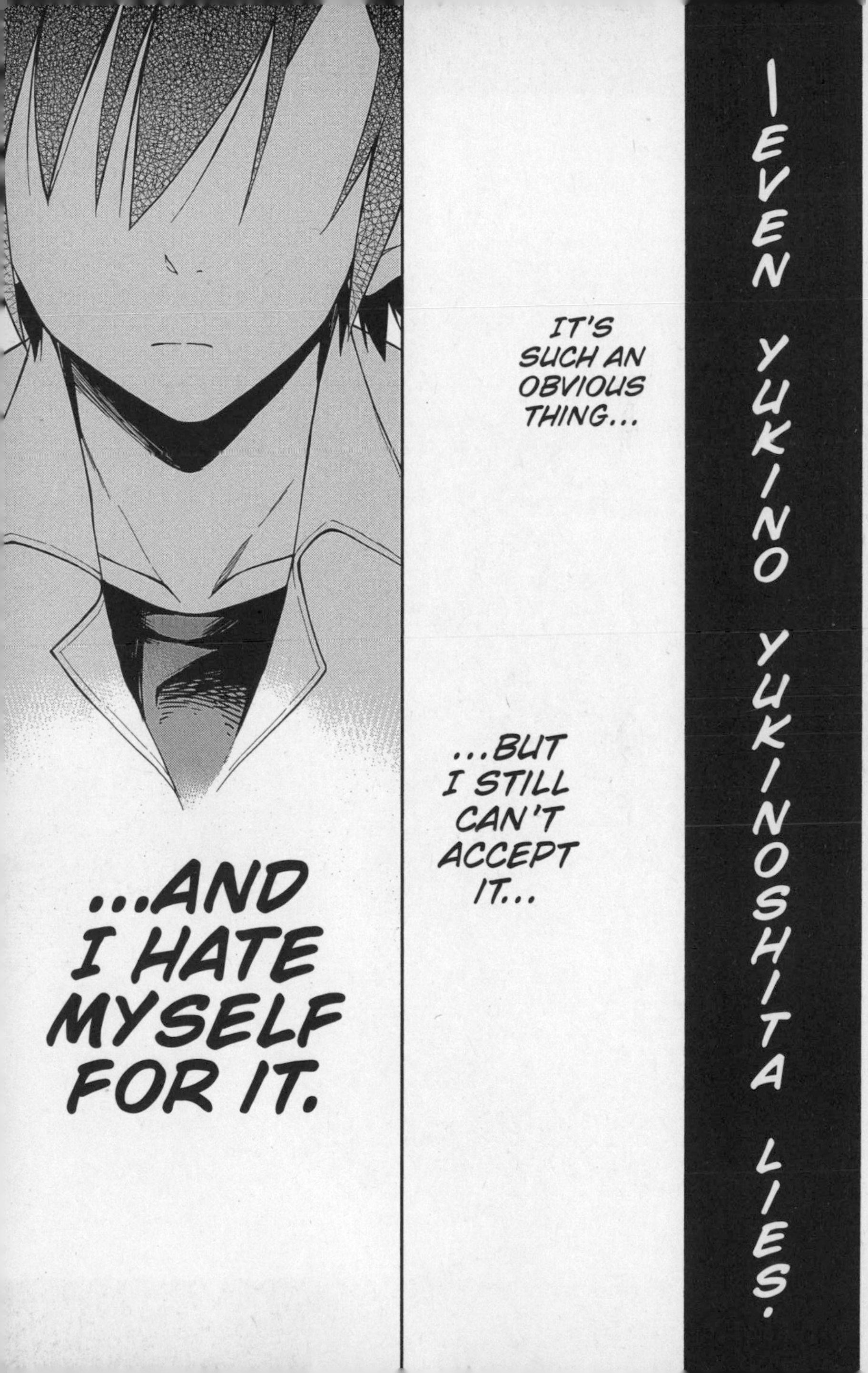
I EVEN YUKINO YUKINOSHITA LIES.
IT'S SUCH AN OBVIOUS THING...
...BUT I STILL CAN'T ACCEPT IT...
...AND I HATE MYSELF FOR IT.

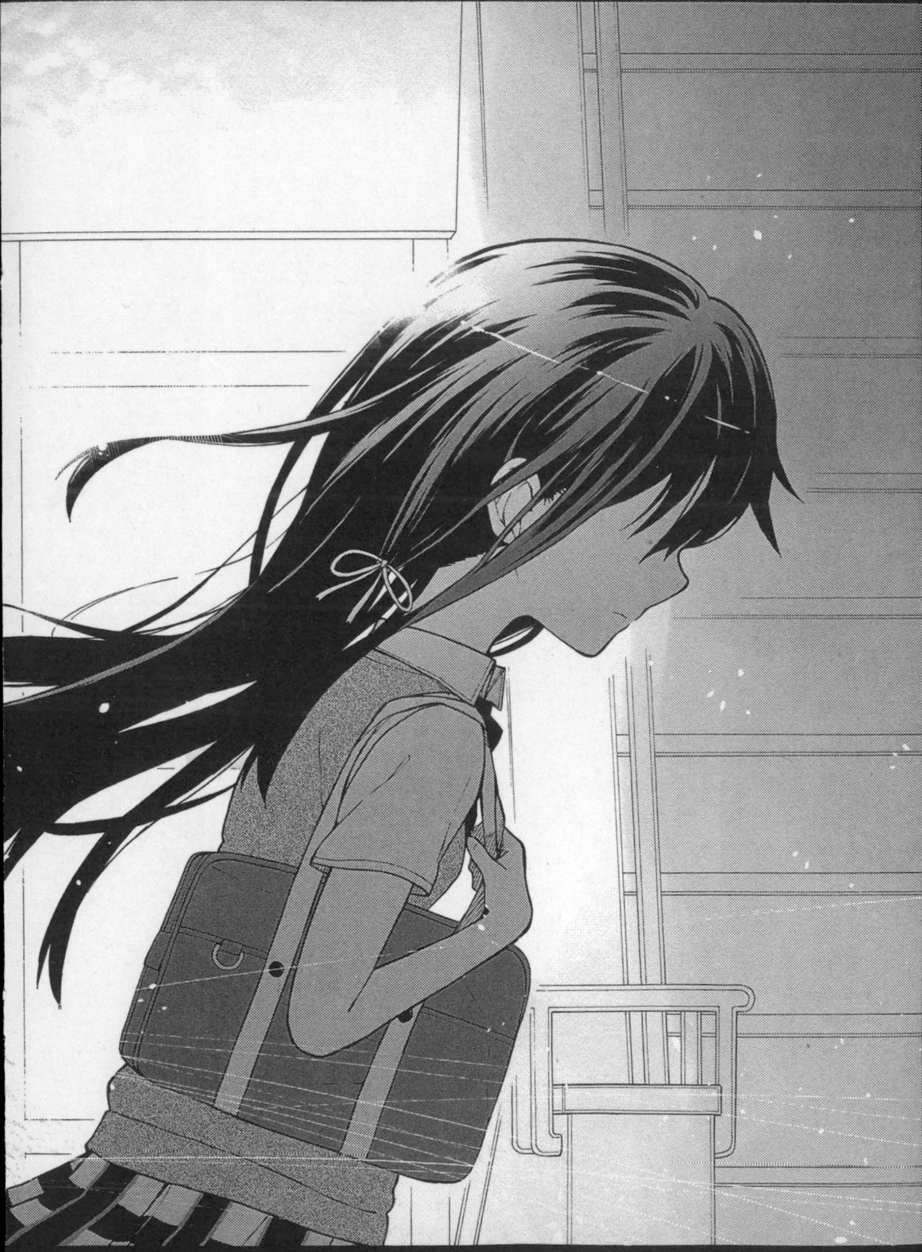

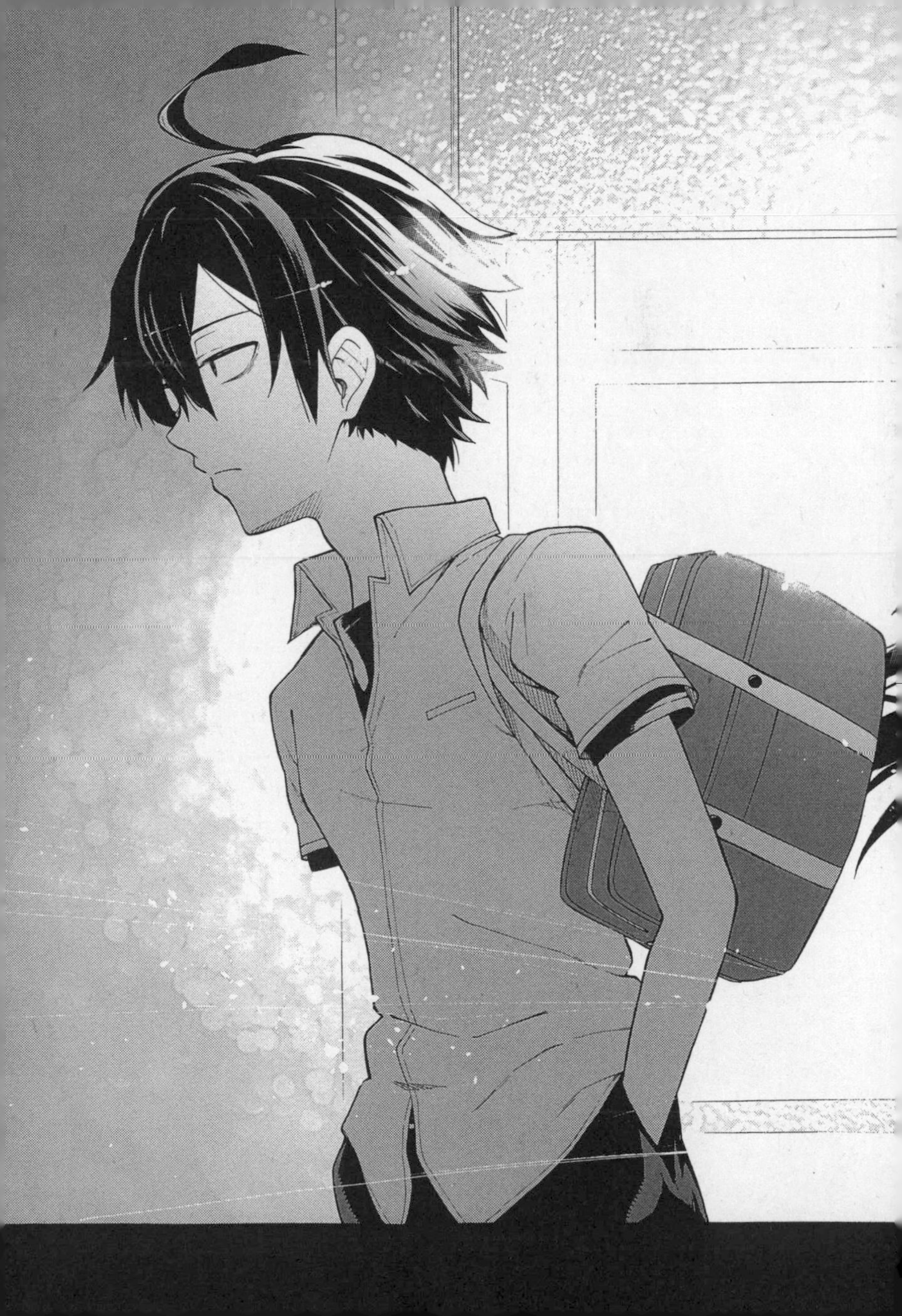

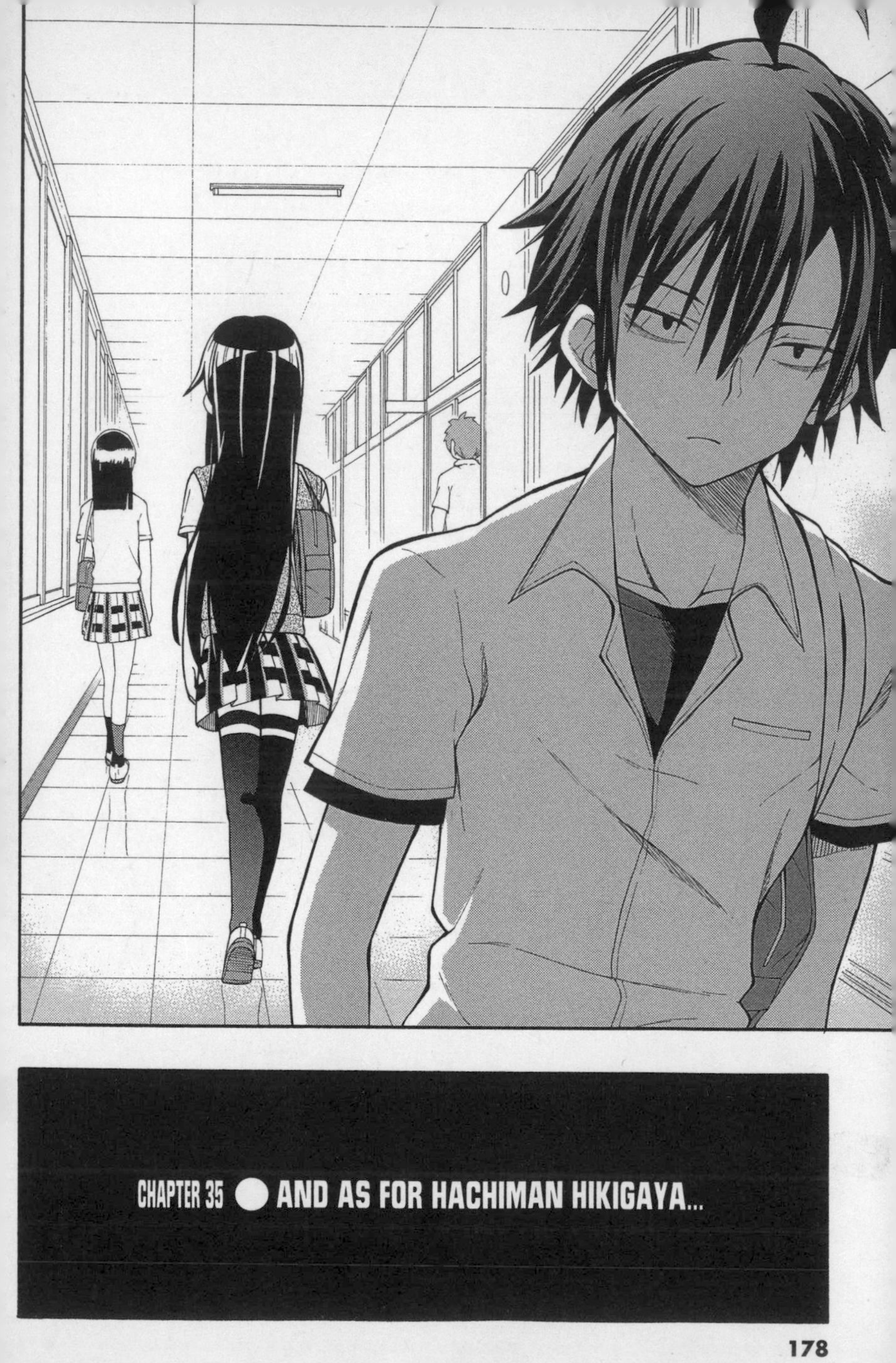

CHAPTER 35 ● AND AS FOR HACHIMAN HIKIGAYA...

MY YOUTH ROMANTIC COMEDY IS WRONG, AS I EXPECTE

...To Be Continued

CHAPTER 29.5 AND THUS THE STARS GUIDE SAKI KAWASAKI.

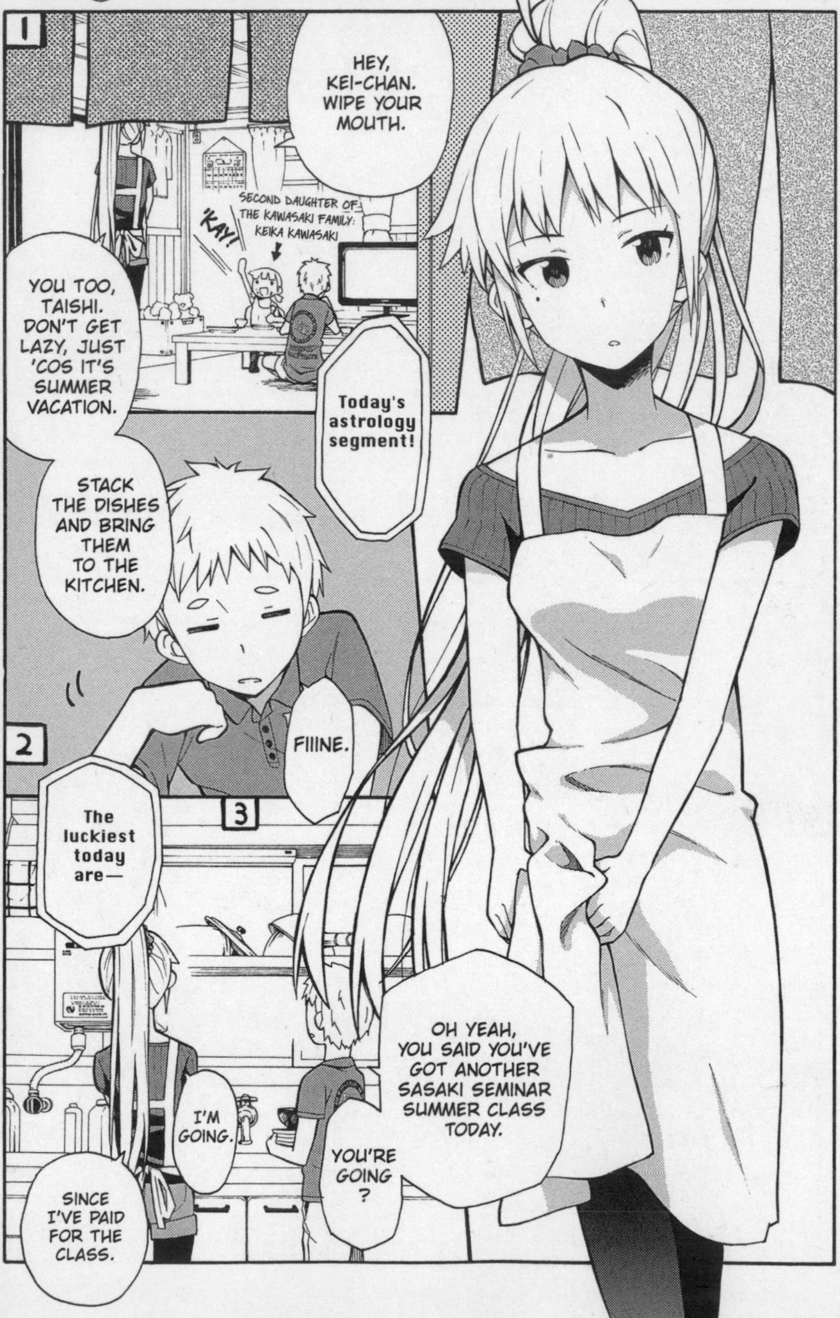
1
HEY, KEI-CHAN. WIPE YOUR MOUTH.
'KAY!
SECOND DAUGHTER OF THE KAWASAKI FAMILY: KEIKA KAWASAKI
Today's astrology segment!
YOU TOO, TAISHI. DON'T GET LAZY, JUST 'COS IT'S SUMMER VACATION.
2
STACK THE DISHES AND BRING THEM TO THE KITCHEN.
FIIINE.
3
The luckiest today are—
OH YEAH, YOU SAID YOU'VE GOT ANOTHER SASAKI SEMINAR SUMMER CLASS TODAY.
YOU'RE GOING?
I'M GOING.
SINCE I'VE PAID FOR THE CLASS.

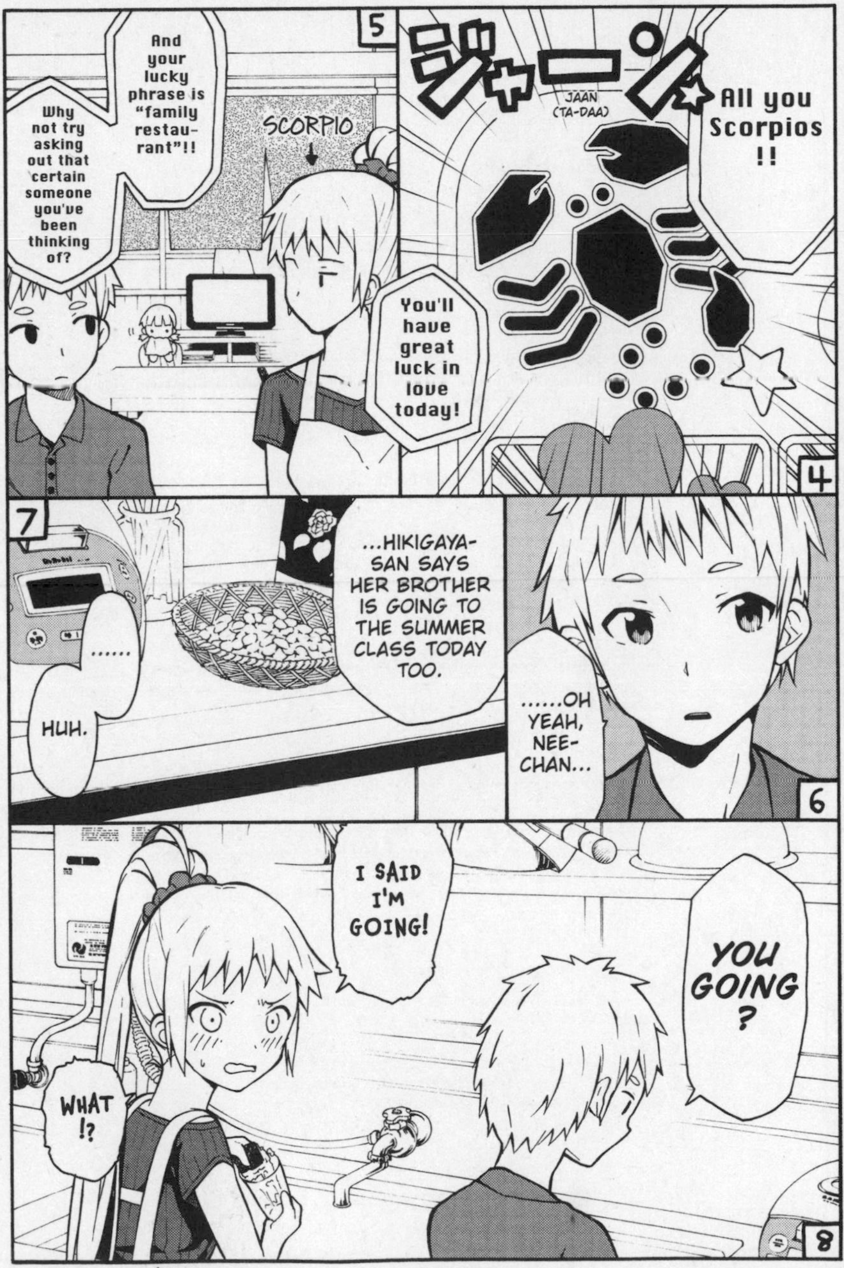
ジャーン☆
JAAN (TA-DAA)
All you Scorpios !!
You'll have great luck in love today!
And your lucky phrase is "family restaurant"!!
Why not try asking out that certain someone you've been thinking of?
SCORPIO
......OH YEAH, NEE-CHAN...
...HIKIGAYA-SAN SAYS HER BROTHER IS GOING TO THE SUMMER CLASS TODAY TOO.
......
HUH.
YOU GOING?
I SAID I'M GOING!
WHAT!?

THE END

TRANSLATION NOTES

Page 4
The word **"scholarship"** here is the actual English word, which is why Saki Kawasaki has trouble recalling it.

Page 6
The **red thread of fate** is a belief or myth in East Asian cultures that the gods tie a red thread to those destined to come together. In Japan, the use of the term assumes a romantic connection.

Page 17
National and public courses are taught at Japanese cram schools to help high school kids improve their chances of getting into national and public universities. In Japan, national universities are held in higher regard compared to public and private ones.

Page 23
The Laws of the High School Student parody the oath of the Shinsengumi, a special police forced organized by the military government in 1863.

Page 26
"I'd like to present him with a variety pack of axes" is a reference to Aesop's fable of the honest woodsman. The story involves a woodsman who is rewarded for his honesty with the present of a golden ax.

Page 30
"Take care" here is *kawaigaru* in Japanese, a term used in sumo stables to mean something along the lines of "tough love." It is not uncommon for newcomers to sumo stables to be hazed.

Page 38
Messe Amuse Z is based on an actual mall in Chiba called Messe Amuse Mall.

Page 40
Hinko 3D is a parody of the horror film *Sadako 3D*, a sequel to *Rasen* ("Spiral") which was in turn a sequel to the very popular *Ring*. The play on words between Hinko and Sadako comes from the fact that the kanji characters for the *hin* ("poverty") in *Hinko* and the *sada* ("chastity") in *Sadako* resemble each other.

Page 49
Shinkiba is the name of a station in Tokyo. *Zaimoku* means "lumber" or "wood." Both words have the character for "wood" in them, like Zaimokuza's name.

Page 51
Lafcadio Hearn (1850–1904) was an international writer best known for his books about Japan, most famously *Kwaidan: Stories and Studies of Strange Things*, about Japanese ghost stories. His Japanese pen name was Yakumo Koizumi.

Page 51
Zaimokuza's speech, including all the various unusual laughs, is based on a Japanese 2channel copypasta, wherein a poster imitates and exaggerates the stereotypical tone of an internet *otaku* when responding to the question "Which *Haruhi* character do you like?" The original post was quite sarcastic.

Page 53
Zaimokuza ending his sentence with **"...foy"** is a reference to Draco Malfoy from *Harry Potter*. The character is often referred to on the internet by Japanese fans as "Foy," and the phrase has become a humorous sentence-ending particle.

Page 55
Portable word processors (*shippitsu debaisu*) are a minimalist device purely used for notes and writing, with no apps or distractions attached. It's about the size of a tablet but with a built-in keyboard. One of the most popular brands in Japan is Pomera.

Page 57
A **Mini 4WD** is a miniature race car that runs on a battery pack without remote control. The ones popular in Japan, sold primarily by the toy manufacturer Tamiya, are often hand assembled and highly customizable. You generally have to run them on a racetrack for them to run properly. They are mostly popular in Asia but are also sold in a number of other countries. There was also a tie-in manga and anime called *Bakusou Kyoudai Let's & Go!!* that was basically a vehicle for selling the toys.

Page 58
The **Brocken G** (Brocken Gigant) and the **Beak Spider** are both Mini 4WDs released in the nineties.

In the *Bakusou Kyoudai Let's & Go!!* manga and anime series, Mini 4WD competitors often attached real weapons to their cars in order to take out their opponents.

Page 59
The change in art style applied to Hikigaya here is based on the aesthetic of *Bakusou Kyoudai Let's + Go!!*

Page 60
The **Avante** model Mini 4WD by Tamiya is an older "classic" model Mini 4WD originally released in the eighties, unlike the Brocken G and the Beak Spider.

Page 71
Both Hiratsuka's face and the words **"Ramen! That's an option too?"** are references to the main character of the manga *Kodoku no Gourmet* (*Lonely Gourmet*) by Masayuki Kusumi. The original line is "To go! That's an option too?" when he sees a man taking pork miso soup to go. He thinks since it will get cold, it won't be any good.

Page 79
"There is always one truth" is the catchphrase of Conan Edogawa, the pint-sized detective from the manga and anime *Detective Conan*

TRANSLATION NOTES (CONTINUED)

(released in the United States as *Case Closed*). It is an extremely long-running and popular series by Gosho Aoyama that began in 1994 about a high school detective trapped in the body of a child.

Future Boy Conan is a 1978 TV postapocalyptic science fiction anime directed by Hayao Miyazaki, based on the 1970 novel *The Incredible Tide* by Alexander Key. The two Conans are totally unrelated; they just have the same name.

Page 82-83
A wide variety of ramen exist in Japan as a result of historical differences resulting in strong preferences that can sometimes be very regional. **Pork bone** (*tonkotsu*) ramen originated in Fukuoka and tend to have a cloudy appearance and milky texture. **Light salt** (*shio*) ramen is popular all over but is especially beloved in Hakodate. Soy sauce (shoyu) ramen is generally associated with Tokyo. **Tomato ramen** is a relatively new phenomenon.

Page 95
"I do not want to find a job, that I do not" is a reference to the manner of speech used by Kenshin Himura, the protagonist of the manga and anime *Rurouni Kenshin*. It is not a line that Kenshin ever said, and it would be completely out of character for him to say, and thus the joke. The copula at the end of the line usd in Japanese, *de gozaru*, is a feature of the quaint and old-timey sort of speech that Kenshin employs, and it's also often used by Internet otaku when talking on message boards, whether ironically or not. Zaimokuza also says it sometimes.

Page 102
"That's my justice" is a reference to *Kamen Rider Black RX*, the ninth instalment of the classic sentai show that ran from 1988 to 1989, as well as a piece of Internet slang used when emphasizing your beliefs in an atmosphere when everyone else thinks you're being stupid. The actual English word *justice* is used here.

Page 109
Souvenirs are a big deal in Japan, and usually, souvenirs means sweets. Every region sells these kinds of boxed sweets—generally they're **boxes of cakes**, crackers, or mochi of some kind—and they often deliberately sell them only in a certain location, as a tourism thing. If you go on a trip—even a business trip—it's considered good manners to give souvenirs to all your family and friends and everyone in your class at school or department at work. The way Komachi is phrasing the gifting of souvenirs, however, implies that Hachiman and Komachi's parents will be Yui's in-laws.

Page 114
"Itchy. Tasty" is a famous line from a journal in the original *Resident Evil* game. The journal describes an animal keeper slowly becoming infected with the zombie virus and losing his mind. The only thing written on the very last page is "Itchy. Tasty."

Page 117
Zexy is a wedding and bridal magazine. The fact that Hiratsuka is reading it plays on her worries about not being married.

Page 124
Like in other parts of the world, Mastercard commercials about unforgettable moments being **"priceless"** also aired in Japan. Instead of using the Japanese term for *priceless*, the ads feature the English word.

Page 128
Yakisoba is stir-fried noodles, usually mixed with a variety of meats, vegetables, and a thick, savory sauce. It is a common food at Japanese street festivals.

Shioyaki is salt grilling and is typically used on a variety of meats.

Gomoku yakisoba is a form of yakisoba that used five different garnishes, hence the name (*go* means "five").

Page 129
Skewers, or *kushiyaki*, are grilled meats and other foods on sticks. *Yakitori* (grilled chicken) is the most well-known, but other ingredients can also be used.

Senbei crackers are Japanese rice crackers that come in a variety of styles. They can be sweet or savory.

Page 136
"Tamayaa!" is a phrase typically yelled when lighting fireworks in Japan as a way to express excitement. It has its origins in a Japanese fireworks factory owned by the Tamaya clan. The name of a rival factory, owned by the Kagiya clan, is generally shouted in response.

MY **YOUTH**
R♥MANTIC C☻MEDY
is **WRØNG,** AS I EXPECTED
@ *comic*

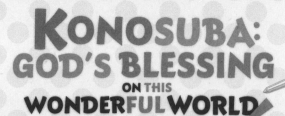

IN THIS FANTASY WORLD, EVERYTHING'S A GAME—AND THESE SIBLINGS PLAY TO WIN!

No Game No Life
1
YUU KAMIYA

No Game No Life © YUU KAMIYA
KADOKAWA CORPORATION

A genius but socially inept brother and sister duo is offered the chance to compete in a fantasy world where games decide everything. Sora and Shiro will take on the world and, while they're at it, create a harem of nonhuman companions!

1
No Game No Life, Please!
Art: KAZUYA YUIZAKI
Original Story • Character Design: YUU KAMIYA

No Game No Life, Please! © Kazuya Yuizaki 2016 © Yuu Kamiya 2016
KADOKAWA CORPORATION

LIGHT NOVELS 1–6 AVAILABLE NOW

LIKE THE NOVELS?

Check out the spin-off manga for even more out-of-control adventures with the Werebeast girl, Izuna!

Yen Press

Follow us on

www.yenpress.com

Two girls, a new school, and the beginning of a beautiful friendship.

Volumes 1-2 available now

Kiss & White Lily for My Dearest Girl

In middle school, Ayaka Shiramine was the perfect student: hard-working, with excellent grades and a great personality to match. As Ayaka enters high school she expects to still be on top, but one thing she didn't account for is her new classmate, the lazy yet genuine genius Yurine Kurosawa. What's in store for Ayaka and Yurine as they go through high school...together?

Yen Press

MURDERER
IN THE STREETS, KILLER
IN THE SHEETS!

MURCIÉLAGO

VOLUME I
AVAILABLE
NOW!

Mass murderer Kuroko Koumori has two passions in life: taking lives and pleasuring ladies. This doesn't leave her with many career prospects, but Kuroko actually has the perfect gig—as a hit woman for the police!

Murciélago © Yoshimurakana / SQUARE ENIX

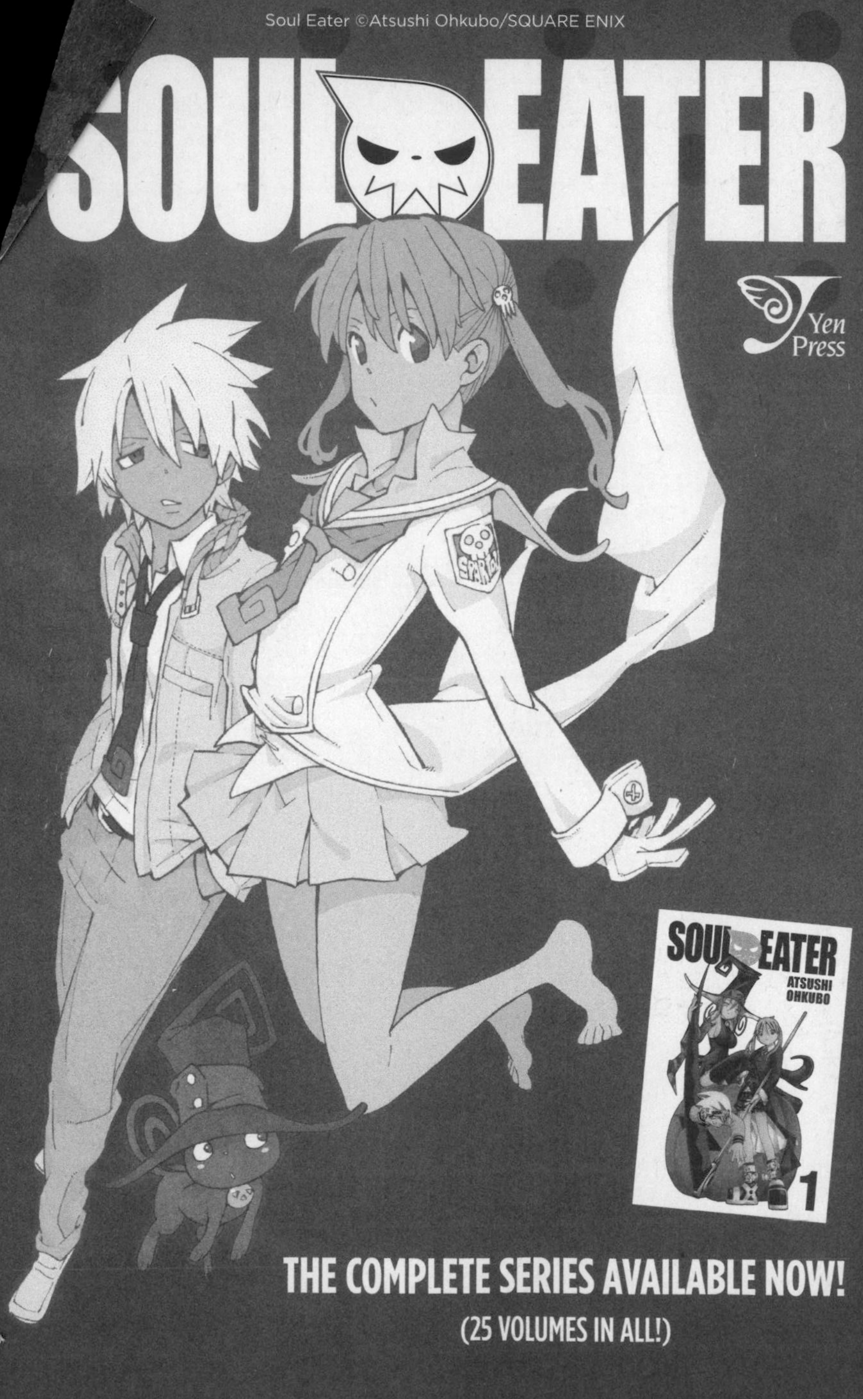
Soul Eater ©Atsushi Ohkubo/SQUARE ENIX
SOUL EATER
Yen Press
SOUL EATER
ATSUSHI OHKUBO
1
THE COMPLETE SERIES AVAILABLE NOW!
(25 VOLUMES IN ALL!)

Hello! This is YOTSUBA!

Guess what? Guess what?
Yotsuba and Daddy just moved here from waaaay over there!

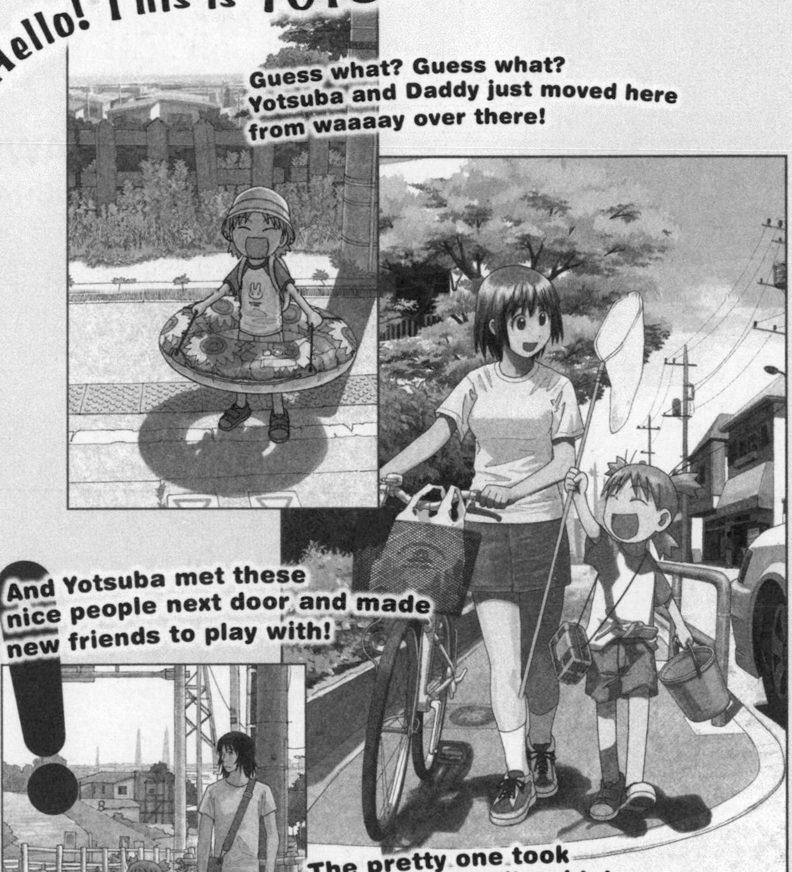

And Yotsuba met these nice people next door and made new friends to play with!

The pretty one took Yotsuba on a bike ride!
(Whoooa! There was a big hill!)

And Ena's a good drawer!
(Almost as good as Yotsuba!)

And their mom always gives Yotsuba ice cream!
(Yummy!)

And...

And...

OHHHH!

MY YOUTH ROMANTIC COMEDY IS WRONG, AS I EXPECTED @COMIC ⑥

Original Story: Wataru Watari
Art: Naomichi Io
Character Design: Ponkan⑧
ORIGINAL COVER DESIGN/Hiroyuki KAWASOME (Graphio)

Translation: Jennifer Ward

Lettering: Bianca Pistillo

YAHARI ORE NO SEISHUN LOVE COME WA MACHIGATTEIRU.
@COMIC Vol. 6 by Wataru WATARI, Naomichi IO, PONKAN⑧
© 2013 Wataru WATARI, Naomichi IO, PONKAN⑧
All rights reserved.
Original Japanese edition published by SHOGAKUKAN.
English translation rights arranged with SHOGAKUKAN through Tuttle-Mori Agency, Inc., Tokyo.

English translation © 2017 by Yen Press, LLC

Yen Press
1290 Avenue of the Americas
New York, NY 10104

Visit us at yenpress.com
facebook.com/yenpress
twitter.com/yenpress
yenpress.tumblr.com
instagram.com/yenpress

First Yen Press Edition: September 2017

Yen Press is an imprint of Yen Press, LLC.
The Yen Press name and logo are trademarks of Yen Press, LLC.

Library of Congress Control Number: 2016931004

ISBN: 978-0-316-41187-5

10 9 8 7 6 5 4 3 2 1

BVG

Printed in the United States of America